Penguí
We werf

Lawson Glassop (1913–1966) was born in the Blue Mountains in New South Wales. A journalist, he joined the army in 1940 and served with the AIF in the Middle East during the Second World War. He was a war correspondent in Korea in 1950-1 and from 1951 to 1960 he wrote for a range of Sydney and Adelaide newspapers; thereafter he was a columnist for the Adelaide *Advertiser*. *We Were the Rats* (1944), his major work, was banned as obscene by the NSW government in 1946, but its accurate depiction of the Australian soldier at war, its raw realism and its vivid characterisations have ensured its place among the classics of Australian war literature. Glassop published two other novels, *Lucky Palmer* (1940) and *The Rats in New Guinea* (1963), and a children's book, *Susan and the Bogeywomp* (1947).

Sir Edward Dunlop, AC, CMG, OBE, KCSJ, MS, FRCS, FRACS, FACS, LLD(Hon.), DSc. Punjabi (Hon.), was born in 1907 near Shepparton in rural Victoria. 'Weary', as he is known, graduated in medicine and surgery just before the outbreak of the Second World War. He served with the AIF in the Middle East, Europe and the Pacific during the war. Captured in Java by the Japanese in 1942, he survived more than three and a half years in some of the most notorious Japanese prison camps; his devotion to his men and his inspirational leadership are legendary. Since his return to Melbourne in 1945 Sir Edward has continued to practise as a surgeon and has been actively involved in community service in Australia and abroad. He was knighted in 1969. *The War Diaries of Weary Dunlop*, his exceptional account of prison-camp life, was published in 1986.

AUSTRALIAN WAR CLASSICS
PRESENTED BY E. E. (WEARY) DUNLOP

WE WERE
THE RATS

LAWSON GLASSOP

PENGUIN BOOKS

Penguin Books Australia Ltd
487 Maroondah Highway, PO Box 257
Ringwood, Victoria 3134, Australia
Penguin Books Ltd
Harmondsworth, Middlesex, England
Viking Penguin, A Division of Penguin Books USA Inc.
375 Hudson Street, New York, New York 10014, USA
Penguin Books Canada Limited
10 Alcorn Avenue, Toronto, Ontario, Canada M4V 1E4
Penguin Books (NZ) Ltd
182-190 Wairau Road, Auckland 10, New Zealand

First published in Australia by Angus & Robertson 1944
Reprinted 1945
New edition published by Horwitz 1969
New edition published by Currey O'Neil Pty Ltd 1982
This edition published by Penguin Books Australia Ltd 1991

10 9 8 7 6 5 4 3 2

Produced by Viking O'Neil
56 Claremont Street, South Yarra, Victoria 3141, Australia
A Division of Penguin Books Australia Ltd

Cover design by Jan Schmoeger
Printed in Australia by The Book Printer, Maryborough, Vic.

National Library of Australia
Cataloguing-in-Publication data

Glassop, Lawson, 1913-1966.
    We were the Rats.

    ISBN 0 14 014924 4.

    1. World War, 1939-1945 – Campaigns – Africa, North –
    Fiction. I. Title. (Series: Australian war classics).

A823.2

FOREWORD

Tobruk, nestling on the Libyan coast between the desert and the sparkling Mediterranean, and hallowed by the gallant dead of a chivalrous conflict, should remain enshrined in our national consciousness. I am therefore particularly delighted that this moving tale is to be republished.

For those Australians who served in the famous 242-day siege of Tobruk in 1941, Lawson Glassop's realistic portrayal of the embattled, shattered town and its valiant defenders will stir proud memories like those of Shakespeare's Henry V as he recalled the Battle of Agincourt on its anniversary, St Crispin's Day. This is more than simply a soldiering story, however. As Norman Lindsay comments in his delightful Foreword to the original 1944 edition: 'All the complexities forced on him by war, action, endurance, fear, courage, love and death are here painted with an enduring visibility in words, and with an unerring selection of types and personalities which reveal the man of action under the relentless test of war.'

We first meet the central character, Mick Reynolds—unwillingly dubbed 'the Wizard of Nerridale' for his legendary cricketing prowess—in his small New South Wales home town. He emerges as a literate, articulate and athletic youth possessed of an easy familiarity with men, girls and booze, and a flair for casual love affairs. His restless, slightly flippant nature is redeemed by an inner seriousness which, under the stimulus of his first sincere love and by the stern crucible of war, is eventually transformed into an admirable maturity. Despite the gravity of his theme, Glassop's touch is light and his characterisations memorable. There is a completely credible, humorous account of Reynolds' enlistment in the AIF, of life in the local training camps, and of the bonds that develop between men of quite diverse educational backgrounds, social circumstances and interests. This interdependence and mateship is seen to flourish in what are, to me, the very familiar army camps of Palestine and Egypt, and later in Libya.

By early in 1941, as we of the 'Lustre Force' suffered defeat and withdrawal at the hands of the Germans in Greece and Crete, the inexperienced 9th Division under General Morshead was assailed by the well organised Panzer divisions of Rommel's proud Africa Corps, 'flushed with the fallacy of its own invincibility'. The threat of outflanking instigated a disorderly retreat—often styled 'the Benghazi

Handicap'—by the Allied forces from El Agheila back to Tobruk. In the dust and confusion, some troops were diverted by Germans posing as traffic police and the British generals O'Connor and Neame, unwisely riding in a spectacular silver-grey Lincoln Zephyr, were lured into captivity.

There the war really begins for Corporal Reynolds. He and his section shoot their way free of the encircling Germans to reach Tobruk, humiliated to be fleeing along the road taken earlier by the victorious 6th Division. Once in Tobruk the poorly equipped and half-trained men of the 9th dig in and fight grimly: they withstand the initial onslaught of German tanks and supporting infantry to stabilise a front around the perimeter of the town, and in the long ensuing siege become a thorn in the side of the German army.

As well as facing constant and almost unopposed aerial attack and shelling, these men endure the cruel extremes of desert heat and cold, and oppressive sandstorms. Their diet is inadequate, water is scarce, dysentery is rife, and their ranks are depleted daily. Morale remains high nonetheless, the grimly resolute confidence of the Australians recalling that of the earlier AIF at Gallipoli. Glassop's descriptions of the fierce fighting at close quarters, of offensive patrols threading through the minefields, of the disheartening work of the medical orderly, of the stealthy night arrival in Tobruk Harbour of small ships exchanging stores for casualties, have a matter-of-fact but powerful authenticity. In the event the 9th Division wins great glory, and with the few survivors from his section Reynolds is recalled home to join the forces in the mounting Pacific war.

This stirring account of an Australian soldier in action is a forceful memento of one of the famous sieges of history, which takes him 'from quiet homes and first beginnings out to the undiscovered ends'.

E. E. Dunlop

CONTENTS

FOREWORD TO THE 1944 EDITION

I THINK it was about ten years ago that I received by post an MS. novel by one Lawson Glassop. It was one of those annoying first novels which are not good enough to publish but which reveal a genuine sense for prose in the writer. A little later Lawson Glassop himself arrived to see me and demand what I intended to do about getting his novel published. He, also, confused a nice critical estimate of personality, for besides being an extremely good-looking youth, aspiration in him appeared to be equally divided between literature and athletics. He talked in the same breath of achievement in both objectives, with some reference to that other quest of all aspiring male egos, girls, in short. I had noticed that in his novel he had a genuine flair for that most difficult achievement in any art, a capacity to project the feminine image with charm, clarity, and reality. I don't remember very clearly what was said in that interview; I have talked to so many young aspirants to the arts, but I did retain a strong impression of Glassop's personality, by turns innocent and sophisticated, arrogant and humble, resolute and uncertain. Youth setting out on a muddled quest for adventure in life and art. All I retained of it was a feeling that he would either do something very good or nothing at all. But I do remember that through it all he insisted on a passionate determination to be a novelist.

Well, he has become one, and a disgtinguished one, too. Wisely, he has let experience of life accumulate before adventuring it as material in art. I did not have a word from him again till he sent me the MS. of *We Were the Rats*. A very bedraggled MS. it was, obviously written under difficult conditions and carried about anyhow in the very restricted baggage of a man on active service. But it rewarded putting in order and reading. I realized as I read that only a driving passion to record truly the spectacle of life could have produced it. It explained, too, Glassop's puzzling duality of writer and athlete. By being one he had acquired material for the other. He could be the men he wrote about while retaining the writer's detachment to analyse and understand them, as they could never have understood themselves. For that reason he has revealed them with astonishing clarity. We have had many brilliant enough sketches of the Digger in action; this is his full length portrait, and painted life size, too. All the complexities forced on him by war, action, endurance, fear, courage, love and death, are here painted with an enduring visibility in words, and with an unerring selection of the types and personalities which reveal the man of action under the relentless test of war.

But this is not only a first-class war novel. It is a first-class novel. A work only episodic of war must have war's time factor attached to it, with its threat of receding in interest as the war it records recedes in time. But Lawson Glassop has wisely presented his central character before the war starts, as youth—with all its urges and discontents over girls, booze, sport and the nagging desire to find some concrete statement of self in life and art—suddenly disrupted by the war, which becomes the motive of a full realization of manhood by the threat of death, by self-understanding, by understanding others, by comradeship, and by the discovery that love, rather than casual love affairs, becomes the apex of life's adventure. It takes the full curve of a beginning, middle, and end, which a novel must have if it is to be a constructed work of art.

Moreover, it is written in the first person singular; a method that rarely succeeds, because the author hardly ever escapes confusion with himself as the hero motive of the novel, and the reader suspects and rejects a too apparent partisanship. But the central character of *We Were the Rats* never once alienates our sympathy by an exhibition of self-esteem. He presents himself starkly, without reservations, and lets us do what we like about accepting him or rejecting him. We accept him because he is an admirable piece of craftsmanship, conscious or otherwise. I find it difficult to recall another novel where the first person singular is used so effectively.

Australia owes Lawson Glassop a big debt for this novel. Historians may record the progress of wars, but they cannot project a picture of the men who fought them. And how much of the country's future tradition exists on the record of its men of action, who supply the material for art, for aspiration, for national pride, for the energy which drives life on into the future. If Australia is destined for a fine future, this book is necessary to its spirit. Our fighting men have made their record of courage and endurance and are making it still, and this book is its affirmation. In it Lawson Glassop speaks for the Australian soldier. And in a book that will endure.

NORMAN LINDSAY

Springwood,
June 1944

"The rats of Tobruk, those self-supporting prisoners of war."
—Lord Haw Haw.

I LOOKED *down again at what was left of Tobruk. Of all the God-forsaken spots known to man, of all the desolate wastes, of all the places on the earth's surface where man had chosen to build a home, surely this was the worst.*

Eddie was right when he said, "Just to live in this lousy place is bad enough without all the rest."

I heard somebody singing, faintly at first. The song became louder and I recognized it as "The Wizard of Oz", the song the Sixth Division had sung when it went into action at Bardia for the first time. I could hear somebody tramping along the escarpment behind me. I did not bother to look round. I heard him stop a few yards away and then the words came clearly:

"Oh, we're off to see the Wizard, the Wizard of Nerridale."

I was dropping a couple of stones from one hand to the other. I dropped them slowly to the ground. So somebody knew.

In the A.I.F. introductions lack the formality of those in civilian life. "Ay, Blue, this is Darkie" was the usual thing. You knew Diggers as "Slim" and "Bill" and "Snowy" and "Tich" rather than Private Jones, Corporal Smith, Sergeant Thompson and Sergeant-Major Williams. With me, it was more a case of "Mick, meet Harry" than "I don't think you have met Corporal Reynolds, have you, Sergeant Johnson?"

It was five years since I had played cricket and I had never played for the State. "The Wizard of Nerridale" had been forgotten. I told those who did remember my name that the Wizard was a cousin of mine.

But now evidently the secret was out. It did not matter. A champion cricketer was not much use in Tobruk. Some of the boys played occasionally and we had read some rot in one of the papers about umpires with loaded rifles; but the presence of a good ack-ack gunner or a soldier with two bottles of beer would have aroused more interest than that of Don Bradman.

There was something familiar in the tone of the singer's voice. I turned to look at him.

For a moment I stared dully at him. "It's George Shammar," I said slowly.

He was standing there, grinning all over his face. His head was as shaggy as ever, his eyebrows as bushy and his dress as unkempt, but there was more than mockery in his beady eyes now.

After I had pumped his hand, clapped him on the shoulder and spluttered in amazement, he sat down beside me.

"That was a pretty heavy raid," he said.

I looked at him sharply. "Sorry, George. It was chicken-feed. Apart from bringing down that Eyetie, it wasn't worth watching."

I saw the crinkles deepen around his eyes. "Oh," he said. For the first time I felt superior to George. His tone acknowledged that superiority. To him I was a veteran, one of the "heroes of Tobruk".

"You ought to see the Jerries turn it on," I said. "They come straight down through that harbour barrage. You wouldn't think they'd live through it. Some of 'em don't."

"Oh," said George.

"Christ, it's good to see you. So you finally got round to it, eh? What about that hollow log out Alice Springs way? I just can't believe that you're here. What are you in?"

"The 54th. I couldn't get with you. I tried, but an officious bastard at base posted me to the 54th. Said the 93rd needed no reinforcements."

"Of course we don't. None of our fellows ever gets killed. We're all Speed Gordons. We're all immortal. Like hell we are! Some of the officers at the reinforcement depot are a lot of twirps. They get into it because they can't take it, or they're rejects who were no bloody good in action, or they're good men who kicked against authority. I'll see if I can get you a transfer to my platoon."

"Good. I was a sergeant in the reos, but lost my stripes, of course, when I got here."

I drew a line in the dirt with the toe of my boot. Then I looked up into his eyes. "What price pacificism now?" I asked.

"You were right, Mick," he said. "It was too big for me."

I had him down and I wanted to see him suffer as he had made me suffer. I saw the crinkles deepen around his eyes again, and I knew I had scored a direct hit.

"You're not going to say 'I told you so', are you?" he asked.

"Of course I am. You had no mercy on me and I'll have none on you. Do you still believe it's easier to enlist than face the silent condemnation of the mob? Do you still think you can pacify a mad dog like Hitler? Do you still believe I'm the kind of man who causes wars?"

George was drawing figures in the dust with a stone. "You sound bitter," he said.

"I am bitter. And, by Christ, when you've been here a few months you'll be bitter too. The iron of Tobruk will enter into your soul.

It's no Sunday School picnic here, George. It's not like doing route marches in the Palestine fields here."

George jabbed at the dust with a stone, and looked up at me. He was pale.

"I'm sorry, Mick," he said. "I was wrong. I apologize. Let's forget it."

"O.K.," I said.

"I couldn't stand it any longer," said George.

"The only difference between us was that your conscience had a delayed-action fuse," I said. "The infantry will win the war in the end despite all their tanks and their fancy planes; but it's a bastard. Why didn't you get a job in brigade or divisional headquarters or ordnance or postal or pay or some base unit?"

"Because I'm a bloody fool like you," he said quietly.

"It's funny. Everybody I spoke to who'd been to the last war seemed to have been in the trenches. I had the idea that if you joined the A.I.F. you had to fight in the front line. I know now how many men it takes to keep one in those trenches. Do you know our divisions have even got a mobile laundry and decontamination unit and a mobile bath unit? Wouldn't it rip you?"

"Yeah. But I suppose we'll all be the same. Every old Digger who tries to bite you for a drink or sixpence for a pie and peas or some lousy verses will have been in Tobruk or Greece and Crete."

I asked him eagerly about Palestine, particularly Beit Hareed, but my questions about Nerridale were half-hearted. Nerridale was a long way behind me now.

"Remember Shirley?" asked George. "The pouter pigeon girl with the beautiful eyes who worked in that sundae shop next to the Mayfair Theatre? Well, she's the 'elegant Mrs 'Aliburton' now. Her husband's over here somewhere. In the A.I.F., too."

"Oh," I said. "Remember the night war broke out and Captain Rissay came and told us it was great news for him?" asked George.

"Yes. I often wonder what happened to him."

"He got killed at Bardia. He was a major."

"Oh. We never see any casualty lists except those sent from home, and most people don't like to send things like that. You might be out on the Bardia Road sector and somebody you knew back home might get killed in the El Adem sector and you'd never hear about it. You wouldn't even know he was in the A.I.F."

George told me he had not seen Margaret. "Is that still on?" he asked.

"Yes."

"Good. You know, you've given me such a faint picture of her."

"Yes. But I've got such a faint picture of her myself. It's a funny business. I've hardly ever seen the girl, you know. Haven't seen her more than about thirty times in my life. It's like—it's like being in love with a stranger, with a shadow."

"It's tough," said George. "Life hasn't been very kind to you, Mick."

"Mahlish.[1] I'm alive, aren't I? Some day I'll make up for it all. Some day."

"Yeah. Some day."

"Did you bring a chess set with you?" I asked eagerly.

"Yes."

"Hooray! It must be the only one in Tobruk. I've tried everywhere to get one."

He told me about the meals he had had in Tel Aviv and Alexandria. "Chicken," he said, "and asparagus and lettuce. Grilled steak, poached eggs, chips and tomatoes. And remember how you used to like grilled kidneys? Well, I had a plateful of 'em in Alex. the other day."

I licked my lips. "Stop!" I cried. "You're killing me. It's practically all bully beef and biscuits here, George. No matter how cleverly the cook disguises the old bully, we always see through it. And we get about a cigarette tin full of chlorinated water to wash, shave and clean our teeth in. I advise you to clean your teeth first, then wash, then shave. And I hope you like flies—to eat, I mean. Because, boy, you're going to eat 'em."

"Sounds grim," said George.

"Remember in The Journal of a Disappointed Man Barbellion disagrees with what Keats—or was it Shelley?—said was the most beautiful thing in the world? Barbellion said, 'The most beautiful thing in the world is a xenophor standing in a glass jar in the sun.'"

"Yes. I remember."

"Well, they're both wrong, George. The most beautiful thing in the world is a grilled flounder standing on a white plate in the electric light."

George laughed. "You're right, Mick. I didn't realize the importance of food until I joined the army."

"Nobody did. George, what is the most significant thing the army has taught you?"

"That's easy. It has taught me something fundamental—the sheer delight of living. It has made me realize that all my life I've been ungrateful, that I've taken things for granted. Things like food

[1] Never mind.

and comfort and security and peace. I've been ungrateful. If I ever get home I'll never complain again."

"I knew you'd say that. It's what everybody says. The whole world has learned that lesson, but I'm afraid the world will, as usual, soon forget. Some of the boys are inarticulate of course, but if I put it into words for them they agree. 'Yeah,' they say, 'it was a bloody good life we led back in Aussie, on'y we didden seem ter think so then.' India, Palestine and Egypt have taught us to appreciate our own country, and our standard of living. And there's something else you've learned, too, and now you're here you'll learn it so well you'll never forget it. And that is that the only decent thing you'll ever get out of war is fellowship."

"Yes," said George, "I can well believe it."

"It must have been funny when you arrived in Palestine. I suppose you were amazed when the first Wog you saw said 'Syeeda, George'?"

George laughed. "Yes. I couldn't believe it was fair dinkum. I thought one of the boys was having a joke. A colonel named George came over with us. You should have seen his face when the first Wog he saw when he got off the ship at Tewfik held out his hand and said 'Bucksheesh, George'!"

We laughed. "Tell me," said George, "How do you feel about the chocos? And the munition workers?"

"Some of the boys are bitter," I said. "The trouble with the world today is inequality of sacrifice, just as it's always been inequality of distribution of wealth. I know the munition workers are doing an essential job, but I wish to hell they wouldn't pay 'em a tenner a week when we get five bob a day for holding the perimeter of Tobruk. Did you know that every Sunday morning some of the boys go up to the cemetery the engineers built out near the Bardia Road? They observe a minute's silence for the fellows injured in Saturday's football games at home. Bitter, isn't it?"

"Tobruk must have gone deep," said George.

"It's gone deep all right. I don't think any man who's been here for long will ever be the same again. You can't get away from it, George. You just can't escape it. Sometimes when you come out of the line you get hell bombed out of you and you're bloody glad to get back into it. Have you ever lived months without seeing a woman, without hearing a woman's voice, except on the radio? You begin to wonder whether there are such things, whether you'll be game to talk to one when you see one. Have you ever lived weeks without having a bath, without putting water on any part of you except your face? Your feet stink, George, and you get desert sores, and the dirt is caked on your body with your sweat, and you feel ashamed. You count the days until you'll be able to emerge from your hole and go down to the sea. And days and weeks and months go past and there is no end to it. It just goes on and on, and you see the hopelessness in men's faces and know there is hopelessness in your own. And then you see the spirit shine through, you see men laugh it off, and if you believe in God you thank Him for men like these, men who will make bets on where the next bomb will fall, men who go in through enemy shellfire with that high-shouldered, swinging Australian infantryman's walk, and laughter on their lips, and cry to each other, 'If the tucker doesn't improve I'm going to get out of this unit.' And you hope that some day you'll deserve to share the same bully beef and flies and fleas with them."

We did not say anything for a while. Then I said, "I'm getting maudlin. Let me tell you something about our perimeter defences, tell you why Jerry will never get into Tobruk. He's a no-hoper, George. He's just not in the race."

"Good," said George.

Book One

NERRIDALE

☆

CHAPTER I

I HAVE never seen anybody else grow older so graciously as my mother. Time, which treats women so harshly, was gentle with her. It tinged her hair with grey, and although lines multiplied in her face they were only faint and her eyes still held the guileless clarity of childhood.

I do not think she thought ill of anybody in her life. An uncle told me that the day after she received a telegram in 1917 telling her that her husband had been wounded she said, "Those poor Germans. The poor men simply don't know what they're doing."

My father had left her barely enough money to live on. The war pension helped, but until Joan and I were working she must have had to scrape to make one obstinate end meet the other. Yet she often gave me money, and I know that she wormed from my schoolmates the names of books at which I had looked eagerly in windows. She gave me so many books that I had to keep my literary longings to myself.

I did not know until later what my five years at Nerridale High School and my visits to Sydney with cricket teams must have meant to her.

She had, of course, been cursed with the outrageously incomplete education of her generation, and at times her ignorance shocked even me, who knew her so well. I shall never forget running home from school, my heart singing with the discovery of "The Nightingale" and bursting into the kitchen with the cry, "Mother, what do you think of John Keats?"

She looked up from the stove, puzzled. "John Keats, dear?" she said. "He's the new tobacconist in Victoria Street, isn't he?"

Although her husband had been at the war she did not have the faintest idea where England was, and she thought that much of America was overrun by Red Indians. In my fierce young intolerance, I was ashamed of these things at first, but later I realized that the other members of her circle, Mrs Parkinson, Mrs Grey, Mrs Curnellan and Mrs Riley, knew just as little.

Often when I came home from school I found them sipping tea and delighting in harmless but scandalized gossip. Years later when I read Oscar Wilde's witticism, "All women become like their mothers. That's their tragedy. No man does. That's his", I recalled those placid afternoon teas; but when I came running in to them with my battered schoolbag they were notable only for delicious hot scones with melting butter.

Twice each Sunday my mother ensured the desirable destination of her soul. That was not remarkable. What was remarkable was that she did not insist on making certain of the destination of mine.

She had grown up in a bigoted age, but she was above its bigotry. She sent me to Sunday School until I was twelve and then, taking me into the sitting-room she said solemnly, "Howard, dear. You are old enough now to decide whether you want to go to church or not. You're getting too old for Sunday School. If you have really heard the call of the Lord you will want to go to church; if you haven't you will want to go surfing. Which is it to be?"

She looked at me eagerly, but I could not tell a lie on this subject, even for her.

"Well, mother," I said, shifting my feet uneasily and mixing my metaphors, "I am sorry to have to tell you the Lord's had a fair crack of the whip and He's missed the bus. It's surfing for me."

I could see her disappointment, but she merely smiled, said "All right, Howard", and kissed me.

I will have to do something to help her, I thought. "Mother," I said.

"Yes, dear."

"Don't be worried, mother. Church might be better for my soul, but the surf'll be better for my body. And bodies are pretty important."

"Yes, dear," she said gravely. "Bodies are pretty important."

Old Dr Baines, who brought me into the world, told me once that it was utterly impossible for my mother to believe anything to my detriment, and I knew he was right.

"Mick," he said, "if your mother saw you kill a man she would not believe her eyes. If she heard you say something foul she would not believe her ears. If she smelt drink on you she would not believe her nose."

I knew it was true. Often I came home smelling of beer, but she did not notice. Sometimes I came home drunk, so drunk that I could scarcely speak, but still she did not notice. Her mind simply refused to accept the evidence of her senses.

I remember what my father had told me when, wide-eyed, I had sat on his knee and listened to him talk. "Mick," he had said, "I saw some great men in France. I saw men who just refused to admit defeat. They were beaten but they wouldn't give in. They were dead but they wouldn't lie down." My mother was like that.

I overheard Mrs Grey say to my mother one day, "I hate to say this, Mrs Reynolds, but I think I should tell you that Mick was seen the other night in a car with a barmaid."

I heard my mother put down her teacup. "Mrs Grey," she said quietly, "if you ever say such a ridiculous thing again I will have to ask you to stay away from this house. Would you like another scone?"

That was my mother. I did not get my cursed restlessness from her. I often wish I had inherited some of her supreme placidity. She had a sublime faith in the British Empire, the Baptist Church, a cup of tea and Mick Reynolds.

Sometimes, when I was not out with barmaids, milk-bar girls, shop assistants or waitresses, I took her to the pictures. One night, as I strolled down Victoria Street with her, she said, "Howard, I've lived in Nerridale for fifty years and I don't know a quarter the people you know."

"I've a capacity for making friends, mother," I said. "Perhaps it's my simple nature or they trust my face or something."

She laughed. "What absurd things you say at times," she said.

A big man swaggered by in a check suit. When he saw me he lifted his green hat awkwardly. I noticed the coloured feather in it. " 'Night, Mick," he said.

"Good night, Mr Newton," I said, for my mother's benefit. I glanced back and saw him staring after me and scratching his head.

"Who was that, dear?" asked mother.

"That was Mr Michael Newton; he has big financial interests," I said.

"Oh, how nice. They were strange clothes he was wearing, weren't they?"

"Oh, I don't know. You have to allow these financial magnates plenty of latitude, you know."

"Yes, I suppose you do. Ask him round to the house one night."

"Yes, mother, I will," I said, turning away to hide my smile. I could see Big Mike Newton drinking tea! Big Mike had the most thriving S.P. betting business in Nerridale and had been sent out for life by Nerridale Jockey Club for "fixing" a field on Cup day.

Then we met George Shammar, who had taught me English at Nerridale High School and guided my halting steps along the literary road. He looked like a bear. His brown hair was shaggy, and he always looked as though he needed a shave. His beady eyes were whimsical when they were not mocking, but they were usually mocking. His shoes were always dirty, and his tie badly tied.

Above all else, I liked George for the way he always spoke to my mother.

"One would think," I said to him one day, "that you were meeting a queen."

"I am," he said.

"Don't forget that appointment for chess next week, George," I said.

"You'll never forget the hiding you'll get," said George, and we laughed and went on.

We passed a muscular fellow with a black shirt, white tie and black and white shoes.

"How yer goin', Mick?" he said, pulling off his cap.

"Good night, Frank," I said.

"Whatever happened to that young man's nose, Howard?" asked mother.

"He had an accident. He's a coming man. He puts people to sleep."

"You mean he's an an— an an——"

"An anaesthetist."

"Yes, dear. I forget these big words. That's very nice. I like to see the young men do well. It only shows you how appearances can be deceptive."

It was Tiger Farrell, the best welterweight who had pulled on a glove at Nerridale Stadium for ten years. No welterweight in Australia had more dynamite in his right cross than Tiger. I knew. I had sparred with him many times at Les Taylor's gym. If Tiger was not ten-seven champion of Australia within a year I would never go to another fight. I would be certain the game was not fair.

A shabby youth planted himself in front of us. I tried to edge around him, but he spoke. " 'Lo, Mick," he said. "Want ter talk to ya a minute."

"Mother," I said. "I'd like you to meet Mr—er—Mr Galsworthy." I had just finished *The Forsyte Saga* and my mind was full of its rare beauty.

"How do you do, Mr Galsworthy," said mother. "I'm pleased to meet any of Howard's friends."

I watched amazement flood ludicrously into his face. "Er—glad ter know ya, ma'am," he mumbled. "Say, Mick, mind if——"

"Excuse me a moment, mother." I said. "Mr—er—Galsworthy wants to speak to me privately. Would you mind looking into that window for a moment?"

"Certainly, Howard."

I drew him aside. It was Spike, who kept the pie cart on the corner of Victoria and Kendall streets. I could not introduce him to my mother as Spike and I did not know his surname.

"Ay, Mick," he said, pulling at his ear. "What's all this———? Are ya havin' me on? What's that there fancy handle ya give me?"

"Galsworthy?" I said. I fell easily into the street corner idiom. "Ya oughta be proud, see? This Galsworthy is a Pommy bloke who packs a punch. He's known as a trump all over the place. He's fair dinkum. And I call ya 'Galsworthy' and ya get off ya bike."

"He was a real big noise, eh? Bowled a lotter blokes over?"

"Yeah. Fair dinkum."

A slow smile spread over his lumpy face. "Well, she's jake. I thought ya was tryin' to be funny. Havin' me on."

"Spike," I said earnestly. "I gotta introduce ya to me mother. I don't know ya other monnicker, see? So I gotta say somethin', haven't I?"

"It's oke. Everythin's jake. I'm not crooked on ya no more. And me second handle's Curran. But listen, Mick. What's yer old woman call ya 'Howard' for?"

"It's me name, but it's too cissy, so I dices it and picks up 'Mick'."

"Aw. I don't blame ya."

"Well I gotta get goin'. She's waitin' for me. What's on ya mind?"

"Oh yeah. Wait'll I tell ya. You know them two grouse sheilas we've got the meet on with tomorrer night?"

"Yeah. Them two from the milk bar."

"Yeah. Let's scrub 'em."

"Scrub 'em. Why?"

"I was talkin' ter Jerry Kinnaird. Ya know 'im. He stopped the abo in three last Saturdee. What a punch! It was a bloody beaut. I leaves me cart outside and sneaks in just in time to see Jerry knock Binghi as cold as a Polar bear's backside."

"Yeah. Make it snappy, Spike. I gotta go."

"O.K. Well, Jerry tells me they're on the nose."

"Yeah?"

"Yeah. Just a coupler ———." He used a word that means that they titillated the passions and then refused to satisfy them. "What sort of mugs they think we are?" he asked in an injured tone.

"They're diced," I said. "Well, I'll be seein' ya, Spike."

"Half a mo, Mick. Whaddaya say to us gettin' two other sorts instead? You seen that new blonde barmaid at the Royal? A real good line. They tell me she's got a bonzer mate. We'll take them two for a spin instead. We'll go through on them two milk-bar sorts."

"O.K., Spike. Only I gotta have the blonde, see? You take the chance on her cobber."

"Suits me, Mick. Ya never know. I might come in on the grouter. I'll have a pint at the Royal tomorrer and put it on the blonde. She'll be jake. I'll be seein' yer."

" 'Bye, Spike."

"So long, Mick."

I found mother staring with lively interest into a window full of those ridiculous things that masquerade as women's hats.

"Howard," she said, "what a strange young man Mr Galsworthy is. Does he always talk like that?"

"No, mother. He was just fooling. He's a great one for a joke."

"That's nice. I like to see young people enjoying themselves. He wanted to talk to you about cricket, I suppose. Everybody wants to talk to you about cricket. Where does he work?"

"Oh, he's in the retail pastry business."

"Is he? Now isn't that nice?"

"Howard," said mother one night. "A curious thing happened today."

"Yes, mother."

"You may go to bed, Joan."

"Aw gee, mum," Joan said, "I always know when you've got anything interesting to say 'cause you always say 'You may go to bed, Joan.' "

Mother went placidly on with her knitting. "There are some things a young girl's ears shouldn't hear, even if they aren't true. Now off to bed you go. Good night, dear."

I had been listening to a description of a wrestling match on the wireless and had settled down to James Branch Cabell's *Jurgen*, which George had lent me, and was delighting in its cleverness. This is something a young girl's eyes shouldn't see, I thought, but of course a young girl wouldn't see anything in it.

"Howard," said mother when Joan had left the room. "I want to make it clear that I don't believe a word of what I heard, but I thought I should tell you just the same."

I looked up, and there must have been a light dawning in my eyes.

"Yes, mother."

"Well, when I was going into town in the tram today I was sitting next to two girls. They weren't very nice girls, dear. They had too much paint on their lips and powder on their faces and not enough skirt on their dresses."

"Yes, mother." I did not know what to do with my hands. I tried biting my nails.

"Well, one of them said to the other, 'You know who I seen'— isn't it disgusting the way girls talk nowadays?—'with Ethel the other night?' "

My palms were becoming clammy and I drew my right hand slowly across my forehead to hide the look in my eyes.

"And the other girl replied 'No. Who?' and the first girl said 'Guess' and the other girl said 'Aw gee, I can't. Don't tease. Who was it?' and the first girl said 'Why, that cricket fellow, Mick Reynolds.' "

"Good heavens, mother. Did she say that?" I have never heard a more unconvincing voice.

"Yes. Isn't it disgraceful? And the second girl said 'Aw gee. You don't say?' and the first girl said 'Spit me death.' What a disgusting expression!"

"Yes, mother."

"Then the second girl said, 'He took me drivin' out to Lake Carraday a coupler times in that green car but he don't hang round no more.' I remember everything they said because I listened carefully and as soon as I got out I wrote it down. I felt so humiliated. I was glad there was nobody else in the compartment."

I licked my dry lips and held the book tightly in both hands. "Yes, mother. Go on."

"Well they didn't say much else, except that this awful girl Ethel told one of them later that she and you—I mean this boy who was supposed to be you—had drunk a bottle of gin and had gone for a swim without—er—without any clothes on. I'm sorry to have to tell you this, Howard, but I feel you should know what stories are being told."

"Yes, mother. I'm glad—glad you told me."

"Well I had to get out then, but before doing so I told them they shouldn't be taken in by such falsehoods and they could tell their friend Ethel to tell her friend that if he didn't stop imperson-ating my son I'd inform the police."

I dragged my right hand down over my chin. When I spoke my voice was hollow.

"What did they say to that?"

"The hussies were too dumbfounded to say anything."

"I'll bet they were."

"I tried to do my duty as I saw it. You don't think I did the wrong thing, dear, do you?"

"What's that? Oh no. Of course not. I'll have a word with one of my friends at the police station tomorrow and see that this doesn't happen again."

"You will, dear? Thank you very much."

"Thank *you*, mother," I said.

I went down the hall, and rang George. "George," I said softly, "you may reef my heart out. You may, like Caliban, cut my wezand with thy knife. You may even send me to a war. But for Christ's sake when you come out here tomorrow night don't come in your green car."

CHAPTER II

"MICK," said Joan, "are you coming to Spellman's dance?"

I was poring over the chessboard and did not answer. George had been doing criminal things with his knights, and I was squirming.

"Howard," said mother, "Joan asked you a question."

George tapped my shin lightly with his shoe. I looked up in surprise. He jabbed his thumb through the air, and I glanced at Joan with a frown.

"I asked you whether you were coming to Spellman's dance on Saturday night," said Joan.

"Spellman's dance?" I said, my mind still hazy with the problem of protecting my king.

"Yes. All the girls from work'll be going. Mary and Betty and Bobbie and Lyla and Sylvia and Martha and Heather, and lots of others."

"Sorry, Joan," I said, "Tiger Farrell's fighting Jacky Peters, and I wouldn't miss that for anything."

"Aw, gee, Mick," wailed Joan, and mother said, "I don't know how Howard can bear to watch two men hurt each other. Mr Shammar, do you?"

"I can't understand it either," said George, with a mischievous glint in his eyes.

"You hypocritical coot," I murmured, for I knew that George would be chewing peanuts in the Press seats with a spurious air of boredom.

"Anyhow, I don't want to see a lot of kids trying to dance," I said, speculating on the dreadful consequences of a rash move I almost made.

"I like that!" cried Joan. " 'A lot of kids' indeed! I'll have you know I'm not a kid. I'll be eighteen the week after next."

Christ, I thought, there goes another five bob. Eighteen, eh? The kid was growing up. I wish George hadn't moved that knight there. His attack had the awful inevitability of a Dreiser plot. You were caught in it, you struggled frantically, but you could not escape and you knew it.

"Aw gee, Mick, won't you come? Cliff'll be away in Sydney with the High School first eleven and I've got nobody to go with. All the girls'll be going with their boy friends and I don't want to be a grape on the business."

"A what on the what?" asked mother, looking up from her knitting in surprise.

"I mean I don't want to be a trouble to anybody," said Joan quickly. "Mary'll be with Sam, and Martha with Johnny and Sylvia with Mac and so on."

"You'll take her, won't you, Howard?" asked mother. "You can see your precious boxing match another time."

I was in a mess. If I moved that pawn to attack his knight it left my queen exposed to his bishop.

"Mick," said George, "your mother's talking to you."

"Eh?" I said, looking up. "Oh yes. What's that, mother?"

"Joan wants you to take her to the dance because Cliff will be away. You'll go, won't you?"

So that was what all this talk was about. It was serious. I could not miss this fight. I had taken too many friendly cracks on the jaw from Tiger Farrell not to want to see him dishing serious ones out to someone else. Besides, I had two pounds I wanted to get set on Tiger.

"Mother," I said. "I've looked forward to this—er—boxing match for months. I've just got to see it."

"And I've looked forward to this dance, too," said Joan, with the corners of her mouth drooping.

"Listen, Joan. You can go with some of the other girls, can't you?"

"But all my girl friends are going with their boy friends and I don't want to be—to have to tag along with them. That's no fun for anybody. And besides, who's going to bring me home?"

"Lots of fellows will want to bring you home. Try one of 'em for a change."

"Gee, I'd like to," said Joan, and her eyes lit up.

"Joan!" said mother. "If Cliff had heard you say that!"

"He didn't, and what you don't hear doesn't hurt you."

"Joan!"

"All right, mother."

"Why not ask Cliff not to go to Sydney?" I asked.

"I like that! And give up his big chance against Parramatta High? If you don't like cricket, he does."

Wasn't I in enough trouble with George getting stuck into me with his full battery without having to worry about taking my sister to some damn-fool kids' dance? A man never got any peace. Cricket again. It was always cricket. If Cliff didn't play the stupid game I'd be able to see Tiger fight without having to talk my way there first.

"I think I have the solution," said George.

We all looked at him. "Mick can do both," he said. "He can take Joan to the dance, go to the stadium, and pick Joan up afterwards."

Good old George. He amused me with his cynicism, provided me with alibis when I wanted to be somewhere else, gave me sage but disregarded advice about milk-bar girls, directed my feet along the literary road, lent me his car for amorous adventures behind the racecourse and out at Lake Carraday, tried to make a golfer and chess player out of me, and now he came to light with the obvious solution.

Good old George. I could have a few drinks at the Majestic, discuss the fight, perhaps take Milly home when she finished at eleven, and meet Joan at twelve.

"Will that suit you, Joan?" I asked.

"Well I would like you to stay and meet some of my friends again—you never take any interest in my friends and they're all anxious to meet the Wizard of Nerridale—but if that's all you can manage I suppose it'll have to do."

"Satisfied, mother?"

"Yes, dear."

"O.K. then. Everybody's happy. I'll miss a few preliminaries, but they don't count. Now let's have silence while I concentrate."

Joan went out and I had the consequence of a move nearly worked out when she returned and pushed a sheaf of photographs under my nose. Curse the girl!

"Joan," I said, "for heaven's sake give me a break, will you? This might all sound like—er———" I looked at George. I couldn't use the word I was going to use.

"Balderdash," said George, grinning. Good old George.

"Yes—like balderdash to you, but it's grimly serious to me."

"It's serious all right," said George.

"So just fold up your tents like the Arabs and silently fade away, will you, Joan? I've agreed to take you and bring you home. Isn't that enough?"

"Don't be harsh with her, Howard," said mother. "She's only a child, you know."

"I am not a child," said Joan.

"All right, all right," I said, "we won't debate that." I noticed the amused glint in George's eyes. "Now go away and don't worry me."

"O.K.," said Joan, ignoring mother's frown; and she went, leaving the photographs near the edge of the table.

Damn him, if he was going to hit me with knights I'd hit him, too. I jumped one of mine boldly into the combat area.

"Good," said George, and I realized that I must have done something really good. I would not admit it was news to me. I would see it in a minute. My left elbow was on the table and my head was resting on my hand. Now what had I done? I moved my head to the left so that I could scratch the right side of my head.

My scratching slowed and stopped. My eye had caught the top photograph. I looked away and then looked back quickly. Yes, it was genuine. She was marvellous. I wondered who it was.

I picked up the photographs. Joan, hawk-eyed, was quickly at my side. I glanced up at her suspiciously. This was probably a trap. No, there was as much guile in her eyes as in mother's. I was vaguely conscious of the fact that George had moved, but I was not interested any more.

"Who's that?" I asked. I tried to make my voice casual. It deceived Joan, but I noticed the end of George's mouth curl.

"That's Martha. You know Martha."

"Not Martha Kellvert."

"Yes. You used to chase her around the peach-tree in the yard at my birthday party every year."

I was amazed. Young Martha Kellvert had become this glorious creature, this luscious, starry-eyed damsel with her strange unawareness of her own beauty. Little Martha Kellvert whose pigtails I used to pull.

I must be getting old. Why shouldn't Martha become a young woman? She must be eighteen now. Good heavens, Joan must be almost a woman, too. I looked at her so frankly she stared at me with wide eyes. I suppose she was pretty, too. I'd have to ask somebody. You got so used to having a sister about the place you just did not look at her.

I looked at Martha again. I could not get over it. I thought she still had pigtails and freckles. I would not chase her around a peach-tree any more. No, sir. I could think of much better things to do with Martha than that.

WE WERE THE RATS

12

"Give," said George. I handed the photograph over reluctantly.

"I'm in this group," said Joan. "That's me in the front row—on the left."

"Yes," I said, looking for Martha. I had not noticed Joan. I found Martha at the back. You could not see her figure this time—blast the fool who had posed them—but she was still enchanting. She must be attractive, I told myself, if I thought so when I could not see her figure.

"That's Mary," said Joan pointing to a plump girl. "Don't you think she's nice?"

She was. So were some of the others.

"I had no idea your girl friends had grown into young women," I said. "I thought they were still kids."

"There you are, mother," said Joan. Mother looked up from her knitting and smiled.

"Will—er—will all these girls be at the dance?" I asked.

"Of course. There's one here of us in bathing costumes."

I glanced up and caught George's eye. I looked away quickly.

"I'd like to see that one," I said. "Is—are you all in it?"

"Yes. Here it is." She handed it to me, and I caught my breath as I saw Martha in the middle of the front row. It was criminal for a girl who looked like that to go round in a bathing costume. I had never seen anything so fresh and sweet as Martha.

"Don't you like my costume?" asked Joan.

"Yes. Pretty good." I had not seen it.

Joan showed me a photograph of Spellman's vigoro team. There were a couple of new faces in it. Attractive young faces, too.

"Do you still want me to give the girls a bit of coaching?" I asked.

"Aw gee, Mick. Would you?"

"Well, I won't promise. But perhaps I'll be able to spare the time one of these days."

"That would be noble of you, Howard," said mother.

I looked at George, and decided not to reply. I went back to the photographs.

"I don't want to distract your attention," said George after a while, "but it's still your move."

"Eh? What? Oh, my move. Yes, we were playing chess, weren't we?"

"I thought we were," said George.

When George was going I walked with him to the front gate.

"Good night, Mick," he said. "You're going to miss a great fight."

I could hear him chuckling to himself as he walked away.

"Gee, Mick," said Joan in the tram. "It's bosker of you to take me to the dance. We haven't been out together for ages. You've never taken me to a dance before. Gee, you're a bonzer brother."

Her eyes were gleaming with excitement, and she could scarcely sit still. Looking at her, with the pink bow in her hair and her young lips faintly outlined with red, I wondered bitterly whether I could ever recapture her ebullient young enthusiasm.

I'm twenty-two, I thought. I'm getting old.

"That's all right, Joan," I said. I felt ashamed. "I ought to take you and mother out more. Remind me to take you both to the pictures one night next week."

"You shouldn't need reminding," said Joan primly, smoothing the lap of her dress.

I always say the wrong thing, I thought. My first impulsive ardour had waned, and I was beginning to regret agreeing to take her. Fancy missing seeing Tiger Farrell put Jacky Peters where he belonged! I was a fool. This kid Martha would probably be another example of the subtle alchemy of photography.

I would not know whether George had got set for my two pounds either. I had arranged for Dan Johnson, who did the broadcast over Station 2PR, to say "This is round two" at the beginning of the second round if the money were covered; but I could not be sure of getting to a wireless set.

George was right, as usual. Why hadn't I gone to the dance and the stadium? I stared moodily out of the open window at the familiar outlines of shops slipping past. I was going away from the stadium instead of towards it.

Gangling High School kids would pester me about cricket, and I'd have to dance with some heavy-footed friends of Joan's. And what would I get out of it? Martha would probably ask me to chase her round the peach-tree or call me "Mr Reynolds" or refuse when I asked her to go out with me. She was only a kid, anyhow, for all her slashing figure and high-pressure glamour.

After a while Joan said, "Mick, why do you have so many different girl friends? Gee, some of them don't last more than a week. Aren't those ones nice to you?"

I scraped a cigarette butt off the floor of the tram with one of my dancing pumps and looked up at my sister. "You're a queer kid," I said. "The trouble is they're too nice. The other ones last. Oscar Wilde was right, as usual. 'In this world there are only two tragedies. One is not getting what one wants, and the other is getting it. The last is the real tragedy.'"

"You know, Mick, it's you who're queer. You don't seem to get a kick out of things. You're a cynic. That's the word, isn't it?"

"Oscar Wilde defines a cynic as someone who knows the prices of everything and the value of nothing."

"Oh, you and your silly old Oscar Wilde. You're unhappy, Mick, aren't you?"

I looked quickly at her. The kid *was* growing up. "I'm restless, that's all," I said. "I don't know what's wrong with me."

"I can't make you out," said Joan. "You've always got a look in your eye as if you're looking for something, and as if you know you'll never find it. Yet about some things you're so—so——"

"Intense?"

"Yes. So intense. About silly old chess, and surfing and golf and poetry and dull books and all those awful people you know. Yet you're not interested in the things you can do really well. Cricket, for instance, and boxing—Cliff tells me Les Taylor reckons you're pretty hot. And you don't care anything about nice people."

"Nice people are dull."

"You know what you ought to do, Mick?" asked Joan, tapping me sagely on the knee. "You ought to get married."

I started. The kid had an acute perception all right.

"And I know who you should have married, too. Mavis Johnson."

I must have been goggling at her now. She was right, of course. Mavis Johnson was one of those girls a young man admires but never marries. She was the substance he always passes by in his hectic pursuit of the shadow. In all our pasts there is a Mavis Johnson.

"She was in love with you, too," said Joan. "Everybody knew that."

"The Mavis Johnsons always are," I said. "That's why we all neglect them so much."

"Whatever are you talking about?"

"Nothing. Nothing."

"You should have married her, Mick."

"Maybe I should have," I said. "But you just can't order yourself to fall in love with the nicest girl you know. Life isn't as simple as all that."

"If she's the nicest girl you should fall in love with her," said Joan dogmatically.

"All right," I said, "all right. Let's forget about it."

The Town Hall was crowded. When I became depressed by the sight of so many shapely but unattainable bodies protruding from and bulging under evening frocks I slipped behind the stage and had a few beers with some fellows I knew in the orchestra. The only trouble was that they wanted to talk about cricket.

Martha was there, too, with young Johnny Fitzsimmons. Although she was in my party I ignored her as much as possible—I could not stand looking at such young beauty for long, and I had implicit faith in the goading technique. I had proved many times that the less interest you showed in them the more interest they showed in you.

I realized immediately that studio portraits were one thing and snapshots another. Joan's friends were even more enchanting than I had anticipated. I had never seen such a congregation of budding radiance. They were so young, so fresh, and so excited, they made me feel excessively blasé—except when I looked at Martha.

For once, with all these eager young faces around me, I found I did not mind talking about cricket. I even exulted in the attention I commanded.

The boys did not seem to mind being neglected. They kept calling me "Wizard" and taking me away to introduce me to friends. Some even called me "Mr Reynolds", although I was only about four years older than them.

"You don't know my friend Mick Reynolds?" they said, and whispered, often behind their hands, "The Wizard of Nerridale, you know."

I could never understand why people got such pleasure from the dim rays of a little reflected glory, yet I liked to be seen with Tiger Farrell myself.

Johnny Fitzsimmons took me aside and asked me to show him how to do a square cut. I had to demonstrate with a pencil. Harry Cooper asked me how I would deal with a fast rising ball on the off stump. How the hell would I know what to do with it? I'd have to see it first, and then I'd just hit it, that's all. How I'd hit it I wouldn't know until I found myself doing it.

"Step across and hook it round to leg," I said inanely.

Harry looked puzzled. "Fair dinkum, Mick?" he said after scratching his head. "I believe you're right. By crikey, I hadn't thought of that. That's corker."

I wondered how Tiger was feeling. He would wonder why I was not there to wish him good luck. And Les Taylor would be wondering where I had got to, too. Wonder could I dash down to the stadium in a taxi? No, it wouldn't be fair to young Joan, and anyhow it would interfere with my patient campaign against Martha. I'd probably have trouble in finding a taxi in the crowd when I came out, and anyhow it was a surprisingly good dance and the lilting frothiness of jazz music always delighted me.

I'd have to hear the fight somehow, though. I told Joan I was going out for a while, promised not to drink too much, and went over to Jim Marks, who was taking the tickets.

"Hullo, Mick," he said. "How ya goin'? I didn't have a chance to have a word with ya when ya come in. Are ya goin' to play against Carter's eleven next Saturdee?"

"No, Jim. I'm through with cricket. For life this time."

He shook his head sadly. "I'm downright sorry, Mick. I was lookin' forward to seein' ya have a go at Carter and Brooks, but it's yer own business. Why aren't ya at the fight?"

"Young Joan wanted me to bring her here. Cliff's away in Sydney. I certainly would like to be there. The fight, I mean. Ay, Jim, where's the nearest wireless set? I want to hear the description."

"Just down the street at Harry Courtenay's. Only bought it yesterdee."

"Good old Harry!" I cried. "I didn't know he had it. See you later, Jim."

"Hullo, Mick," said several people when I went into Harry's hamburger shop. "Going to play against Carter's team?"

Cricket, cricket, cricket. Only for cricket I'd be at the fight now. I could hear music. Good. I hadn't missed any of the fight.

"No. I'm through with it for life," I said.

"Oh gee," they said. "Can't understand why you don't play regular."

Harry took me out to the kitchen. "Mick," he said dolefully. "Why aren't you at the fight?"

"Had to take young Joan to Spellman's dance. Her boy friend's away. Playing cricket, too. It's always cricket."

Harry did not smile. He never smiled. "Think Tiger will win?" he asked.

"He's a moral," I said. "A lay-down misere. I might have two quid on him."

"What do you mean 'might'?"

"I don't know whether I'm set or not. George's getting it on for me. I won't know until the second round starts. If Dan says 'This is round two' we're on."

"I'll be five bob with you if it's jake."

"O.K., Harry."

The music stopped, and a few minutes later we heard Dan's voice telling the world of the rare qualities of Itsrubbed Tobacco.

"Christ, I wish I was there," I said. We heard a roar. "That's Tiger getting through the ropes," I said.

"It's funny, Mick," said Harry. "I suppose Nerridale's proudest of three things—Tiger Farrell, Slippery Sally and Mick Reynolds."

"Bullo," I said. "Where do you get dat stuff? I'll bet Tiger knocks him in five. Come on, Tiger, you beaut. If Tiger wins I'm going to put it all up on Slippery Sally in the Cup on Saturday week."

"Good," said Harry dismally.

Tiger's opening attack failed. This Peters was no mug. You could not just walk up to him and drop him with a right swing. He lived through the first minute, and consequently the first round. There wasn't a sound in the shop. Even the chewing of hamburgers had stopped.

Harry shook his head dolefully. "He didn't stop him, Mick," he said.

I slapped him on the shoulder. I was strangely elated. I was always elated when I had forgotten my haunting restlessness. "Snap out of it, Harry," I said. "Tiger's a moral I tell you. Now see what Dan says when he finishes all this bullo about Itsrubbed."

"There goes the bell," said Dan. "This is round two."

"You beaut!" I yelled.

"Shut up in there!" called somebody from the shop.

I stuck my head out the door and grinned. "Sorry, Mick. Didn't know it was you."

I waved, and went back to Harry. The fight lasted only two more rounds. Tiger knocked Peters cold.

"You bloody beaut!" I cried, and there was so much excitement in the shop nobody complained that his girl friend's sensibilities had been ruffled.

"Five bob," said Harry in his usual mournful tone.

"Thirty-five bob," I said. "Harry, don't you ever smile?"

"Once when we were in Flanders a visiting brass hat stepped off some duckboards and went up to his chest in mud. Some of the boys reckoned I smiled then. If ever I see anything funny enough to smile at I'll smile," he said doggedly.

It was only when I was half-way back to the Town Hall that I realized that I was elated because someone had been battered into unconsciousness.

I told all the boys that Tiger had won, and was surprised to learn that none of the girls except Joan had heard of him.

I spoke to everybody but Martha. Once I walked past her to have a dance with Sylvia. I saw her eyes light up expectantly as I approached and saw the light go out as I passed. The fish was biting.

When the dance finished I still had not had a dance with Martha. While Joan was getting her coat I waited near the door, and when Martha and Johnny were saying good night I asked, "Could I speak to you alone for a moment, Martha?"

I saw the suspicion die out of Johnny's eyes when I added,

"Sorry, Johnny, but I want to give Martha a message from Joan."
I was his idol, and, in any case, I had not had a dance with Martha
so what justification was there for suspicion?

I drew a puzzled Martha aside. "Martha," I said, "I want to
see you later. Can you get rid of Johnny quickly?"

Her blue eyes and soft lips opened wide. "Oh gee, Mick," she
whispered. "I didn't think you liked me. You didn't even have one
dance with me."

"I couldn't bear to hold you in my arms without kissing you,
Martha," I said.

She was gaping at me now, but there was adoration in her eyes,
too. "Oh, Mick, you're wonderful. Did you really think that? Oh
gee, I didn't think I was in the race. Oh gee, Mick. Course I'll get
rid of Johnny. I don't really like him very much. I'll meet you
at the side gate."

She told me her address. I took her back to Johnny, who looked
surprised when he saw her flushed face and sparkling eyes.

"Must have been good news," he said.

"It was," said Martha.

"Crikey, I wish you'd play against Carter's team," said Johnny.
"No chance?"

"None," I said.

"Crikey, Mick, I wish you would. Good night."

"Good night," said Martha with a radiant look that made me turn
away to find Joan.

As we were walking up the street from the tram Joan put her
arm through mine and said, "Thanks for taking me, Mick. I had a
scrumptious time. It was bonzer of you."

"That's all right," I said awkwardly. I was thinking of Martha's
provocative body and the light in her eyes.

"You liked my girl friends, too, didn't you?"

"Yes."

"Thanks for being so nice to them, and to the boys, too. Which
girl did you like best? I'll bet it was Mary. Mary's nice, isn't she?"

"Yes. Pretty nice. Nice lot of girls."

"You didn't have a dance with Martha, did you? Don't you like
her? All the boys think she is pretty."

"Martha? Which one was that? The one in the red dress? She's
a nice girl. Just didn't get round to her, that's all."

I heard a car toot, and, turning, found that it was the leading
one on a taxi rank. The driver got out and came over. It was Frank
Andrews, the Secretary of the Cricket Association.

"Hullo, Frank," I said.

"Hullo, Mr Andrews," said Joan.

"How are you both?" asked Frank. "Sorry to worry you, Mick, but——"

"All right, Frank. I detect the link between your official position, the two-day match against Carter's eleven next Friday, and the 'Sorry to worry you but——'. Sorry, Frank, but the answer is 'No'."

"Mick, you've given me more sleepless nights than anybody I know."

"He's a fool, Mr Andrews," said Joan. "It's no use arguing with him. We gave up years ago."

"I've tried everything, Joan. He just gets wild."

I stood in the road and kicked moodily at the gutter. "I don't want to have to go through it all again, Frank," I said. I could see Martha standing at the gate with the moonlight caught in her golden hair and gleaming on her ivory neck. That was something urgent, vital, elemental, and they prated to me of cricket.

"I don't like the game, that's all," I said. "Surely there's something you don't like."

"I dunno," said Frank, scratching his head so that his driver's cap tilted on to his nose.

"There must be. Something you hate. Think for a moment."

"Well, Mick, I s'pose I'd rather take poison than eat mushrooms. I hate 'em."

"Good. Now people. You must hate some fellow."

"Well," said Frank slowly. "Nobody I know. But there's one feller on the screen I can't stomach. Mickey Rooney. I hate the little twirp."

"Excellent. Now something else. There must be something else."

"Well I don't like tomato sauce either. Got into the pantry when I was a kid and drank a bottle of the stuff. Ugh!"

"Good. Now, Frank, imagine yourself sitting in the pictures looking at Mickey Rooney and eating mushrooms and tomato sauce."

"Christ!" cried Frank, falling back with his hand up in an involuntary gesture of protection. "Sorry, Joan. Mick, I wouldn't wish such a thing on my worst enemy."

"Good. Now you'll have a faint idea of how I feel towards cricket."

"So that's how it is, eh?"

"That's how it is."

"You don't know how much it would mean to me to have you play, Mick."

"You don't know how much it would mean to me to have to play."

"There's only one way to make him play," said Joan. "You've got to hurt him. Then he fights back."

"Joan. Please."

"Well, perhaps this'll hurt him," said Frank. "It's current talk in the cricket clubs that you're no good, that the reason you don't play is that you're not game to spoil your average. They reckon that since you got bowled for three against the State you've lost your nerve."

I could feel the blood surging into my face. "What do I care what they say?" I said, but I knew I did care.

"It's not only that, Mick. They say your father was the same. He couldn't take it either, they reckon. They say he was yellow."

"Yellow? My father?" The hot blood was pounding through my veins now. The words "yellow" and "father" sounded so incongruous together. "The rotten coots," I said. "I s'pose they brought my father back from France on his back because he was yellow? By Christ, they can't get away with that. Who said it?"

"I can't pin it down," said Frank. "If I could I'd knock the man down first and have him up before the committee afterwards. It's just vague talk."

"So I'm yellow, eh? And my father was yellow, too? Tell 'em from me, the whole rotten pack of dirty liars, that I'll meet 'em at Les Taylor's gym any night they like. The rotten bastards."

"Mick," said Joan in a little voice, "I'm here."

"Sorry, Joan," I said, "but I'm sore. They can't get away with this, Frank. What sort of a batsman was my father?"

"The best. I saw every innings he played. Played with him, in fact. He was just like you, Mick. Hardly ever played, but by Christ —sorry, Joan—when he did you saw something."

"Joan," I said.

"Yes, Mick."

"Will you see Cliff tomorrow?"

"Yes. Why?"

"Tell him to get all the bowlers from the High School first and second elevens and have 'em in our backyard at 6 a.m. and 5 p.m. every day next week. I'll show those so-and-sos something."

"Oh gee, Mick!" screamed Joan. "I told you you had to hit him, Mr Andrews." And then I had to submit to the indignity of being kissed by my sister in front of a friend.

Frank did not say anything. Evidently he could not, but I saw the gratitude in his eyes. He just pumped and pumped my hand.

He drove us the rest of the way in his taxi. I took Joan to the door and told her I wanted to talk to Frank about the match. I found out next morning that she rang all her girl friends to tell them the news before she went to bed.

I got Frank to drop me a hundred yards from Martha's place—he was so elated he would have driven me to hell if I had asked him—and I walked the rest.

There was moonlight in the lane, but no Martha. I was a fool. Perhaps Johnny was still there. I did not know what I could say to him if he came through the gate. Another message from Joan would seem a bit thin. Anyhow, Martha was only a kid. What was I wasting my time for? Cradle-snatching, they called it. Imagine me making love to a girl Joan's age. It was absurd. Why didn't I wake up to myself? Surely I was old enough to resist a pretty face and a shapely leg. The old restlessness was back on me again, curse it.

I went down to the gate. It swung open and Martha was standing there, with the moonlight caught in her hair and gleaming on her ivory neck, just as I had imagined it. Some women might have the delectable poise of maturity, but Martha was young and fresh and vivid. This was what I wanted—this budding beauty and the adoration in her clear blue eyes.

"Oh gee, Mick," she said softly, "I thought you weren't coming."

I leaned against the fence and looked at her. I realized again that there was nothing to equal the delicious ingenuousness of a young girl.

"I was frightened to wait in the lane," she said.

"Frightened? You're not frightened of me, Martha, are you?"

"Of you? Golly, no. Aren't—aren't you going to kiss me?"

I did not answer. I lolled there, arrogantly conscious of my own power, with my hands in my pockets and chaos in my heart. It was no good. I could not do it. She was Joan's friend and only a kid. It would not be fair to Johnny. He thought I was such a great fellow, too. I would just look at her for a minute and then I would go.

"Oh gee, Mick, I'm sorry. I shouldn't have said that, should I? You'll think I'm bold. But I'm not, Mick, really I'm not!"

I did not speak. She looked at me eagerly, doubtfully. She was lovely, standing there in the moonlight with apprehension in her eyes and her golden hair about her shoulders.

"Say something, Mick. Oh, Mick, please say you forgive me."

"There's nothing to forgive," I said. It would not hurt to kiss her good night. I would just give her a friendly kiss, something like the kiss I gave Joan when I was going away, and then I would go.

I put my arms lightly around her. I trembled as I felt the exquisite softness of her young body merge with mine. I told myself haltingly that I would give her a platonic kiss and then go. I bent my head, she threw her arms around me, and her red lips opened and met mine.

The blood was pulsating in my veins now, and there was an elemental urgency in me. This was one of the few things in life worth while. You could dam rivers, you could move mountains, but this was a force you could not stop for it was as old as life itself.

I slid my hands from her waist over the satin of her dress on to the trim beauty of her hips, and marvelled at the dimpled hollows at each side.

"Oh, Mick. Oh, Mick," she whispered, and kissed me again, hungrily.

My heart was racing now. I could scarcely breathe. I could not struggle any more. It was no use, with this vast, elemental force sweeping me on.

"Gee, Mick," she said, "you're a marvellous cricketer."

"Cricketer?" I said dully.

"Yes. I've kept a scrapbook about you ever since you first became the Wizard of Nerridale after you scored a hundred and twelve and a hundred and twenty-seven against the Grammar Schools that time. You know, Mick, I cried the night after you got out for a duck against Sydney Tech."

My passion was dying fast. "Martha," I said, taking my hands away, "you like cricket?"

"Course. It's a great game. It'll be bonzer to be able to say I've been kissed by the Wizard of Nerridale."

I did not speak.

"Gee, Mick, it's corker to see you scoring those centuries. You fight back as if you were hurt."

I was hurt all right, but I could not fight back. I was licked.

"And when you played against the State last year. I cut out all that stuff in the paper. You know, 'Wizard Uses Schoolboys to Prepare for Test Bowlers'. I got all that stuff."

I was leaning against the fence now, with my hands back in my pockets, watching her and listening to her ecstatic chatter.

"I got pictures of you, too. Golly, I wish you'd give me one of you, one with a cricket bat in your hand and 'To Martha, with love from Mick' on it."

"Martha," I said, "what would you think of me if I never played again?"

"I just couldn't think of you like that, Mick. I always think of you with a bat in your hand. You're going to play against Carter's team next Friday, aren't you?"

"Good night, Martha," I said.

She gaped at me. "Good—good night?" she repeated, bewildered.

"And when you get to work on Monday," I said, "stick a notice on the wall, 'All appointments made by me on Saturday night with members of this staff are hereby cancelled', and sign it 'Mick Reynolds'."

CHAPTER III

"Fair dinkum, George," I said as we walked down the aisle of the Plaza Theatre one Saturday afternoon. "There's as many people on the stage as in the stalls."

"The trouble with this generation," said George, "is that it prefers the two-dimensional shadow to the substance. It's not satisfied unless it gets everything out of what the Americans call a 'can'. Here, at least, we have the pleasant possibility of the male lead getting hiccups or the leading lady's pants falling off."

"Sssh!" I said from an acoustic rather than a moral point of view.

Our seats were in the second row. It was *The Country Girl*, one of those hardy, tuneful old musical comedies like *The Arcadians*, *The Quaker Girl* and *The Chocolate Soldier* that even talking pictures could not stifle. Only about two flesh and blood shows came to Nerridale each year.

We had been in the theatre about ten minutes when I nudged George. "George," I whispered, "have you noticed the little blonde second from the right end of the ballet?"

"I haven't noticed anybody else," whispered George.

"Christ," I whispered, "she's bloody marvellous."

At the end of the first act I was infatuated. At the end of the second I was in love. Stanley Armstrong and Judy Hampden might have the dubious distinction of being the outstanding second-raters on what was left of the Australian musical comedy stage, but I found them tiresome now. I knew that Johnny O'Connor was the best comedian I had ever seen, but I wished he would get off and make room for the ballet.

Whenever one of those strange creatures the programme called "gentlemen of the chorus" took the hand of the blonde or put his arm lightly around her waist I knew what jealousy was.

I gaped at her. She was plump and young and sweet. Her fair hair flowed down to her shoulders. Her pink cheeks glowed. She seemed to be enveloped in a golden light. Her attraction for me was so strong, so vital, that I was convinced that it was some kind of radial magnetism. I would have given my right arm to have discovered that her professional smile was not professional and that it was meant for me.

"Why, oh why," asked George at the end of the first act, "does a girl like Judy Hampden, who does quite well merely by looking delectable, try to wring glittering drops of melody from an arid voice?"

"George," I said gravely, "sometimes your singular profundities amuse me. Today is not one of those days. I know it sounds like madness, but at last my eye is in a 'fine frenzy rolling'. 'Lead on, Macduff.' Bring on the second act."

When she was pulled back on to the stage and I heard the words, "You're the prettiest one", I wanted to cry ecstatic confirmation, but I just sat in the front stalls, gaping at her.

I walked out in a throbbing daze. "George," I said. "I've simply got to meet her. I'm in love."

George bought a paper and held the front page before my eyes with a wry smile. The headlines shrieked something about Hitler. I pushed it roughly aside.

"I remember," said George, "a girl named Edna."

"But this is different," I said.

"That was different," said George.

"George," I said earnestly, "this is the real thing."

"I also recall," said George, "a girl named Eunice and a girl named Meryl."

"But this is different."

"O.K.," said George, with a tolerant grin. "We'll hover."

"Hover?"

"Of course. Hover in middle distance, like villain with designs on Poor Blind Nell. There is stage door. Stage door opens into lane. All members of cast must come down lane. Show is from Sydney therefore all members of cast must stay somewhere. No law to stop reasonably restrained amorous swain following girl down street."

"George," I cried, "We'll hover."

We hovered. At last she came down the lane with two other girls. She was wearing a blue coat with a fur collar. She was beautiful. I was exultant because I knew now that no miracle of make-up or lighting had deluded me.

We followed her to the Majestic Hotel.

"George," I said, "I need a drink. In fact, I need drinks. Come on."

We went down the street to the Royal. "What can I do?" I asked hopelessly over the third gin. "I don't know her. I don't know anybody who knows her. The show won't last more than a few weeks at the most, and judging by the empty seats this afternoon it won't last as long."

"They're hitting you," said George. "Go in and fight."

"I want to, but I can't. I don't know who to have a crack at."

We had four more gins; they might as well have been water for all the effect they had on me. George was looking at me with his mocking smile.

"George," I said, "to think that this show's been running a week and I didn't know she was in it. Can you see the picture reviewers of the *Mail* and *Times* and get them to give the show a good run? That might make it last longer."

"Your innocence is appalling," said George. "The provincial Press is in fetters, and the great god Advertising hammers them on."

I had another gin. "What can I do?" I wailed. It was years since there had been such urgency in my tone.

"Perhaps she plays cricket," said George, jiggling his silver jiggler in his gin. He had his right foot on the brass rail, and was leaning on the bar. "Lots of girls do."

I shuddered. "God forbid," I said.

"Lou Anderson does," said George slyly.

"Lou Anderson? What do you mean?"

"He plays cricket."

"Jesus! So he does. But I don't know him."

"He knows you."

I looked at George. He was looking down into his glass, but I could see the way his lips curled at the corner.

"Thanks," I said, and I had never meant anything so much.

We went down to the post office, and I rang the Majestic, which was only across the street.

"Mr Anderson? It's Mick Reynolds speaking. I don't think you know me."

"Know you? Of course I know you." His voice was oily. "Everyone knows the Wizard of Nerridale, Mr Reynolds, even if he hasn't played for a long time. What can I do for you, Mr Reynolds?"

"You have some of the girls from the R. K. McGuinness show staying there, I believe. I wonder would you do me a favour and introduce me to one?"

"Of course, Mr Reynolds. Only too pleased. By the way, we're playing the Royal tomorrow week. I'd be delighted if you'd be good enough to play for us."

"Certainly, Mr Anderson." If he had asked me to grapple with a tiger I would have said "Certainly, Mr Anderson."

"You would? That's fine. That's splendid. Now what is the name of the young lady?"

I shuddered at the phrase. "I don't know," I said, feeling ridiculous. "But she's wearing a blue coat with blue fur around the top and she's a blonde and is about five feet three."

"Just a moment. I'll ask Joe."

I heard faint voices. Then Anderson said, "That would be Miss Murchison. Miss Margaret Murchison. Can you come round?"

Margaret. Margaret Murchison. The name sounded wonderful. I turned, and saw George standing outside the box, watching me quizzically. I nodded in triumph, and he grinned.

"I'll be round straight away," I said.

"Well?" asked George when I came out.

"It's jake. Anderson'll do the right thing if I go round. Fancy having that obsequious coot introduce me! It'll make a great impression, won't it?"

"A pity, but nothing else for it."

"No. Listen, George. I must get a shave and do my hair. Where can I go? All the shops are shut."

George smiled. "Come down to my room. I've got some shaving gear there."

"George," I said with what must have been pitiful gratitude, "you don't know what you're doing for me. I'll never forget this. Never. Come on."

"You think I've got the dingbats, don't you?" I asked as I lathered my face.

George was sitting in a tilted-back chair with his feet on his untidy desk. Tobacco was scattered everywhere from the drooping cigarette he had just rolled.

"There is a tide in the affairs of men," he said sententiously. "Dive into it and swim like hell. You've actually got some sense at last."

More than half an hour later I took a deep breath and went into the Majestic Hotel. I was going to meet her, to talk to her!

Everything was sharper, clearer. I seemed to be looking at the world through a telescope. Joe was standing in the passage. "Good night, Mr Reynolds," he said. "The trump tells me ya goin' ter play for us on Sundee week. Gee, that's bonzer. I seen ya score that century against the Poms that time. Crikey, ya didden half get stuck inter them Poms! Ya won't crack a lay about playin' against the Royal, will ya? If they're not a wake-up I can get set for a caser like steam."

"I won't say anything, Joe," I said impatiently. "Is Mr Anderson in?"

"Yeah. The trump's got his foot on the old rail. I'll pull him out."

What an odious prawn this Anderson is, I thought, as he came towards me rubbing his pudgy hands and peering through his horn-rimmed glasses. "I'm so sorry, Mr Reynolds," he purred, "but Miss Murchison has gone back to the Plaza. It's after seven, you know. Perhaps you could come round in the morning? Then you could take the girls for a drive."

"Yes. That'd be pretty good." My voice was dulled with disappointment. "I'll come back in the morning."

"You haven't forgotten about the match tomorrow week, have you?"

"I'll come back in the morning," I said, and went out.

It was no good. Obviously she did not want to meet me. She had gone out purposely or was still in the hotel. Five past seven seemed a ridiculous time to go back to the theatre. It was not far, after all. But I did not know much about these things. Some people even said that they put drops in their eyes to make them gleam. But she would not need any of that.

Good heavens, he would probably tell her I was going to take them for a drive! I had no car, and George's was in dock. I was mad. Why didn't I admit I hadn't a car? Was it a crime not to have a car? I'd like to push that oily swine's face in.

I could not face George now, so I decided to wander down to Nerridale Beach and walk along the sand. When I reached the beach I stopped suddenly. My God, I was a fool! There was only one place to go. To the theatre, of course. I hurried there, fearful that all the seats were gone.

There was plenty of room. I got a seat in the third row. The fat girl who took my ticket gave me a puzzled look. "Ay, Mick," she said. "Have you got shares in the show or something?"

"No. Why?"

"Don't tell me you weren't here this afternoon. You must be sweet on one of the girls."

Curse the infernal intuition of women! "I'm madly in love with one, Jean," I said. "I saw her for the first time this afternoon."

She laughed. "Oh yeah? You're a one."

I came out of the theatre even more fascinated than ever. I waited in the street. Margaret came out, and I followed her until she went into the Renown Café. I decided to go in, but then my courage wilted, and I went down to the beach.

Mother and Joan were away at Lake Carraday so I did not have to bother about telephoning. I realized with a shock that I would have forgotten to ring about not going home to tea, anyway.

It was no use going home. I would not sleep. I walked down to the beach, scowling in the gloom at the dim but eloquent outlines of amorous couples.

It was four miles to the lighthouse on the point, but I walked to it and sat on the sand, watching the waves wash up the beach and glide away again. I looked up at the flashing light. Old Mac would be up there, doing the night shift, playing patience and watching the great light stab its golden finger across the sea; but I could not bear to talk to anybody with such turmoil in my heart.

I sat there for a long time, letting the fine sand trickle through my fingers and tracing the initials "M.R." and "M.M." on a flat, patted patch. I watched the moon slide up, and saw it transform the sea from eerie menace to sparkling beauty, but it did nothing to combat the depression that had routed the lilting cadence of my earlier mood.

I must be mad, I told myself. She was only a chorus girl, anyhow. I knew what chorus girls were. Fair game for anybody. Easy on the eyes and easy on the virtue.

But no. Not Margaret. Margaret was different.

I wandered back along the beach, stamping viciously on blue-bottles that had trailed their long stings across the sand like railway lines on a map. I went home through the deserted streets. Somebody had put a note under the door. I picked it up abstractedly. It was addressed to me. It read:

If this is your idea of a joke, it's certainly not mine. I called at seven, as we arranged, and have been back three times since. If you think I'm going to wait around the streets half the night until you choose to come home you've got another think coming. And don't bother to call at the shop to explain. I'm through with you for life.

JULIE.

"And I'm through with you, too," I murmured, tearing the note up. That I had forgotten all about her was final proof of my absorption in Margaret. I went to bed and dreamed of a ballet of plump lighthouses kicking their legs about, saying "You're the prettiest one," and singing "Try Again, Johnnie" while Lou Anderson rubbed his pudgy hands together and purred "You won't forget tomorrow week, will you, Mr Reynolds?"

CHAPTER IV

I GOT up early, called at George's hotel, combed my hair again and borrowed his new suit. I strolled into the Majestic.

"Mr Anderson please, Joe," I said.

"Sorry, Mr Reynolds," said Joe. "He's gone fishing. To the lake. Won't be back till tonight."

I turned and walked out into the street. Next day four people complained that I passed without recognizing them.

It was no good. It was always the same with everything. I just had the irritating faculty of making a mess of all the things that mattered. I went home and mooched around the house. Suddenly I remembered that I was still wearing George's suit. I did not even smile.

Lunch-time came and went, but I could not eat anything. I had not thought of eating for twenty-four hours. I simply had no appetite. Just as well mother was not home or she would be worrying.

Finally I could not stand it any longer. I rang the Majestic and asked for her. Seconds drifted indolently into minutes. My hand holding the receiver was clammy.

At last I heard, "Hullo." It was a sweet voice—young, musical, cultured. I knew it was hers. "Is that Miss Margaret Murchison?" I asked. Nothing Keats had written sounded sweeter than that name.

"Yes." Her tone was puzzled. "Who's speaking, please?"

"Are you the one who comes back on to the stage when the comedian says 'You're the prettiest one'?"

"Yes. Whoever is it? I don't know anybody in Nerridale."

"Yes you do."

"Who?"

"Me. Or you're going to. You know, you *are* the prettiest one, too."

My God! What drivel I was talking.

"I'm sorry, but I'm afraid I'll have to go. I don't know you."

My hand clutched around the receiver trembled, my right hand opened and closed spasmodically, and I kicked myself savagely in the left calf. I told myself that, by my stupidity, I had ruined any chance I had had.

"Just a minute, Miss Murchison, please." My voice was strained and urgent. "I saw you yesterday afternoon for the first time, and felt I'd like to meet you."

I'd have to bring that simpering Anderson into it. "Mr Anderson,

the manager of your hotel, promised to introduce me but he's gone
fishing for the day, and I thought—perhaps—I couldn't wait—er—
I thought I'd ring instead and—er—not wait for him. Oh, I've forgotten to tell you. My name is Reynolds. Mick Reynolds."

"I'm sorry, Mr Reynolds. I appreciate your interest, but I really
can't see you." Her tone was courteous but final.

"But Miss Murchison—I know it's not conventional, but conventions are merely barriers to be torn down. I must meet you." My
voice faltered.

"I'm sorry. I just don't do things like that, that's all. I'm afraid
I must go now. Good-bye."

"I'm sorry, too," I said dismally. "I'm sorry to have worried
you. Good-bye."

The phone clicked. It was all over. But even in the bleakest
depression I had ever known, a depression that put my sullen moods
in a new perspective, I was exultant that she had refused to meet
me. Thank God she wasn't "easy". She wouldn't go out with the first
fellow who rang her up. For the first time in my life I was grateful
for conventions.

The full significance of my failure soon laid its heavy hand upon
my heart. I could never meet her now. Why the hell hadn't I waited
until tomorrow, and been nicely introduced by that oily manager?
I roamed around the house, kicking viciously at the furniture.

I went into town, saw George, and changed into my own suit. I
was fearful he would laugh at the sorry affair, and I knew I would
never speak to him again if he did.

He did not laugh. "Christ, man!" he cried, pacing up and down
his untidy room, "Is this the Mick Reynolds I saw belting Carter
all over the place and doing criminal things to Brooks? Snap out
of it! If you want anything worth while you've got to go in and
take it. You don't get any plums on silver platters these days. You
pick 'em off the tree and hope to Christ you won't get a barrelful
of buckshot in your backside."

"I can't do any more, George. I've messed up the whole business."

"Rubbish!" cried George. "For three years I've watched you go
from frustration to frustration. Now you've found, for the first time,
something that makes your eye light up, something that has burst
smack bang through that colossal indifference of yours, and you tell
me you're licked just because you've taken one on the chin in the
first round. You give me a touch of 'em."

I stubbed my cigarette viciously. "I can't do any more, George,"
I said. "I can never see her again."

I waited outside the hotel for ten minutes next morning. Then
I took a deep breath, and strode purposefully up the steps. I did

not know what I was going to do, but I had to do something. I could not just sit supinely and take it any longer.

Anderson greeted me effusively, rubbing his soft white hands and peering at me through his glasses. "Ah, Mr Reynolds," he murmured, "I'm so pleased to see you. Lovely day, isn't it?"

"Yes," I said, and forced myself to ask, "Enjoy your fishing trip?" I hoped he had been seasick and dragged overboard by the kellick.

"Yes. It was very nice."

"Catch many?"

"Yes. Had a great day. Went outside the heads and got on to the redfish and flathead. I like the redfish myself."

"Of course."

"But you can't always get on to them. We landed thirty-seven redfish and sixteen flathead. Pretty good, wasn't it, for five of us?"

"Oh yes. Yes." Wouldn't the moron ever stop talking about his stupid fishing and his stupid redfish?

"It was a bit rough, but that didn't worry me. I'm a pretty good sailor, you know."

"I'm sure you are." What depths a man had to sink to to get an introduction to a girl. I'd like to grab this servile fawner by the neck and tell him to send for the girl or I'd tear his fat throat out.

"I believe in keeping fit, you know," he said. "Always in good condition."

I looked at the bulge of his pot belly and felt sick. "Miss Murchison," I said.

He nodded and his two chins became three. "Oh yes. To be sure," he said. "By the way you'll be available for the match against the Royal next Sunday?"

He had me, and he knew it. I saw the sly, gloating light in his eyes. But he hadn't got me after all. Once he had introduced me to Margaret his power over me had vanished. If he thought I was going to play cricket with a lot of hotel loungers and urgers he had another think coming.

"No, I haven't forgotten," I said.

"Good. Good. I'm sure we'll have a nice day." He rubbed his puffy hands together. "Joe," he called. "Get Miss Murchison, will you? Tell her Mr Reynolds is here."

I heard the lift go up, and heard it stop. Anderson was babbling something about cricket. I just said "Yes" at the end of every sentence. The lift was still there. She wouldn't come. I might have known.

What would any decent girl think? Some amorous, incoherent fool who had seen her semi-naked figure from the front stalls rang her up, told her she was the prettiest girl, talked a lot of rubbish about tearing conventions aside, and, despite a courteous rebuff, insisted on being introduced to her by a slimy man who happened to be manager of the hotel where she was staying.

The lift was still there. What a cheek I had! Joe, thinking of his "caser", was probably trying to persuade her and telling her what a great cricketer I was. As if that would excuse my blatant bad taste!

Anderson, rubbing his pudgy white hands together, was still talking. Something about redfish. I kept saying "Yes" whenever he stopped. Suddenly I heard the lift move, and my heart jumped. Then I remembered that Joe would have to return to tell me that she would not come.

I picked up a match from an ash-tray. The lift stopped, and I heard the door open. Somebody came out. I screwed up my courage and looked. She was coming towards me.

Years later, in Tobruk, Gordon C. Harday often posed grandiloquently and said, "There are unimaginable moments in one's life." This was one of them.

She came up to me, and I was dimly conscious of Anderson purring and scraping, rubbing his odious hands and introducing us. I was breaking the match up and dropping the pieces on the carpet. I stammered something. Soon the last pieces of the match had fallen, and I did not know what to do with my hands. I picked up a match-box, and began to pull pieces off it.

A few minutes later I found myself sitting in the upstairs lounge with her. In my daze, I had sat down before her. I felt light-headed. I was listening to her musical voice and looking at her. I was glad she was talking—something about the stage—because I was incapable of more than yes's and no's for a while.

I was conscious only of the fact that all I wanted from the world was compressed into a space five feet three inches high. Her voice was slow and sweet, and she spoke with delicious precision. Her gravity was disarming, her complexion perfect, her poise ingenuous. There was something in her face I had never seen before.

I struggled through somehow. I do not remember much of it, but I do remember how enchanted I was when she said that she had to be at the theatre "one-ish".

I can remember only one thing I said—"Do you like cricket?"

"Good heavens, what a strange question," she said. "No. I think it's a silly game."

I did not speak, but my heart was singing.

I found myself out in the street with an appointment for lunch the next day, and a throbbing realization of triumph. I could scarcely believe it. I went down the street, singing jubilantly to myself. There was a blind man on the corner. I gave him ten shillings.

I went to the theatre again that night—I was relieved to find that it was *The Arcadians* now—and next day, with George's suit on and Galsworthy's *Apple Tree* in my hand, I strolled into the Majestic Hotel.

Anderson was standing in the lounge, and he came over, rubbing his soft white hands together and purring. "You haven't forgotten about next Sunday, Mr Reynolds, have you?" he asked ingratiatingly.

"No," I replied. "Don't keep bothering me about it. Is Miss Murchison ready?"

"Ah," he said, and I thought I saw a gloating gleam in his little eyes. "I'm so sorry but Miss Murchison is ill."

I gaped at him. "Ill?"

"Yes. Just a heavy cold. Nothing to worry about. She said to say she was sorry."

I went out into a day that had become bleak. The old depression was back on me, but now it was overwhelming. It was no good. She was only laughing at me. I stopped, aghast at a terrible possibility. Perhaps she was seriously ill; perhaps she was going to die.

I went to a bookshop and bought *Precious Bane* by Mary Webb. I remembered that a photograph of a grinning negro boy had appeared in the *Nerridale Mail* that morning, so I bought a paper, went to the office, cut the photograph out, scribbled a note, enclosed the photograph, and sent the two books, the letter and a bunch of red roses to the hotel in Frank Andrews's taxi.

I do not know how I got through that afternoon. I forgot my slick line of sales talk entirely, and went through the mechanical act of thumping tables and beds with my fist and saying "A good solid job, sir", in a voice that must have been flat and unconvincing.

I could not wait until the curtain went up that night, and I did not know whether to be relieved or frantic when I saw her in the ballet.

Probably she did not want to go to lunch with me. But the excuse was too obvious not to be genuine. Probably she chose it because it was so obvious, chose it so that I would give it up as hopeless. But why did she agree to see me at all? Probably to see what I looked like, and she was so disappointed that she could not bear to go to lunch with me. But why did she agree to go to lunch? Probably to gain her revenge for my shocking lack of taste. But why——?

They formed a vicious circle in my mind—these dismal doubts

and desperate hopes—a mind already taxed with trying to cope
with the lilting music of *The Arcadians* and the still overwhelming
realization that I was in love.

I lurked in the darkness, and followed her to the hotel. Then I
went down to the beach and walked the four miles to the lighthouse
and four miles back before I got Frank Andrews's partner to drive
me home.

I rang her from the office early next morning. She said she was
sorry, was feeling much better, and was delighted with the flowers.
She thanked me for the book. She had read *The Apple Tree* straight
away and thought it was beautiful.

"Thank God," I told myself, "she's intelligent as well as beautiful.
I'll bet she doesn't read Henry F. Gates." Suddenly I realized that
she could easily have been one of the "I-seen-yous-was-follerin'-me"
type. I had been out with chorus girls before.

"Tell me," she said, "why did you send me the picture of the
nigger boy?"

"Oh that. I thought it might cheer you up, that's all."

"Oh," she said slowly, "you're funny."

So I was "funny". I did not know whether I was pleased or not.
I took a deep breath and asked her to lunch. At one o'clock, still
wearing George's suit, I went into the Carnarvon, Nerridale's
smartest café, with Margaret, nodded to a few friends who stared
at her, and directed her to a quiet table in the corner.

I never forgot the red hat she wore that day. I was enchanted
by it as I was enchanted by her.

I let her talk—I was still unable to trust my voice—and she
told me she was eighteen, that she liked violets even better than
roses, that she had been dancing since she was seven, that the
one interest in her life was to make good on the stage, that she
often posed for advertisements and worked as a mannequin.

I was half an hour late getting back to work, but I was singing.

After work I saw one of the gentlemen of the chorus in the
Hotel Moderne. He was alone, so I bought him a drink and tried
to get him talking about the ballet. He was deep-chested, and had
a booming voice and a disturbing permanent wave.

He told me that some of the girls were going to the Mayoral
Ball after the show that night. He put his mug down on the bar,
looked me in the eye, and asked abruptly, with a knowing grin,
"Which one is it?"

I grinned back, and told him. "Good God!" he said. "Why don't
you have a crack at something easy? There's half a dozen who'll
play ball."

"Don't like ball games," I said. "Is she going?"

"She's undecided. Can't understand it, though." He shook his head, and his elegant black curls shivered and slid back into place. "Now that little redhead third from the left. Nell her name is"—and he told me an anecdote about how gin, which was reported to have ruined a mythical auntie, always caused the redhead to behave in an extraordinary manner.

" 'And there was where he met poor Nell and sent her on the road to hell, doomed forever to walk the town, a painted whore at half a crown'," I said.

"Did you write that?"

"Break it down. My name's not Masefield."

I realized how greatly I had changed. A few days ago the information about the redhead would have been invaluable. Now all I could do was pass it on to Spike. No. I would not take any risks of Margaret's associating me with fellows like Spike. Perhaps I had said too much to this gentleman of the chorus already.

Sick at heart, I went out into the street, plagued by a new fear.

CHAPTER V

I WENT to the theatre again that night, of course—I reserved my seat on the side of the stalls where the usherette I knew would not see me—and afterwards I waited near the corner and followed her to her hotel. I was grateful just for being able to follow her down the street.

I wandered down to see George.

"I've got tomorrow night free," he said, turning away to hide his grin, "and I've got a couple of slashing lines who've come from Sydney for the Mayoral Ball. They're a couple of pushovers. How about a drive to the lake."

"Break it down," I said, "nothing would interest me less.

"George," I said, "how do you explain my singing as I go down the street—my hiding in a telephone-box just to see her go past on the other side of the street?

"George," I said earnestly, "I go round asking the other salesmen can I do their work. I even found myself offering to help old Creeping Jesus shift a pile of chairs and three ice chests."

George grinned. "You've got it bad," he said.

"Can I borrow your dinner-suit tonight?"

He stared at me. "Of course, but it's a bit late, isn't it? Want to go to the Mayoral Ball, I s'pose. I thought you refused Old Joe's invitation?"

"I did, but that was before I got the drum, as Spike would say, that Margaret might be going."

"Might?"

"Yes. The elegant hermaphrodite who told me wasn't sure. What about going down to the Town Hall and seeing if she arrives? If she doesn't I'll go home to bed. If she does we'll dash back to your hotel and, hey presto, I become the languid man about town."

"O.K.," said George.

We sat in the gallery.

"I can't see her," I said.

"Jazz," said George, "——I will not say jazz music—is the prime fatuity of man. If people really turned in their graves Beethoven would be the perfect example of perpetual motion. The other day I actually heard a number entitled 'Don't be a Ninny, Mr Paganini', and I believe there is a song which asks a question which is evidently of paramount importance to the future of the world—'Does Santa Claus Sleep With His Whiskers Under Or Over The Sheet?'"

"I can't see her," I said.

"Jazz is defensible," said George, "only as an excuse for holding a luscious blonde against your body while you jiggle in close juxtaposition and propinquity, to use two deplorable words of an O. Henry character who was addicted to Bowery couriers. It is inconceivable that a girl will allow you to merge her curves with your angles on a dance floor, but will clout you one in the mug and scream blue murder if you put your arm around her in a public place. I cannot——"

"I can't see her," I said.

"I cannot understand how that disgusting cacophony——"

"She's not here," I said.

"Your mother is."

"I know. It's one of her treats of the year, the Mayoral Ball."

"Why don't you take her?"

"Because I'm selfish. I don't think she's coming. Margaret, I mean."

"I remember," said George, "a few years ago a jazz number that stunned me. I just couldn't believe it. It went like this:

> I didn't know that anyone in his right mind
> Could treat another human being so unkind
> As to run away and leave a note behind.
> Was that the human thing to do?

Incredible, isn't it?"

"I don't think she's coming."

"And it goes on:

> It's no use trying to make it up.
> What must be must be.
> I wouldn't even treat a pup
> The way you treated me."

"She can't be coming."

"And then there was the redundant phrase I heard in a jazz number —'Something, something, something love, under the something stars above.' Well if you're under the stars they must be above you, mustn't they?"

"She's not coming."

"You're not listening. Ah well, ah well. Woman has blighted a beautiful friendship. Let's go and have a drink."

"It'll be all right to have a drink now. There's no chance of meeting Margaret."

"How come?"

"I haven't been drinking before eleven p.m. most of this week. Frightened I'll meet Margaret and she'll smell it."

George stared at me. "My God," he said, "you *do* need a drink."

We walked down the marble stairs and out into the cool night air. We were going down the cement drive when I saw her. She had a blue bow in her golden hair, and her apricot evening dress was the most beautiful I had ever seen. She had passed me before either of us realized the other was there.

I turned and stared, my heart thumping. The girl with her said something, and Margaret looked back. I hesitated, and then went on. She hesitated, and then went on. I hesitated, and then went on again. She waved, and disappeared through the door.

"What a bastard," I said.

"She's beautiful," said George.

"Of course," I said, "but I've missed her. I always mess things up. But I'm glad you liked her in her apricot dress."

"Apricot dress? Oh, you mean Margaret? I was talking about the brunette."

"You rotten coot!" I cried, grabbing at him, but he eluded me. "George, I'm going to marry that girl. Come on." I hustled him into the street, and dragged him into a run.

"What the hell's wrong?" he asked, puffing.

"Everything's jake," I said. "The dinner-suit. Shake it up."

There were no taxis, so we caught a tram. It was held up a hundred yards from his hotel. We jumped out, and I made him run the rest. We raced up the stairs in the mistaken idea that it would be faster than the lift.

George rang for a taxi, polished his dancing pumps for me, clamped a ready-made tie around my neck, and fumbled with the studs.

"George," I wailed, "for Christ's sake and mine hurry. Every minute is a minute less with her."

I got a taxi and told the driver—it was Jim Williamson, who used to bowl spinners for Shadbury—to step on it. I strolled into the Town Hall as though twelve-thirty a.m. was my usual time for arriving at balls.

I went over to old Joe Louden's party. "Why, Mick," he cried, "I thought you weren't coming."

"Whatever gave you that idea, Mr Mayor?" I asked as blandly as I could. "You know I wouldn't let you down. Sorry I'm late."

Old Joe looked perplexed, but he had had too many whiskies to try to puzzle it out. "Would you prefer to join your mother's party?" he asked.

"No, thanks," I said. "I told you I'd be in your party, Mr Mayor, and here I am." I had noticed from the gallery earlier that there was a surplus of girls in mother's party and a surplus of men in Old Joe's.

"That's very nice of you, Mick," said Old Joe. He introduced me to the people I did not know, which meant that he introduced me to two girls from Sydney. I would have found them attractive if I had not met Margaret.

"This is Mick Reynolds," said Old Joe, "the Wizard of Nerridale, you know", and went off to have another whisky.

They seemed bewildered. "Wizard?" said one, a brunette who protruded agreeably from a scarlet evening dress. "Is it quite safe to dance with you. You won't put me under a spell, will you?"

But I was looking for Margaret. She passed in the arms of one of the gentlemen of the chorus, caught my eye, looked surprised, and smiled faintly.

The brunette, who smelt of whisky, looked at Margaret and at me, and said, "I get it. There's that look in a man's eyes again. And I was going to tell you I'm in room forty-four at the Royal and have a strange habit of leaving keys under doormats."

"You city girls are miles ahead of us yokels," I said. "But you've come into my life just four days too late."

"A pity," she said.

"A great pity," I said. I had not looked at her. I was staring after Margaret. "With you, I gather, one dispenses with the preliminaries."

"Yes," she said. "They're tiresome. They bore me."

"A scarlet woman," I said, "after my own former heart. I should have met you months ago. A pity."

"A great pity," she said.

I had two dances with Margaret. With her in my arms I was merely a palpitating mass of incoherence. Her attitude was still courteous but distant.

I struggled through a dance with mother. "Whatever are you doing here, Howard?" she asked. "I thought you weren't coming?"

"Well, mother, I wasn't, but I thought it wouldn't be fair to let the Mayor down, so I came along."

She held me away from her a little, and said, "You know, Howard, you're a wonderful son. You're always so considerate and understanding."

"Yes, mother," I said quietly, and looked away.

I stood with Margaret while a pimply youth gave an exhibition of tap dancing. I thought Margaret would think he was futile.

"He's rather good," she said.

I looked at her. "Yes," I said. "That's Arthur Harris. His father teaches."

Arthur and his fat little father eked out a living with a second-rate studio, but now this youth I had despised had become a somebody. Margaret had said, "He's rather good." I looked at him in awe. All she had said about me was that I was "funny".

It was the same with everything she said and did. Everything she said seemed to be vitally important; everywhere she went became hallowed ground.

The ball came to its inevitable rowdy end. Margaret went off with some girls from the ballet and gentlemen of the chorus—how I envied them—and I took mother home.

"Who was that nice fair girl I saw you dancing with?" asked mother in the taxi.

I hesitated. I was tempted to tell her. "That was Margaret Murchison," I said. "Just a girl I know."

CHAPTER VI

I FOUND myself utterly unable to cope with Margaret Murchison. She was not clever, she was not complex; she was just a plump, and, to me, beautiful ballet girl with whom I had fallen in love.

I had made girls, as it were, my life work, and I had been able to keep the wheel of conversation whirling equally well with milk-bar girls and society women; but it was different with Margaret. I was so fearful I would make a mistake that I scarcely said anything, and practically everything I said was banal.

The result was that I was convinced that I had made an entirely negative impression. My silence forced her to talk, and I learned a lot about her. I learned more about her absorption in her ambition.

When I asked her why she did not have the small part an incompetent girl was playing, she replied bitterly, "Oh, she's a friend of the manager of the company. I'd rather be dead than get on that way."

It was the old story. So it happened to more than the barmaids of the world. It was probably why so many prominent Hollywood actresses were so hopelessly incompetent.

Her attitude to me did not vary. It remained distantly courteous. Later, I told myself, when she gets to know me better, it will change.

I went to the theatre every night, took her out to lunch a second time, gave her *The Forsyte Saga*, hid in the telephone-box every night to watch her arrive at the Plaza, and was more obsessed by her than ever.

I borrowed George's car, and took four of the girls for a drive. Margaret got in the back, and her girl friend Greta sat next to me. I did not recover from that for twenty miles. I soon turned the small mirror so that it reflected Margaret's face, and forgot all about the traffic behind me.

From the start Greta showed a lively interest in me, and I showed a complete lack of interest in Greta, except when she talked about Margaret. Whenever I looked at Greta, Nereda, Marie or Hazel, I realized how far I had come in a few days. They were just the type of girls I had regarded as perfect parking partners—all exotic perfumes, silk stockings, high heels, blonde hair and pencilled eyebrows. Overnight they had become as dull as a sermon by a Methodist lay preacher.

I did not say a word to Margaret about how I felt. I could scarcely bear to mention her name to anybody, let alone admit to her the urgent longing in my heart.

I sneaked into the theatre in the mornings, sitting inconspicuously in the back row of the stalls, and watched the company rehearsing. The girls wore high heels, black shorts, and white blouses, and stalked about the stage like cranes. I watched Margaret hungrily, watched her go through the new routines, and when I went out into the street it was not only the sudden sunlight that made me feel dazed.

The show came to its excruciating end a week after I saw Margaret for the first time. I got a taxi, helped the driver put Margaret's and Greta's luggage in the boot at the back, helped him get it out and carry it on to the station, and tipped him lavishly.

Then I endured that most depressing experience life holds for anyone—waiting for a train to leave. I was haunted by the fear that I would never see her again, that the train would crash into another, that she would be killed. I was desolated by the realization that she was going away, and scourged by my inability to decide whether I would kiss her good-bye. I was crucified by having to remain silent when I had such a clamorous insistence in my heart.

The last few minutes were enlivened by the discovery that the luggage belonging to Nell, the red-headed girl, was there but Nell was not. The girls clucked and shrilled, and finally, with half a minute to go, the manager of the theatre and Nell, whose hair was ruffled and dress creased, came rushing on to the platform, trying to look at ease. The manager had a faint lip-stick mark on his cheek.

A sudden clanging of the bell crashed discordantly against my jangled nerves. I would have to decide now. Greta solved the problem for me by kissing me on the lips. I bent awkwardly towards Margaret. I thought I saw her lips tremble. My lips touched the dimpled softness of her cheek. She had turned her head deliberately. It was like a blow in the face.

"Good-bye," they said.

"Thanks for being so nice to us," said Greta, and Margaret said quietly, "Yes. Thanks for being so kind. Thanks for the nigger boy. You're funny, you know."

The engine tooted, and the train drew away. Margaret waved until the train had gone about ten yards, and then withdrew her head. Greta kept waving until she had vanished around the turn.

I walked out of the station with my hands deep in my pockets, my eyes on the ground. So I was "funny". She had said it again. And even Arthur Harris was "rather good".

I walked home, kicking moodily at a match-box part of the way. All she could say about me was that I was "funny".

I was wondering what I could do when suddenly I remembered mother. Instinctively I turned to my mother as I had turned to her when I was hurt as a child. I would tell her. She would think of a way. She would invite Margaret to Nerridale for a week-end when her tour was over; she would even call at the Murchisons at Croydon when she went to Sydney to do some shopping. Mother would fix everything. Margaret could not fail to like mother.

My head came up and I found myself walking briskly. Mother would fix everything, I told myself. I would tell her.

CHAPTER VII

I DID not believe that anybody could have been so unresponsive as Margaret Murchison. I sent her violets in Townsville, Brisbane, Sydney, Melbourne and Perth—George or I had friends in each place. I sent her boxes of Snowballs, a sweet with soft white stuff inside and chocolate outside, regularly. I gave her copies of every great novel I had read, and I wrote to her every few days.

The dam of my reticence broke when I wrote to her, and I poured forth the flood that had gathered in my heart. I cannot quote much that I wrote to her, for it is sacrilege to repeat the tumultuous out-pourings of a young love. I wrote verse—I cannot call it poetry—to her, and I turned to some of my favourite writers to express the emotion throbbing in my heart.

Shamelessly, from tormented Rupert Brooke, I took "The dear pain of your remembered face" and "Oh! Death will find me long before I tire of watching you", and from Shelley, "My heart is too fully laden ever to burthen thine".

I took the agony of Robert Louis Stevenson, spending a night among the pines in the Cevennes with his donkey, and sent it to Margaret as an expression of my own travail.

"The flower of you," I wrote, "is blooming still within my heart."

Her replies were always the same. "I have caught a cold at rehearsal. The stage is too draughty. Greta sends her love. I must close now."

"The weather has been fine but it is raining to-day. We will do *The Arcadians* next week, and then *The Quaker Girl*. I had a letter from mother yesterday. She is well. Greta sends her love. I must close now."

"The train trip to Melbourne was tiring. We are staying at a nice hotel near the theatre. It was nice of you to send the violets. They were lovely, Mick, you are *funny*. Greta sends her love. I must close now."

So it went on, this hopeless fight of mine against something with which I could not come to grips. Her mother, who liked me and sent me photographs of Margaret without her knowledge, told me that Margaret did not have a boy friend.

I stayed up until three o'clock one morning to see Margaret for two minutes at Nerridale Station as she passed through on her way to Sydney, and did not dare to kiss her when, bleary-eyed from sleeping, she came wearily to the window to speak to me.

I went to Sydney especially to say good-bye to her when she was leaving for New Zealand with a new company. I even considered getting my holidays early and going to New Zealand. I intended to keep my presence secret and watch Margaret from the stalls every night and the other side of the street every day. The only reason I did not do it was that I knew she would be angry if she found out.

All the way up in the train I was trying to pluck up courage to ask her to marry me. I knew it would be hopeless but I was determined to show her my sincerity. It was ten months since the day I had said to George, "There's as many people on the stage as in the stalls", but I had made no progress. Her attitude was always the same. She was courteous but distant; that was all.

I rang her from Central Station as soon as I arrived. She said she could not see me. She had packing to do. She would see me on the ship.

I wandered gloomily around the city, staring disconsolately at the green water at Circular Quay. I looked dejectedly at the towering outline of the Harbour Bridge, sat dismally in a corner of the ferry that took me to Manly and back, and scowled at two pimply youths who were ogling a couple of typists.

Then I went morosely down to Darling Harbour and waited at the entrance to the wharf. I called out to Marie, who drove past in a gleaming car with a middle-aged man, and she replied that she had not seen Margaret. I waited and waited, and my misery deepened. She was not coming. Something had happened to her. She was ill. She had had an accident.

Finally I hurried through the barrier, and strode up to where the liner crouched beside the wharf. I went up the gangplank. She had been on board all the time.

"Hullo, Mick," she said in the quiet tone she always used to me. "Thanks for the flowers and the books and sweets. It was nice of you to think of me."

"Of us," said Greta.

"You're always nice to Margaret," said Mrs Murchison.

I mumbled something. We walked around the deck together. I had the feeling, as I always did at these farewells, that I was intruding, that I had forced myself brutally into a private family affair, that, by my crude assertiveness, I had desecrated a family intimacy.

Most of the time they were talking about people I did not know. What luck I had had, falling for Margaret! If it had been Marie, who always gave me an encouraging smile, or Greta, who kissed me smack-dab on the lips, or Nereda, who stopped me in the street one day and startled me by saying, "Why don't you give me a break, darling? You'll get nowhere with Margaret", it would have been different.

I knew that, with the typical perversity of women, they were interested in me only because I was not interested in them. Perhaps if I pretended to be interested in them Margaret would become interested in me. But I could not do that.

The dreaded time had slipped insidiously upon me again. We had to go ashore. Mrs Murchison kissed Greta and then Margaret. I stood there, a quivering mass of indecision. Forthright Greta came to the rescue, as usual. She kissed me on the lips.

"Here we go," I told myself grimly. I turned to Margaret and bent towards her. She turned her cheek.

I did not even say good-bye. I turned and walked off the ship.

Mrs Murchison and I held streamers as the ship drew away. Margaret was throwing kisses; she was throwing them to her mother. The streamers broke, and the ship drifted out into the stream.

When we reached George Street I turned to Mrs Murchison and said, "Your daughter's lips are evidently sacred."

"I'm sorry, Mick," she said. "I don't know what's wrong with Margaret."

"There's nothing wrong with Margaret," I said, "but I'd like to know what's wrong with me. I'm beaten. I give up."

"Don't give up, Mick. There's nobody else. You've still got a chance."

"I've got two chances," I said. "Mine and Buckley's. Do you know where I'm going?"

"No."

"Well, I'll tell you. I'm going to get drunk."

I wrote to Margaret next day. I told her that for ten months I had poured out my heart and that I would have received as much response from a stuffed mule; that I went to Sydney especially to ask her to marry me; that I was disgusted when she would not see me, and horrified when she turned her cheek.

The only trouble was that I had been too considerate, I wrote. If I had treated her badly she would probably have come back for more. I knew where I stood now and would not trouble her any more. Not once in all that time had I tried even to hold her hand, not once had I embarrassed her by protesting my love except in letters. Well, it was all over now. I was through. I was sorry I had made a fool of myself, sorry I had annoyed her by my sustained insistence. I was finished with girls for life.

It was a bitter letter, and I meant every word of it.

I carried her reply about with me for two hours before opening it.

She was sorry she had hurt me, she wrote, but it had been hopeless from the start. She respected me as a friend, but that was all. Nobody had ever been so kind to her as I had.

"I'm sorry, Mick," she wrote, "that there can never be anything between us. My career is my life. I'm not interested in anything else. My estimate of my ideal man is so high that I'm afraid nobody can ever come up to it. I'm sorry. I don't think we had better see each other again."

So that was that. But it wasn't. Three months later I got a letter from her—my hands trembled when I opened it—saying that her mother was coming with her when the company visited Nerridale next month, and asking me could I find them a cheap flat.

I haggled with estate agents and owners of flats for hours, and all I could get at the low price the Murchisons wanted to pay was a small, scantily furnished flat in a dismal building in a side lane. I was tempted to engage a luxurious flat, pay the agent the difference and swear him to secrecy, but I was afraid that Margaret would find out.

Mother was away, so George and I went round to all our close friends and borrowed and begged odds and ends of furniture, blankets, kitchenware, and cushions. I even borrowed furniture from old J. B. Turner, my boss, for a week.

I smothered the flat with flowers and, with the additions we had made, it did not look too bad. I was fearful that Margaret, her mother and the inevitable Greta would be horrified by its gauntness when I took them to it in a taxi, but they seemed pleased. In any case, they could not have expected much at the price.

The week was a repetition of the one so long ago. I found again the old turmoil in my heart. All my latent feeling came surging to the top again, and again it encountered that distant courtesy, that aloof disinterest. Sometimes, when I looked at her unexpectedly, I found her watching me, and I thought I saw something unusual in her face; but the veil came down again and I was baffled. I must have imagined it.

I went to the theatre every night again, and hid in the telephone-box.

"It must be genuine," I told George. "Good God, man, it's over a year now and I haven't even looked at another girl. It must be genuine."

"I believe it is," said George.

When I saw them off at the station I kissed Mrs Murchison and Greta and held out my hand to Margaret. I saw her eyes half close as though she had been hurt, and then the look was gone.

"Thanks again," she said. "You've been very kind. The land-

.lady told us that a lot of the stuff wasn't hers. It was sweet of you to make us so comfortable."

"Am I still funny?" I asked.

"No, Mick. You're not funny any more."

I walked out into the street with my hands deep in my pockets, trying to puzzle that one out. Eventually I shrugged my shoulders and wandered down to my hotel to get drunk.

CHAPTER VIII

AND then my mother died. I realized too late, of course, what my home life had meant to me. It was not grief for my mother—I was sensible enough to treat death as inevitable and not, as so many people did, as an opportunity for disgusting displays and preposterous advertisements in the papers. It was simply that I could not adjust myself to my new way of living.

I could not fight the loneliness any more. I was beaten and I knew it. It was all right when I was working, but I just could not fill in from five-thirty p.m. until eleven p.m. each day, and the week-ends were hell.

Most of my school-day friends were scattered all over New South Wales, or were married and had drifted away from me. It was not the same any more. They had wives and children. They had to think how much they spent, and how late it was, and there was no more pirating of likely looking girls on beaches or in cafés, no more trips to Lake Carraday when the moon was full and the gin flowed freely.

I knew the solution. I ought to get married. There was only one girl I could marry, and she turned her cheek when I kissed her. I was drinking too much, goaded by a loneliness I had not dreamed existed. I haunted the hotels seeking drinking companions, and did not find many. I could not be bothered with people unless they were my friends, and my friends were fewer than ever. I knew thousands of people but there was only a handful with whom, in my acute restlessness, I cared to drink, and only a handful, as I soon found out, who cared to drink with me.

I had not played cricket for years—not since the match between Nerridale and England—and not many people remembered the Wizard of Nerridale. At twenty-six, I felt I was finished. Something had gone sour in me.

Everything I did was purposeless. The flavour had gone out of everything. I still liked lolling in the sun on Nerridale Beach and getting the big shoots, trying to catch them expertly as they broke, but it was not the same any more. I could not even raise a laugh at the mugs who fell for the old cry "All on!", caught a dumper and were smashed into shallow water, went through a miniature earthquake, and came up through sand-darkened chaos.

I still could not do well all the things I longed to master—chess, golf, swimming, writing poetry.

I understood, at last, the bitter truth that lay behind George's cynicism; but I did not respond to his satirical thrusts at Galsworthy any more, and I went to his room to play chess less and less.

The war clouds were gathering, but I turned and looked the other way. In my blind faith I told myself that these things could not be. The newspapers shrieked the truth at me, and every time I went to the pictures the sonorous voice of Lowell Thomas proclaimed the diabolical menace of the Nazi war machine.

I agreed with George when he told me that I ought to get married. All my friends told me that as I looked bitterly at their children. Oh, it was easy. Just get married. It was easy all right when the only girl who could make me happy turned her cheek.

I still went to the stadium every Saturday night, but it was more from habit than inclination. I had to go somewhere; at least I could not get drunk at the stadium. I had even lost interest in boxers. All they could do was fight.

On the way back to the hotel from the stadium one night I went into Happy Joe Simpson's sundae shop next to the Mayfair Theatre.

"Hullo, Mick," said a plump girl behind the marble counter. She had a musical voice. "I haven't seen ya for ages. How's things? What ya gunna have?"

I found myself looking at her with a flicker of interest that surprised me. "You amaze me, Shirley," I said. "You're the only person I've ever known who is illiterate without being uncouth."

"A whatta without being a whatta? Gee, Mick, ya've swallowed a dictionary."

"I don't want anything. I just came in for a yarn with Happy. Where is he?"

"If ya referrin' ter Mr Simpson he went mad and they shot him," she said with a delightful gravity that transformed banality. It was always the same with Shirley. She spoke like a fishwife and had the charm of a Hollywood starlet; but she had God's greatest gift —a capacity for happiness, an almost bovine unawareness, a blind, invincible serenity of temperament.

She was just eighteen. She had an almost ludicrous rotundity, and I often looked in awe at the swelling amplitude of her bosom. She had the roundest face and the most beautiful brown eyes I had ever seen. She had eyes like my mother's, the eyes of a child, and she knew even less about the world than my mother had known.

"He won't be in, Mick."

"All right." I was about to walk out. I remembered that it was too early to go back to the hotel with only drinking awaiting me there. "Give me a vanilla ice cream," I said impulsively, with a smile that mocked myself.

I lingered over it. I did not know what was going to happen to me. There was no way out. I was through.

I wandered over to the Palais, where a thousand dancers were flinging themselves about to a devastating pulsation of sound. The dreadful breath of the place came up and smote me. I remembered how, in *Julius Caesar*, "the rabblement . . . threw up their sweaty night-caps and uttered such a deal of stinking breath . . . that it had almost choked Caesar."

I strolled back. The crowd in the street had thinned. The raucous cries of the proprietor of a pie cart echoed dolefully down the empty street. I went into the shop, sat in a quiet corner, and surrendered myself to a brooding contemplation of my own misery.

Shirley came around the end of the counter and sat beside me.

"Ya not happy, Mick, are ya?" she asked.

I looked at her for a while. There was a warmth, an intuitive understanding, in her face that was more than mere beauty.

"If I knew what happiness was perhaps I'd know whether I was unhappy," I said. She reached over and pressed my hand. It was the only decent thing anybody had done for me in weeks.

"Golly, Mick, I'm sorry. Ya oughtn'ter feel crooked on things. I s'pose it's because Bertha's outa town."

I grinned ruefully. If I were miserable because Bertha was away at least I could look forward to her return. "Say, aren't ya on the square with her?"

"Afraid not. Why I like you more than I like her." I had just realized it was true.

"Golly!" she cried. "I give up hope long ago."

"You did hope then?"

" 'Course I did. But when I seen I wasn't in the race, well I started goin' with Snow 'Aliburton. He's a boilermaker's labourer."

"Oh."

"Gee, Mick, ya oughtn'ter get like that. Doan get crooked on things."

I'm like a lonely mongrel, I thought, and the only person who'll take pity on me is a fat girl in a sundae shop.

"Shirley, are you happy?"

"Yeah. 'Course I am."

"Always?"

" 'Course. I gotta good home. Me old man's dead, but that was a break, a real good riddance, 'cause he drunk himself ter death. Me mum takes in washin'. She doan make much, but with what I get workin' here and what me bruvver Jim gets as a bricklayer an' makes fightin' we get along good-o."

"Yes, I can see you're pretty well off. Shirley, it's obvious you've never known the torture of a tormented spirit or the dreadful anguish of a restless soul."

She gaped at me.

"Do you like cricket?" I asked.

"Cricket? No, why?"

"Who am I?"

"Say, listen. Have ya got dingbats or somethin'? Mick Reynolds, of course."

"Never heard me called anything else?"

"No. Ay, wait a minute. One day a bloke told me ya first name was 'Oward, but I tells him he's up a tree. Everyone knows ya name's Mick."

"Yes. Tomorrow's Sunday. If I borrowed a car and asked you to come for a drive to the lake for a swim would you come, Mr 'Aliburton notwithstanding?"

"Golly! 'Course I would, Mick. Snow's playin' cricket all day anyhow. Hotel Moderne *v.* Royal Hotel and four nine gallons of grog to stop 'em dyin' of thirst."

"Good," I said.

I was thoughtful on my way home. For a while I wished I was a boilermaker's labourer.

Shirley and I swam at the baths at Kedron Point, and lay in the warm sunlight, looking across the unnaturally calm bay. Her skin was milky white, and I had to struggle with myself to keep my eyes from being drawn back to the jutting magnificence of her breasts. She was unconscious of the goading revelation of her striped costume.

"Shirley," I asked, "do you smoke?"

"No."

"Do you drink?"

"Aw gee no."

"Do you swear?"

"Golly no. Break it down."

"Don't you do anything interesting?"

"Say, listen," she said indignantly. "I'm not one of them immortal girls."

I must have gaped at her because she looked puzzled and said quickly, "There I go again, gettin' inter trouble tryin' ter use big words."

She told me about her mother. "You know," she said, "me mum always reckons I was made to be a great lady."

"I'm sure you were, Shirley."

"Yeah. Me mum reckons I was born to wear nice clothes and go to nice places and travel. Maybe I will some day."

"Yes. Maybe you will. I'm sure you'll make an elegant Mrs 'Aliburton."

"Yeah. Say, that's pretty good. Elegant Mrs 'Aliburton. That'd be me."

She let her mind play with the delectable prospect of being the elegant Mrs 'Aliburton. I could see the salt whitening on her face and her long lashes.

"The other day I went over to see Snow about the boilermakers' picnic, but he wasn't there, so I stops talkin' to Mrs 'Aliburton for a while. I says, 'Mrs 'Aliburton, I haven't seen Snow since the day before yesterdee. He hasn't diced me, has he?' "

" 'Gee, Shirley,' she says, 'he musta got another girl friend.' As if he would dare!"

"Shirley, that's a queer name, 'Aliburton. How do you spell it?"

"Haitch-a-l-i-b-u-r-t-o-n."

Later she said, "You know I sing."

I looked at the maternal expanse above her waist, and said, "I can well believe it." Spike would have called it "a decent sort of an upper deck".

"Well," she said, touching herself on the bosom, "I get me singin' from here. I wants ter get on the community singin' at the Mayfair next door, see, so I goes up to see Mr Wilkerson in his office. 'Mr Wilkerson,' I says, 'I wants ter sing at the community singin'.' He looks at me with that you-know look in his eye, looks at me like as if I haven't got nothin' on. You know, Mick, the way you looks at some girls. Not at me though."

"Thanks," I said.

"She's jake. Well Mr Wilkerson gets through lookin' at me that way and then he says, 'Lift up ya dress so's I can see ya legs.' Says it just like that. 'Lift up ya dress,' he says, 'so's I can see ya legs.' The hide of 'im!

" 'Listen, Mr Wilkerson,' I says, 'Ya don't see no legs, see? I come here ter sing not ter give ya a leg show. What sorta girl ya think I am, anyway?'

" 'Ya a very nice girl, Shirley,' he says, oily-like. 'Ya oughtn'ter be in a milk bar.' 'Listen, Mr Wilkerson,' I says, 'I'm awake-up, I am. Ya doan need ter come that stuff with me. I didden come down in the last shower. Where d'ya think I come from? Woop Woop? Now break it down, will ya, and let me get on with me singin'.' Are ya listenin', Mick?"

"Yeah. Sure. Haven't missed a word."

"He stands up and comes round the table ter me. 'I'm sure we understand each other, Shirley,' he says. 'I can do a lot for a girl like you.' And he slips his arm around me waist and tries ter kiss me. I slaps him on the gob good and hard. 'Mr Wilkerson,' I says, 'Cop this. I'm no common sheila. I'm not one er them. What ya think ya comin' at? If that's the way a girl's gotter act ter get on I doan wanter get on, see?' and I walks outa his office. What sorta sheila does that bloke think I am, anyway?"

I lay on the grass with the warmth of the sun soothing my back, my chin cupped in my hands, and my eyes looking into her beautiful brown outraged ones.

"Shirley," I said after a while, "you're the only attractive girl I know I'd never try to kiss."

"Yeah? Why? Frightened I'd slap ya on the gob?"

"No. I'd be frightened I'd fall in love with you. It's time we went home."

CHAPTER IX

I WENT on my frustrated way, haunting the bars looking for drinking partners, picking up new girls and dropping them as soon as I tired of them, feeling a twinge amid the bitterness in my heart when, sometimes, I saw a photograph of Margaret in an advertisement.

And all the time, like so many millions of people who were afraid, I kept my head in the sand. Even when, on 2 September 1939, I sat in George's room and saw the flames leaping up to engulf the world, I tried to stiffen my waning faith, my futile optimism. I was like a man who, sentenced to death, hopes for a last-minute reprieve.

"But George," I said desperately, "the Germans can't do this evil thing. Why, man, they produced Beethoven."

"Yes," said George, looking up at me slowly with his mocking smile, "and they produced Adolf Hitler."

A little later, on the wireless, we heard the sonorous voice of the Prime Minister of England say, "It is my melancholy duty to inform you that Great Britain is at war with Germany."

I looked up at George, and as I looked I knew that my eyes were staring and my mouth had fallen slackly open. George was looking at me. His lips were twisted in a smile, and there were crinkles of pain around his eyes.

"I hope you'll like France," he said.

"I won't go," I said. "I tell you, I won't go."

He was smiling.

"The militia," I said. "They'll have to go. They've been playing at soldiers long enough. Let them go. There're precious few of them, I know, but let them go. Let 'Nerridale's Own' go. I'll have nothing to do with this barbarity."

George shook his head. "They won't go," he said. "The ones who do'll get all the commissions, of course; but it'll be mainly fellows like you who'll go, poor bastards who've got a conscience."

Before I could answer the door was flung open, and Captain Rissay, adjutant of the 85th Battalion, "Nerridale's Own", burst in. His eyes were shining.

"Mick! George!" he gasped. "Heard the news? Great, isn't it?"

We were gaping at him. "Great?" asked George.

"Yes. It's wonderful. Why, George," he cried, "you don't know what this means to me!"

We sat there, staring at him. "You don't know what this means," said George, "to the world."

Through the eight months of the "phoney" war my determination not to enlist did not waver. A few of my friends, including Captain Rissay, sailed for Palestine—I had to look it up on a map to find out where it was—or England, and periodically the papers announced that another convoy of the A.I.F. had arrived safely in the Middle East. That was all the war meant to me.

I watched marches through the streets with a cynical detachment, and once, after winning fifteen pounds at Randwick races, I took a group of A.I.F. men into a hotel in George Street, Sydney, and shouted them two rounds of drinks. I was patronizing, as though they had an unfortunate disease for which they were not responsible.

On Anzac Day—the anniversary of the day on which Australia "found her nationhood", as the newspapers told us every year to remind us of the day on which thousands of Australians were butchered on Gallipoli—I watched, with a superior smile, the A.I.F. march down Victoria Street, and went down to the Royal Hotel to see the men who had been through the last war get drunk and tell each other what good times they had had in France and at Anzac Cove.

Then the blow fell, and suddenly my conscience stood up in me and smote me and I was alone and afraid. Men were dying in France, in Belgium, in Holland, to save me, and I was selling furniture. I was selling furniture.

"Well," said George, as we strolled into the Majestic Hotel, "I suppose we'll soon be seeing our brave boy in khaki."

I turned on him in sudden anger. "I'm not going to join the A.I.F.," I said, "and if I do decide to join it'll be my own bloody private affair and nobody else's!"

My God, I thought. What have I said?

The old mockery was back in George's eyes. "Ah," he said, " 'if I do decide to join'." And suddenly I noticed that he was laughing.

CHAPTER X

I STARED moodily out of the window of the Nerridale express and cursed myself for a fool. The realization was drummed into my mind by the regular clicking of the wheels on the lines, and the monotonous sight of gum-trees streaming by.

I picked up the *Nerridale Mail* again, listlessly this time, and glanced over the headlines. Things were bad in France. God knows what it meant. I remembered what Harry Courtenay had said dolefully: "You'd better hurry up, Mick, or it'll be all over before you get there."

I looked out the window. I could see the blue Pacific caressing one of the beaches that stretch like a string of golden beads down the coast of New South Wales. The Pacific. Perhaps soon there would be war here, too, making a mockery of its name.

A man was a fool to join the A.I.F. The Home Defence Forces—officially known as the A.M.F., the Australian Military Forces—were what the boys would call "the lurk". Join the militia and salve conscience, and you would not have to do anything more serious than a few days on manoeuvres. It was the Pacific all right; war would never come here. Join the militia and get a uniform. Get a uniform and stay in camp in New South Wales for the duration. Let the other silly bastards go overseas. Stop home to defend your homeland. Fight for your own flesh and blood. Repel the invader who sought to defile the sanctity of your native country. The more copybook the maxim, the more trite the catch-cry, the better it sounded.

But no. What was good enough for my father was good enough for me. If he could take it so could I, or the breed had watered down in a generation. Join the militia? No, never! People were dying in France and Belgium, had died in Poland, to save me, to save the world. This insane slaughter would have to stop, and the only thing I could do to stop it was to become part of it, and help kill the madmen who had let this horror loose on mankind.

I cursed myself for a fool once more, but it was not for deciding to join the A.I.F. I was doing that because it was the only thing to do. I just could not stand it any more. I cursed myself because I was travelling one hundred and fifty miles each way just to look at a house because a girl lived in it. A girl who, I suppose, if the truth were known, was not as kind or intelligent as that brunette in the opposite corner of the box compartment.

I pulled a piece off the corner of the *Mail* and tore it into shreds, slowly. Surely a sane man would not travel three hundred miles just to look at a house. Ah well, perhaps I was insane. Poor hopeless Romeo, doting over his Juliet, was even such a one as I. But Romeo had a reason for his dotage. He did not batter himself desperately against the brick wall of distant courtesy.

I could not help it. I just had to go to Sydney to look at Margaret's house. I would not tell her I was going to join the A.I.F., but I could not join it without being near her. It was irrational, I knew, but I was in love.

> Lovers and madmen have such seething brains,
> Such shaping fantasies, that apprehend
> More than cool reason ever comprehends.
> The lunatic, the lover and the poet
> Are of imagination all compact.

I had a "seething brain" all right, with my distress over the agony of the world, the almost incredible importance of the decision I had made, the most vital in my life, and now this crazy trip to Sydney.

The brunette smiled at me as I got out at Wollongong, but I did not do anything about it. Stray brunettes seemed so futile now that a great country was being battered into bondage on Flanders fields, where, twenty-five years before, my father had fought and bled so that I might never have to go to war.

I wandered up and down the platform, kicking a cigarette box moodily before me. It reminded me that I was smoking too much. Even now, when hope had been finally dissipated, I did not dare to drink for fear that I would meet Margaret. A fat lot she'd care whether I was rolling drunk or not; but I couldn't do it.

I went back to the compartment, avoided the eye of the brunette, settled down in the corner, and watched the green fields skip by.

Suddenly the Nerridale express seemed to be Man hurtling to destruction. This poor creature who was being destroyed by the machines he had built, this Frankenstein with his impressive trappings of civilization, his music, his art, his letters, his fine clothes, his rich foods. He had conquered the sea, chained the river, impressed the air. By his own ingenuity, his skill and courage, his steadfast toil, he had emerged from the darkness into the light, he had made a way of living such as the world had never conceived. He had done everything but conquer his own soul.

I threw an unlighted cigarette out of the window and glared at the brunette, who stared at me in amazement. I pulled my hat down over my face and hunched myself up in my corner.

I got out at Central, went down a gloomy tunnel and up another one to another platform, and caught another train, an electric one this time. At Croydon I went down the yellow platform and up the wooden steps, and thrust my ticket savagely into the collector's hand. Now I was here my trip seemed crazier than ever.

I wandered down the street, past the house where a former Premier of New South Wales lived, and up to the Western Suburbs Hospital. Soon I was walking along Chandler Street and looking across at Margaret's home. I went down to the next corner, crossed the road, turned, and came back past the front of the house.

"Well now you've seen it," I told myself. "Now you can go into the city and get drunk."

But I could not leave it. I tried not to admit it to myself, but I knew what it was. The longer I stayed near there the better chance I had of seeing Margaret. I cursed myself for a fool. I had not seen her for years. She might even be married by now. I stopped suddenly. Good God, she could have had a child by now!

I loitered about so long that people sitting on a front veranda looked at me suspiciously. I turned for one last look at the house. One never knew. Perhaps I would never see it again. After all, I was going to a war, and not everybody who went to a war came back.

I went back to Parramatta Road and waited for a bus. It was a red double-decker. We had had them in Nerridale for a few years, but I could not overcome my delight in their novelty, and I always rode on the top. I was about to step on to the bus when I noticed a girl getting out. It was Margaret.

She was wearing the most fascinating hat I had ever seen. It was even more delightful than the red one she had worn the day I had taken her to lunch at the Carnarvon the first time. It was just a few strands of blue and yellow wool twisted into a coronet.

She gaped at me for a moment, and I gaped at her. Then I raised my hat awkwardly and helped her down. For a moment I thought I saw something strange in her eyes, and then it was gone.

"Why, Mick," she said in her quiet voice which still had that enchanting precision, "I haven't seen you for ages."

I did not think I would be able to speak. I made an effort and said, "It's over a year, Margaret."

"Is it? Doesn't time fly? What are you doing out Croydon way? You haven't called to see mother, have you?"

"No. Just had some business out here. Funny meeting you."

"Yes," she said. She looked at me, opened her mouth to say something, and shut it again. Neither of us said anything for a while. Then I asked her how Greta was, and she said, "She's all right, thank you." There was another awkward silence.

"Anything interesting happened to you lately, Mick?" she asked.

"No, nothing much," I said, scraping the toe of my shoe over the edge of the gutter. Then I decided to tell her. She would not be upset about it. And if I couldn't have anything else I wanted her respect. I wanted her to know that I might look like a clumsy oaf whenever I met her but that I had a bit of guts, anyway.

"Nothing much," I said, trying to make my voice casual, "except that I'm going to join the A.I.F."

I was looking at my shoe. She did not say anything. I thought she had not heard me. My voice had been faint.

"I'm going to join the A.I.F.," I said.

She did not say anything. Evidently she was not even interested in what happened to me.

"I want to give you a letter, Mick," she said. "Wait here, please, dear."

I heard her turn and walk away. I could not believe it at first. It was so strange. She had called me "dear". I looked up slowly. She was walking down the street. I saw her turn the corner. She did not look back.

I put my hand up, pushed my hat forward over my eyes, and scratched the back of my head. She had called me "dear". Margaret had called me "dear". Well what was funny about that? I had been a friend of hers for years, and perhaps it was a habit with these stage girls. My aunts called me "dear", didn't they?

She was a strange girl, though. I told her I was going to join the A.I.F., and she merely said, "I want to give you a letter, Mick. Wait here, please, dear."

Evidently the letter was for somebody at the recruiting office in Nerridale or somebody in Ingleburn Camp. Funny to get me to deliver it though. Funny how she had called me "dear". Why hadn't she asked me to walk down to her home with her?

I saw somebody coming in the distance. It was her young brother Bill. I stood with my hands in my pockets until he came up. I did not like meeting Bill because he had a Murchison face. He reminded me poignantly of Margaret.

"Hullo, Mick," he said.

"Hullo, Bill."

"How's things?"

"Not bad. Things O.K. with you?" I was always irritated by an exchange of banal greetings.

"I'm O.K.," said Bill, "but I think Margaret's off her rocker. She's given me a letter to give to you."

He handed it to me, and I put it in my pocket. "Thanks," I said. "It is a bit queer. But girls are strange creatures."

"They certainly are." He was looking at me as if I were a bit queer, too.

"What's wrong?" I asked. "Got a smut on my nose?"

"No. It's just a bit queer, that's all."

"What is?"

"You are. I give you a letter and you just shove it in your kick. You just south it."

I looked at him in growing bewilderment. "Listen," I said, "what's wrong with you? Has the Murchison family gone nuts today or something? Why shouldn't I put it in my pocket?"

Bill shook his head as though he needed to clear his brain. "Mick," he said, "aren't you going to read it?"

"Read it? Are you drunk, Bill? I don't make a habit of reading other people's letters."

He started to laugh. "A great light breaks," he said. "You silly fool, it's for you."

I stared at him. "For me? But Margaret——"

"Margaret's behaving like a girl with dingbats. Read the bloody thing, for Christ's sake."

I took out the letter and stared stupidly at the name on the envelope. It was for me all right. I opened it and read the words without comprehension. The whole business was too fantastic for me to grasp. She behaved like an eccentric old maid, and now she was writing drivel about O. Henry. It didn't make sense, none of it. Not even the letter, which was scribbled in pencil.

I read it again:

Mick. Among the many books you gave me is the Complete Works of O. Henry. In this book there is a story called "By Courier". My brother is not a Bowery boy and you are not sitting on a "bench", but in other respects this message is the same as the last one the girl sent.

MARGARET.

I was trying to puzzle it out. It was evidently some new kind of conundrum.

"Mick," said Bill, "Margaret's nuts. She gave me two bob, told me to hurry and said something about stupid people who disapproved of kissing in the streets. You don't think she's been drinking, do you?"

"Drinking? Kissing in the streets?" I asked, frowning. I looked at him dully. Suddenly something clutched at my heart. I grabbed him by both shoulders, shook him, and cried, "What's that about kissing?"

"Cripes, are you nuts, too? She said people disapproved of kissing in the streets. Hey, let me go! You're both crazy!"

My heart was racing now—there was a wild flare of hope in it —and I was biting my lip hard.

"Jesus!" I cried. I swung Bill roughly aside and ran down the street like a madman. My hat went flying, and I was mumbling triumphant profanities over and over to myself.

For I had remembered that the last message the girl sent in the story was, "Tell that guy on the other bench that his girl wants him."

CHAPTER XI

THE night porter woke me at five o'clock. As I stood in my bare hotel bedroom, shivering, the full meaning of what I had done rose up and smote me. Suddenly I realized that I was leaving Nerridale, leaving all this old life, and perhaps I would never come back. Perhaps I would lie mangled in some Flanders field.

For a moment all my former fears overwhelmed me, and then I shook them off and was strong again. I was going into a new world. Great events and experiences lay ahead, and if death were there, too, at least it would not be dull. I grabbed my towel and went to meet my new life, via the bathroom.

The night porter was the only person to say good-bye to me. "Good-bye and good luck, Mick," he said. It was the first of many times I heard that depressing expression. They meant well, I suppose, and a man would need luck. It is luck that "shapes our ends, rough hew them how we may." It made one man blind and another rich; one a corpse and another a hero. Every man with the V.C. or even the M.M. was lucky to be alive.

I went into that cheerless place—a city street at five o'clock in the morning—and the old loneliness settled down on me like a pall. A milk cart clattered by, and a few cold and silent people were dragging themselves towards the station.

The Wizard of Nerridale was going forth to war. Going forth to save the world for democracy. It would not even be worth a line in the *Sydney Morning Herald*.

Harry Courtenay was on the station, looking dolefully at me

through his glasses. It was good to see him. I had one staunch friend, anyhow.

"Typical of the army, Mick," he growled. "Won't give you a rail warrant for the Nerridale express. Second class in an old slow train will do for a soldier of the King."

"The express passes us the other side of Wollongong," I said. "We shunt on to another line. It takes us six and a half hours to get to Sydney. I told you not to come, Harry."

"Had to do the right thing. You know how it is."

"Thanks," I said.

We did not say much. There was not much to say. I found a seat in a bare box compartment, and we wandered about the station, rubbing our hands together.

"Nice time to go into camp," growled Harry. "Too bloody cold."

"Yes," I said.

We passed the place where Margaret had turned her cheek the first time, and I smiled. How long ago that seemed. How different my world was now.

"I can't tell you much, Mick. Mainly you've just got to take your chance with the rest. Remember one thing, always. There's a helluva lot of places a shell can land except on you. When you hear 'em come whistling over remember that."

"I'll remember it," I said.

"It helps," said Harry. Anyone would think I was sailing to-morrow instead of just going into camp. "Your old man was a good soldier. You'll be a good soldier, too."

"And my son, and his son, and his son," I said bitterly.

"Yeah. That's the way it is."

"I hope I'll be a good soldier, Harry." I shivered in a gust of the chill wind. We had to keep moving to try to get warm. After a while I said, "Harry, I'm afraid I'll be afraid."

He took my arm quietly. " 'Course you'll be afraid," he said. "Everyone is. It's not being afraid that hurts; it's showing it. Never show it, Mick, for then you can keep the one thing you've got to keep—respect for yourself."

"I'll try," I said. "Harry, what time have you got to get up in camp?"

"Dunno for sure. I reckon reveille'd be about half-past five."

"Jesus! Every morning?"

"Yeah. What do you think the A.I.F. is? An old woman's home?"

"But that's the middle of the night."

"Your lazy old days have gone, Mick, gone with the wind of war, and the sooner you realize it the better. Things are going to be tough from now on."

"Yeah," I said. The bell rang. I hopped into my compartment, and we shook hands through the window.

"Good-bye and good luck," said Harry.

"Thanks," I said.

The train began to move. Harry's eyes gleamed through his glasses. "By Christ," he said, "if I was only twenty years younger I'd be going with you!"

I poked my head out of the window and watched him limp away. A bit of shrapnel had hit his leg at Lone Pine. If the last generation could take it surely this one could. I hoped I could, anyhow.

At Central a soldier met half a dozen of us and took us over to a group of about twenty other recruits. We waited about for an hour, looking curiously at each other—I felt as though we were waiting to be executed—and then a truck drove up. I wondered how it got on to the station. We were driven to Sydney Sports Ground, and we sat about there for another hour.

Then we went up into one of the grandstands and had lunch. We had to line up for it with plates, a knife and fork and a mug they gave us. I heard one of the garrison soldiers on duty there say something about a mess parade, and marvelled at the extraordinary jargon of the army.

After lunch we waited about again, and finally we were herded to another part of the ground, and a door opened and we trooped into a big room. The tedious delay in this place amazed me.

I thought England needed men and needed them badly. Wasn't there a war on? Wasn't France battered to her knees and bleeding? From all over New South Wales we had come, butchers, bakers, candlestick-makers, clerks, salesmen, labourers, journalists, steelworkers, electricians, shearers, taxi-drivers, milkmen, graziers, tramdrivers. We had come with our bags in our hands and determination in our hearts, and fear was there, too, a goading fear of the unknown, but we kept it pressed down; we did not dare to look it in the face.

We had come streaming from the cities and the towns, from the wheat and the sheep, from the mountains and the plains so that men might know freedom again and so that women could submit to the agony of childbirth without fearing that, twenty years later, there would be a greater agony—the agony of waving a son good-bye.

Men from the farm and the factory, the mill and the meadow, the cows and the corn, a thousand men a day from a population of two and a quarter million. Men in reserved occupations putting down "labourer", boys of fifteen saying they were twenty, men who fought in Flanders and Gallipoli cutting a few years off their ages, joining the "lying thirty-nines", pleading for a chance to go and get killed, going forth again to join their sons and brothers. The Poles could say with Malcolm,

> Our country sinks beneath the yoke:
> It weeps, it bleeds; and each new day a gash
> Is added to her wounds.

and the Czechs with Macduff,

> O nation miserable,
> With an untitled tyrant bloody-scepter'd,
> When shalt thou see thy wholesome days again?

but, by Christ, Australians would never say it!

We wanted to get into camp, to learn to fight, to learn to kill so that a megalomaniac would never see his crazy dream come true. And here we were, enmeshed in the machine we were to know so well, the machine that we had to accept eventually for the ponderous but inevitable thing it was.

The youth in front of me was asked what he wanted to join.

"I'm easy, mate," he said. He had a cigarette butt stuck over his right ear.

"The infantry do?"

"I'm easy, mate," he said.

The man marked his papers. Silly bastard, I thought. I'm a silly bastard, too, but at least I know I am.

The manpower officer asked me what I did in civil life. I told him.

"You're O.K.," he said. "Next please."

The next man asked me what I wanted to join.

"The infantry," I said. "The 2/93rd Battalion."

"Can't promise any special unit," he said abruptly. "Anyhow, they might be in Palestine or England."

"They're not. It must be the 93rd. My father was in it."

"Oh," he said, "so that's it. What name?"

"Reynolds. Mick Reynolds."

"Didn't know him. I was in the engineers myself." All these men had returned soldiers' badges. I looked at them in awe. They had been to a war. "I'll put it in your papers. Good luck, son."

"Thanks," I said.

"What do you want to join?" he asked the fellow behind me.

"Anything, I'm easy."

"What about the provosts?"

"What the hell are they?"

"Traffic control."

"Traffic control?"

"Yes. They direct military traffic. Keep the roads to the front open. Important job."

"That'll do me, mate."

He did not know it and neither did I, but he had become a military policeman. Six months later I met him at Beit Hareed, Palestine.

"There's only one way to get out of the provosts, mate," he said. "When you hear somebody say, 'Who goes there?' don't answer."

So it went on—an evidently interminable succession of men and forms. Finally we reached the doctors. First we had to urinate in a bottle.

"———in this for me, will yer, cobber?" said the man behind me. "I got diabetes."

"O.K."

"Jesus, they'll be testing your ——— next."

"Hey, don't spill any. The ——— house is downstairs."

"Dunno how this collection's gonna help us win the war."

"I'm not sayin' ya yella, mate, but ya ——— is."

"Look, there's a bloke boilin' it. Queer jobs some blokes get."

Two old men with grey hair and that intent look of doctors had a look at intimate parts of me and shoved a stethoscope over my heart. "You're all right," they said.

I was going to be a soldier.

Downstairs again, four of us put our hands on a Bible and took a solemn oath. I smiled cynically to myself as I repeated the words. Then I went down a long row of clerks. One gave me a paybook, a thin, brown book, with, on the front, spaces for my name and number, "Australian Military Forces", the Australian crest of kangaroo and emu, and SOLDIER'S PAY BOOK in capitals.

A tall, mournful middle-aged man began to fill in my details.

"Surname?" he asked.

"Reynolds," I said.

"Christian names?"

"Howard William."

"Religion?"

"None."

The grey head came up slowly, and two puzzled eyes looked at me through horn-rimmed glasses. "I asked what religion," he said.

"And I said 'None'," I said.

His eyes widened, and a faint frown creased his forehead. "There must be some mistake," he said. "You must have some religion."

His dark eyes were disturbed. I remembered something about which I had always wondered—why religious people always looked so miserable. The line of men behind me was growing. I could hear whispers.

"I have no religion," I said slowly. ."That is, I have no religion of your church kind. I have what an Englishman would call a code. It's pretty elastic, I admit, but I believe in it all the same, and I live by it."

He was staring up at me in amazement. "You—you don't go to church?" he asked.

"I don't go to church," I said. "I will never go to church again. I gave religion a fair go. It just didn't make the grade, that's all."

"But surely you're not telling me you——" he hesitated as though it was unthinkable—"you don't—don't believe in God?" He mouthed the word "God" in the way only ministers and middle-aged churchmen can mouth it.

"I don't believe in God," I said.

His mouth dropped ludicrously open, and he gaped at me. "But Mr—er——" he looked at my paybook—"Mr Reynolds. I can scarcely believe it."

I laughed. As if it mattered.

"Listen, mate," I said. "You can shove a bayonet through a man's guts just as well whether you believe in God or not. Believing in God won't make you live any longer if a shell hits you."

I could see the puzzled, hurt look in his eyes. "But, Mr Reynolds," he said, "I'm at a loss to understand. I just can't conceive it."

"Look here," I said, "you're wasting everybody's time." There was a long line behind me now. "Please put down 'None' and let me get on. There's a war on."

"But, Mr Reynolds, I want to speak to you a moment. Why don't you believe?" His dark eyes peered hopefully at me through his glasses.

"Why don't I believe?" I cried. "I'll tell you why. I don't believe in God because there are wars. People are slaughtering each other, blowing each other to bits and—what's worse—maiming and blinding. And Christ said 'Thou shalt not kill'. If there were a God I wouldn't be here. My conception of a God is a merciful God, a protecting God. You talk about 'the fear of God'. I don't want a God to fear. I don't want to fear anything."

I was leaning over the table, thumping it with my fist. I heard a murmur of approving voices from behind, and somebody said, "Good on you, mate."

"Ah," said the man, with smug complacency, "You do not believe now, but someday you will. When you come back from the war you will."

"Listen, feller," I said. "I'm twenty-seven. I'm old enough to know my own mind. I don't believe now and I never will, war or no war. For Christ's sake put down 'None' and let me get on!"

I could feel my voice rising. I was getting angry.

"Ah," he said again, unctuously, "when you come back from the war you will."

"I tell you I won't," I said. "I don't need you to tell me what I believe. I won't, see? Put down 'None', will you, and give us a chance to get into camp before midnight."

"Yes," cried somebody in the crowd. "Get on with the job, for Christ's sake! What a bloke believes is his own business."

"But, Mr Reynolds," he pleaded, "can't I put down some denomination?"

I thumped the table again. "Are you asking me to tell a lie?" I demanded. "I've just taken a solemn oath to serve my country faithfully, and before I get out of the building you ask me to break my word."

"Good on you, mate," said somebody behind me.

"Er—no," stammered the man. "I don't ask you to tell a falsehood, but it seems—I don't know—I can't understand it, that's all."

"You can't understand it," I said. "Well, can you understand this? We're fighting for democracy, aren't we? And democracy means freedom. And yet you deny me the freedom to think as I like. You amaze me, the whole mournful tribe of you deists amazes me. You must prod, and pry, and stickybeak. Why the hell can't you leave a man in peace?"

"Good on you, mate!" cried somebody behind me. "Give it to him."

"That's unjust," said the man quickly. "I'm only trying to help you, to guide you."

"Dice it," I said. "You're sabotaging the war effort. Put it down, man, put it down!"

"But I—I've never had to do this before. I——" He looked dismally at me through his glasses. I knew his mind was crying out "Unclean! Unclean!" and I grinned. He shrugged his shoulders, filled in my rank, the military district, the date of attestation, the age on enlistment, and the date I joined camp, and handed me the book.

"Good luck, son," he said, looking earnestly at me.

"Thanks," I said, and moved on.

"I hate to stick my nose in, mate," said the next man, a hard-bitten Digger. "I know how you feel, but I was in the last stink and, take it from me, your paybook's your Bible. It goes everywhere with you. Your religion's important in the army. It goes on every sick report and keeps cropping up. If you'll take my advice you'll shove something down. Anything'll do. If you get a C.O. who goes for this religious bullo you'll strike trouble. It might stop you getting promotion. Every time you report sick you'll have to go through the sort of thing you've gone through this afternoon. I hate to butt in but I think you'll regret not having any stated religion in the long run."

I looked at him for a moment. "Thanks, pal," I said. "I'll do it."

I went back to the first man. "I've changed my mind," I said grudgingly, handing him the book. "I'm an Anglican."

His eyes gleamed in triumph. He wrote "C.E." carefully in the space provided for religion, handed me the book, smiled and said "Thanks".

CHAPTER XII

GOING out in the bus from Liverpool, I sat next to a soldier who had jumped the rattler.

"This bus's s'posed to be for new men," said the corporal in charge.

"O.K., corp.," said the soldier, grinning. "I won't pool ya."

"Give him a go," said somebody, and somebody else said "Yeah. Don't be a standover merchant."

The corporal mumbled something and let it pass.

"How long've you been in camp?" I asked the soldier.

"A fortnight," he said, and I stared at him in awe.

"What's it like?"

"You'll be sorry," he said. The words sounded ominous; we were to come to know them well. Every soldier we passed on the road yelled, "You'll be sorry." Every soldier we encountered in camp until we got our issue clothes said, "You'll be sorry."

Three days later I wandered up to brigade to watch the recruits come in, and I lifted up my voice with the rest. "You'll be sorry!" I yelled. I was a veteran.

"Ya goin' ter be sick," said the soldier.

I looked at him with a start. "Sick?"

"Yeah. Bloody sick."

"I feel all right. The food's not so bad, is it?"

"It's not the food. Ya got vaccinated, didden ya?"

"Yes. Why? It feels all right."

"Oh, it's all right now. But you wait. Five days, and then—boom! Ya goin' ter be sick."

"Oh," I said.

"Yeah. Ya goin' ter be real sick." I could see some of the others craning their necks and listening. "Why, a feller died in the C.R.S. yesterdee. Died from vaccination."

"Died?" I asked incredulously.

"Ay, what sort of an army is this?" asked somebody behind me. "They kill you first just to see if you're tough."

We laughed, but it was a false laughter.

"What's the C.R.S.?" I asked. I had never been so conscious of my own ignorance.

"You got a lot to learn," said the soldier. "The Casualty Receiving Station."

"Oh," I said. Christ, they had casualties already. Perhaps I'd better get out and go back home. But I'd signed up for the duration and one year after.

"Yes," said the soldier, grinning. "The M.O. sends me from the R.A.P. to see the C.O. at B.H.Q. about being A.W.L. from the P.A.C., and I says I seen the C.Q.M.S. about the L.M.G. on my F.200. The D.A.D.O.S. asks the A.D.M.S. about the L.A.D. but the B.M. says the D.A.A.G. won't get the O.C. to see the D.A.A. and Q.M.G. to O.K. the M.T. return of the S.O.M.E."

We were gaping at him "You're in the army, mate," he said. "You'll be sorry."

"Break it down," said the corporal. "You'll give these blokes the tomtits before they get their first lot of C.B."

There was another one. I wondered what C.B. meant. The only C.B. I could think of was C.B. Ale or Connie Boswell. Or it might be Before Christ reversed.

I was surprised to find that there was no fence around Ingleburn Camp, one of the biggest in Australia. The main road went right through the middle of it. It was dark when we got there.

The soldier dropped off the side of the bus at the first cross street. "Doan let them get ya down with their 'You'll be sorry'," he said. "Good luck, Digger."

"Thanks," I said. A glow went right through me. He had called me "Digger!" It dawned on me suddenly. I was in the A.I.F. I was a Digger, too!

I got off the bus in a daze, lugging my suitcase with me, and I was still in a daze when we lined up at what I discovered later was 20th Brigade Headquarters. I could see huts scattered about. Somebody who sounded like an officer was calling names and sending groups of men away with what he called runners.

"Runner from 2/93rd!" he called in the tone I came to know so well. It was the voice of authority.

"Yes, sir."

"Take—er——" He looked at his papers. "Maxwell, Reynolds and Taylor down to the 2/93rd. See if there's anything hot left over from mess for them."

"Yes, sir."

I looked at the watch they had given me at the shop. It was nearly eight o'clock. It seemed a week since I had got up fifteen hours before. I picked up my suitcase and overcoat and followed the runner down the road.

"You'll be sorry," he said.

We kept passing groups of soldiers who called out the same thing. It had become odious already.

We stopped at a hut with a notice board outside and a few soldiers lounging in the doorway. "You'll be sorry," they said.

We did not say anything. We went inside, where an officer looked appraisingly at us and asked what company we wanted to be in. He looked as though he was buying fat stock.

One of the others, a stocky fellow with an open-neck shirt and an unshaven face, said awkwardly, "Well it's like this, if you doan mind me sayin' so—we was in a pub yesterdee and we seen an officer."

"Strange place to see an officer," said the officer.

"Yeah. Lieutenant Hill his name was. An' we told him we was goin' inter camp today and he says to ask to be put in his company. A Company it is, and he seemed a bonzer bloke, so that's what we want. Eh, Bert?"

"Yeah," said Bert, "That's what we want. If it's not too much trouble."

"Nothing's too much trouble," said the officer, smiling. "I don't know why everybody wants to join A Company. Perhaps it's this hotel recruiting. It's over strength now, but we'll fit you in."

"Now what about you—er—Reynolds?"

I had been finding a cynical amusement in the fact that a chance meeting with an officer in a hotel had decided the destiny of two men. Some companies were sure to have a worse time than others. But how could you know which? I suppose their way was as good as any.

"I'm easy," I said. "Any one will do me." I did not know which one my father had been in so it did not matter.

"I'll put you in C Company," he said.

Feeling that my fate had been settled one way or the other, I followed the others outside.

"See you again, mate," said the other two, and went off with a soldier.

A soldier standing next to the steps was slapping his thigh with a stick. He was wearing what I learned later was called a forage cap. We had a much more vivid and obscene name for it. It was small, and fitted on the side of the head.

"Where's the company orderly corporal?" he asked. "Hey, runner, go down to C Company and get 'em to send up the orderly corporal straight away. Tell 'em a draft's in."

I never forgot that soldier. He stood there, slapping his thigh and saying, "Where's the company orderly corporal?" I had never heard such a ponderous phrase. For the first time I realized that I was irrevocably in the army.

The runner came back with the news that the company orderly corporal could not be found.

"Where the bloody hell is he?" asked the soldier with the stick. "Where's the company orderly corporal?"

Much as I hated his title, I began to feel sorry for the company orderly corporal. Finally the runner took me down the gravel road to C Company, where my particulars were taken and I was shown to a hut a couple of hundred yards away.

A few soldiers who were lying on palliasses looked up with faint interest. I could see them looking at my new blue suit and grey overcoat. "You'll be sorry," they said.

Then I was taken to a smaller building where a grubby soldier cursed and demanded to know whether cooks had to work all bloody night and get up at bloody four o'clock, too.

"Cook?" asked the soldier with me. "All you cookhouse jokers are a lot of bludging bastards. You're not a cook's backside. You're only the cook's bloody offsider, anyhow."

"Go and get ———," said the cook's offsider.

"I'm sorry, mate," I said. "I don't like troubling you, but I've been up since five myself, and I'm hungry. Haven't had any tucker since lunch-time."

"I'm not crooked on you," said the cook's offsider. "It's the way they ——— you around. That's what gives me a touch of 'em. They ——— you around."

"Of course they do," said my guide. "You're in the army, aren't you? You're being ——— around by experts. They can do anything to you. Anything except make you love the child."

Full of foreboding, I tackled a plate of warmed-up stew. Then I was taken to a hut with "Q.M." on the door. My guide said to the soldier behind the counter, "New bloke just marched in. Got some stuff for him?"

"Nothing," said the soldier. "You know what it's like, Curly."

"I know," said Curly. "We're in the army."

"I can only give you two blankets, mate," said the soldier behind the counter.

"No palliasse?" asked Curly.

"No."

Curly turned to me. I did not even know what a palliasse was. "Dig," he said ominously, "tonight is going to be one of those nights you'll never forget."

"I can take it," I said. "I'm in the army now."

But I couldn't take it. I lay awake all night. I had put one blanket on the board floor, and on top of the other one, which I put over me, I had put my overcoat and a greatcoat I had borrowed.

I had never felt so cold. I had never felt so uncomfortable. I had never felt so miserable. The wooden floor beneath the blanket was as hard as stone, and before I had been lying there five minutes my hip was sore. The cold came in through the cracks in the doors, came seeping up through the spaces between the boards, came beating down on me from the galvanized iron roof.

I was alone in an icy world. I was shivering all over. The shadows made vague and menacing forms all round me, and the occasional stirring or talking of a soldier in his sleep gave a fearful reality to these menacing shapes.

I kept shifting my position to ease the pain in my hip, but it was useless. I pulled the blanket, greatcoat and overcoat closer around me, but nothing could keep out that insidious cold. It had me in its unfaltering grip, and it squeezed me into an almost whimpering impotence.

It became colder and colder. I rolled over on to my other side, but that hip was soon throbbing, too. The cold became more than an irritating inconvenience; it became the epitome of all the malevolent forces in the world, a symbol of the implacable enemies of all mankind.

I was shivering from the top of my head to the tips of my toes. I remembered, with a grimace distorted by my chattering teeth, that they had said, "You'll be sorry." I was sorry already.

CHAPTER XIII

IT was the longest night I had ever known. At last a soldier opposite me got up and bellowed, "Rise and shine, my lucky lads!"

I have never heard such sustained abuse. "Go and get ———, you bastard!" "You rotten old ———, go back to ——— bed!", "The old codger's mad", "Get ———, it's the middle of the ——— night", "You're not still workin' in the ——— mine", and "You might've won the M.M. and the D.C.M. in the last ——— war, but by Christ, you won't live to get to this bloody one."

The M.M. and D.C.M.! I sat up, shivering, and looked towards him, but it was too dark to see anything except his vague outline. He laughed. "Ya a lotta pansies," he said mildly. "Why in the last stink———"

That started it again.

"——— the last war."

"Pull ya head in."

"You old Diggers are all the bloody same."

"Will all you bastards shut up and let us do some spine bashing?"

"Jesus, it's only five o'clock. We've got half an hour yet. Shut up, the lot of yous."

I got up and began to get dressed. My hands were so cold I could scarcely pull my trousers on. The buttons were like ice cubes. The soldier sleeping on the palliasse on the floor on my right said, "Take it easy, Dig. Reveille's not till half past. Jesus, is that your teeth chattering?"

"I'm cold," I said. "Only getting dressed to try to get warm."

"They didn't give you a palliasse? The bloody bastards. Christ, you're freezing to death. S'pose the Q.M. can't help it. I've been here two months and haven't seen a bloody rifle yet. Squad drill and route bloody marches all bloody day long."

I heard a click from the other side of the hut, and then an odiously ingratiating voice said: "Good-morning, everyone! Good-morning to you all. And a very good morning it is, too, isn't it? This is, of course, the Good Morning Man of Station 2YB calling you. And how are you all this morning?"

If the Good Morning Man of Station 2YB could have heard what the thirty members of hut No. 5 in C Company of the 2/93rd Battalion, Ingleburn Camp, thought of him he would never have dared to defile the pristine air again.

"Turn that pansy bastard off, for Christ's sake," called someone. "He gives us all a touch of 'em."

"I hate his guts."

"Why doesn't the coot join the bloody army?"

The Digger from the last war had turned it on, and he merely laughed. Nobody bothered to get up and switch the disgusting voice off. I did not blame them. It was too cold.

It happened every morning. The Good Morning Man inflicted

his saccharine servility, his false ebullience on us with oily and detestable verve.

Soon they were all getting up, cursing the A.I.F., the Germans, the N.C.Os, the cold, each other.

"What time's breakfast?" I asked the soldier who had spoken to me.

"Six-thirty," he said. "There's a parade first. You'd better shave before that parade. You won't have much time between it and mess. Ay, haven't you got a giggle-suit?"

"A what?"

"A giggle-suit. Ordinary working dress. S'pose they call it a giggle-suit because it makes people giggle to look at it. Haven't you got one?"

"I've got nothing. Only my eating gear and two blankets."

"Christ, what an army!"

After the inevitable series of "You'll be sorrys," I went over to parade, and lined up in the rear ranks with the others from my hut. I could see the raw edging of red where the sun was coming up behind the hills.

"Stop that fidgeting, men," said a corporal standing in front.

"We're not fidgeting, corp.," said somebody. "We're shivering."

It was true. I would never have believed it could be so cold.

"Who're those fellows over there?" I asked the soldier next to me.

"Sick parade," he said. "No matter how sick you are you gotta be on sick parade, gotta walk two hundred yards in the cold and stand round and shiver like Christ. It's the army. Fellers from Brigade Headquarters gotta go a mile down the road to the C.R.S. for treatment. Got no M.O."

My loneliness was deepening. I cursed myself for not having joined the A.I.F. with somebody. Harry Courtenay had advised me not to make friends, but a man needed a mate; I knew it already.

I had thought the A.I.F. was a perfect example of mechanical efficiency, that behind the façade of saluting and parades, the shining show window, the wheels turned with crisp exactitude; but I was encountering the first of a series of devastating breakdowns in the lumbering machine.

I admired the men of the 1st A.I.F. more than ever. They had achieved it all—Gallipoli, Verdun, Amiens, Polygon Wood—despite this humbug, this inescapable adherence to a ponderous system.

I stared in amazement at a soldier out in front—I learned later that he was the company sergeant major. He marched across in front of the parade with his arms stiff and his hands swinging nearly to his shoulders. At first I thought there was something wrong with his elbow joints and wrists but I soon learned that that was the new way to march. We laughed at the goosestep, but we marched like this!

That first morning was a revelation. The C.S.M. handed the parade over to a lieutenant, who handed it over to a captain, who handed it back to the lieutenant, who handed it back to the C.S.M., who dismissed it.

"My God," I whispered to the soldier next to me. "Is this usual or just for my benefit?"

"Wouldn't it?" he said. "It's the army, mate, it's the army."

My God, I thought. What have I done?

Later, when we were on the mess parade, I was astounded by the way in which the troops talked to the corporal in charge. I had thought a corporal must be a pretty important fellow. They did not. I thought years of mixing with boxers, starting-price bookmakers, cricketers, and street corner loungers had made me tough, but some of the comments shocked me.

They told the corporal what they thought of him and his dubious ancestry, and gave him explicit but impossible advice about what he could do with his mess tin. The corporal grinned amiably. "Wouldn't it?" he asked the world.

Dressed in my blue suit and black shoes, I spent the morning marching up and down the parade ground. We marched in threes; I thought it would be fours. We marched up, and then we marched down. We did right turns, we did left turns, we did about turns. We did left wheels, we did right wheels. We formed squad on the right, we formed squad on the left. We formed squad at the halt. We formed squad marking time. We left-formed. We right-formed. we left-formed at the halt. We left-formed marking time. We right-formed at the halt. We left-formed marking time.

There was another fellow wearing civilian clothes. He was short, and had gleaming black hair and a small black moustache. Evidently he had come into camp last night, too. I noticed how anxious he was to learn, how shocked by the coarse talk of the others.

There was another mess parade at lunch-time; we lined up again with our mess tins, plate, mug, knife, fork and spoon. The food was plain but surprisingly good, and I was starving after a morning's marching in the sun. An officer came through with the routine call "Any complaints?"

In the afternoon, after a long time in which the ridiculous ritual of the army was observed, we had a battalion route march. We marched out of the camp and down the hill towards Ingleburn Railway Station. The battalion band was out in front. I had never known anything so inspiring. I found myself swinging along like a veteran, and suddenly I was ashamed to find that my arms were going as high as anybody's. I could scarcely bear it when the band stopped, and when it began again I subdued my suspicions about the insidious propaganda of flag-waving and band-playing and was proud to be in the army.

After we got back and had been dismissed on the company parade ground, I sat on the steps at the back of the hut and was conscious only of a pervading loneliness, of my feet that were hurting and of my utter weariness.

The other soldier in civilian clothes was sitting on the bottom step, and a few other fellows were lounging about. The soldier in civilian clothes stood up and went down to the latrine. He was soon back, and I noticed that he was white.

He sat down. "I can't do it," he said suddenly. "I can't do it."

"Can't do what?" I asked. The others were looking at him strangely.

"Take a coupler number nines," said one of them.

"I can't do it," he said again. "There are no partitions between the places. Everyone can see everyone else. It's disgusting. A soldier on one end throwing orange peel at one on the other. I can't do it."

Everyone gaped at him. "What's wrong with this galah?" asked somebody and another said, "Well wouldn't it rip you? What do you expect him to throw?"

"I can't do it," said the little fellow with the gleaming black hair and black moustache. "I won't do it."

"Don't do it," said one of the loungers, winking at his mate. "Just stay right where you are. Don't let 'em bluff you."

The little soldier sat down on the step near me, and after a while I saw his face become tense and he got up and went down to the latrine.

The loungers laughed. A soldier came towards the steps. As I stood up to let him pass one of my feet slipped and I fell forward. My shoulder struck his chest a hard blow, and he went sprawling on his back in the dust.

"I'm sorry," I said and, forgetting my weariness, went to pick him up. "I slipped."

The loungers laughed again. I could see his eyes gleaming as I reached out to help him up. He pushed my hand away and got slowly to his feet. He stood there for a moment, bent forward, and I could see his hands clenching and unclenching at his sides.

"I'm sorry," I said. "My foot slipped just as you went to pass me."

"God stone the bleedin' crows," he snarled. "Think ya bloody funny, don't ya? Think ya can make a mug outta me in fronter me mates?"

I sighed. "I'm not trying to make a mug out of anybody," I said. "I slipped. I said I was sorry."

"You'll be sorry all right," he said.

"Now listen," I said, "I'm not looking for trouble."

"Yer may not be bloody well lookin' fer it, mate, but ya'll bloody well get it."

Resentment was rising in me now, an insistent resentment I knew I could not suppress for long.

"I said I'm sorry," I said, and I noticed my voice was louder. "What else do you want me to do?"

"Ay, Eddie, would you like him to massage the thick head you got from drinkin' too much grog you scrounged from the sergeant's mess last night?" called someone.

Eddie did not look round. "You keep outa this," he said grimly, "or ya'll get a crack on the bloody jaw, too."

I noticed the word "too".

"I found out ya name," said Eddie. He was still standing there, leaning forward, and his eyes were still gleaming. "It's Howard Reynolds. Where'd ya get a pretty monicker like that from?"

"My mother gave it to me," I said quietly, and I heard some of the boys laugh.

Eddie's mouth closed suddenly. Then he said, "That's a pretty suit ya got on, too."

"It's paid for," I said.

The boys laughed again. Eddie's hands were clenching and un-clenching. "Think ya smart, doan cher?" he snarled. "We doan want no bloody pansies in this battalion."

"Don't worry," I said. "They mightn't find out about you."

The boys guffawed, and I saw Eddie go slowly red. He came towards me, stopped in front of me, and pushed his face into mine.

"I don't like ya bloody face," he said.

He was tall, even taller than I was, and I was five feet eleven. He had an ordinary face, the sort of face you would pass a thousand times in Sydney any day of the week. His blue eyes were hard now, and I noticed that he had a few pimples on his brown skin.

"I can't say," I said, "that I've fallen in love with yours. When you become a big boy you'll grow out of the pimply stage. I wouldn't worry if I were you."

A crowd of soldiers had gathered, and they roared with laughter. Eddie said nothing. He went white. Then he stepped back and began to undo the white tape at the bottom of his giggle jacket. His hands were trembling, and he fumbled with it.

"I joined the A.I.F. to fight the Germans," I said. "It'd be a pity to kill one of my own countrymen first."

Eddie looked up with contempt blazing in his eyes. "Don't say pretty little Howard is a dingo?" he said.

"O.K., soldier," I said, taking off my coat. "I'll take you apart to see what makes you get that way."

Soldiers were running from two lines of huts, and I could hear cries in the distance of "Brawl on! Brawl on!" A circle was formed and somebody took my coat. "Do this galah over," he whispered in my ear. "He's a king-hit merchant."

I knew fellows who went out looking for what they called a "blue". Evidently this Eddie was one of them. There was a gloating leer on his face as he came towards me, his hands up and his fists still clenching and unclenching. How could you convince a man like that? It was like trying to reason with Adolf Hitler.

Eddie led with his left. I slipped it easily, but he ripped his right to the body. I dropped my left elbow mechanically, but it did not take the full force of the blow, and I felt my ribs stinging and heard the roar of the crowd.

Eddie was grinning. He thought I was easy. He came in again, but I spiked him with a left lead that jolted him ludicrously back on to his heels. There was a new note in the noise this time, and I heard somebody call, "Take six to four and back blue pants."

Eddie bent his head and looked at me from under his eyebrows. He was sizing me up. He came in cautiously this time. I was deceived. Suddenly he let go with both hands in quick succession, his left to the face, his right to the body again. I expected him to try something else. I pushed his left aside, but his right got home and I felt the harsh impact of knuckles on my ribs. My feet, moving back, struck a tuft of grass and I went down. I heard the crowd roar. It seeemed to be a long way away.

"Two's on Wilson," came the cry. "I'll bet a pound to ten bob Eddie. All right, Alan, ya set."

As I got up I saw Eddie's gloating grin hanging like a full moon in the sky. My God, I thought, what would Les Taylor and Tiger Farrell think of me if they could see me now? Knocked down into the dust in a brawl with a lout. Suddenly my resentment crystallized into a grim purpose. This knockdown artist couldn't do this to me. I was Mick Reynolds. One of the few things I could do was fight.

Anyhow, Eddie Wilson was ruining my new suit. My new blue suit. I had paid eight guineas for that suit only a few weeks before. I wanted it for after the war. No Eddie Wilson would do that to me. Instantly this defence of my suit became an obsession. Nothing else mattered. Eddie Wilson had probably never had a suit like it in his life. Well, by God, he was not going to ruin mine!

I walked straight into Eddie Wilson. I feinted with my left, and as he ducked I uppercut him with my right. I misjudged it slightly. It hit him on the edge of the mouth. He went down, and that mad roar, that blood-lust roar I knew so well, was pounding in my ears.

Wilson lay on his back. I did not see anybody else, only Wilson lying there. I heard somebody say, "What the bloody hell is all this about?"

"Get up, Wilson," I said. "I'll teach you to ruin my bloody suit."

"What the bloody hell is this all about?" said the voice again. I looked over my right shoulder. There was nobody there. I looked back at Wilson. Then I realized that the soldiers had vanished. I looked back again. They were gone.

I looked over my left shoulder, straight at Lieutenant-Colonel Russell-Francis, the C.O. of the battalion. I shook my head, and looked again. He was still there.

"What the bloody hell is all this?" he barked. "Answer me, man. Don't stand there looking like a bloody idiot. What's going on here?"

I knew now why they called him Old Gutsache. His mouth always had the querulous expression of a man with a pain in his stomach, the peevish distemper of a dyspeptic.

"Nothing—sir," I said stupidly. It was an effort for me to say "sir"; I had never called anybody "sir" before.

Old Gutsache snorted. "Why the bloody hell you don't keep your fighting until you meet the bloody Huns I bloody well don't know," he growled. "Why the bloody hell are you dressed in those clothes?"

"I haven't been issued with anything else—sir."

Old Gutsache swung round and glared at a lieutenant standing behind him. "See this man is fitted out with his issue first thing in the morning, Briggs," he said testily. "What the bloody hell is this battalion? A hiking club?" He turned to me quickly. "What the hell's your name, soldier?" he barked.

"Reynolds—sir." I drew a deep breath and said, "Howard Reynolds."

"Hmmmm. Pretty name that."

"So is Michael Hugh Russell-Francis."

"What's that?" he barked.

"I said, 'So is Michael Hugh Russell-Francis.'"

Old Gutsache shoved his chin forward and growled. "That's insolence, soldier."

"That's not insolence, sir," I said. "That's justice."

Old Gutsache reached up and stroked his chin quickly three times.

"I believe you're right," he said suddenly. "How the bloody hell did you know my full name?"

"Looked you up in *Who's Who*. You're a good soldier."

"Thanks," said old Gutsache. "Can I mention your name next time I see the General? What did you say your name was?"

"Reynolds. My father was in the 93rd with you in the last war."

Old Gutsache's eyes lit up. "Well I'll be damned!" he said. "Mick Reynolds's son, eh? Should have recognized you at once. Mick Reynolds, eh?" He did not say anything for a while, and I knew he was back in France, slopping about in the mud with my father, going over the top with him, getting drunk with him on leave, bringing him in the time he got wounded at Villers Brettoneaux.

"Do you play cricket?" asked Old Gutsache suddenly.

"No, sir."

"Too bad. I remember once we persuaded Mick—your father— to play against a Tommy unit on leave. He was a hundred and fifty-six when we declared. Well I'll be damned. Mick Reynolds's son, eh? Another Reynolds in the 93rd." He was off again, back in the past, and I thought there must have been some good in something that gave a man memories like these.

The lieutenant shifted his feet uncomfortably. Eddie Wilson had got to his feet and was wiping his mouth with his giggle-jacket. I could see heads poking out of hut doors, and faces at windows.

"Who the bloody hell started this?" asked Old Gutsache suddenly. "By Christ, I'll put you both on a charge. I'll crime both of you, that's what I'll do. What's your name?" he asked Eddie.

"Wilson, sir."

"Wilson, eh? Oh. You're the man who was in Bendigo jail when the Sixth Division sailed, eh? They thought a change of scene might do you good, so they foisted you on me. You're a trouble-maker, Wilson. I've a good mind to drum you out of this battalion, too. Get that?"

"Yes, sir."

"It was my fault, sir," I said. "I picked on Wilson."

"No, sir," said Wilson quickly. "I picked on him. It was my fault."

"Briggs," said Old Gutsache. "Privates Reynolds and Wilson will spend tomorrow on fatigue duty. Perhaps they'll get to know each other better in the salubrious atmosphere of the cookhouse and the latrines. That is all, gentlemen."

He glared at us both and stalked away, followed by the dutiful Briggs, who was saying, "Yes, sir, yes, sir."

I looked at Eddie Wilson. Eddie Wilson looked at me. He grinned sheepishly. "Er—me name's Wilson," he said awkwardly. "Eddie Wilson."

"Mine's Howard Reynolds," I said, "but my friends call me Mick. You call me Mick."

Eddie smiled. I liked his smile. "I'll call ya Mick," he said. He held out his hand. I shook it. "I'm sorry," he said. "I thought ya was a bit of a queen. I done me block. Ya not crooked on me?"

"Forget it."

Eddie shifted his feet uncomfortably in the dust. I could see a purple stain on his chin. "Ay listen, Mick," he said with the diffidence that is inevitable when you use somebody's Christian name for the first time, "I reckon where we're goin' a joker's goin' ter need a decent sorta backstop, and I was thinkin'—well, if ya doan mind—I reckon a bloke what can use his mitts like the way you done—that last one was a beaut—well, how about you an' me bein' cobbers an' sharin' what we gotta take, good or bad? Is she jake?"

He was looking at me eagerly, self-consciously. The last words had come out with a rush.

"Eddie," I said, "what I need right now is a friend. She's jake."

A cloud came over his face. "I've gotta give ya the dinkum oil," he said. "I gotta tell ya this before ya go sayin' ya'll be in it. I gotta be fair dinkum. Ya see, I got more red ink in me paybook than any joker in the Sixth Div. I was in the Sixth Div., see, but I was in the boob in Bendigo when they sailed. Nothin' serious it wasn't. Just another case of A.W.L., but I just wanted ter tell ya before ya said ya'd be me cobber." He was scraping the toe of one of his brown boots in the dust. "An' I won't have no money for a long time. I'll still be payin' fines for months."

"Eddie," I said, "she's jake."

"That's bonzer," he said, and when he looked up I saw the relief in his face. "Let's take a bo peep at what they got in the canteen. It'll only be milk, but it'll do. The bastards won't give us poor privates wet ones."

"Lead on, Macduff," I said.

"Mac who?" asked Eddie. "Me name's Wilson."

"Wilson or Macduff. Who cares?"

"I don't give a bugger," said Eddie.

"Neither," I said, "do I."

CHAPTER XIV

THE cold was not so bad that night. Eddie had moved over next to me, and before lights out he said awkwardly, "We'll share our blankets, Mick. It's warmer that way."

We folded the blankets and put them across the bed. This gave us several more thicknesses. "Good night, mate," said Eddie.

I grinned in the darkness. "Good night, pal," I said.

We spent the next day in the latrines and the cookhouse.

"Strange places," I said, "for a noble friendship to flower."

"Yeah," said Eddie doubtfully. "I remember an old record we had. Somethin' about 'Ya can take me away from Dixie but ya can't take Dixie from me'. Well I wish somebody'd take these dixies away from me." He glared at a pile of dirty ones.

The following morning, in the first break in squad drill, Eddie introduced me and the little dark soldier, whose name was Clive Fenstone, to the others in the section. Clive had told me he was a wool-classer. We were sitting in the shade of a great white gum. The ground between the two lines of huts had been worn bare of grass by marching feet. We were dressed in giggle-suits, cloth giggle-hats, and tan boots.

"I want ya ter meet Pat McDonald," said Eddie. I looked at the giant before me. These were the men on whom my life might depend, the men with whom I'd have to live, possibly with whom I'd have to die.

"We ought to be a good pair," I said. "Pat and Mick."

"Yeah," said Eddie. "Pat's a queer bloody mixture—a Scotch-Irish-Australian. And if he starts talkin' about Edinburgh hit the poor coot with somethin'."

I saw at once that Pat had that enchanting Irish smile. "Don't take any notice of that ape," he said amiably. I was nearly six feet but he was several inches taller. I estimated that he weighed sixteen stone, but he was not fat. I had seen him shaving that morning, seen the muscles bulging on his back. He had fair hair and frank eyes.

"Pat's an insurance clerk," said Eddie. "We'll have ter get him ter insure us all before we go off ter die for the Empire."

We laughed. "You'd all be a better risk than you taxi-drivers," he said to Eddie.

"An' this here's 'Happy' Curben. He's an electrician. His laugh'd crack the ears of the galahs in an old gum half a mile away. Wonder

they doan ban him from the front line, 'cause he'll give our positions
away to the bloody Germans."

Happy, who was short and fat, began to laugh. I had never heard
a laugh like it. You ceased to fight against it, for it overwhelmed
you.

"This here's Harry Creege," said Eddie. "Not satisfied with the
D.C.M. and M.M. from the last stink. He's after the V.C. in this.
He's a miner. You'd uv thought he'd uv joined the pioneers so's
he could go on diggin' holes."

Harry grinned. As he shook my hand I felt the callouses on his. He
was small, his brown hair was getting thin on top and his brown
face was weather-beaten.

"Pleased ter meetcher, Mick, Clive," he said, "pleased ter
meetcher." So this was the stuff heroes were made of. This ageing
little man had been capable of sustained courage, and was coming
back for more. I looked at him in awe.

"And this is Jim Mills. The original bastard from the bush. You
know the poem—

> "If ya had a harlot to support ya
> Would ya give up work for good?"
> And the bastard from the bush replied,
> "My ——— oath I would."
>
> "Would ya knock a man down and rob him?"
> Asked the leader of the push.
> "I'd knock him down and ——— him,"
> Said the bastard from the bush.

Well this is the bloke the poem was wrote about."

"Glad ter know yous both," said Jim awkwardly. He was small
and so colourless he attracted attention. He looked as though the
sun had bleached him—his hair, his skin, even his eyebrows and
lashes.

"Still got the hay in his hair," said Eddie. "First mornin' he come
here he says, 'Cripes, this is good-o. You don't have ter get up till
five o'clock.' "

"The mug aleck prowls around at four o'clock each morning,
looking for cows to milk," said Pat.

Jim grinned. "Strike me pink," he said, "yous city blokes dunno
nothin'. Yous think five o'clock's the middle of the night. Why up
at Wattle Creek——"

"Some other time," said Eddie. "Meet Ingleburn's Darby Munro.
The one and only Bert Trevine."

"Urgers to the ——— house," said Bert in a slow stupid voice.
"Yous can laugh. I'll show yous all one er these days. I got sent

out fer life, but I'll come back, don't yous fear. I'll show yous." He was short and his legs were bandy. He had a freckly face, and an earnest, inane look.

"And last comes Gordon C. Harday," said Pat. "God's gift to the business world. The man whose only ambition is to amass smash."

"Last," said Gordon, "but not least. Harday speaking. My card, gentlemen." He handed us, with a flamboyant gesture, a card each. We read, "Gordon C. Harday, M.L.A."

"Christ," I said, "I didn't know we'd got a member of the Legislative Assembly with us."

The others laughed. "How dare you laugh at the future biggest business magnate in Australia," said Gordon in mock annoyance. "If anybody questions me about the M.L.A. part I say it means, 'Melbourne's Leading Advertiser'."

Clive and I laughed. We thought it was a joke. Gordon was podgy. His plump face and double chin betrayed a taste for rich food, an avoidance of exercise and a natural tendency towards fatness. His hair was ginger, his face pale, his nose substantial and his movements awkward.

"There's room for you in my organization," he said to me. "Stick to me, buddy, and you'll wear diamonds. It'll be a sad day when Harday can't light his cigar with a pound note."

I was staring at him. I still thought it was a joke.

"Don't worry," said Bert in his inane voice. "The poor bastard's hopeless. He'll come back to the field."

"A Harday," said Gordon solemnly, "does not take any notice of the remarks of the lower orders. They haven't got any smash."

"That's all right, Blue," said Eddie.

"And don't call me 'Blue'," said Gordon. "It sounds—er—un—un——"

"Uncouth," I suggested.

Gordon bowed slightly. "Thank you, my friend," he said. "That's the word. It sounds uncouth. By the way, can I interest you in a fifty-year calendar or the blueprint of the Harday gastroscope? You see, the calendar is rather unique"—I shuddered at the phrase—"for by turning the dial you can tell the day of any date in the next fifty years."

"How interesting," I said. "I can't bear to wait till I hear what day 9 October will fall on in 1989."

"Dear me," said Gordon, "I haven't got the calendar here. Later, my friend, I'll be pleased to oblige."

I looked at them as they lounged about on the ground in their giggle-suits and ridiculous cloth giggle-hats. I found it difficult to realize that some of them—no, some of us—were going to die; probably all of us to know fear and pain and misery.

We were sitting there, laughing about the Harday gastroscope and the Harday fifty-year calendar, just as thousands of Australians were laughing in the camps of the sprawling continent of the South Pacific, Australians who had left their mines, their desks, their taxis, their horses, their farms, their shops, had come flooding into recruiting offices to try to stem the red tide of an outrageous tyranny.

I looked at Pat's magnificent body as he lay on his back on the bare ground. That body, perhaps, would be torn and maimed, shattered and crushed. I shook my head, but I could not shake the fear out of my heart.

"You don't think so?" Pat was saying. "I tell you it's fair dinkum. He's got four or five other names, all known to the demons. Don't think he knows which is his right one himself. Gordon C. Harday, Alastair Y. Glendenning—wait till you hear the story of the Alastair Y. Glendenning Mining Corporation—Kyne B. Peterson——"

"He got that from the writer bloke, Peter B. Kyne," said Eddie.

"——Francis Bartholomew, Erskine P. Chiverton and Artemus C. Carstairs."

"Funny about the last one," said Gordon. "I walked into a country hotel in Queensland without a cracker, but with my fur coat and black homberg on. I was wondering what name I'd sign in the register when I remembered that some fellow in the train had said something about somebody named Artemus Ward— I think he was a Yank writer or something—and I remembered the hero of a story in the *Boys Own Paper*, a remarkably dashing boy named Carstairs. So you see—Artemus C. Carstairs I became."

He was smiling. "Certain hotel-keepers and business associates of mine in the southern and western States would go white at the mere mention of some of them names," he said.

"Those names," said Pat.

"I said 'those names'," said Gordon.

"You're a bloody liar," said Pat.

"He's left so many dogs tied up all over Australia it's a wonder there're enough of 'em left to hold tin-hare meetings," said Eddie.

"I resent that, gentlemen," said Gordon. "I'll have you know I pay my debts promptly."

"Yeah," said Pat. "By cheque. And, boy, do those cheques bounce back!"

"I'll admit that at times," said Gordon, coughing behind his hand, "certain difficulties have been encountered with certain bank managers half an hour after I have left town, but we won't go into that. I attribute my success to a nimble wit and a fast car. You admit I've got ability? You admit that?"

"God stone the bleedin' crows," said Eddie, "after the way I seen ya snaffle that bayonet from the Q.M. store, doctor it up so it looked old and sell it to that old sheila as the one Jacka won his V.C. with in the last blue, I'll bloody well admit you've got ability."

"Enterprise and ability, gentlemen," said Harday. "It was one of my lesser deals, but still it just shows you. I believe in amassing smash."

"Smash?" asked Clive. "What's that?"

"Smash, dough, fiddlies, coin, tin, hay, oot, shekels, sponduliks," said Gordon. "I'm still the highest paid member of this company."

"Bullo!" said Pat. "What about the O.C."

"The O.C.," said Gordon, "receives a paltry seven pounds seventeen shillings and sixpence a week. It's chicken feed. It wouldn't keep me in cigars. There's only one thing that matters and that's smash."

"That's his main, his only, idea in life," said Pat, "the poor misguided bastard."

"It's a good one," said Gordon. "You can buy anything in the world with money."

"Not anything," said Clive earnestly. "No, not anything. You can't buy love."

Gordon threw back his head and laughed. "Every woman's got her price," he said. "You only fail because you haven't got enough smash."

"Haven't you ever been in love?" asked Clive.

"Of course I've never been in love. There's no dough in it. It's not a business proposition."

Clive had lines of pain around his eyes. "Harday," he said earnestly, "why did you join the A.I.F.?"

"I didn't join the A.I.F.," said Harday. "The A.I.F. joined me."

Before Clive could reply Eddie said, "Come on. More bloody squad drill."

We got up—a furniture salesman, a miner, a farmer, an insurance clerk, a taxi-driver, a wool-classer, an ex-jockey, an electrician, and a charlatan—and went swinging across the parade ground, some of us grumbling obscenely to ourselves when the corporal shouted at us to get our arms up.

I could see Clive, who was beside me, with his elbows locked, his wrists pointed down, his hands "lightly clenched". I could see his obdurate determination to do his best, come what may. His black moustache was bristling with martial ardour.

Suddenly he turned his head slightly, looked at me, and gave me a quick smile. I saw something in his eyes, and I knew that of us all only he and I had the slightest idea of what lay ahead, only he and I knew that, "somewhere on a foreign field", some of us would lie dying.

CHAPTER XV

THAT was how it started. I wondered how it would end.

We drilled all day and went at night to the canteen, the pictures, a concert, the Y.M.C.A. or Salvation Army hut. I soon found that Eddie had extraordinary ability as a scrounger, and sometimes he got beer from the sergeants' mess—all the canteens were dry at that time; or we slipped out of camp, got a lift, and hopped off at the hotel on the corner a few miles up the road to Liverpool.

"Christ, Mick," said Eddie to me at a concert. "What price that little blonde sheila? And they reckon they put bromide in the tea!"

This bromide question caused many arguments. "I tell ya it's all bullo," said Eddie earnestly. "Ya oughter see me when I wake up in the mornin's."

"They doan put it in ya tea," said Jim. "They put it in ya bread. The babbling brook give me the drum."

"I'm going on long leave this week-end," said Gordon, "going to the couch of purple passion. I'll trick 'em. I won't eat any bread, or drink any tea on Thursday or Friday. They can't do that to Harday. It's a wonder some wives don't write to Mr Menzies. Wilson, make a note on my memo pad."

I asked Eddie what the blue light on a tent behind the C.R.S. was for.

"Gee, doncher know? That's the blue light joint. On ya way back from leave ya go there. That's if ya been doin' the wrong thing. Haven't ya seen them blue light outfits? They stop ya gettin' what ya shoulden get."

"Oh," I said. "You don't mean to say the army has realized at last that the problem of venereal disease has to be tackled realistically despite the horrified protests of wowsers? Cripes, will the Church howl its pious head off when it hears about this!"

I had been there a week before they issued us with rifles.

"Christ," said the corporal who had been in the militia, "no gauze." Practically all the N.C.Os had had militia experience. They got into a unit early and got all the stripes. Evidently it was a tragedy that there was no gauze. I began to fear that, after waiting so long, we had been issued with defective rifles.

Mine felt as if it were made of lead. "Cripes," I said, "this bloody thing's heavy."

A corporal laughed, "You'll get used to it, Mick," he said. "Feel like a stick later." He was right. I was amazed at the way in which it seemed to grow lighter.

I watched Clive when he was issued with his. He hesitated, and then took it in a firm grasp. He looked up, and his eyes met mine. He smiled wanly. He and I were the only ones who knew.

Then followed the travail of rifle drill. I was convinced that I should never master even sloping arms. I felt as awkward as a man wearing skates for the first time. But slowly it came to me, as it came to us all, under the ceaseless repetition of army training, day after day, week after week, month after month.

"Look after your rifle," said the corporal instructing us. "It's a soldier's best friend."

We looked after it. We did not "clean" it; we "pulled it through". We became expert with the pull-through and pieces of what we called "four by two" but the Q.M. and the corporal insisted was "service flannelette". We were becoming soldiers.

After we got our rifles we started guard drill—up till then the guard had been done by former militiamen—and I was amazed again at the inevitable ritual of the army and bored by the sheer monotony of guard duty.

Week-end leave was a break. One week-end we had short leave, the next long leave, and the next we spent in camp. Some week-ends I saw Margaret and we had a few precious hours together before I had to go back to Ingleburn to master the art of killing. Going back to camp on the leave train was like going back to jail. Time was so short, the latrine wireless insisted that we would sail any day —and there was such a store of love in my heart.

A horde of tired and ill-tempered troops poured out of the train at Liverpool and overwhelmed the ticket collectors at the bottom of the wooden bridge. Some of us had tickets to Redfern, the first station, and most had no tickets at all. We did not care; neither did the ticket collectors. It was no use trying to stem this khaki flood.

There was practically no equipment. I learned later that Australia sent thousands of rifles to England to replace the losses at Dunkirk. We were trained with Lewis guns, which were so antiquated that there was no prospect of using them in action. We did not even know what a Bren or a Vickers looked like.

Then I was issued with my khaki uniform. It did not fit, of course. The tunic was too big and the trousers too short, and the tunic was slightly darker than the trousers. I took out my issue housewife, sewed my colour patches on my shoulders and hat band with awkward fingers, put up a metal "Australia" on each shoulder, and metal rising suns on my hat and lapels, sat looking at my work for a while, and then put the uniform on.

Eddie was sitting on his palliasse and grinning. We got up and went for a walk in the winter air. I did not say anything. I was wearing my slouch hat, with its rising sun badge on the turned up side, and I had my hands in my pockets.

"Well, Mick," said Eddie as we neared the artillery lines, "How's it feel? Ya feel like a soldier?"

"Soldier? No. I feel as if I'm going to a fancy dress ball."

I was in the A.I.F. It seemed like some strange dream. I could not believe it, not even when Harry woke me up with his "Rise and shine, my lucky lads", or the Good Morning Man burbled about the birds singing in the leafy trees, or when I struggled out of bed, pulled on my giggle-trousers with cold, stinging fingers, and tramped up to the cookhouse in the raw dawn to steal some hot water for shaving.

I realized it only when I went to Sydney on leave, and found myself changing step to conform with that of my companion. It was the first real impact the army had made on my civilian life, and it made an irrevocable impression on me.

I soon came to curse the demon who had endowed me with the formerly priceless faculty of imagination. I was tormented by a recurrent thought—that many of these men were going to die. On route marches, in the late leave train with its bottles of beer and its drunken troops, at concerts, at picture shows, in the canteen— it came to me suddenly, this bitter realization of lurking tragedy, this haunting fear for the destiny of mankind.

CHAPTER XVI

THERE was a light in George Shammar's room. I went in. George was sitting in his chair. His table was as untidy as ever, and so was his hair. There were stains on his suit, and the dandruff on his shoulders had probably been there a week.

He looked up, and I noticed that he looked older, that the lines in his face were deeper. He was thirty-six now, and I wondered again why my best friend was about ten years older than I.

It was a tame welcome. "Hullo, Mick," he said. "Sit down. Is this it?"

"It's it," I said. "I shouldn't disclose security information but we sail in about a fortnight, probably on the Big Ship."

"Funny how the Sydney Harbour boatmen are only allowed to call out 'A shilling to see the Big Ship' when everybody knows it's the *Queen Mary*. Well only the best is good enough for our brave boys in khaki."

"Yes," I said.

He was doodling with a pencil, drawing pictures of Hitler on the small part of his blotter protruding from the litter on his desk.

It was not the same any more. George was a stranger. I was a soldier and he was a civilian. His clothes shrieked the word at me, and although I maintained in camp, in the face of hostile opposition, that a man had the right to choose his own way of living and his own way of dying, that the liberty of the individual was what we were fighting for, I could not suppress a feeling of resentment towards the people who were living in houses and sleeping in beds, people who could look to the future without wondering whether there was really a future to look to, people who received more than "five bob a day".

"How's Bathurst?" asked George. "Any better than Ingleburn?"

"About the same. Too far away from Margaret. You know, the army treats you fairly well. Pretty good food and free medical and dental treatment."

"Yes," said George bitterly. "The only time the State will do anything for you is when you're willing to die for it. Where are you going?"

"I've got the drum from a friend in the Seventh Div. Headquarters in Melbourne. We're going to Bombay—at first they said Kenya—for three months' training in India, and then, if things are still quiet in Malaya, we're going on to Palestine."

I tried to say these strange places as if they were Sydney or Melbourne, but did not succeed.

"Oh," said George. He sat there, still doodling, and an uncomfortable silence enveloped us. I stood it for a while, and then, realizing that we had nothing in common any more, I was about to go when he looked up suddenly and said, "You're a bloody fool, Mick."

I felt the blood come surging into my face. "Why?" I asked.

"My God!" he cried. "It's fools like you who make wars!"

I pulled my chin strap off my chin and pushed my slouch hat back with my forefinger. I wanted to be able to think clearly.

"If everyone in the world was like me," said George, "there'd be nobody to fight wars."

"Of course. But there's just one point you're overlooking. Everybody's not like you."

"Unfortunately," said George, "they're not. Good God, man, you don't believe all this claptrap about a better world, about fighting for democracy, do you? Christ, our fathers sailed away to all that hooey—twenty-five years ago. And where did it get them? It got them 'honourable graves' and it got us another world war within a generation. And now the sons of those men are going to spill their blood too. Egged on by fanatics who've never been to a war, they go out to spill the 'red sweet wine of youth'. And I thought you were intelligent! You're just like all the rest. Wave a flag, beat a drum, appeal to your hot young blood instead of to your reason, and you shed a century of civilization. The atavism of Mick Reynolds. It makes me laugh."

I ground my cigarette out viciously. "Get one thing straight, George. No fanatic persuaded me to enlist. I enlisted because I couldn't stand it any more, and I fail to understand how any human being could stand it. If you saw a big man bullying a small man, you'd hop in, wouldn't you? No real Australian has ever liked a bully. Well, that's how it was with me. I just couldn't go to football matches and picture shows and parties while the world was in flames all around me."

George was smoking quickly, nervously. "It sounds so beautiful," he sneered. "Young Lochinvar riding out of the west, a handsome knight coming to the rescue of his fair maiden, a youth carrying a banner with the strange device 'Excelsior'. It sounds so romantic. Christ, Mick, that's the lure—the romance of it all. The bands play and the flags wave and the suckers go off to get themselves killed. There's nothing romantic about a shell splinter in the guts, Mick. There's nothing romantic about that.

"My God, we've still got hospitals full of what is left of men who went to the last war. Thousands of them. And thousands didn't come back. But their families lived on, lived on on the pittance our glorious democratic system allowed them. Oh yes, they'll promise you everything. There will be a new deal, there will be no more poverty, no more misery. The world will be beautiful and everybody will be happy—until the next war. Of course they'll promise you it—because you're the little people, you and your fighting mates, the little people, and they can't fight wars without the little people to fight them with."

I was walking up and down behind him. I was smoking too, now. I had to do something. "So much you say is right that the truth clouds the mistakes," I said. "We get nothing out of it, I suppose, if you call a better world nothing. I'd be a fool if I believed that there will ever be no poverty and no misery, but I'd be a fool also if I chose the way of Adolf Hitler. We've got a great country and, by Christ, we're going to see that it stays that way, that no arrogant bastards who've set a man up as a god are going to come tramping on all we hold sacred with their hobnailed ersatz boots. You can say what you like about Britain; she's not out to dominate the world."

George laughed hollowly. "I can say plenty about Britain," he said, "and even in this glorious democracy I'd get put behind bars if I got caught saying it. Britain's history stinks, Mick, and you can't deny it. What about India? What about Ireland? What about America? She even took Australia from the poor old abo, and New Zealand from the Maoris. Oh no, Britain doesn't want to dominate the world. She already dominates it, or most of the richest parts of it. She doesn't want to rob anybody of their land, because her maw is full of her undigested spoils from centuries of warfare, of aggression, of pillage."

I stopped behind him. "I don't agree with you," I said. I watched a python take shape under his pencil. It had a big bulge in it. He labelled the python "Britain".

"No, you don't agree," said George; "but you can't tell me where I'm wrong. Don't think I admire the gentle methods of Adolf Hitler; but, by Christ, he's arisen out of the mistakes of thousands of stupid Englishmen, and when you get a stupid Englishman, my friend, you get what the Americans call a new high."

"I don't agree with you," I said.

"You're like all the rest," said George. "You stand there like a bloody fool saying, 'I don't agree with you.' Britain the peace lover. Britain the hater of aggression. Britain's fought France, Germany, Russia, America, Ireland, Scotland, the Boers. Ever heard of a man named Mohandas Gandhi? You're going to Bombay. Ask the Indians what they think of Britain. Take my word for it, some-day there'll be blood shed in India. I must sound like an arch-fiend of sedition, a fifth columnist of the first water. I'm neither. I'm trying to look at this bloody mess impartially, as a man and not as a member of the British Empire. I never had any faith in man, thank God, because if I had had I'd have committed suicide long before this."

Resentment was rising in me all the time. I could not keep it down. "George," I said, "I've known you a long time. You've done a lot for me, and I'm grateful. But I'm telling you now that the time is past for this sort of talk and that I won't stay here much longer and listen to it."

"You won't listen to it," he said. "You won't listen to it. That's the trouble; the world won't listen to it. It hurts because it smacks right through your conventional acceptance of the conventional and rings the bell. It's so easy to take the easy way."

I dropped my cigarette on the floor and stamped viciously on it. "Easy way?" I said incredulously. "I've taken the easy way? Do you think it was easy to leave Margaret just when she was mine after all these years of longing and hoping, easy to give up my job and accept five bob a day, to cast aside my whole civilized life, to live in a hut and call men 'sir' and drill like an automaton —I can't read any more, George; just got no stomach for it—to devote my whole existence to learning to kill, to sail away to meet the war instead of sitting safely here at home and reading about it? Do you think that was easy?"

George laughed. "Of course it was easy," he said. "Don't you think it takes more guts to stick to one's principles, to refuse to go when the casualty lists come out, when the women, who send more men to wars than all the Adolf Hitlers of the world, point at you in the street and whisper. They can do it," he said, getting up and facing me. "but, by Christ, they won't break my spirit! They'll never break my spirit!"

There were new lines in his face now, and a grim defiance. "Not me," he said. "My father, but not me too. They can put me in jail first. They had their chance when they won the last one. Why didn't they destroy every munition factory in Germany? They can go to hell. Let them fight this one out among themselves."

I stood facing him, looking deep into his eyes. There was something new in them, an awareness that something strange and terrible lay ahead. I had seen the same thing in Clive's eyes the second day we were in camp, when we were marching together, and when he was issued with his rifle.

"If a mad dog came at you or your mother, you'd try to kill it, wouldn't you?" I asked.

"Ah," he said, "but no mad dog's coming at me."

"It's coming at the world," I said, "and you're part of it. The Belgians and the French and the Dutch and the Poles—they fought for us, and now they can't fight any longer it's our duty to fight for them. And, by Christ, those of us who see this blight that is settling on mankind, this foul canker of Nazism, are willing to risk everything to wipe it out."

George shook his shaggy head. "Don't be a bloody fool," he said.

"After all these years you've still got a Nerridale mind. So this is what I've made you?"

"You've made me?" I said hotly. "You haven't made me anything. I'm myself. I'm Mick Reynolds. What I am I've made, not you."

"You're a bloody fool," he said.

Resentment was welling up in me now, vigorous and burning. "It's hard," I said. "A man looks into his conscience, brings it out into the open so he can see it clearly, and it tells him what he should do, and then you tell him he's a bloody fool."

"Won't you see it?" cried George passionately. "It's people like you who cause wars!"

I could not stop it any more. It overwhelmed me. I grabbed him by the neck of his shirt, twisted it until his collar became tight around his neck, and shook him.

"My God!" I cried. "Don't you talk to me like that! You poor spineless bastard, you're frightened to go; that's what's wrong with you. I'm getting out of here. I don't like the smell of the place. And let me tell you this—you think you can beat it but you can't. You'll be in it sooner or later. You see."

I let go his shirt. He stood there with his hands at his sides. I shuddered. I had never seen such a look in any man's eyes. I could see his mouth working.

"That's all you understand," he said. "Force."

I went to the door, and made a mocking gesture of farewell with my hand near my hat. "I'll see you overseas," I said.

"I'll see you in hell first," he said in a strained voice. "Unless a man with your beautiful principles goes to heaven."

I slammed the door behind me and went out into the street.

CHAPTER XVII

I WENT to Sydney next day, booked in at the King George Hotel in Elizabeth Street, and went out to see Joan, who was married now and living at Kensington. I liked Joan—I had always congratulated myself on having avoided the almost inevitable tragedy of domestic incompatability—but the sight of her settled life distressed me.

"You're a fool, Mick," she said. "You didn't have to join up. It's got nothing to do with Australia. Peter wants to go, but I won't let him."

"It's a matter between every man and his conscience," I said. "Let's forget it."

I left early and went into the hotel lounge to have a drink before going to bed. I lingered over a new beer with a dash, marvelling at a system of control that insisted that bars be closed at 6 p.m., but did not care whether lounges stayed open all night. I wondered whether the police were really corrupt.

Why had Margaret's company picked this month to go to New Zealand? What would she be doing now? What time would it be in New Zealand? I could quote Shakespeare and Rupert Brooke and Oscar Wilde and Ben Jonson, but I didn't even know whether New Zealand time was the same as ours.

I noticed that a girl sitting near the wall was staring at me. She was dark, attractive and wore a veil. I wondered why a veil made a woman look so seductive. It would do a woman good to have five minutes' talk with a knowledgeable man. He could give her invaluable hints—tell her how alluring she looked in a veil, how the insidious odour of perfume made a man's resolution falter, how charming she looked in a floral frock or an evening dress, how silly she looked when she was smoking, how much more attractive she became when she had a dress that fitted tightly around the hips, how much more interesting when she appeared disinterested.

The girl was still staring. Perhaps she was, as Eddie would say, "on the battle". I had been told some of those girls hung about this lounge. Perhaps she would come over and say, "Well, love, how about it?"

Good heavens, she *was* coming over.

She stopped in front of me and said, "Do you mind if I sit here?"

I put my glass down and looked up casually. "It's a free world," I said. "Or it was."

"Thanks," she said. I did not bother to get up and help her with her chair.

"Drink?" I asked.

"Yes."

I called a waiter.

"Whisky and water," she said, "and remember, Alphonse, I'm allergic to water."

The waiter grinned and went away.

"How much?" I asked.

She looked puzzled. "How much what?"

For a dreadful moment I realized that I had almost made the worst *faux pas* of my life. "How much water?" I said glibly.

"Oh. At first I thought——"

"Thought what?"

"Skip it. I nearly did you an injustice."

I looked at her again. She bulged in the right places, too. I liked her hat. I liked her dress. I liked her veil. I liked the gentle mockery in her eyes. She had dark hair and blue eyes. I had never been able to resist that combination.

The waiter brought the drinks.

"Good luck, soldier," she said.

"Good luck," I said. I wondered who she was. Perhaps she was just a friendly girl with a boy friend or husband overseas, a friendly girl who had noticed I was lonely.

"Have another?"

"Thanks, corporal." When she picked up her second whisky she said, "Here's to the Wizard of Nerridale."

I put my glass down. I looked at her. She was drinking. I was grateful for not having made the *faux pas*.

"I haven't played for years," I said.

"No. Not since you made the century against England. I read about it. Nice work."

"I'm sorry. I don't remember you."

"Too bad; but I didn't think I made much of an impression. You didn't seem to have your mind on your work. Doesn't my dress remind you of anything?"

I looked at her again. She wore a red dress with a low neck that made me realize that she had infinite possibilities. Her exotic perfume was in the air about me.

"Come again," I said.

"Now, Wizard," she said with mock coquetry, "don't tell me there's been more than one scarlet woman in your life?"

It all came back to me now. "A scarlet woman," I had said, "after my own former heart." "I've got a strange habit," she had said. "I put keys under doormats."

"Good Lord!" I said. I picked up my glass and drank. "I thought for a moment it must have been a dark night and you were going to accuse me of being the father of your cheeild."

"I wasn't nominated," she said. "You were goggling at a blonde. What happened to her?"

"New Zealand," I said.

"Still goggling?"

"Still goggling."

She sighed. "Some girls get all the breaks," she said.

"She took a risk and went. Then they gave me final leave."

"Tough luck. You need a drink."

As I ordered them, I remembered Ronald Colman quoting Dowson in the film *Cynara*: "I have been faithful to thee, Cynara!

in my fashion", and his simple explanation that is so credible
to a man and so incredible to a woman: "If only you could have
seen her I think you would have understood."

His affair started just like this. I shook my head. Rot. This girl
probably wouldn't be interested in me even if I were interested
in her. And there was Margaret. I could never be unfaithful to
Margaret. Oh, Margaret, why have you forsaken me?

I looked up again. "What's your name?" she asked. "I've
forgotten."

"Howard Reynolds," I said. "But my friends call me Mick. You
call me Mick."

She smiled. "I'll call you Mick," she said. "Just call me Scarlett.
Scarlett O'Hara."

"I hope the analogy ceases with the name. And who am I? Rhett
Butler or Ashley Wilkes? Or perhaps Charles Hamilton. They all
went off to a war, anyhow. I think I'm more like poor hopeless
Ashley, but I'd rather be like Rhett."

"You're none of them. You're the Wizard. And once a woman
comes under your spell she can never feel free again."

I looked up sharply. There was something strange in her tone,
and she was smiling a queer smile. I did not say anything.

"I live in a flat at King's Cross," she said. "My girl friend's away
tonight. I'm frightened of the dark."

"I'm frightened of it, too," I said, "if there's a woman in it."

"There will be," she said.

"I need a drink," I said.

We did not say anything for a while. "Take your veil off," I
said. "I can't give away any start."

She smiled, and turned the veil up. "Sorry," she said.

"You would be," I said.

"I wouldn't," she said with sudden earnestness, leaning forward.
"I know I wouldn't."

I could see her eyes plainly now, and there was a candour in
them I had never known before. "It's madness," I said. "I've got
a girl in New Zealand."

"And I've got a boy in Palestine," she said, reaching over and
pressing my hand. "Don't be a fool. Get what you can out of life
while you're still living."

I saw George Shammar saying ponderously, "Everybody's
expectation of life is less than ever before. Don't be a fool. Make
the most of what you've got while you've got it."

I shook my head, not to indicate dissent, but to try to shake
off the thing that was soaking insidiously into my mind. I looked
up. She had let go my hand and was sitting quietly, but her eyes

were still on me. She was attractive all right, too attractive. And the faint perfume had me in its alluring grip.

"New Zealand is a long way away," she said, "and soldiers get killed in wars."

I lit another cigarette. My hand was shaking. If only I was not so lonely I could fight this thing.

"I'm lonely, too," she said, and I looked up, thinking I must have spoken. I saw something in her face that I had not seen before, something lurking in her eyes. "I've waited four years," she said.

I picked up my empty glass and turned it round and round in my hand. "You women," I said, "you make a tiger trailing a bleeding deer through the jungle look like a benevolent old lady."

She laughed, a delicious, tinkling laugh.

"I'm a bloody fool," I said at last, "but I'll come."

She reached over and pressed my hand. I did not look up. We stood up and went out. She took my arm as we went down the stairs. I took a quick look at her. She was smiling.

CHAPTER XVIII

WE sang as we drove down to the wharf through the almost deserted Melbourne streets. It was six o'clock on Sunday morning. We sang the haunting "Maori Farewell", which merely deepened the loneliness in our hearts.

"Now is the hour for me to say good-bye. Soon we'll be sailing far across the sea."

We had come all the way from Bathurst, come hundreds of miles because there was no more room on the *Queen Mary*.

"Wouldn't it?" asked Eddie. "It's the army. They certainly muck you about."

People waved to us from windows, and we waved back. At Port Melbourne we drove on to the wharf, and after the usual delay we carried our brown universal kit-bags and white sea kit-bags up the gangway into a big hole in the side of the grey mass of ship huddled against the wharf. The bags were tied together, and the cords cut into our shoulders.

Eddie and I had a cabin on C deck. It was bright and clean, and had running water. Clive and Jim, who were next door, had a private lavatory. We were amazed by the size of the vessel. It was like an underground city, and sometimes we got lost while going to the mess deck through passages deep in the ship.

We were like children at their first Sunday School picnic. We went exploring. We climbed up a dingy stairway inside one of the great funnels. At the top workmen were repairing something and from there we watched the crowd gather at the entrance to the wharf. The ship stayed there all day, but we did not sail.

There were rumours about submarines in Bass Strait. Eddie and I were at mess next day, eating pork of all things, when we noticed a slight movement. We went up on deck to watch.

"We're moving," said Eddie. "We're on our way."

A tug went with us to the entrance to Port Phillip, and an aeroplane dived around us, and then the tug whistled mournfully and left us. I had never known anything so depressing as that tug's whistle. It was as dismal as the tolling of a funeral bell, as desolate as the cry of a bird in a wailing storm; it seemed to sever every connexion we had with civilization, and send us forth alone into an unknown world, a world of strange countries and strange people, a world from which, perhaps, there was no return.

I turned to Eddie with the doleful notes of the tug's whistle sounding in my ears, and I saw at once that he understood.

"Well, Mick," he said, "that's that."

There was no turning back now. We were going forth to meet the future.

"Yes, Eddie," I said, "that's that."

We headed for the open sea, and not long afterwards we saw two ships in the distance, and as we approached we recognized them as a cruiser—we found out later that it was the *Perth*, which went down in the Sunda Strait sixteen months later—and the *Queen Mary*, whose immense grey bulk I had seen in Sydney Harbour when I was on final leave.

Day after day we watched the *Perth* out in front, tossing about in the rough seas of the Great Australian Bight. Its grey shape was dwarfed by the big ships, and I was often amused to think that it could sink the great liners in a couple of minutes. It was the epitome of power. It was all we had to protect us from the awful might of the German war machine.

I watched the *Queen Mary* keeping pace with us on our port side and found a juvenile delight in noticing at times that we were slightly ahead. Day after day we drove through the green sea without seeing land, and I was amazed by the size of the country I was leaving, a country about which I knew so little.

We gloated over the troops on the *Queen Mary* at Fremantle. The ship was too big to go into the harbour, and the soldiers on board glared at us as we steamed slowly past.

A naval rating was standing alone at the end of Fremantle breakwater. He was standing at ease with his rifle thrust forward. A wit who had clambered into the rigging shouted, "Why don't you join the army and see the world?"

The naval rating waved his spare hand and grinned.

They kept us waiting on board at Fremantle—the army always keeps you waiting—and, lined up on the deck, impatient to get at the fleshpots of a new capital, we sang "Abie, Abie, Abie my boy, *what are we waiting for now?*"

We were supposed to be back by midnight, but at 11 a.m. next day drunken soldiers were still returning. Two were brought back by military police. Still drunk, they insisted on kissing the M.Ps good-bye and telling them what great fellows they were. Leaning over the rails, the troops cheered raucously. Coming up the gangway the drunken soldiers met a lieutenant-colonel and said heartily, "How ya goin', corp.?"

On we went, on across the Indian Ocean. It became hotter and hotter, and meal-times came to be dreaded. Hundreds of men were packed into one mess room. There were two sittings, but the heat and smell of the place were almost unendurable. As we reached the top of the stairs the stinking breath of the room came up and smote us. Often, nauseated, I turned away and bought biscuits from the canteen. If I ate in the mess room I gulped the food down with sweat pouring down my chest and dripping off my face, and fled to the cool breeze on the forward deck.

"It's crook," said Harry, "but you should have seen how we went to the last blue. Herded in holds like cattle, we was. We didden travel in no posh ships like this."

It was a strange new world. I had not been on a bigger ship than the *Nerridale*, which made a nightly trip from Nerridale to Sydney or Sydney to Nerridale. The pulsating power of the great ship, driving inexorably through the rough sea, amazed me.

We had sports and lectures every day and, with the inevitable ardour of the amateur, wrote many letters, most of which were not answered. All our mail was franked by unit censors, and we were careful to write only about "the other ships" and not even to mention "big ships".

It became hotter and hotter. From the forward wet canteen, a former drawing-room, a queue of thirsty soldiers stretched twenty yards down the passage. In the room troops stood about, drinking watery beer from glass mugs, and clustered around the crown and anchor boards, urged on by raucous cries of "What about the old hook?" "A few bob on the sergeant-major?" "If you don't speculate you won't accumulate." "Another few bob before they go." "O.K., they're racing."

I saw a soldier lose twenty pounds in five minutes and go out, laughing, to get some more.

"Gordon," I asked, "why don't you run a board? They make a lot of smash. I know a bombardier who's made a hundred quid already."

Gordon struck the pained attitude we knew so well. "Reynolds," he said, "are you inferring that I'm a piker? A Harday run a crown and anchor board? Am I one of the plebs? I'm a business man, an investor, a master mind of the commercial world. I do not depend for the amassing of smash on a couple of dice. How dare you suggest such a thing."

We could not open the windows because of the blackout, and the air was stifling. Our shirts were open to our waists, but the sweat streamed down our chests. I could not stay there for long, but some remained for hours, risking a fortnight's pay on one throw of the dice.

It became hotter and hotter. One day Eddie grabbed my arm and cried "Look! Flyin' fish! Look at the little bastards."

After that we stood at the bow counting the little flying fish as, startled by this monster, they scuttled across the surface for a few yards and fell back with a plop. They did not fly; they floated, and the water on their blue wings glistened in the sun.

It was a strange new world, and a prelude to a stranger one. Our most violent complaint was about the beer. We lined up in a long sweaty queue and eventually were served with mugs of pale beer that tasted like muddy water with a little sugar in it. It was draught beer, and it was so bad that I stopped drinking it.

Boat drill was dull. One night somebody saw a sandbag fall overboard and reported that it was a man. The rigid blackout was shattered by searchlights playing on the water, and the *Perth* darted about for half an hour. When the roll was called next morning everybody was there.

One day, in the middle of the Indian Ocean, the cruiser *Canberra*, which went down nearly two years later off the Solomon Islands, met us, and the *Perth*, with its crew lined up on board in their white uniforms, glided majestically down the middle of the convoy. It was going home.

There was the usual ceremony when we crossed the equator, and finally we reached Bombay. We steamed slowly into the muddy harbour, one of the greatest roadsteads in the world. As I stood on deck and looked around me at the first foreign country I had seen I marvelled again at the beauty of Sydney Harbour with its towering heads, its green slopes and green water, its bays and inlets, its mighty bridge.

Bombay was nothing like that—it was just a colourless city of white buildings, a big circular harbour of muddy water full of ships and small craft. The propeller was churning up more mud. It was too shallow for the *Queen Mary*, which remained outside, "a painted ship upon a painted ocean".

"See that queer circular building on the waterfront," said somebody standing next to me. "That's the Gateway to India. And I think that's the Taj Mahal Hotel just near it."

"Is it?" I asked politely. I supposed I should have been impressed, but it meant nothing to me.

Thousands of troops were lining the rails on all decks and clinging to the rigging. Swarms of hawkers came out in their crude, snub-nosed dhows. Bewildered by the Indian money I had received for my Australian notes, and my first contact with natives' methods of doing business, I bought a green cloth money belt, congratulating myself on beating the hawker down from eight rupees to three. I found out later that it was worth about a sixth the price I had paid for it.

We lowered a rope with a tin attached over the side, and pulled the goods up. Then the bargaining began.

"Get to hell, you robbing coots," cried Eddie when asked ten rupees for a knife.

"Yes, sare. Yes, sare. Very good knife. Very good, sare."

We flipped annas and threepences into the hawkers' boats to see them fight for them.

"They won't go overboard for anythin'," said Eddie. "I seen sixpence bounce into the water, but they don't make a move."

"I wonder would they dive in if I threw a ten bob note over," I said.

"Listen, mate," said Eddie. "You throw a ten bob note over and I'll bloody well dive in meself!"

Pathans—the hillmen of India—had come aboard and had the winches going, already lowering cargo from the holds to native boats. We spoke to some, and they offered us what they called "Indian tomacco". We gave them Australian cigarettes.

One said "You want nice girl? Me show you where get nice girl. Only fourteen. Two rupees."

"Break it down, Eustace," said Pat, "I've got a girl in Sydney." We laughed, and the natives laughed too.

Eddie, Pat, Gordon and I wangled it so that we were detailed for wharf work and stayed in Colaba Camp, a series of tents and huts only a short distance from the heart of the city. The rest of the battalion went up to a big camp on a plateau in the hills.

As we marched through the stinking streets in the heat, we passed the Taj Mahal Hotel, where two Australian nurses waved to us.

"If only I had some hay in the bin and could get a fair go at those sheilas I'd show the officers they weren't even nominated," said Eddie.

"White masters," said Gordon. "I wonder what the commercial prospects are in this town?"

We passed a blackboard with a sign "Best Australian Chops".

"There's enterprise for you, Gordon," said Pat. "We haven't been in the place more than a few hours."

Gordon laughed his deprecatory laugh. "Small town stuff," he said. "A Harday has no truck with the pheasantry."

We laughed. " 'Peasantry'," I said.

"I said 'peasantry'," said Gordon haughtily.

"O.K.," I said. "It's too hot to argue."

Bombay amazed us, with its foul smells, its filthy streets, its appalling squalor, its persistent beggars, its teeming natives. The main impression we took away was dirt, an outstretched hand, pleading eyes, an imploring voice, and the word "*bucksheesh*", the eternal cry of the East.

Everywhere we went we were plagued by sellers of walking-sticks, and swarms of people, mainly children, demanding *bucksheesh*. Later we found Palestine and Egypt bad enough, but they could not be compared with Bombay.

One night we went into the native quarter. We had been told that sometimes troops were attacked, so we bought sticks from one of the persistent walking-stick sellers and, holding them tightly, we ventured into a side street crowded with hundreds of natives. Many of them were sleeping on the footpaths. We were told that, in the summer, thousands of natives slept in the streets every night. Evidently they had no homes to go to, so they just lay down where they happened to be when it was time to go to sleep.

"I forgot to tell ya," said Eddie. "I found one. Comin' round?"

"Found what?" I asked.

"A drum," said Eddie. "Comin'?"

"My oath," said Gordon. "I don't mind dallying on the couch of purple passion."

"I'll come, but I won't be in it," said Pat. "I've got a girl in Sydney. What about you, Mick?"

I put down my glass and scratched my head. "I dunno," I said. "I've never been in a brothel before and you know my good resolutions. I knocked back a good thing in Perth, and I'm determined to do the right thing all the time I'm away."

"God stone the bleedin' crows," said Eddie, "ya doan need to be in it. Just hold me hat."

"Gentlemen," said Gordon, with a patronizing gesture, "I would like you to be my guests," and he pulled out a wad of Indian money.

We gaped at it. "Where'd you get all the smash?" asked Pat.

"The Harday organization," said Gordon, "works fast. I reefed it off a few Parsees like steam."

"Oh," said Eddie, "ya pulled a full hand off the bottom of the pack."

"How dare you," said Gordon in the slow voice he always used when he pretended to be insulted. "I'll have you know a Harday never sinks so low as to use his skill at cards for mercenary gain. This was strictly a business proposition."

"All right, all right," said Eddie. "Ya got the smash and I got the drum. That's all that matters. Come on."

So I went. It was in a street behind Green's Hotel. A couple of Tommy M.Ps were standing outside. As soon as I saw them I had a feeling of guilt. I thought they would forbid us to go upstairs. They merely grinned and said, "Hullo, Aussie."

We tramped up the stone stairs to the second floor, and went into a room containing a table and several chairs. Two girls were standing near the table. One had black hair done in a bun at the back, and gleaming black eyes outlined with mascara. She was wearing a kimono with red and yellow stripes.

She squealed a welcome. "Come in, Aussies!" she cried. "Come in, my beeg Australian soldiers! We will make you so happy."

"Not me you won't," murmured Pat.

I was ashamed to find that she attracted me.

"How ya goin', love?" asked Eddie, slapping her affectionately on the buttocks. She laughed and wagged a finger at him in mock reproof.

"No, no, no," she said. "You do that you and me must marry one another."

Eddie introduced us by our Christian names. Mine sounded profane in that place. There was another girl there. She must have been unattractive because I do not remember her. A door opened and a Digger with an artillery colour patch on his hat came out with a soft-eyed girl wearing a light blue sari. Like the others, she was Indian. She had a wide, flat face, and her eyes had a dewy innocence. I liked her smiling indolence. She could not speak a word of English, but her smile broke down all barriers of race and creed. It reached over and took you by the hand.

Her sari was loose but it did not conceal the voluptuous undulations of her magnificent body. She merely stood and smiled.

The soldier grinned. "G'day," he said, nodding his head and

turning it in the same quick movement. "Take a tip from me, mate. Have a go at this sheila. She's a beaut." Still grinning, he went out.

Eddie was whispering to the girl in the striped kimono. She nodded and looked at me. Then she came over. I backed away.

"You want make love, yes?" she asked. "Make love good, yes?"

I was still backing away. "No," I said. "No, no." I turned and ran, pushing chairs out of my way. The girl chased me, crying, "Why you no want make love?"

Eddie was screaming with laughter, bending over with his hands on his knees. The other boys were laughing, too.

"Look out, Mick! She's gaining on you!" cried Pat.

I was afraid. Incongruously, I recalled Francis Thompson's line, "I fled Him, down the nights and down the days". I fled her. Eddie was pushing chairs in front of me, and I was pushing them away.

"If only we had Clive here!" cried Eddie. "Oh, if only we had Clive!"

The girl stopped, puffing. She turned to Eddie with a puzzled look. "You say corporal want make love," she said. "Why he no want make love? All men want make love. He no want ——?"

She used the first Indian word we had heard on the ship, a word that has many counterparts in English, none of which is in any dictionary. Later we were surprised to find the same word in Palestine, Egypt and Syria.

"He's shy," said Eddie. "He's shy with so many of his cobbers here."

"Break it down, Eddie, for Christ's sake," I said. Eddie grinned.

She came towards me again. I backed away. "No," she said. "Me just want talk to you. Just like shy virgin girl."

I could hear the others laughing as she drew me aside. I went doubtfully. "You beeg strong Australian," she whispered. "Me like you. You come back half past ten, eh? Just me here then. We make love. You come back?"

"I'll come back," I said. Turning to Eddie, I said, "For God's sake let's get out of here. I'm weakening."

Eddie laughed, and he and the others followed me down the stairs. "Not bad for chromos, are they?" asked Eddie.

I did not look at him. "No," I said, "not bad."

"There's another drum down here," said Eddie.

"I think I've seen enough for one night," I said.

Later, after we had undressed, Eddie and I were standing in the doorway of the tent, standing on the stone floor and looking up at the big round moon. We could hear in the distance one of the guard arguing with some drunken soldiers who had just come back from Green's Hotel.

"Well, Mick," said Eddie, "what did ya think of the drums?"

I looked up at the moon and across at the gleaming white finger of moonlight it had laid across the water. I wondered how there could be such beauty amid such squalor.

"I dunno, Eddie," I said. "It was like this morning when I saw those women working in the camp, carrying those bricks and baskets of dirt on their heads. I feel as if I've encountered something unwholesome. I feel—I feel tainted."

Eddie laughed. "I been in more drums than ya could poke a stick at," he said. "In Surry Hills in Sydney, in Dandenong Road in Melbourne, in the red light joints in Brisbane, in Roe Street in Perth. They doan mean nothin' to me. A girl's gotta live."

I turned away from the moon. "Yes," I said. "I suppose so. A girl's gotta live."

Later, when we were in bed and I was looking up at where one of the bamboo poles disappeared in the blue lining of the tent, Eddie said "Mick?"

"Yeah?"

"Ya still goin' ter be true to Margaret? Still goin' to keep knockin' back the sheilas?"

"Yeah," I said.

"But it might be years, Mick. And we mightn't get back at all."

"I know. But I've got to do it. It's all I've got to cling to. I failed her once in Sydney. I can never fail her again."

Eddie did not say anything for a while. Then he said: "Ya know, Mick, yer a funny bloke."

"I dunno," I said. "Maybe I am. Maybe I am."

The next day we met a Tommy who told us we must see Grant Road before we left. "It's out of bounds but it doesn't matter," he said. "It's not really Grant Road, choom. It's the lanes off Grant Road. The women in cages."

"Women in cages?" we asked incredulously. "What do you mean by 'women in cages'?"

"You go and see, choom," said the Tommy. "That's what I said. Women in cages."

We got a taxi near the Flora Fountain. "Grant Road, Eustace," said Gordon.

"Ah," said the driver, leering at us over his shoulder. "Women in cages."

We looked at each other. "It must be fair dinkum," said Pat.

We drove through the teeming thousands in the streets.

"A definition of perpetual motion," I said. "Putting in men's shirts in Bombay."

Most of the natives had their shirts hanging out all round. At first I thought it was untidiness. They had the front of their long shirts hooked up so that their movements would not be impeded. Practically everyone wore white clothes.

We were amused by the gaudy dress of the traffic policemen, who wore bright blue uniforms with yellow socks, a yellow sash and yellow caps, and looked as if they had stepped out of the chorus of a Gilbert and Sullivan show.

We stared down the filthy side streets and marvelled again at the dense population and infinite squalor of this island city. The taxi turned off into a narrow street crowded with pedestrians. The driver had to keep honking his horn. We had noticed already that drivers of cars in Bombay regarded their horns as a child would a new toy. They honked them at the slightest opportunity, but the result of all this "crying wolf" was that scarcely anybody took any notice of it.

"Cages," said the driver, pointing. "Women in cages."

We looked. At the fronts of the houses lining the street were what looked like cages. They were rooms opening on to the street, and in each one, behind their wooden bars, we could see an Indian woman. They were staring out at the crowded street or sitting in front of their mirrors combing their beautiful black hair.

There were couches and tables in the rooms. The women were fat, painted, repugnant. They leered and called to the passing troops, exposing teeth darkened by chewing betel nut.

There were hundreds of them. Some had their parents and children in the "cages" with them. As we drove slowly down the street men put their heads in the windows of the taxis and asked, "———— Aussie? Very nice, very good. You want ————?"

We turned at the bottom of the street and drove up another. Both sides of this street, too, were lined with the "women in cages".

It was the most degrading thing we had ever seen. It shook us, even Eddie.

"As long as I live," said Gordon, "I will never go to the couch of purple passion with a prostitute again."

"Hey, Eustace," said Eddie, "drive us back to Green's Hotel, quick. I want a drink."

CHAPTER XIX

A few days later we were on our way again. The *Queen Mary* and our ship had disgorged their troops into a number of transports. It made us realize again the immensity of those liners.

My company was crowded into a deck near the waterline at the bow of the *President Doumer*, a French steamer. It was almost unbearably hot so deep in the ship, and instead of sleeping there, as we were supposed to, we lay our hammocks on the deck and slept on them. All the officers had cabins; their accommodation was superb. I asked the boys what they thought about the fact that nine-tenths of the ship was occupied by one-tenth of the men.

"White masters," snorted Gordon.

"We're fighting for democracy," said Pat.

"Wouldn't it rip ya?" said Eddie. "The army can make ya do anything. It can even make ya love the child."

"I dunno," I said. "We're the little people, and the little people never get a fair go and never will. Sometimes I think if you had an army in which the officers got exactly the same treatment as the men you'd have the greatest army in the world."

Nothing happened. We ate in our "black hole" near the water-line—it was stifling at night with the port-holes closed for the blackout—slept on the deck, were awakened every morning by Harry's inevitable "Rise and shine, my lucky lads!" did our sub-marine picket and guards on the forward and stern gun, the wet canteen and the mess deck, did P.T., listened to lectures and the experiences of officers in the last war, read the news pasted on the notice board, were pleased to hear a denial of a rumour that Mr Eden was dead, looked longingly at the nurses, wondered what was happening on the top deck, which was out of bounds to anybody but officers and nurses, and stood at the stern, drinking beer out of bottles, putting them on the rail and sending them spinning into the churning wake with a sweep of our hands.

One day while we were standing at the stern drinking beer, Eddie told me something.

"Mick," he said, "I'm gunna be a father."

"But Eddie," I said, "I didn't know you were married."

"I'm not," he said.

"You're not? Cripes, aren't you worried? What are you going to do about it?"

"Nothin'. Her husband'll think it's his."

"Her husband? Oh my God, Eddie!" I was shocked, really shocked. "But Eddie," I said, "you don't care? You don't care that another man has your child?"

"Why should I? I won't mind as long as it's brought up right. I'll just see that it's brought up right an' see it occasionally. Everythin's jake. Why, what's wrong, Mick?"

Often, at night after I had picked my way along a deck cluttered with sleeping troops, I stood at the rail, looking at the golden beauty of the moon and the changing beauty of the sea. I was happy now, free from the shackling restrictions of Nerridale. It was going forth to meet the future, into strange lands and strange adventures, driving forward across the Indian Ocean, going to meet the war. Perhaps, in a foreign field there would be some corner that would be for ever Australia. Here, with the moonlight gleaming on the sea and in my face, I did not care.

But when, later, I woke from a fitful sleep, I lay there trembling, with strange malevolent shadows all around me. I was Mick Reynolds, the former Wizard of Nerridale, and I was too young to die. Every turn of the screw drove me forward towards disaster, forward away from Margaret, the only stable thing in my unstable life. I rolled over and pulled my blanket over me, trying to get away from the stark reality of the moon. I was young, and I did not want to die. I wanted to go home to Margaret, to sell furniture, and to be the father of her children. I did not want to die.

And when, with the sunlight streaming up over the horizon, Harry sat up on the lifebelt chest behind me and bellowed "Rise and shine, my lucky lads!" I was grateful for that cry. I grinned at the profanity of the others, and sitting up and yawning sleepily at Harry I was conscious only of the fact that I was happy and that it was a day less of the war.

Nothing happened. We did our guards, we drank our beer, we used the officers' latrines because of the shocking state of the men's, we cursed the monotonous food.

Soon we were in the Red Sea, and we were told that within a few days attacks by Italian bombers were likely. "Zey will not heet us," said a member of the crew. "Zey are Eyeties," he said scornfully. "Zey come over at twenty thousand feet, drop a few bombs. Two bursts of anti-aircraft fire, and pouf, zey are gone!"

He was right. We were sitting on the deck one day, listening to Captain Herbertson, our company commander, telling us how many thousands of vehicles Britain lost at Dunkirk and that they were replaced from Canada in three months, when we were startled by a *whoomph, whoomph!*

We stared at each other, our mouths falling slackly open. "Ack-

ack," said Harry, as if he were saying, "Today is Thursday." I
looked quickly at Clive. I wondered whether he was as afraid as
I was. He was going green.

Free Frenchmen with their distinctive peaked helmets were running up ladders to the gun on the top deck. The alarm rang shrilly.

"Everybody down below," said Captain Herbertson. We got up
and went along the deck and down the stairs to the bow. Many of us
were looking up at the clear sky. We could not see anything except
a few white puffs where the ack-ack shells had exploded. We were
ordered down below, and we went. I wanted to stay on deck to see
what happened, but a nagging fear impelled me to go below.

We tramped down the steep iron stairs and when we got down
there I felt the sides of the ship pressing against me, hemming
me in as if in a coffin. A coffin. I shook my head, but I could not
shake the fear out of my heart. I could hear the water swishing
along the side of the ship, and I thought what a shambles it would
be if a bomb scored a direct hit on the bow. It seemed such an
obvious place for a bomb to fall, too.

I remembered that somebody had told me that convoys were
dispersed so that each ship occupied only one sixty-third of the total
space, which meant that only one bomb in sixty-three should hit
something, but it was no consolation. I was certain that the first
bomb would hit the bow of the *President Doumer*. Even a near miss
would kill us all, because there was little chance of us getting up
those steep stairs if the side of the ship were blown in. I looked at
Clive. He was still green, but he did not whimper. I saw fear in
Gordon's eyes, too. Only Harry was normal. And Jim. I was surprised to see that Jim was unconcerned. I had to do something with
my hands. I picked up a pack of cards.

"Like a game of rummy?" I asked.

"Yes," said Clive.

I began to deal. Somebody said, "Fancy playing cards in an
air raid. No other troops in the world would do it!"

It was false. It was horribly false. I knew he was afraid, afraid
just as I was. I dealt the cards. Suddenly the all-clear signal went,
and I saw the relief flood into their faces. I was ashamed when I
realized that it was flooding into my own.

Somebody said he had seen fifteen planes; somebody else said
there were only eight. We learned later that it was an Italian
reconnaissance plane.

A few hours later we saw a plane swoop down fairly low over
the convoy. I expected the heavy escort to open up, but it did not,
and I was about to flee to the stuffy mess deck when I noticed the
R.A.F. markings. A few minutes later we saw a plane crash into

the sea a long way away on the starboard bow, a vivid flash and a swift eruption of black smoke. A destroyer following us darted over to investigate, and we had topic of conversation and rumours that lasted until we reached Suez.

Every afternoon at four o'clock the alarm clanged and we started; then we realized sheepishly that it was the daily practice. There were no more genuine alarms.

As we steamed slowly into Suez we passed a convoy going the other way. I was lonely. I wished I was going back. We anchored off Port Tewfik, and away to the left we saw the old town of Suez, which appeared to be what we came later to describe as "just a Wog village", and next morning we entered the canal.

We hurried up on deck, excited at a sudden contact with history.

"Well what do ya think of it, Mick?" asked Eddie.

"I dunno," I said. "I hardly remember all the junk they teach you at school. You know, ten years to make, finished in 1869, Disraeli's brilliant purchase of the shares, Ferdinand de Lesseps's mad dream come true."

"Didn't get that far," said Eddie. "Ran away from home and schoolin' when I was twelve. Ay, what's that?"

"That must be de Lesseps's statue," I said. "There's another one farther up, they reckon."

"It must have cost a lot of smash," said Gordon.

"I thought it was wider," I said, looking at the green water with its regular buoys marking the channel and its white stone walls. It was only about a hundred yards wide.

We saw two natives harnessed like horses and pulling a snub-nosed felucca with its mast stretching more than fifty feet into the air. Two other natives were sitting in the felucca and staring stupidly at us.

"The bludgers," said Eddie, and he yelled, "Why doan ya give the poor bastards a fair go? Get out and pull, ya bludgers."

We stared eagerly at everything. On the Egyptian side the banks were green; on the other side the undulating desert stretched away to the horizon. At regular intervals on the Egyptian side there were trim houses with flagpoles and red tiled roofs and signs, all starting with "garde". They were stations occupied by officials of the canal company.

Suddenly a fog came down and the ship stopped. It was fantastic to be enveloped in a fog in the Suez Canal. I kept telling myself, "You are in a French ship in a fog in the Suez Canal," but I did not believe it.

At Tewfik several boatmen had clambered on board and we helped to haul their boat on to the deck. They went among the troops,

selling wallets, knives, bangles, lockets, bogus scarabs. I looked at
them curiously. They were the first Egyptians I had ever seen. They
were swarthy, unshaven, dirty, stolid. They did not seem much
different from Indians except that they were stockier. I haggled
with one of them and congratulated myself on having bought a
wallet for eight rupees instead of the fifteen he asked. I found out
later I could have bought it in Cairo for the equivalent of half a
rupee.

We passed through the Little Bitter Lake, and anchored for the
night in the Great Bitter Lake. I was on guard on the forward and
stern guns—two hours on each—and as I walked around them I
tried to tell myself that I, Mick Reynolds, was on guard on one
of the guns on the *President Doumer* in the Great Bitter Lake, in
the Suez Canal; that that afternoon I had bought Turkish delight
from an Egyptian and drunk Chinese beer on a French ship near
Arabia. I scratched my head and grinned in the darkness. I did
not believe it. It was too utterly fantastic. I was back in Nerridale,
asleep in my hotel bedroom, and any moment now Joyce, the maid,
would open my door with her duplicate key and snuggle in
beside me.

The next day we stopped at El Kantara. As we steamed slowly
into the wharf on the eastern bank droves of children crowded
down the bank and into the water, howling "*Bucksheesh*!" They
waded out into the shallow muddy water at the edge of the canal
and we flicked coins to them. They swam and fought and yelled,
diving for coins.

A policeman in a coloured uniform chased some of them away
from the edge of the canal and tried to take another's clothes. The
troops yelled threats at him.

"Give 'em a break, you bludging bastard!"

"What the hell's wrong with you, you rotten coot!"

"You bloody demons are the same the whole world over!"

"Why don't ya be fair dinkum or I'll come down and push ya
face in, ya big mug!"

"Give the kids a fair go, Charlie, or I'll smack you in the chops!"

After waiting about for an hour, watching a punt drawn back
and forth across the canal on thick cables, we lugged our universal
kit-bags, sea kits, web equipment, tin hats, respirators, packs, haversacks, and blankets down the gangplank and up to the station,
which was only a hundred yards away.

We passed several men with "War Correspondent" on their
shoulders. There was a green truck with "A.B.C. Field Unit" on it
near the wharf, too, and a mass of complicated radio equipment
in it.

I did not know it, but I was at the most important troop junction in the Middle East, the vital railway link between Egypt and Palestine. To us it was just El Kantara, just a few buildings and a railway station, just somewhere to stretch our legs before going on into the unknown.

We waited about for hours. A group of us stood under the station sign "Kantara East", and Gordon climbed on to the top of the train and took a photograph. We looked curiously at a few natives —loungers, canteen attendants, railway employees.

Arab children came along the line, dirty Arab children dressed in filthy *ghalabeers*,[1] and with festering eyes. "*Syeeda*,[2] George," they said. "*Bucksheesh!*" they cried, holding out their grubby hands, "Gibbit *bucksheesh*!" and then they said "*Shufti*[3] ———" and with their free hand they pulled up their tattered garments to their waists. They were not wearing anything underneath.

Bucksheesh! Syeeda, Shufti and ——— were the first Arabic words we learned.

They sang an obscene Arabic song.

> *Shufti* ———, *Shufti* ———.[4]
> *Ana muskeen ma fish fuloose.*
> *Wahed whisky, etneen beer*
> *Talarta* ———, *Wwyees kateer.*

"Aussie, Aussie, come from Melbourne," they said. "Me Ned Kelly. Me from Gundagai."

Some of them were selling oranges. "Very good, very clean, very nice, very sweet," they howled, and some of them cried, "Very syphilitic."

"I detect," I said, "the presence of the Sixth Division."

We had changed our money into Palestinian, and we threw them a few small coins. We had no idea how much they were worth. Evidently the currency of the country was "mils".

Finally the train came in, and we found that we had to travel in cattle trucks.

"Jesus," said Eddie. "It's no use sayin', 'Pull ya head in, they'll think it's a cattle truck.' It bloody well is a cattle truck!"

Cursing, we clambered in, carrying our heavy equipment with us, and after another long wait the train started. We stared out at the desert slipping by, but it was too dark to see much. We still

---

[1] Long garments.
[2] Hullo.
[3] Show me, or look at.
[4] Show me your ———, show me your ———.
I am poor. I have no money.
One whisky, two beers,
Three ———, that's very good.

did not know whether we were going to some strange place called Heliopolis—somebody had said that the Australian Light Horse camped there in the last war and that we would probably camp there, too—or to Palestine. Nobody had a map, and there we were cursing ourselves for letting our geography slip so badly.

We peered into the darkness, but there was nothing to see—only undulating desert broken up by stunted bushes and occasional palm-trees. Every time we stopped Arab children appeared. They were dirty, and they exposed themselves, crying "*Syeeda*, George", "*Bucksheesh!*" and "*Shufti* ————", holding out their hand.

We went on and on, sitting in our cattle trucks and peering through the bars at the desolate desert.

"Ay, Mick," said Eddie, yawning, "if we go much further we oughter be in Berlin."

Once I saw the sea gleaming through the palm-trees, but thought I was mistaken. Eventually we stopped at what appeared to be a railway siding. We climbed up to the top of the side of the truck and asked an Australian soldier who was passing where we were.

"Gaza, Dig," he said, and walked on.

"Eyeless in Gaza," I said. The others stared at me. So this was Gaza, this drab railway siding. I peered into the darkness, but all I could see were stationary trucks.

"We're in Palestine," I said. "In Gaza, one of the oldest places in the world."

The others yawned. "So what?" asked Eddie. "I wanter go ter bed."

We went on, and not long afterwards the train stopped again. We were ordered to get out. We got out, cursing, and dragged our gear after us. Then we formed up in the darkness—I could see high sandhills outlined faintly against the dark sky—hoisted our heavy loads on to our backs, and marched across the railway line, along an asphalt road, up a gravel road next to an orchard—the sweet smell of oranges was strong in the air—and dumped our gear near a wooden cookhouse.

We were given a hot meal (we discovered we were not too tired to eat it) and I stared in awe at the mess orderly, a Digger with a Sixth Division colour patch.

"Where are we?" I asked.

"Beit Hareed," he said as casually as a man would say Sydney or Melbourne.

"Where's the Sixth Divi.?" asked Eddie.

"Moved out a few weeks ago," he said. "Looks as if there's somethin' doin'. Wanter get back to me mob instead of gettin' camps ready for you bastards. We'll show the ———— who've been callin' us 'five bob a day tourists' and the 'Palestine militia'! Looks like I might miss some fun. A man's just a crumpet. I reckon you Seventh Div. jokers have come in on the grouter."

I felt ashamed. "Our turn'll come," I said. "We've got to do some more training yet. Haven't even seen a Bren gun."

"Who has?" he asked. "S'pose they expect us ter fight with waddies, nulla-nullas an' boomerangs. We've been sittin' on our arses here since last March. What a bloody war!"

"Yeah," we said. We were looking at him in even greater awe. He had been in Palestine eight months. Christ! We hadn't even been in the A.I.F. as long.

"Some blokes aren't nominated," he said dismally. "They cop all the strife that's goin'. Look at Keith McMillan. Lance-bombardier he was."

"Was?" asked Gordon. "Don't say he did his oner."

"No, he didden do it, mate. Five months ago he loses his leg in a road accident near Beit Jirja, just down the road. They reckon he swerved to miss a coupler Wogs. He's boarded see, and all set ter go home. He takes a day's leave in Tel Aviv with a coupler sheilas from one of the A.G.Hs an' what's he cop? Only cops a bomb when the Eyeties drop a few eggs. Knocks him fer six. He doan go home. He doan go nowhere. He's *khaloss*[5]."

We did not say anything. Then Jim asked, "Dead?"

"I said he's *khaloss*, didden I?" said the soldier. "First A.I.F. casualty over here from enemy action. Strike me pink, some jokers are stiff."

"God stone the bleedin' crows," said Eddie, "that poor bloke drew the crow."

This was what happened to the A.I.F. I thought. The Italians killed them with bombs.

"How do you like Palestine?" asked Gordon.

The orderly scratched his head. "I dunno mate," he said. "It's funny. It's only now that a bloke realizes Aussie's *kwyess kateer*."[6] We wondered what *kwyess kateer* meant. It did not sound too good for Palestine.

"I dunno," said the orderly again. "It's not too bloody bad, I s'pose. Too many bloody Wogs for my likin'. They'll *cliftie*[7] the bloody shirt off ya back. Take a tip from me. Be careful. These Wog bastards'll cut your ———— off and sew 'em in ya mouth. Yeah. Fair dinkum. They got a coupler our jokers in a village. When we found 'em their ———— were cut off and sewed in their

5 Finished.
6 Very good.
7 Thieve.

mouths. We went down to the village next day and done it over properly. Fair dinkum." And with this grim warning he went away to get some more stew.

So this was Palestine. Italians dropped bombs on you. Arabs imperilled your life on the roads by not having sense enough to get out of your way. Children demanded *bucksheesh* and pulled up their clothes. Trains took six hours to go about a hundred miles. Village men liked to cut off essential parts of you and sew them in your mouths.

So this was Palestine. I fell into a fitful sleep in our tent and dreamt that I was being chased by hundreds of bloodthirsty Arabs with knives in their hands and a grim purpose in their eyes.

CHAPTER XX

"THEY'RE lining up for mess," said Harry. "Any starters for the Mungareer[1] Stakes?"

Eddie stuck his head out of the tent and said, "The line's too long—Anyone know what's on?"

"They reckon the babbling brook's done some rissoles," said Happy.

"Christ," said Eddie. "Rissoles!"

"Bully beef in disguise," I said.

"What a bastard," said Eddie. "I shoulden er even hoped."

"Nobody ever should," I said.

"It's funny," said Clive. "Before I joined the A.I.F. I never worried much about food."

"Now," said Jim, "I doan worry much about anythin' else."

I was lying on my rickety palm bed. We had had a hard day, doing boring rifle drill and marching doggedly over the sandhills between Beit Hareed and the sea. We had come straggling into the tent, pulled our kits roughly off the beds, made the beds haphazardly, and slumped down on them. All except Clive. Clive had made his carefully and put his gear into orderly piles beside it. He had tidied the dressing-table he had improvised out of a couple of kerosene-cases and had gone for a hot shower before mess. Now he was parting his black hair immaculately, and his nail file was ready.

[1] Food.

"Got a meet on with a Wog bint?" asked Eddie.

"Yes," said Clive. "If she asks me nicely I'll consider sleeping the night with her."

"You wouldn't have said that before you joined the army," said Gordon.

Clive smiled. "I've selected a beautiful village maiden," he said.

"A maiden?" asked Eddie. "Ya'd have ter take her from her cradle."

I got up and washed my hands and sluiced my face in water from my water-bottle. I was tired. I lay down again. All of us except Clive were lying on our palm beds with our muddy boots protruding over the ends.

"What's on at the pitchers tonight?" asked Gordon.

"The word," I said, "is 'pictures' not 'pitchers'." It was strange that Clive and I picked on Gordon every time he made a mistake, but let the mistakes of the others pass. I often wondered why we were so ruthless with him.

"I said 'pictures'," said Gordon.

"I won't bother to deny it," I said. "It's useless. You're a queer study. You're a remarkable personification of ambition. You have the native shrewdness of the sewer rat. You're dominated by a greed for gold."

"Listen, Reynolds," said Gordon in mock annoyance, "don't psychologize me."

Clive, Pat and I roared with laughter. The others grinned.

"Would somebody please change the subject?" asked Gordon. "I am seriously displeased."

"You got them words outa a pitcher," said Eddie. "I seen it with ya the other night. Talkin' of pitchers, there's a pretty good one on ternight. Alice Faye in *Lillian Russell*."

"Christ," I said wearily, "have we got to go through all this again? I can't stand that sloppy, baby-faced, putty-nosed blonde."

That started it. It was usually Mrs Simpson or the barmaid in the saloon bar of the Regal Hotel in Bathurst or an English girl we had seen in Green's Hotel, Bombay; but tonight it was Alice Faye. The sides were about equal. I'm sure some of the boys had no opinion on the matter—they just argued for something to do—but I was serious. I liked her as much as Frank Andrews liked Mickey Rooney.

"The line's just about *khaloss*," said Harry.

"I'm not going to mess," said Gordon. "Anyone coming up to the canteen?"

Nobody spoke. "The canteen menu," said Clive, "is confined to the inevitable eggs and chips and Spinney's Special[2]. I'll take the rissoles, bully beef and all."

Gordon went up to the canteen by himself, and, resuming our argument about Alice Faye, we picked up our mess gear. "What mug aleck pinched me knife again?" asked Eddie, and wandered through the mud to the mess tent.

The orderly officer came through asking, "Any complaints?"

"Yeah," said Eddie. "I might be in the land where Christ was born but I wish to Christ I was in the land where I was born."

The officer smiled. There were catcalls, hoots and hisses, and many comments.

"What's wrong with ya? There's Victorian beer on."

"I'll put you on to a bonzer bint in Tel Aviv."

"Frightened yer girl'll dice yer?"

Eddie grinned and went outside for another mess tin full of tea.

Later we gathered around a tub of clean hot water provided for washing our mess tins. Our eyes lit up.

"Jesus," said Jim, "look at that. Hot water. Clean hot water."

As we walked back across the muddy camp I marvelled that we had reached a state of living in which we were grateful for a tub of hot water.

"They shot a Wog up at Julis last night," said Eddie. "Tryin' ter pinch a rifle. Didden know they was chained ter the tent pole. Goin' ter have a kick?" he asked, fishing a football out from behind his kit-bag.

"No thanks, pal," I said. "You drop-kick artists give a man a touch of 'em. Why don't you play a decent game?"

"God stone the bleedin' crows," said Eddie. "A decent game? Ya listen ter me. Ya New South Wales twirps woulden know football if ya seen it played. Why——"

"It's on," said Harry. "It's on again."

Eddie made an effort and controlled himself.

"Go kick your football like a good little boy," I said.

Eddie grinned, made a rude gesture, and walked away.

"These Victorians," I said. "Talk about a red rag to a bull!"

Jim was sitting on his tin hat outside the tent scraping the mud off his boots and trying to forget that he had influenza. Harry, who had what we called "Wog gut" or "Palestine ache", was walking patiently up to the latrine for the fifth time that day.

Clive was filing his nails and reading a play in French, smiling quietly to himself. Bert had picked up an old *Sydney Morning Herald* turf supplement in the latrine and was following them.

[2] A brand of sausages made by Spinney, the leading supplier of food in Palestine.

Pat was sitting up on his bed, looking over towards Happy and telling him how the Black and Tans hanged his grandfather on a lamp-post. At any moment now Happy's bellow of laughter would smite our ear-drums. Gordon was still up at the canteen. He was probably handing out copies of his cards to the Arabs behind the counter and telling them about the Alastair Y. Glendenning Corporation.

The others went up to the wet canteen and I remained behind to write to Margaret.

Later I tramped through the mud up to the canteen on the hillside. I grinned as I went past the door marked "Corporals' Bar"—"And we're fighting for democracy. Bloody junior white masters," said Gordon the first time he saw it—and went into the main bar.

The canteen was full of smoke and thirsty soldiers. At one end I heard cries of, "A hundred in the guts", "A hundred mils to see 'em go", "Are yous all set on the side?" and then the old "Come in, spinner".

I forced my way through the crowd to where Eddie, Gordon, Clive, Harry, Jim, Pat, Bert and Happy were drinking. I stood near them for a while, listening.

"So I says ter him," said Eddie, " 'What makes ya think I'd know where ya could find a chromo?' An' he says, 'Come on, come on. Doan muck around the fountain. You taxi-drivers know everythin'.' 'Maybe we does,' I says, 'but what's it worth? Do ya sling? Ya might be a demon.' 'Demon be ———,' he says. 'Make it snappy. I want one bad. I'll give ya a caser.' 'Hop in, Alphonse,' I says, 'ya practically in bed right now.' An' next day I calls round at the drum and gets me chop from them, too."

"Bullo, bullo, it all sounds like bullo to me," I sang.

"Hullo, Mick," said Eddie. "Have a drink." He thrust his bottle of Abbott's lager into my hand. I wiped the mouth of it with my fingers and took a swig. "Luscious beer," said Eddie, "bloody luscious beer. What I reckons is that I'm entitled to me chop at both ends. I done the bloke a good turn, didden I? And I done the old tart what runs the place a good turn too."

I looked seriously at him. "You regard it then," I said, "as strictly a business proposition?"

"Yeah, well wasn't it?"

"Yes, I suppose it was. But I'll bet you charged the poor bloke ninepence a mile."

" 'Course I did. Mugs was made to have their smash reefed off 'em."

"Somebody else," I said, "said it another way: 'A fool and his money are soon parted.' "

"That's it," said Eddie.

"That's certainly it," said Gordon, "thank God. Did I ever tell you gentlemen about the Alastair Y. Glendenning Corporation? No? Well——"

"Come back to the field," said Eddie. "Why doancher buy a drink? Get them death adders outa ya pockets."

"How dare you insult a Harday," said Gordon, with the old mock annoyance. "Why right through the ages the Hardays have been noted for their hospitality. My grandfather, for instance ——"

"Pat's was hung, too," said Eddie.

The boys laughed. "How dare you——" began Gordon, but somebody interrupted.

"We've got bayonet practice and a bloody long route march tomorrow," said Gordon, "and the bestiality of bayonet practice distresses me." He looked at Clive and me for acknowledgement of the phrase.

"You musta got them words outa a pitcher, too," said Eddie.

"How dare you——" began Gordon, but we grabbed him, and carried him out into the night air and dumped him on the ground.

"How dare you uncouth oafs touch Harday," he said, but we were running down the hill, laughing and leaving him to come down by himself.

Next day I stood just outside the tent and watched Eddie haggling with a dirty Arab. "How much for socks, George?" asked Eddie. "Very nice, very clean, very sweet. How much for socks?"

The Arab felt the socks and said, "Thirty mils."

"Thirty mils? Why ya *cliftie*[3] bastard, they're *tamarm owie*[4]. You *mush kwyess*[5]."

"Thirty mils," said the Arab doggedly.

"You ungrateful coot," said Eddie indignantly. "To think that women sit at home in Australia workin' their fingers to the bone makin' them Comforts Fund socks and ya only offer thirty mils for 'em. You rotten ungrateful bastard."

I chuckled in the fullness of my friendship and sat down on a box to try to scrape the mud off my boots.

[3] Thieving.
[4] Very good.
[5] No good.

CHAPTER XXI

"Christ," wailed Eddie, "how far're they goin' ter take us? We must be gettin' near Aden by this."

I hitched my rifle into a more comfortable position on my shoulder and grinned at him. Two files were marching on one side of the road and one on the other. Eddie was in the file next to mine.

"Now you know why they still call it the P.B.I.," I said. "It's poor, it's bloody, and it's infantry. And they reckon this is the age of mechanized warfare!"

Eddie pushed his slouch hat back with one finger and scratched his head. I could see the sweat running out of his hair. His chin strap had slid up under his nose. "Remember when we came ter Melbourne from Bathurst before we sailed?" he asked. "Remember how we chalked 'Berlin or Bust' on the carriages? And the same thing in Fremantle? Well, we've marched far enough since comin' over here ter be in bloody Berlin be now."

I looked out across the brown, fallow Palestine fields to the lush green slopes beyond. On a hilltop, a row of stately pencil pines stretched their lean olive-green shapes tautly against the sky. An Arab with a donkey, a cow and a camel hitched to his primitive plough did not even look up as we tramped by. Here, in this placid land, the war seemed far away.

No wonder none of us ever talked about our war future. Already nostalgia had begun to nag and we spoke about what we would do when we got home, but we never spoke about next week, or next month. Although we had been in the A.I.F. for from seven to ten months we could not believe that, some day soon, we would be killing Germans and Italians or being killed by them.

There was leave in Tel Aviv at the week-end, and a shipment of Australian beer, Victorian this time, thank God, was due tomorrow. Somebody had said there was an air mail in, and New South Wales letters were included in it at last. Ten days from Australia. A pretty good service. But it hurt to pay ninepence for an air mail stamp when you got only five bob a day, and you had a solid allotment.

The hot showers were working again. The cook had got drunk for the last time and was up on a charge, and Dodger Harris, from Don Company, had taken over. They reckoned he was pretty good and knew some fancy ways of making stews. Those were the things that mattered.

"Berlin," I said. "Have you ever thought about it, Eddie? It must be a beautiful place."

"Beautiful me eye!" said Eddie. "I hope every coot in it dies, and the sooner the better. I hope the R.A.F. blows it off the bloody map. Only for those mug alecks I woulden be here, trudgin' through this 'beeyoutiful ancient land rich in Biblical history', as the padre calls it."

"A lot of them will die," I said. "But you can't get away from the fact that Germany is a beautiful country, and so is Italy. Isn't it a pity a few people have been allowed to do so much harm? All over Germany there are troops tramping just like us, up and down the roads, across the fields. Only they can't say they're hot or tired or that their feet hurt. We can. That's democracy."

"To hell with democracy. I'm not fightin' for democracy. I'm fightin' for Aussie, an' what the hell I'm doin' ten thousan' miles away from it I'm damned if I know.

"They reckon there's Victorian beer on termorrer night," said Eddie. "Gee if I ever get ter Germany I'll have a go at their slops. In one er them beer gardens with them big mugs. An' plenty er music an' bonzer sorts. I won't worry about them being Aryans or whatever ol' Adolph calls it. No sir! I won't ask 'em ter produce a certificate showin' that they're fair dinkum Germans an' haven't any Jewish blood."

Gordon was tramping awkwardly in front of me. "Private Harday," I said, "pick up the step there."

He looked over his shoulder with an air of affected superiority. He looked like a camel, which has the most supercilious expression, apart from that of an English aristocrat, of all God's creatures.

"Reynolds," he said, "don't mechanize me."

We went on, trudging along the wet road.

"It's goin' ter rain again," said Eddie. "This place is worse than North Queensland. The slit trenches are half full now."

"The climate of Palestine," I said in the sing-song tone of a jaded geography teacher, "is notable for the fact that all the rain falls in the winter. The average annual rainfall is twenty-eight inches, and this falls from September to March."

"Shut up," said Gordon. "My feet are wet. They can't do this to Harday."

I looked down at our tan boots.

"Ours aren't," said Eddie. "Ours are all bright an' shinin'. Doan give us a touch of 'em, Gordon. You're not sellin' fifty-year calendars to the Afghans now."

Gordon turned with his head in the air and an indignant expression on his pudgy face. "I am seriously displeased," he said. "I'll have you know I've never sold anything to the Afghans. Of course, there was one little trip I made into the Northern Territory in which I interested the members of an aboriginal tribe in shares in the Alastair Y. Glendenning Corporation, but we won't mention that."

"That's ya form," said Eddie. "Robbin' the poor bloody blacks. Yer in ya right class, with the abos."

Gordon looked over his shoulder and put his nose in the air like a petulant schoolgirl.

"Gordon," said Clive, "you're so ignorant you think Havelock Ellis is a brand of tobacco."

I laughed so loudly that heads turned for twenty yards up the road.

"Get ———," said Gordon amiably.

"God stone the bleedin' crows," said Eddie. "It must be funny but I can't see the bloody joke."

We passed a group of Arabs breaking white stones on the edge of the road with hammers. We had to make a slight detour along a muddy track. The Arabs stopped work and gave us the thumbs up sign. Some of them, without knowing it was rude, had copied an Australian gesture. We grinned at their innocence. "*Syeeda*, George," they called, and we replied, "*Syeeda*, George." Some of the boys said, "*Syeeda*, Wog."

"By cripes," said Bert in his slow voice. "When I get back ter Aussie and start ridin' again I'm gunna tell one er the owners ter name a horse 'Syeeda George'. I reckon every Digger at Randwick'd be on it."

"I doan like Wogs," said Eddie.

"Harday speaking," said Gordon. "I don't have anything to do with the lower forms of human life. They haven't got any smash. If you held the bloody lot up by the seat of their pants, or what goes for pants in these parts, you wouldn't get five mils."

"You'd clout on that much, anyhow," said Eddie. "You'd reef it off 'em like steam."

"Five mils," said Gordon disdainfully. "It'll be a sad day when Harday can't light his cigar with a pound note."

We let it pass. We had heard it before. I looked at the loutish expressions of the Arabs, their discoloured teeth, their festering eyes, their almost inane smiles, and thought of their filthy mud villages, their dull existence, their asinine contentment. But was it asinine? I had often told myself that I could not recognize as deplorable any state of contentment, even contentment in a lunatic.

"You wouldn't get five mils," repeated Gordon.

I came back to earth. "Listen," I said, "if you held our section upside down by *their* pants you wouldn't get five mils either, so what? Anyhow, you're a bit light on too, aren't you?"

"Purely a temporary state of poverty, Reynolds old boy. I'm still the highest paid member of C Company."

"I know. 'And it'll be a sad day,' etc. All right. The trouble with you is that you spend the smash as fast as you make it. You make it all right, but then you blue it. You'll never amass smash that way, Gordon."

Gordon smiled the self-complacent smile he reserved for discussions about his future. "I will make, at a conservative estimate, one million pounds. The only thing that could stop me amassing smash would be the abolition of the monetary system. In the Harday organization even the janitor will be a public figure. You know, Mick, after the war it will take you twenty minutes to get in to see me."

I grinned. "Yeah," I said, "and then only on visiting days."

"How dare you——" began Gordon.

"It's all right," I said. "You've been in jail before, so it won't be a novel experience for you."

"I shall consult my solicitors. I am seriously displeased."

"And Victorian beer's on tomorrow night," said Clive. "The Australian Army Canteen Service is a great institution——"

"Oh yeah," said Eddie. "That's why we've got to drink that New South Wales muck——"

"—and I would like to say a few words of congratulation to the organizers of the Australian Comforts Fund——"

"I wouldn't," said Eddie. "About time we got an issue er smokes, isn't it?"

"—but that millenium——"

"That whatta?" asked Eddie.

"—that millenium when either of these commendable institutions will dispense largess to the troops in the form of fermented hops has not yet arrived."

"God speed the bleedin' crows," growled Eddie. "I don't wanter be a grape on the business, but what's Clive gettin' at? Won't somebody drum me?"

I grinned. "To translate it into English," I said, "Clive reckons that before we can get stuck into the slops *bookra*[1] we've got to have smash, and at the moment we *coolo*[2] *ma fish fuloos*[3]."

"Christ," said Eddie in an aggrieved tone, "why didden he say so?"

[1] Tomorrow.
[2] All.
[3] Have no money

"If we had ten mils," said Gordon, "we'd put a guard on it."

"The Lord," I said, "or Private Wilson will provide."

"Private Wilson will," said Eddie, grinning. "This Lord of Clive's must be a pretty good sort of a bloke to have as ya backstop in a blue, but if anyone thinks He can snaffle five pounds er butter from the sergeant's mess for a caser for every two pounds, I'll see bloody fly do it. Doan worry about the Lord. Ya stick to Eddie Wilson."

"We'll stick to Eddie Wilson," I said, "but that doesn't debar Clive from using a bit of influence with the Lord on the side."

Clive changed the subject. I knew he would. "The war's done one good thing, anyhow," he said. "It's made a tremendous difference in the transport facilities of Palestine. More roads have been built since the A.I.F. came than ever before. It's not so much new roads as good roads."

"By the way," I said, "anyone seen Jewesses working on the roads?"

"Yeah," said Eddie. "Not on the main roads, but on the camp roads. I seen them at Deir Suneid an' other camps. Workin' in blue dungarees an' caps. Fat sheilas, they was. Seemed to do 'em good. Why?"

"It interests me," I said. "I'd like to hear the feminists on it."

"It's funny," said Clive. "War brings money flooding into some countries. Look at Palestine, for instance, and Egypt. And it has certainly given woman an opportunity for her much vaunted emancipation."

"They'll never get it," I said, "never get it while they go on having babies. And I haven't heard of any move to shift that responsibility to the male."

Eddie told us what to do to women.

"Of course," said Gordon, looking over his shoulder with a mischievous grin, "by all means. By all means known to man. I know woman's place."

"All right," I said. "Don't tell us. Don't be crude. Cripes, it must be ten to. We're stopping for a spell."

"Thank Christ," said Eddie. "Where the hell are we? Somewhere near Aden, I s'pose."

"About eight miles from Gaza, I'd say," I said. We sat down at the edge of the road. Our platoon commander, Lieutenant Douglas Jackson, came along and told us we could get a drink at Deir Al Balah Cemetery, behind a nearby hedge.

Bert and Happy stayed behind to mind the rifles, and Harry, Jim, Pat, Gordon, Clive, Eddie and I went into the cemetery, walked along the neat graves, and drank deliciously cold water from a well. Two Arab boys pulled it up by a simple mechanism. A rope fitted into a groove in a wheel. They dropped an empty bucket down and pulled a full one up on the other end.

"Let's have a look at the graves," said Clive. "I noticed some rising suns."

"Too tired," I said. "Rather lie down. Forget 'em. They're dead."

"That's right," said Eddie. "When a bloke's dead he's *khaloss*. The livin' matter, the dead doan."

I looked at him sharply. "I've never heard it said so succinctly," I said.

"God stone the bleedin' crows," said Eddie, and his face shone in admiration. "You come out with some corkers, some real beauts."

"That's a selfish view," said Clive. We were looking at the details on the graves. The regimental badges were carved on the head-stones. "I'm going to take a note of the Diggers and write to the Returned Soldiers' League so their people'll know their graves are well cared for."

"You would," said Eddie, but there was no scorn in his tone.

"Clive," I said quietly, "what does it matter what their graves are like? They're dead, aren't they? Nothing matters if you're dead."

"It does matter," said Clive doggedly. "It matters a lot."

"Well I'll go jumpin' to Jesus," said Eddie. "I didn't know all these units were in the last stink. Look at these: the Royal Scots Fusiliers, King's Rifle Corps, Suffolk Regiment, the Cameronians, the Royal Irish Regiment. Funny, isn't it? We're just the 2/93rd or the 2/13th or the 2/48th. No fancy names to us."

Jim called, and we went over. "Look at this," he said. It was a marble headstone—the rest were of stone—and on it in black were the words "In memory of a Member of the German Flying Korps".

"I didn't know there were any Germans here in the last war," said Harry.

"Neither did I," I said.

We had forgotten about lying down. We strolled among the graves, with that morbid interest any cemetery induces. Eddie and I chuckled over some of the inscriptions. Clive thought they were beautiful.

"When I die," said Eddie, "I doan wanter cause no trouble to nobody. I doan want no funeral. I just wanter be shoved in a hole so's I won't stink. I doan want any bible-bashing bastard who's never seen me before mumblin' any bull—— over me. I doan want nothin' except a hole in the ground. No headstone, no nothin'."

I turned and looked at him. "Me too," I said. Sometimes I believed that Eddie and I had more in common than Clive and I had. Often, when Eddie talked, he said exactly what I would have said. More crudely, but he said it.

"That's horrible," said Clive. "You must have respect for the dead."

"Respect for the dead?" I said bitterly. "By God, it's a pity someone doesn't have a bit more respect for the living."

"Black arm-bands," said Eddie, "an advertisement in the paper with poetry in it. An' wreaths——"

"They call 'em floral tributes," I said. "They would."

"Yeah. An' stoppin' goin' ter the pitchers. They prob'ly stay home and use it as an excuse ter get blind. An' messages er sympathy——"

" 'In their recent sad bereavement'," I said. I was amazed. I thought Eddie would have exulted in things like:

> A year ago this very day
> God called our little child away,
> He is gone but not forgotten
> Because we will always remember him.

"It's incredible," I said. "It's a pitiful commentary on the intelligence of the masses. They publish things like 'dearly beloved husband of so-and-so'. They make a public proclamation of their love at six bob an inch. If you have such widespread ignorance how can you fail to have wars?"

"I doan even know where me mother's grave is," said Eddie. "But, by Christ, let any bastard say I've got no respect for me mother an' I'll knock him rotten. I'll belt the bloody daylights outa him."

"I can't understand it," said Clive, who was copying names from the graves of Australians. "I simply can't understand it."

"You amaze me, Clive," I said. "You're an otherwise intelligent man. Religion's soured your soul. It's part of the devastating cant of the church to invest dying with mystery and significance. The Church couldn't enslave you unless it could frighten you. They must give dying the panoply of ritual. Religion's full of pagan rites. I'm not ashamed to tell you I don't know where my mother's grave is either. When my mother died I'd have preferred to have her put in a deal box and taken to the cemetery in a cart. I'd rather have given the money to some poor wretch who was living—if you can call it living. Most of the people who attend funerals do so for business reasons. As Gordon would say, it all comes back to smash."

Clive looked up from his notebook, and I saw the lines of pain around his eyes. It was unfortunate, but it had to be done. We had to toughen him or God knew what would happen when things got really hard.

"Please, Mick," he said slowly, "if you don't mind."

"All right, Clive," I said. "I'll shut up."

We wandered among the graves. Every time I saw a fatuous inscription I nudged Eddie. There were many different inscriptions. "Whilst fighting for freedom God called him home", "Asleep in Jesus. Time nor space debars this precious hiding-place" (what ever that meant), "A soldier of the Great War. Known unto God" (there were many of these), "Loyal and faithful unto death", "Thy will be done, O Lord", "In the arms of Jesus", "Promoted to Glory", ("That's one promotion I doan want," whispered Eddie. "Rather become a lance-jack."), "A worthy son, a loving brother, and a true soldier".

"Incredible," I was muttering to myself, "absolutely incredible."

Eddie said, "What's a Q.M.R.? Here's a Captain and Q.M.R. A. Levingston, 11th Australian Light Horse, killed 17 November 1917."

"Must mean 'Regimental Quartermaster'," I said. "We just call him Q.M."

Suddenly Eddie nudged me, and nodded at Clive. Clive was standing in front of the next grave and staring at it with horror flaring starkly in his eyes. He was as white as a marble headstone, and his notebook and pencil had dropped to the ground.

I was at his side in two strides. I grasped his arm. "What's wrong, Clive?" I asked. "Not well?"

He was staring at the headstone in front of him. He pointed at it. "Read that," he said. His voice was so low I could scarcely hear it. I glanced quickly at Eddie, who raised his hands in a baffled gesture.

I read it. "It says 'Lieutenant F. L. Zouch, 7th Australian Light Horse, 17 November 1917'," I said "Why?"

"It doesn't say that," said Clive slowly. "It says 'Private C. Fenstone, 2/93rd Battalion, 23 August 1941'."

"That's two days after my birthday," said Eddie mechanically.

I shook Clive's shoulder. "Don't be a bloody fool!" I cried. "It says Zouch, I tell you! Zouch, not Fenstone!"

Suddenly he burst into sobs, horrible, racking sobs. I shook him madly. "Clive! Clive!" I cried. "Snap out of it, son! You're all right, don't do that, Clive. Can't you hear me, Clive? For God's sake stop it! Stop it, for God's sake!"

I knew what to do, but I couldn't do it. I took my left hand away from his shoulder and rubbed the knuckles of my right up and down the palm of my left. I closed my fist and lifted it up to my chest. Then I dropped it again.

I turned to Eddie. His right hand was at his side. I saw it clenching and unclenching.

"Let me, Mick," he said. I stepped aside and looked away. I

heard a sharp crack, and heard something fall to the gravel path.

"Thanks, Eddie," I said.

"Out like a light," said Eddie, bending over him.

"That's the way to go out," I said. A whistle blew in the road.

"Eddie," I said, "go and tell Doug that Clive has fainted, and that you and I'll stay and see he gets back all right. And bring the three rifles back."

"O.K." he said.

"And Eddie—not a word to anybody about what he thought he saw."

"Mum's the word," said Eddie. "She's jake."

I watched him as he walked away. I shoved a tobacco tin under Clive's head to keep it out of the dirt, sat down on the path, and began to roll a cigarette.

"Never knew any good to come out of a tombstone yet," I muttered.

CHAPTER XXII

THE three months we spent in Palestine seemed so long then and seem so short now. After we had been at Beit Hareed a month we seemed to have been there a lifetime.

Three weeks after we arrived I went out into the mud as usual one day to look for the elusive Arab who came round every morning calling "*Palesteen Post, Palesteen Post!*" I floundered back through the mud as quickly as I could and startled the others by crying, "It's on! It's on in Egypt! The Sixth's in action!"

Blankets were thrown off, and the boys came crowding round me in their pyjamas, reading the brief announcement.

A few weeks later Clive bought the paper, and as he came into the tent he said in his precise voice, "Now what do you think of that? Wouldn't that rip you? The Wizard."

I had been trying to decide whether I would have another five minutes in the warm blankets or get up. I looked up slowly. So the boys would know my secret at last. However did the *Palestine Post* hear about me?

"Read it out, Clive," I said.

"They're tigers, the Sixth, all right," he said. "They went into action at Bardia singing 'The Wizard of Oz'."

"Oh," I said, "is that all?"

The smashing success of the Sixth Division stunned us. We were delighted that it was doing so well—the number of prisoners astonished us—but we were fearful that we would let it down.

"The trouble is the world expects so much of Australians," I said to Clive after we had read about the fall of Tobruk. "They think we all swear like troopers, drink like fish, and fight like wildcats, and that we don't know the meaning of the word 'fear'. We can blame our fathers. It makes it hard for us, particularly now the Sixth is cleaning up the Eyeties with such gusto. All our lives we've read about the Diggers being the best troops in the world. They say Hitler thinks the Turks are, but I think the Germans must be pretty near the best. They've taken on the world twice in twenty-five years and given it a good run for its money. I hope to hell that when our turn comes we don't let everybody down."

"Yes," said Clive, and his face was troubled. "I'm sure the others won't, but I'm worried about myself."

"So'm I," I said. "About myself, I mean. I'm sure you'll be all right, though. Why do you think Australians are such good soldiers? I've often wondered."

"I have too. It's hard to explain. I think it's because we're a young and virile country, because we play so much sport and get so much sunshine we're always fit, and because we've still got the initiative and spirit that helped the pioneers to fight drought, fire and flood."

"I suppose that's it," I said, "plus an adventurous spirit and, among many of us, an unawareness of what lies ahead. You can't, for instance, imagine fellows like Eddie and Jim knowing what danger means. They just don't give a damn. Australians, like Americans, have still got the virility of a young nation. We haven't had time to go to seed. And we don't have to depend, as the Tommies and Germans do, implicitly on our officers. Most of our platoon sergeants could be company commanders, and if a section leader got knocked somebody, anybody, would just take over and the rest would follow without question. An Australian's used to fending for himself. If he can't do something the ordinary way he'll soon find another way to do it."

"I suppose you're right. I only hope we're as good as the Sixth, that's all."

"Yes," I said. "They're tigers all right. What price the 'Palestine Militia' now? Some people at home reckon the Sixth's comprised of fugitives from justice and fellows who want to get away from their wives. And the Sixth calls us the 'Long Thinkers'. If only we can fight like 'em, that's all; but it doesn't look as if they're going to leave us anybody to fight."

In Tel Aviv one day Eddie and I met a private from the 2/3rd Battalion. He was bitter because he was going to be boarded[1]. We stared at him in awe. He had been in action. He had been wounded.

"Want to get back," he said. He was tall and sunburnt. I looked at his Sixth Division colour patch with a strange respect. "Copped one in the foot. Funny thing, but my mob had a lot of wounds in the legs and feet. We were wearing leather coats, and the Eyeties must have thought they were bullet-proof because they kept shooting low. We were dancing about, trying to miss the bullets zipping past. Fair dinkum. Their artillery was pretty good, but their infantry wasn't worth a ———— full of cold water. Just turned it in like steam. We threw our respirators away. Too much of a bloody nuisance. The only danger of gas from the Eyeties was when they breathed garlic on you."

"Threw them away?" I asked incredulously. We were horrified.

"Yeah, corp. Got in our bloody way. Did those Eyeties have plenty of cognac? All the boys got blind. And we reefed watches and rings off 'em like steam. Only you didn't want to pick up fountain pens. They were booby-traps and would blow your hand off."

"Oh," we said. "We must have a lot of troops up there to take all those prisoners."

"Troops me eye! There's not much more than the Seventh Armoured Division and the Aussies. Wavell put one over the Eyeties all right. He only had about 30,000 troops, but he ordered enough stuff for 300,000 vaccinations and made sure the fifth column in Cairo heard about it. Our 'I' tanks are the goods. The shells just bounce off 'em. Fair dinkum. What? No, hardly any bombing. Our Aussie No. 3 Squadron saw to that. Just blasted the Eyeties out of the skies. The Eyeties dropped bombs in one raid and killed three hundred Eyetie prisoners. The desert's crook. Just miles an' miles of bugger all. Looks as if you blokes are going to come in on the grouter. Well so long, boys. Gotta meet on with a bint down in Hayarkon Street, a *Yehudi*[2] sheila. See you again some time."

We came to know the names of the A.I.F. camps that stretched along the fertile coastal belt from Gaza towards Tel Aviv as we knew the suburbs of our cities and towns—Gaza Ridge, Kilo 89, Deir Suneid, Dimra, Beit Jirja, Beit Hareed, Barbara, Julius and Qastina, with Khassa, Hill 69 and Hill 95 back off the main road.

We were anxious to go into Gaza—we thought it was an attractive city. But a driver who had been into Corps Headquarters there told us it was a glorified Wog village that looked as though an

[1] Go before a medical board for re-classification.
[2] Jewish.

earthquake had hit it, and later, when I saw it, I realized that that was a perfect description. The debris lying about had probably been there since British and Australian troops had swept the Turks out of it in the last war, or perhaps it was the same debris the Crusaders had found there when they conquered it.

Blood had been shed in all the fields around our camps, and we found many battered trenches in the hills and picked up rusty pieces of shrapnel.

Drivers who had been to Tel Aviv and Jerusalem came back with stories of those cities, particularly of the Jewesses in Tel Aviv. Since arriving in Palestine we had seen no women, apart from a few dirty Arabs and the members of the Troupers, a Jewish concert party, and we listened open-mouthed as the drivers told us about the way the bosoms of the Jewesses bounced up and down as they walked down Allenby Road.

"We gotta get leave," said Eddie.

"Yeah," I said.

And so it happened that one day we went into Tel Aviv in the leave bus. It was an adventure to go beyond the range of our route marches, an adventure just to see the other camps along the road. The orange groves stretched for miles on both sides with the oranges gleaming golden among the dark green leaves, and then the green fields sloped away to the horizon, with stately pencil pines deeper green against the sky. There were fallow fields, too, of rich chocolate loam.

I turned and saw Jim staring out the window. He saw me watching him. "Mick," he said, "after the war I'm comin' back here. Why, with up-to-date methods this country could feed the world. There's wealth here, Mick, wealth in the soil, an' some day I'm comin' back to get it out."

For the first time I saw the poetry in him, understood his love for the land, understood why he was so embarrassed when we pulled his leg about his cows and the narrowness of Wattle Creek.

"Good on you, Jim," I said. "But once I get back to good old Aussie gelignite or an earthquake won't shift me."

So we went on, along the asphalt and then the white roads, through the orange and grapefruit groves, through the Arab villages of mud huts and the modern Jewish settlements, on to Tel Aviv, which means "The Hillock of Spring".

Thirty-five years ago a few Jews walked out of the ancient town of Jaffa to found a new city. The leader, Meir Dizengoff, stopped among the sand-dunes. Turning to his companions he said, "Here we build. Here we shall construct our city."

Today, instead of the sand-dunes, there stands the youngest city in the world, a city of gleaming white buildings, a city of exiles —Tel Aviv. Twelve years after Dizengoff stopped among the sand-dunes with his great decision made, the population of Tel Aviv was 3600, but in another ten years it had increased to 46,000, and in 1933 it was 80,000. Then a man named Adolf Hitler arose from the gutter with bitterness in his heart against the Jews and he inflamed a nation to hatred, and from all over Europe they fled to Tel Aviv, where there was sanctuary from pogroms, haven from tyranny. In the next ten years the population leapt to 160,000, and Tel Aviv became a modern miracle, a city almost without indus-tries, a city in which men and women who had known fear and persecution were free again.

What a contrast there is between the gleaming metropolis of Tel Aviv, robust in its lusty young growth, and the ancient stones of Jerusalem—Jerusalem, with its Mosque of Omar, its Wailing Wall, its Stations of the Cross, its Convent of the Sisters of Zion, its Garden of Gethsemane, and all the rest.

The guide was a Jew with a beret, horn-rimmed spectacles, a torrent of textbook talk and a habit of saying "Kink of the Jews" and "I sink" for "I think". He swept the boys off their feet with his overwhelming flow of verbosity, only a little of which they understood.

I lagged behind and slipped away. Let the dead past bury its dead. I had no time for the stodgy monuments of a musty past. There was the important present and the vital future. I wandered about by myself, looking at the poverty of the people and the squalor that seems to be the Arab's heritage, for he had known no other.

I wandered about by myself, for here there was a problem much more profound than the problem of the origin and significance of Jesus Christ; it was as old as life itself—the clash of race, creed and colour, the inevitable dispute of ownership. Here, living together, with hostility smouldering underneath, were the Arabs and the Jews, people who, a few years before, had spilled each other's blood, and who if ever the British troops left Palestine would spill each other's blood again.

In the camps and on the roads of Palestine the Arab children had cried "*Yehudi vandook*[3]", their bitterest insult, and we had laughed at them; and only a few of us had known that there, in microcosm, was the problem of the world, the problem of the ages, the problem that all the religions of all the saints and all the saviours had been unable to solve.

[3] Jewish bastard.

Going home in the leave bus I was silent. Eddie, sitting beside me, understood vaguely and was silent too. We went up across the rugged back of Palestine and the others laughed and cried abuse at the driver as the bus struggled around the hairpin bends and up the steep grade of the Seven Sisters. But I did not laugh because anger was burning in me, and I was afraid. For it had come home to me again that people I had seen today were going to die, and some of the men who were laughing beside me now were going to die, too; and all because man had failed to rise above the level of the beasts.

I turned and found Eddie watching me, and suddenly I smiled. "I dunno what it is, Mick," he said awkwardly, "but I'm sure whatever it is it's gunna be all right."

I looked into his anxious face. "Eddie," I said, "if only you were right."

CHAPTER XXIII

ONE night we had snuggled into our blankets and were lying back, listening to the rain on the roof and sides of the tent. There was a desultory conversation about Old Gutsache and the almost incredible success of the Sixth Division in Libya.

"Well," I said in a lull, "Good night, everybody."

Most of the boys said "Good night", but Eddie said, "Ay, Pat, that should affect the price er wheat in Argentina."

"No," said Pat, "but it might have a serious influence on the love life of the Duke of Windsor and Mrs Simpson."

"But I say a cat should wear green pyjamas if it wants to," said Eddie.

"Have you both got dingbats?" I asked, and the others expressed it much more coarsely.

"There's a lot of influenza among the Scowegians," said Pat.

"But that should make no difference to the use of 'I' tanks in the attack on Tobruk," said Eddie.

"I dunno," said Pat. "You've got to consider whether kangaroos would carry their young in their pouches if they had zip fasteners."

So it went on, a series of irrelevant remarks varying from grasshoppers in Saskatchewan to the silk scanties of Lana Turner. We protested, all except Jim. We protested bitterly, but Pat and Eddie merely laughed and were encouraged. That was what they wanted,

Finally I could not stand it any longer. I got up, cursing, pulled my muddy boots on, and wrapped my greatcoat around me. Then I went grimly out into the night, tramped a hundred yards across the slippery mud with a mess tin, filled it with water, and slithered back. As I opened the flap of the tent Pat knocked the tin out of my hand. I stood there, cursing foully, and they laughed at me. Then I offered to fight Pat and Eddie, singly or together, and called them poor misguided bastards and bloody dingoes.

Cursing and shivering, I went back to bed. Pat and Eddie started again, something about smallpox in Turkistan and the size of tadpoles at the North Pole.

"For Christ's sake let us sleep," said Jim. He had not spoken before.

Eddie was out of bed in a flash. "What's that ya said?" he cried, leaning over Jim's bed.

I hopped out of bed, too. My threat to fight Pat and Eddie would be forgotten tomorrow. It was only an incident, part of a joke, but this went deeper; this was serious.

"What's that ya said?" demanded Eddie again.

"Eddie," I said, plucking at his sleeve, "break it down."

"I just said ter let us go ter sleep," said Jim mildly.

"Well, keep ya trap shut or I'll shut it for ya," said Eddie. "Get that?"

"Eddie," I said quietly, "break it down. Please."

"Ya keep outa this, Mick," said Eddie. "I haven't forgot what he did ter me back at Bathurst; how he pooled me with the Q.M. Just a top-off merchant, that's all he is."

"Eddie," I said, and I shivered in the cold night air, "we're going to have this out once and for all. I've told you before, again and again, Jim didn't pool you. He picked the ammo box up in the road without knowing it'd fallen off your truck, and naturally he handed it in to the Q.M. I tell you he didn't know."

"Well I doan believe it," said Eddie. "Ya can't kid me. He pooled me, and I haven't forgotten, see? And if there's another squawk outa him I'll pull him outa bed an' down him like a tack. Why doesen he get up an' fight?"

"For two reasons," I said. "First because you're about twice as big as he is, and second because he's got no squabble with you. Now get back to bed, or, by Christ, I'll bloody well have a go at you myself."

We stood there in the semi-darkness, facing each other. I was trembling, and I knew it was not only from the cold. Eddie did not speak for a while. I could see his mouth working. Then he said, "Listen, Mick, ya me mate. I don't want no trouble with ya. But

I'm tellin' ya now that someday I'll give this bastard what's comin' to him. And he can put that in his ———— pipe an' smoke it!"

Glowering at me, he went to bed. I went to bed, too, and after I had pulled the blankets over me and my shivering had died down slightly I said, "Good night, everybody."

There was silence. Evidently everybody was pretending to be asleep. Then one of them spoke. "Good night Mick," he said. It was Jim.

A few days later Eddie came into the tent when Clive and I were talking about the glory that was Rome, and how a fanatic had doomed a once-great nation to years of misery and bondage.

"Yes," I was saying, "there was no doubt about Caesar."

"By cripes," said Eddie, "he was a good galloper although he had to breathe through that tube in his throat. I seen him win at Randwick the same day as High Caste and Royal Chief won."

We laughed. We could not help it. Eddie stared at us. "We were talking," I said, "about Gaius Julius Caesar, the Roman general and statesman."

We saw his face darken. "Oh," he said, "er course, I woulden know that. I'm just a poor ignorant bastard what never had no schoolin'. Ya give me a touch of 'em. I'm goin' ter Tel Aviv ter get drunk."

I stood up. "I'm sorry we laughed, Eddie," I said. "Anyone could have made the mistake you did. Everyone knows Caesar the race-horse. You only heard one sentence."

"I apologize, Eddie," said Clive quietly. "We didn't mean to offend you."

"Ya give me the gripes, ya high-falutin' bastards," said Eddie. "I'm goin' inter Tel Aviv ter get drunk."

"But Eddie," I said, "You're on guard."

Eddie picked up his greatcoat and strode out into the mud, making for the road. I sat down again hopelessly.

"Oh Christ," I said. "If we can't get somebody to do his guard for him he'll be court-martialled again. You know how he'll go with his record. And just when he's getting his fines paid off from last year, too. Oh Christ. Can't we get someone to do it for him, Clive? I'll tell the C.S.M. a tale about him being sick."

"But nearly all of us are on guard," said Clive.

"I'm not," I said, "but I'm a corporal and I can't volunteer for him. Oh Christ."

I turned and looked round the tent. The boys were putting on their web equipment, getting ready for the monotonous ritual of guard duty. I noticed that all of them were putting on their equipment. "But, Jim," I said, "you're not on guard."

He looked up at me with a shy grin. "I wasn't, Mick," he said, "but I am now."

I sat there, looking at him for a moment and then I smiled. "Thanks, Jim," I said.

One day we heard the news that the Ninth Division would be formed overseas from troops who had been in England and from reinforcements. We did not think that this decision would affect us, but suddenly we found that two brigades, including ours, had been transferred to the Ninth Division from the Seventh; that Brigadier Morshead had become a Major-General and was commanding the division; and that the division, half-trained and ill-equipped, was going to the Western Desert "to continue its training".

"Well wouldn't it rotate you?" said Eddie as we lugged our heavy equipment down to the train.

"It would," I said.

The Arab children from a nearby village, dirty children in dirty clothes, stood about in groups. The tears ran down their dirty faces and their howling echoed dolefully about us.

"Good-bye Aussies," they cried. "Kill rotten German bastards. Then you come back. Hitler rotten bastard."

"My oath," I said.

CHAPTER XXIV

THE confusion that was the retreat to Tobruk early in 1941—we always called it the Benghazi Handicap—has rarely been equalled in the history of a war full of confused retreats. Tommy tank crews who had been in the glorious fiasco at Dunkirk said that at least they had known the strength of the enemy and their flanks had been reasonably protected.

The Ninth, like all Australian divisions overseas, was an infantry division; and now, half-trained and half-equipped, it was fighting armoured forces, and, moreover, Germans. The Sixth Division had shattered the Italian African army, but now we were meeting a German corps fresh from the hot-houses of German training camps and flushed with the fallacy of its invincibility.

We Australians who had driven into Tobruk shouting, "Where's this bloody war?" had found it and were running away. That was what hurt most. We were going back as fast as the Sixth Division had gone forward a few months before.

When I look back on it now, long after the mad confusion of that retreat, I wonder that we were able to get back to safety so comparatively intact.

We had no idea of the size and location of the German Afrika Korps that had arisen, like a phoenix, out of the ashes of Mussolini's shattered army. Desert warfare is even more difficult than sea warfare when it comes to assessing the strength of the enemy. Reconnaissance planes can operate over the sea, but they are useless when the khamsin blots out the desert. Planes cannot even get into the air, nor can they see anything if they do. And a whole division can move behind you overnight. What little air reconnaissance we had often misled us with reports of German troops that proved later to be British.

The failure of the British Intelligence Service to learn that the Germans had landed an armoured division at Tripoli was one of its worst blunders of the war. We had seen German planes, but the first inkling of what was to come was given by the observer of a crashed Italian reconnaissance plane.

He was wearing a German uniform and, like so many German prisoners, he talked. I could never understand why the Germans, who were so magnificently trained in other respects, were so unrestrained when captured. If our troops had been so indiscreet our Intelligence officers would have gone grey. Number, rank and name were all that we were told to tell the enemy if we were captured, and we were determined not to tell any more.

That German talked, and our officers told us that we would soon see some fireworks. Bombing and ground strafing increased; there were three or four raids a day. We looked up at the German planes and said, "So this is the Luftwaffe, is it? Where's the R.A.F.?"

How well we were to know that cry later! "Where's the R.A.F.?" It echoed among the olive-trees in Greece, in the hell that was Crete, in the dun waste of Tobruk, in the dank jungles of Malaya.

Our patrols encountered German patrols, and it was common talk that our G.O.C., Major-General Morshead, was sending urgent messages for equipment and air support, and getting no results. It was not expected that we would have to fight so soon. General Wavell has admitted that it was one of his mistakes; one of his few, thank God.

The Sixth Division, the Kiwis and thousands of Tommies had gone to the rescue of gallant Greece as it waited for the German blow, and with them had gone most of the equipment in the Middle East. Down in Abyssinia the Springboks were battering the Italians into submission; and more forces were required in Irak to thwart a Nazi plot.

The Seventh Division, the only other Australian division in the Middle East, was waiting in Palestine with even less equipment than we had. It knew it was going, but nobody seemed to know where. It was either the desert or Greece, and in the canteens at night there were many arguments about which it would be. One day a few lines in black type on the front page of the *Palestine Post* stunned the boys of the Seventh Division. They stated that it was officially announced that Benghazi had fallen.

The division was going to Greece, it did go to the desert, and it fought in neither. Its only campaign was in Syria. The German push from El Agheila cancelled the Seventh's voyage across the Mediterranean. It went only as far as Mersa Matruh, and then, five weeks later, it went back east to kill Frenchmen.

The Ninth Division had only one of its four brigades in the forward area—neither of the other two divisions had four brigades. Two of our other brigades were between Alexandria and Tobruk, coming up leisurely with practically no equipment. Like us, they believed that they would continue their training in the desert.

One day in March our planes saw some eight-wheeled German vehicles west of El Agheila, and a patrol of King's Dragoon Guards was attacked, also west of El Agheila, by a small armoured force. Soon the British patrols were withdrawn from El Agheila, and the enemy moved in. It was the beginning of the rout. Our Intelligence officer told us that at first it was believed that the Germans merely intended to keep our forces occupied while it launched its blitzkrieg on Greece; but they were encouraged, as our troops had been encouraged a few months before, by remarkable initial success. They soon had us on the run and they kept us running.

Our one brigade in the forward area was supported by eight guns. We did the only thing we could do—we got out. The 2/93rd was in the forward brigade, and we moved back to defend a line running through Tolmeta, Tocra, and Er Regima.

Parts of the weak British armoured units came limping back from rearguard fighting with German medium tanks. The Ninth Division was ordered to slow up the enemy advance along the main coastal route to Benghazi, and the armoured division units were to cover our left flank.

Cyrenaica Command, however, reported that enemy forces were at Msus, sixty miles inland, and outflanking us. Suddenly we were told we were going back to the general line Wadi Derna-Mechili.

Confusion followed confusion in those nightmare weeks. We scarcely saw the enemy, but his menace was more demoralizing because he was unseen. I remember watching Pat standing with his rifle in his hand, thrusting his head forward and saying, "Where are the Jerry bastards? Why don't they come after us and fight? I'll give them something for their bloody corner."

A rifle against a tank, a man against a platoon—it was typical of the whole sorry mess. It was typical of the first two years of war.

We discovered that the troops reported at Msus were not the enemy but our own. Communication was lost with the British armoured units. "The coots are runnin' so fast they're back in Alex. by now," growled Eddie.

"After all, old boy, there's a code," I said, with an exaggerated English accent. "They've got no equipment either, you know."

And so, just after April Fool's Day, we were told we had to move back to Wadi Derna. Later it was discovered that the troops reported by air reconnaissance on the road from Er Regima to El Abiar were members of a British armoured brigade, and not Germans.

"We're being mucked around by experts," said Gordon bitterly.

"What do you expect?" I asked. "We're in the army, aren't we?"

Orders were issued and countermanded, and the confusion deepened. One minute we were going, the next we were digging in. I overheard the Intelligence officer, who was almost frantic by this, say, "I think the Jerries are headed for Bardia in a wide sweep inland. They've evidently got plenty of M.T. and petrol. We're in the soup. We've got to get a battalion out at a time and send the trucks back for another. This isn't war, it's bloody murder. Soon it'll be a case of every man for himself. We've got one brigade's equipment split up among two brigades. What a bloody mess!"

"The high and mighty Cyrenaica Command didn't waste any time getting out of Barce," said a platoon commander who looked as if he had just left school. "They're not playing tennis in their cream duds now, or drinking in their mess in the hotel, or amusing themselves at the brothel. I heard that the Wogs looted everything and set fire to buildings and murdered some Eyeties. They reckon about six hundred Eyeties were released."

"Released! The Jerries would have shot 'em if they'd been us."

"Yes, sometimes I think we don't know how to make war. These Eyeties were orderlies and workmen. I'm sorry for the boys who had to be left behind in Barce Hospital. We'll lose a lot of troops in this wild retreat. A lot of the boys have had to fight their way out already."

"Ah well, *mahlish*. We'll get no promotion this side of the ocean, so cheer up my lads, bless 'em all."

Finally German columns were reported at Mechili. This was the last straw. Units of the armoured division had lost touch with each other, were short of petrol, and had degenerated from a fighting machine to a rabble. They had been ordered to Mechili. When what was left of them got there they found the Germans waiting for them. They were surrounded and overwhelmed.

We set out for Gazala. We were using Italian trucks, and some of the Germans were using British and Australian trucks.

"Christ," said Eddie, "what a bloody mess."

The only consolation was that there was no bombing and little strafing. The khamsin the night we were headed for Gazala was the worst we had known in our slight but eventful acquaintance with the desert. It was as thick as pea soup, and the driving grains of dust hurt through our clothes. It was like the searing breath from the mouth of hell.

"What a bloody country to fight for," said Pat as we jolted along in the back of a three-ton truck. "It's only miles and miles of bugger all."

There were seven of us in the back—Pat, Eddie, Gordon, Jim, Harry, Clive and myself. We had lost Happy and Bert in the confusion. Happy turned up in Tobruk, but we never saw Bert again.

The air was stale and stifling, and the dust blew in through the back, where there was no tarpaulin. The heat was almost unbearable, and sweat poured out of our hair and down our faces. I could feel my shirt sticking to me, and little rivers coursed down my clammy back.

We lay in a jumbled mess of rifles, packs, haversacks, web equipment, greatcoats, tin hats, respirators, rations, tins of petrol and white water cans, and cursed the Germans, the Italians, the British armoured units, the desert, the khamsin, the heat and ourselves.

Jim said that he had heard that the 2/13th Battalion had been chopped to pieces at Er Regima the previous day by a hundred tanks and ten thousand infantry—we found out later that it had been attacked by thirteen tanks and three thousand infantry and had fought its way out after being surrounded. Eddie said a gunner in the 52nd Royal Artillery had told him that the 2/15th Battalion had had its entire H.Q. Company captured, including the C.O. We thought this was just another furphy, but it proved to be true.

We did not talk much. For nearly two weeks we had been retreating, taking a few shots at the enemy and retreating again across the arid desert, going back as fast as the Sixth Division had gone forward a few months before.

It was bitter to have to give back so quickly all the ground the Sixth Division had won, even if it were mainly a desolate waste, and I often caught an ashamed look in the eyes of my friends.

I tried to tell them that it was not our fault, that we could not fight tanks with rifles, but it was not much good. We had lost a lot of the fight that had been in us. We were tired, dreadfully tired, unshaven, unkempt, uncomfortable. We huddled in our filthy clothes and on our blankets and the litter that you find in a truck on any troop convoy, and wondered whether we should get through all right and what the Sixth Division and our fathers of the First A.I.F. would think of us.

We were outgunned and outnumbered—Eddie reckoned that our two brigades had one anti-tank gun, two shanghais, four bows and arrows and three stones.

Harry crawled over the piles of equipment to where I sat in the back of the truck, trying to keep the driving dust out of my eyes. I looked into his lined face, and noticed the crinkles of pain around his eyes.

"Dysentery worrying you again, Harry?" I asked.

"Yeah, Mick," he said. "I'll have to get out. Can't stand it any longer."

The merciless khamsin, dry and scorching, was driving the dust into his face and into his matted hair.

I hated to do it, but I was in charge and these men's lives were in my hands. "Sorry, Harry," I said. "We can't stop. The Jerries might be right on our hammer for all we know. We can't afford to take a risk."

"Oh," said Harry quietly, "I see." He reached up and wiped the dust off his forehead with a weary gesture. "Well, just stop for a minute till I hop out. I'll find me own way back somehow."

I saw his lips straighten out as pain clawed at his stomach.

"You'd never make it," I said. "I admire your guts, but you'd never make it. They'd get you, Harry, and, by Christ, you didn't win the M.M. and D.C.M. in the last war to spend the rest of this one in a German prison camp. Sit up on the tailboard. We'll hold your legs."

Through its coating of dust, Harry's face went red. "But, Mick," he said. "I couldn't—I couldn't do that."

"I'm ordering you to do it," I said. "We'll hold his legs, won't we, Eddie?"

"Yeah, sure," said Eddie. "She's sweet."

"But Mick. I—I feel so ashamed."

I reached over and grasped him by the shoulder. "Harry," I said earnestly, "as long as you live you need never feel ashamed of anything. Never."

CHAPTER XXV

"JERRY'S supposed to be in Derna," said Clive later.

"They reckon he dropped parachute troops at Derna Pass and they're sniping and making it difficult to use the Derna Road."

"We're not goin' that way, are we?" asked Eddie.

"Don't know," I said. "Hope not."

"No," said Clive. "When I got out last night Hughie told me we're going to skirt Derna. We'll go through Giovanni Berta. This might be it now."

He sat up and peered out as we stopped. "I'll get out and have a look," he said.

"Stop here, you silly coot," said Gordon. "The dust's too thick. You can't see anything, anyway. Let Hughie worry. He's driving."

"I'll have a look," said Clive, and got out. When he came back he climbed over the tailboard, wiped the dust off his face, and said, "The convoy's splitting up. A Red Cap advised Hughie to take the desert track."

"I doan give a continental what track he takes," said Eddie wearily.

"Jesus, I'm tired," said Pat. "It's bloody hot in here. Pity we can't open this tarpaulin at the sides, but the dust's too thick. I'm half buried now. All I can say about the Western Desert is that the bloody Jerries can have it. Wake me up at Alex."

The truck started again, and I heard muffled curses as we jolted slowly along the rough track. We tried to sleep, but the lurching of the truck made it almost impossible. Sweat was pouring off us. I remembered my first night in Ingleburn Camp and how I had lain awake all night shivering. If only I could have had some of that cold air now. That was the trouble with Nature. No restraint about her, absolutely no restraint. The burning wind was still driving dust into the truck. It was in our hair, our eyes, our mouths, our shirts, our boots. It was everywhere.

"Cripes," said Clive suddenly, "the dust's clearing."

We sat up. He was right. We could see the moon now, and pick out stunted camel bush at the side of the road. The truck stopped again. Clive got out. When he came back his voice was high with excitement. "Who do you think's up the front?" he asked.

"Mussolini?" said Eddie.

"No," I said, "Jesus Christ."

I saw Clive wince, but I was too weary to be sorry.

"It's two generals," said Clive.

"Not Morshead?" asked Gordon.

"No. Two Tommy generals. General O'Connor and General Neame. Neame's that Tommy general with the V.C. They've got a marvellous silver grey Lincoln Zephyr, too."

"O'Connor?" I asked. "He's Wavell's right-hand man. The armoured warfare specialist."

"Well woulden it rip ya?" asked Eddie rhetorically. "In a car like that. When will these galahs wake up? It's a wonder there aren't no gum-trees around fer 'em ter nest in."

"There are," I said. "Up at Benghazi."

"Did ya see the trumps?" asked Harry.

"No," said Clive, "but a Tommy told me they were up in front. We seem to have lost most of the rest of the boys. They're mainly Tommies in front. The two trucks behind are full of Aussies."

"I wonder where the rest of the boys are?" said Jim. "We've lost Bert for a while anyway. Hope he's all right."

"Doan worry about him," said Eddie. "He'll find a camel an' ride it ter Alex."

"Private Fenstone," said Gordon with affected authority.

"Yes, sir," said Clive.

"Please inform Generals Neame and O'Connor that Harday wishes to see them."

"Yes, sir."

"And tell General Neame to bring his V.C. I wish to choose the design for mine."

"Yes, sir. Anything else, sir?"

"Yeah," said Eddie. "Tell Harday ter go an' get ———"

"Yes, sir."

"I am seriously displeased," said Gordon. "The weather is rather enverating don't you think?"

"You mean 'enervating', don't you?" I asked.

"I said 'enervating'!" said Gordon. "A Harday never makes uncouth mistakes."

"All right. You said 'enervating'," I said. "I'm too bloody tired and hot to argue. It's getting better now though, and we're moving again."

"I wonder how the old codger got his V.C.?" said Clive.

"Doan care," said Jim. "Tell him we've got a bloke here what's got the D.C.M. and M.M. an' if that's not equal to a V.C. I'll jump in the lake."

"I agree," I said. "Are you all right, Harry? You haven't said a word for half an hour."

"I'm O.K., Mick," said Harry, who had crawled up to the front and was lying in darkness with Pat. "It's been too bloody hot ter talk, but I'm damned if I can sleep. I'll say this for France; it was never like this. It might have rained, but we never had none of these dust storms."

"I dunno how this dust still keeps comin'," said Eddie. "Must blow one way all one day an' back all the next. Funny how it's stopped so suddenly ternight. Gettin' cooler, too."

We had stopped again. I stuck my head out the back, but there was nothing to see. Just the dull desert and a big moon.

Harry crawled down to me. "Might as well get one in while we've stopped, Mick," he said, and smiled a wan smile.

"Yeah," I said. "How're you feeling?"

"She's sweet," he said.

Eddie and I helped him over the tailboard. He came back just as the truck was starting. We reached out and pulled him up. His face was creased with pain, but he did not murmur.

Jim started to sing, "Cheer Up, My Lads, ——— 'Em All", but stopped when Eddie growled, "Shut up, for Christ's sake, will ya?"

I could not remember ever having felt so tired. A respirator container was sticking into my back, but I did not bother to move it. It did not matter, anyway. I had slept on the hard ground with my respirator as a pillow too often to worry about a container sticking into my back. My feet felt gritty and clammy, and I would have given all my deferred pay for a cold shower.

Some day, I thought, there will be an end to all this killing. Some day we will go home. Home, Sweet Home. The hackneyed words were hackneyed no longer, and although home to me had been no more than a room in a hotel it had become something precious, something that meant security and peace, the true heritage of the common man.

And when we went home these men would be my friends, or what was left of them. There I go again, I thought. Falling into one of the traps that made wars. I had read somewhere—and I believed it—that every soldier knows that many men are going to die, but never believes that he will be one of them. His ego cannot conceive that he will cease to exist. By a stupid faith, he assumes that fate has singled him out for immunity.

Suddenly I remembered that I had known these men only since the day when, in my new blue suit, I had marched up and down the dusty parade ground at Ingleburn Camp. How long ago that seemed; yet it was only nine months. I had never seen any of them in civilian clothes. I tried to imagine what they would look like.

Gordon, of course, would be dressed as he was always telling us —with an over-smart suit and a black homburg. Too much of a white handkerchief would stick out of his pocket and he would probably carry a cane. Jim would dress in a cheap and shabby suit, and Clive in sober but expensive tweeds. Harry would be a working man and look it. Pat—I could not place Pat. He was such a mixture of Australian, Irish and Scotch, but he could not wear a kilt, a green suit and a Digger hat. Bert would look like a racecourse urger, and would have a feather in his blue hat. I could not dress Happy. You would not notice what he was wearing, anyhow; the only thing you ever noticed about him was his laugh. And Eddie. How would Eddie look? Bert was more the "two-bob lair" type than Eddie, but Eddie's taste would not be restrained. He would probably have a feather in his hat, but not such a clamorous one, and his suit would not be so blatant.

I did not care what they wore. They were my friends, and if anybody in Nerridale slung off at them they would have to settle with me. I had made one great discovery: what Harry Courtenay had told me about the fellowship that developed in the last war was true.

I nudged Eddie, "Ay Claude," I said. I got dust in my mouth every time I spoke.

He yawned. "Yeah, Eustace. What's on ya mind?"

"What're you thinking about?"

"Thinkin' about? Matter er fact, I was thinkin' about how *kwyess kateer* it'd be to be knocking back a dirty big pint in Young an' Jackson's right now."

"Christ," said somebody, "break it down. Yer always thinkin' er somethin' ya can't eat."

"Who said that?" said Eddie, sitting up. He thought it was Jim. It was Jim, but Pat said, "Me. Want to make something out of it?"

"Get to hell," said Eddie amiably, and lay down again. "Jesus," he said, "I wish this bloody truck woulden hit so many bloody bumps. Ya know, Mick, before I was thinkin' about the pint in Young an' Jackson's I was thinkin' about a sheila I met just up the street. On the corner it was."

"Yeah?"

"Well, one Sundee night I'm standin' on the corner watchin' the sheilas go past an' wonderin' if I can pirate somethin'. I doan seem ter be doin' any good for meself, so I'm about to go through an' give St Kilda a go when a Salvation Army mob comes along."

I shifted slightly to a more comfortable position and said "Yeah?"

"Well if there's one thing I think does a good job it's the Army. Not this bloody army. The Army of the Lord. Ya know I doan fall for this religious bullo like Clive does——" I heard Clive move slightly—"I'm like you. I'm a bloody ath—ath—ya know the word. A bloke what doesen believe in God."

"An atheist."

"Yeah. That's it. One of them. Well I doan reckon the Army's *kwyess kateer* just because it saves blokes' souls. No, Mick. Not at all. But I reckon it does a good job when it fills blokes' guts. I been pretty hungry meself in me time—that was when I was battlin' —an' I never got a knockback from the Army."

"It's odd," I said, "that Christianity is so intent on saving man's soul for the next world and so little concerned with ensuring three square meals a day for him in this."

"Yeah. That's what I said."

"You're pretty right about the Army. I've never been hungry back home, but if I had been I'd have gone to the Army. I wouldn't have considered myself one of the 'undeserving poor' like Doolittle."

"Doolittle? Who's he?"

"He was in Shaw's play, *Pygmalion*, the girl's old man."

"Yeah. That's right. I remember the bloke now. I seen him in the pitcher. Bloody good actor, too. Ay, Mick, how'd ya like ter have the girl in it here right now?"

"Don't," I said. "You're killing me. I certainly wouldn't teach her to talk correctly."

"Christ, no. Neither would I. Ay, Mick. I doan talk too good, do I?"

"Not too good, Eddie, but what the hell?"

"Yeah. *Mahlish*. Maybe some day when we got some time ya'll give me a few lessons like the professor bloke in the pitcher, eh?"

"Any time you like."

"Ya know, Mick, before I met you I uster think blokes what talked like you an' Clive were a lotta queens. Didn't think they had no guts. Coulden seem ter come roun' ter thinkin' they was real." He dropped his voice. "Harry an' Bert thought so, too. They didden cotton on ter you an' Clive at first an' I had ter say, 'Ya treat them two decent or over ya go', before they come roun'. But in the end they come to jerry to it that you an' Clive was decent blokes for all ya big words, and all them fellers ya always quotin' from. An' I got ter thinkin' that the blokes that can use them words are the blokes with the best jobs an' good homes an' fancy tucker, an' that, after all, it's a lot ter get for a few extra years er schoolin'. If ya'll help me, I'll have a go at learnin' some er them fancy words meself after the war, so's maybe some day I'll be able ter get a little taxi business on me own. Nothin' big, mind ya. Just a coupler cars."

I levered myself up on my elbow and glanced over to where he lay on his back, with his head on his pack. His face was in the moonlight and I could see that he was sweating from the strain of saying so much, of bringing these things out from the sanctuary of his mind.

"Just say the word any time, Eddie," I said, "and I'm your man."

"Thanks, Mick. But ya won't get nothin' out of it. I'll bet the professor got in for his chop from that good sort."

"Break it down. She wasn't a good sort at first. He didn't expect she'd turn out as she did. I believe his interest was solely scientific —at first anyhow. In the play she marries that twirp Freddie and not Professor Higgins."

"Yeah? Well I'll be ———! Well, ter get back ter another pretty good line. I watches the Salvation Army march by an' sees a sheila who looks *kwyess kateer*, so I follows ter have another squint at her; she's a crackerjack all right. They goes up the street an' they stops at a corner. Well, they're singin' an' prayin' an' halle-lujahin' there for a while an' a coupler mug lairs starts ter chip 'em. They jus' doan take no notice of the lairs. Then the girl comes inter the middle of the ring—gathered round just like a swy game they was—an' starts ter tell how she seen the light an' come safe home ter Jesus."

"Yes. What happened then?"

"Well, when she started ter put over her sales talk for the Lord these jokers chip her, too, an' me an' a few others tell 'em ter cut it out. They doan take no notice. 'I know who ya are,' she says ter them. 'I doan hate ya. I'm just sorry for ya. Yer just poor sinners who have yet ter see the light.'

"'I'd like ter see yer without the light,' yells one, an' the rest laughs. I can't stand no more. I turn round an' lets one have it, fair on the bloody jaw, an' he goes out like a light. Well, then it's on, an' it's the best blue I seen for years. Everyone's stuck inter it. One old girl's hittin' a bloke with a tambourine. I hits one bastard an' knocks him right through the bloody drum. Then I grabs the girl's hand, pulls her outer the mob an' gets her on ter a tram."

"Her name wasn't Barbara, was it?"

"No. Damned if I can remember now, but it wasen that. Well I takes her home. She was tremblin', poor kid. I never seen nobody so grateful. We sits in a park an' she tells me all about herself. What ya think? She tells me how she useter be on the battle, and then she seen the light. Ya could've knocked me down with a feather when she tells me. To think she'd been a chromo all the time!"

"It's not surprising," I said. "You certainly meet some queer people."

"Well, she—er—she was pretty grateful, ya see, an' well—well she offered ter turn it on."

"I have always maintained," I said, "that women are highly emotional creatures. Now I'm sure."

"What d'yer think, Mick?"

"What?"

"I knocked it back."

"No!"

"Yeah. Just coulden take advantage of the kid's gratitude. Just coulden do it, that's all. Just took her home, kissed her good night, an' I've never seen her since."

"Well I'll be damned!" I said. "You tried to be normal, but chivalry would keep breaking through, eh?"

"What?"

"Skip it. We've stopped again. Wonder what the hell's wrong this time?" I sat up and looked out. The moonlight was bright, and I could see the driver and an Intelligence officer in the front of the truck behind us on the rough track. At the sides of the road the undulating desert, studded with camel bush and stones, stretched away to the horizon.

Nothing happened. Eddie sat up beside me and stared sombrely into the moonlit night. I looked at him. His hair was full of dust, his eyelashes were caked with it, and a week's growth hid half of his face. His face was dirty with dust, and there were lines, new lines, around his eyes.

Nothing happened. "Jesus," said Eddie plaintively, "why doan we get goin'? We doan know where these bloody Jerries are."

"Perhaps it would've been better if we'd taken the Derna Road," I said.

Nothing happened. Then a soldier with a rifle and fixed bayonet walked up to the front of the truck behind us and spoke to the driver.

"What's wrong with this bastard?" asked Eddie.

We heard the soldier say something that sounded like "Hein hush".

The driver looked out the window and spoke to him. "Hein hush," said the soldier. "Hein hush."

The driver jerked his thumb towards the officer, and we heard him say, "The other side, mate. Don't ask me. Ask the boss."

"Who is this bloke?" asked Eddie petulantly.

"Dunno," I said. "Probably a Free Frenchman bludging a lift. There's a unit of 'em lost around here somewhere."

"Well, I wish ter hell he'd hurry up. We gotta get on."

"For Christ's sake go round the other side, mate," said the driver.
"Go round there and see the trump. I can't understand that bloody
lingo you're talking."

"Why doesn't he hop in the back if he wants a lift?" asked Eddie.
"We got no time ter argue. Too many Jerries headin' for Bardia
for us ter waste time."

"Jerries?" I said, and then I knew. "Oh Jesus," I said, and my
heart leapt. My hand went instinctively towards my rifle, and then
I realized that the rifles were in a hopeless mess of equipment.

Suddenly we heard shots and shouts from up the front, and tracer
bullets went whistling past in fiery streams on both sides and over
the top of the trucks. The boys sat up quickly, bewildered and
sleepy.

"The rotten bastards!" cried Pat. "Bloody Jerries."

A soldier came round the end of the truck, shoved a rifle and
bayonet towards us, and said, with a pronounced German accent,
"Everybody get down. Quickly. And keep your hands up."

"Jesus," said Eddie. "The salt mines of Siberia."

"No talking," said the German. "Put your hands up and get
out."

My heart leapt again, faltered, and then raced. I must have gone
pale beneath the hair and dirt on my face. For I had remembered
the two men at the front of the convoy.

CHAPTER XXVI

WE climbed out. Our rifles were too deep down in the pile for us
to do anything else. I noticed that only five of us had got out. Who
was missing? I glanced around quickly and realized that Pat and
Harry were not there. Christ, they must be still in the truck! It
was dark where they were sitting. I began to turn to look, but
remembered that I might give them away.

Perhaps all was not lost yet. An experienced soldier like Harry
and a wild Irish-Scottish-Australian like Pat might be able to do
something about us; but could they do anything about the two men
up front? Harry was sick, too. I knew what it was like to have
dysentery clawing at your stomach. What could a man do when
he felt so ill that he did not care whether he lived or died?

Two Australians from the truck behind us made a dash for the
side of the road and disappeared. I thought one was the Intelligence
captain, but could not be sure in the semi-darkness.

We could not do anything. Two other Germans had joined the two we had seen, and they had lined us up on the track between the two trucks. We were standing with our hands above our heads. There were about twelve of us.

"This is the end of the war for us," I whispered to Eddie.

"No talking!" barked one of the Germans.

Suddenly I remembered Margaret and what this would mean to her. As long as I was not captured or wounded and did not get a decoration I would have been able to maintain my deception of still being in Palestine; but now my name would be among the missing, and, later, among the prisoners of war.

The only consolation was that when she knew I was a prisoner she would not have to worry about my safety. I hoped it would not take long for my name to go from the "Missing" list to the list headed "Previously Reported Missing, Now Prisoner of War".

Fighting flared up again in front, and at times bursts of tracers zipped by on both sides of us and above us. I did not dare to look round at the truck to see whether Pat and Harry were still there. Perhaps they had remembered the generals and were stirring things up up there. If Harry rescued two generals he ought to get the V.C. to add to his D.C.M. and M.M. That ought to make him unique. I did not think even Jacka or Sergeant York had the three.

So this was how my military career had ended. "A good soldier is never taken prisoner." How often had we had that drummed into us? I remembered an epic order of the last war, the one General Blamey was supposed to be so keen about: "If the section cannot remain here alive, it will remain here dead, but in any case it will remain here."

Lieutenant Bethune, a Tasmanian clergyman, had written that order. A clergyman. And a long time ago someone had said "Thou shalt not kill". Bethune was determined not to surrender, but he had weapons. We were caught empty-handed. Suddenly a goading consciousness of guilt swept over me, and I was ashamed, bitterly ashamed. I was the section leader, I was responsible, and we had been caught with our rifles under piles of equipment! If our rifles had been where they should have been, where I should have insisted that they be, we need never have been captured. Perhaps we would have saved the generals up at the front.

I looked down bitterly at the two stripes on my sleeve. A soldier? A corporal? I wasn't fit to be a cook's offsider. I spat into the dust, and for once I was grateful that my father was dead.

If only my father could see me now, my father, who had had three years in the mud and death of France. If he could see me standing in this dusty, rutted track with Diggers beside me, Germans in front of me, Italian trucks on each side of me, and my hands in the air.

Suddenly there were shots and shouts up at the front again. The boys were putting up a fight anyhow. There was still hope. Tracers were still zipping sporadically by overhead and on each side of the truck.

Wonder where Pat and Harry are? They couldn't get out the back of the truck, but they should be able to undo the tarpaulin at the side, get two rifles from under the pile of junk, and hop out on the blind side. There might still be hope, but they were taking long enough about it.

How many of these Germans were there? There were only four with us but there might be thousands of them around us in the desert. Christ, I hope Pat and Harry are all right. A bloody shame that a fellow like Harry, with his D.C.M. and M.M. from the last war and dysentery clutching at his vitals, was in the Libyan desert playing hide-and-seek with a pack of Huns and likely to be chopped to pieces by a supporting Spandau at any moment. He ought to be home with his wife and kids.

One of the Germans was moving down the line, searching us. The other three were standing in a group in front. I looked curiously at the approaching German, the first I had seen at such close range. He was dark—what price the pure Aryan race now? He wore a field grey uniform and a peaked cap and his uniform was open at the neck. He was small. He did not look like a superman to me.

Christ, these Germans were well equipped. His rifle was slung over one shoulder, several stick grenades were protruding from his belt, and a gleaming compact black automatic rifle was hanging over his other shoulder. Two of the other Germans had automatic rifles, too. We hardly had a Tommy gun to the whole battalion, we had one Bren gun to a platoon, and one Boys anti-tank rifle to a company. Some day, perhaps, it would be different.

The noise up the front had died down again. The German was looking at Eddie's paybook. "Wouldn't it?" said Eddie. "This is where I do all me back pay."

"Stop talking!" barked the German without looking up.

I heard somebody approaching behind me. My heart pounded. As I glanced round a hand grasped my shoulder and pulled me aside, a voice—an Australian voice!—said, "Where's this bloody Hun?" a hand grasped the startled German by the throat, another hand shoved a Berretta into his stomach.

A moment later that German had two bullets in him and was lying dead on the ground at our feet with his hands clasped to his middle. I caught one glimpse of his contorted face and the blood oozing through his hands before glancing up at the other three Germans. A burst of rifle fire from my left, coming so soon after the sudden death of their companion, made them panic. One dropped dead, and the other two ran.

I found myself crying, "Harry and Pat! You bloody beauts!" and running for the protection of our truck. Everyone scattered for cover. I dropped into the dust behind the rear wheel. The only sound now was the pounding of my heart.

I heard a voice saying jubilantly, "That's fixed the bastards." It was Pat. He and Harry came round the other side of the truck. "You old bastards," I cried, jumping up and throwing my arms around them, "I knew you'd do it."

There was no answering fire from the Germans, who had disappeared over a slight rise.

The man who had shot the first German—it was the Intelligence officer—took charge. "We've got a chance to make it," he called. "They've got the generals. We can't do anything to help 'em. Everybody get back into their trucks, turn 'em round and get to hell out of here. At the double, everybody."

Eddie ran over to the dead German on the track and picked up his paybook. "Whatdyer thing er that?" he asked. "I've got plenty er red ink inside it, an' now I've got plenty er red blood outside it."

The driver of an Italian wireless truck was so excited he turned it over when he was backing it. He and his mate scrambled out with only a few bruises. They got in our truck—it was crowded with nine of us in it—and we set off, going back the way we had come.

"I hope Hughie gives it the works," said Gordon. "That experience was most humiliating. There are unimaginable moments in one's life. I am seriously displeased. They can't do that to Harday. Wait till they find out they've had Harday in their hands and let him escape! How dare they take me prisoner! They can't do that to Harday."

"They've done it," I said.

"Cripes," said Pat, "I'll have to have a new issue of pants in the morning."

"These bastards might do us up at any moment," I said. "See if you can fish your rifles out of this mess. We might need them. Oh boy, what price the Siberian salt mines, which Eddie mentioned so ridiculously, now?"

"Funny," said Eddie, "but it was me first thought."

Our voices were unnaturally high, almost hysterical. We were talking like men who had been sentenced to death, and at the last moment reprieved.

When we came to the track where we had turned off there was no sign of the Red Cap. We heard later that he was believed to be a German.

"That's another thing I've got against the bloody Red Caps," growled Eddie.

We drove all night. When any of us wanted to urinate he had to do it over the back of the truck. We had learned long since that when it came to a choice between delicacy and expediency, expediency won every time.

We could see flashes in the distance at times and hear heavy explosions. Evidently other fleeing British troops were encountering patrols.

The truck stopped. Clive put his head out and looked down the road. "There's a big column of parked vehicles ahead," he said. "They look like Eyeties to me. And there's more of 'em parked off the road, too."

"It don't mean nothin'," said Eddie. "We're in Lancias an' Fiats. They might be Eyeties, they might be Tommies. They might even be Aussies."

The captain sent a message back that the trucks were probably full of Italian troops, but that the only thing to do was to take a chance and drive straight past. We held our breaths and did it, passing truck after truck. Some of them were Australian. We still do not know what troops were in that convoy, but it's ten to one that they were Italians.

Finally we came to a bitumen road, joined the stragglers pressing back to rejoin their units, went past Mechili and drove on to Gazala, Tobruk and safety.

Between Gazala and Tobruk we passed the white blockhouse with the drawing of a bottle of beer and the words "Foster's Lager: A bloody good drink but bloody hard to get" on it—a relic of the Sixth Division. Nobody commented on it, and as we drove into Tobruk nobody said anything. There was nothing we could say.

CHAPTER XXVII

THERE, in Tobruk, we turned at bay. We were ill-equipped and half-trained and, according to all German standards, should have been demoralized; but you could not demoralize men like Eddie Wilson and Pat MacDonald. We were fighting mad, too, for the wound was deep in us, a throbbing wound of resentment at having to flee down the roads along which the Sixth Division had advanced in triumph. We remembered, too, how, when we had passed them on the way up, they had called us the "long thinkers" and "rainbows". "Rainbows?" we had asked. "Yeah," they replied, "you're rainbows all right. You always see a rainbow after a storm."

I remember the day Lieutenant Doug Jackson, our platoon commander, came over to see how we were getting on with the digging. All over Tobruk, Australians, stripped to the waist, were digging, scraping holes out of the reluctant earth of Tobruk, holes from which to fight.

"If you'll pay attention for a minute I've got something to say," said Doug, standing there with his fair hair gleaming in the sun.

I liked Doug Jackson. He was a Great Public Schools boy and even I had suspected him, his English accent and his rapid promotion, at first. "He's a bloody cissy," said Eddie. "Yous mark me words, he won't be worth a crumpet in action, not worth a bloody crumpet." And nearly all the others agreed with him. All except Clive and myself. But there came a time when we all owed our lives to Doug Jackson; there came a time when Eddie went to him, rubbed his hands awkwardly down his trousers, licked his dry lips, and apologized for that doubt. That was something worth seeing. Eddie always called him "sir" after that, and there could be no higher tribute from a man like Eddie Wilson.

I remember saying to Doug one day, "Ay, Doug, a platoon commander can be defined as a lieutenant who blows a whistle, says 'Come on, boys', and that's all he ever says."

He looked up at me and grinned. "That's wrong, Mick," he said. "A platoon commander never has a whistle."

When he came to us a couple of days after we had driven into Tobruk we rested our arms on our shovels and tried to forget the agony in our backs. "This is no time for talk, I know," said Doug earnestly, "but I just want to say this: Wavell and Lavarack were here talking with Morshead the other day and Wavell said, 'Morshead, you've got to hold Tobruk for eight weeks.' Within the next few days Jerry's going to have his smack at us. They're not asking you to do much. They're only asking you to do what's never been done before—to stop Hitler's army. I know how you feel; I want to go out there and take them by the throat, too; but we've got to wait. They'll come to us to get killed. To kill them efficiently and avoid having us all killed we've got to dig these weapon pits. Every spade of dirt you take out is another blow for victory. Within a few days we'll know who's going to have Tobruk. We've got to hang on until Wavell can reorganize down on the border and come to our rescue. That's all, chaps. From now on it's all action and no talk. Hand me that spare spade."

"Doug wants you," said Harry one day. We were manning a perimeter post on the Derna Road sector. We knew somehow that the time had come, that the giant beast of the Afrika Korps had drawn itself up out there in the darkness and was about to leap. It would soon be dawn.

I found Doug striding up and down his room in the side of the post. "I've got to talk, Mick," he said. "My God, man, history's about to be made all around us. Now we'll have a chance to show what sort of stuff we're made of. The 'long thinkers' and 'rainbows' will get their chance now. Not us, damn it, for the attack will not be made here, but the brigade over there"—and he pointed in the direction of the El Adem sector.

"Oh, Doug," I cried, "don't we get a chance to have a go at 'em?" And he cursed in his cultured voice and said all we would get was a grandstand view.

"Mick," he said earnestly, "we've got 'em on toast. I've been talking to Ralph and he's got the dinkum oil. Late yesterday after- noon the Jerries approached in strength from the south, and a few hours ago the 17th Battalion reported that many tanks—big bastards, too—had crossed the little anti-tank ditch in front of them and passed between their forward posts. These tanks were forming up *behind* them in close order. Then hundreds of Jerries moved up and got into the anti-tank ditch only a few hundred yards away from the 17th's wire. They've moved their arty up to within rifle range of our forward posts, too. It's fantastic, isn't it?"

He was striding up and down the room, trying to keep his excitement pressed down, but it was in his shaking voice and his shining eyes. I sat down on the dirty cement floor and put my hands under my buttocks to stop them trembling.

"It's incredible, isn't it?" he said. "My God, what strange creatures these Jerries are."

"But Doug," I asked, "why are we letting them do all this? Why don't we get stuck into them?"

"Stuck into them? Why, Mick, when they attack they'll run into such a hell of fire they'll be lucky if any of them get out alive. You see, Mick, this is not just a mistake they're making. It goes much deeper than that. Morshead describes it as a 'contemptuous tactics', and he's right. They're arrogant, Mick. They've crushed Czechoslovakia, Poland, France, Holland, Belgium, Denmark, Norway. So far the war's been just one big parade. This arrogance is deep in the German character, this myth of the superman, and I swear to you now, Mick, in God's name, that one day this arrogance will destroy them, just as it is going to destroy a big part of their Afrika Korps tonight. One day they'll make this mistake on a vast scale, and that day will mean the turning point of the whole war."

"I believe you're right," I said. "But what are we doing to stop them? Is everything jake?"

"Everything's jake," said Doug. "The reception committee is doing its work efficiently, don't you fear. The infantry has orders to ignore the tanks and counter-attack the enemy infantry as soon as dawn comes. Their main job is to keep the infantry separated from the tanks. The R.H.A. is anxious to add its English hospitality to the party, and all anti-tank units are being moved to positions on the flank of the enemy advance. A cruiser tank force is moving to hull-down positions on the flank too. This gives us the advantage of the morning sun. The arty's been warned what to expect, the R.A.F's been warned to have all fighter planes up at dawn, Western Des. Force has been asked to let us have all its bombers and as many fighters as possible first thing in the morning. The stage is all set to give Jerry the biggest hiding he's ever had in his life. Oh Mick, if only we could be there to help dish it out to him! If only we could be there!"

"Yes," I said quietly, "if only we could be there," and I often wondered afterwards, whether I meant it.

We stayed in our post all day, listening to and watching the battle. All we could do was wait. This impotence was maddening. Men were dying, Australians among them, a few miles away, in this vital struggle for Tobruk, and all we had to do was sit there and watch the stretch of desert out in front of us. It remained wrapped in its heat haze, mocking us with its barrenness, its singular quiescence.

I was talking to Doug in his room later when Captain Ralph Trevennan, the battalion Intelligence officer, burst in, wild-eyed. "It's over and we've won!" he cried. "My God, the things I've seen."

We wrung his hand, clapped him on the back and yelled, "The boys have done it! The bloody beauts, the bloody beauts!"

"Everything went as Morshead planned," said Ralph. "The 5th Tank Regiment came forward at dawn with battalions in close battle order in depth, keeping four hundred yards between each. Their Mark IIIs started up with a roar, with plenty of Mark IVs in support. They came on at twenty miles an hour, leaving their infantry toiling along behind them, and went straight for the first R.H.A., which was disposed in echelon of troops in a broad arc. It was terrific. Sixty big tanks came at the Tommy arty in close formation, came like Old Rowley finishing in the Melbourne Cup. They opened fire at a thousand two hundred yards—we could hear the Jerries barking fire orders over their wireless. One shell scored a direct hit on a twenty-five pounder and killed all the crew, but still we did not fire a shot. If you hadn't known you would have thought the defenders had been turned to stone. For a moment I had a horrible fear in me that something had gone wrong. On they came, on to eight hundred yards. Then, suddenly, the whole twenty-five pounder regiment opens up with a terrific roar. All hell broke loose then. It was a mass of burning tanks, guns booming, the roar of a terrific barrage, the thud of armour-piercing shells hitting tanks point-blank. Those tank crews never knew what hit 'em. Many of the bastards hopped out and ran in all directions and the others tried to get their tanks back, but lots of them collided and in the middle of the confusion in come our bombers, sneaking in on them and dropping death from a few hundred feet up. The noise and dust were terrific. What's left of the Jerry tanks manage to get back to our forward area, and there's another terrific battle there. Our dug-in tanks, with the advantage of light and position, start to dish it out and our anti-tank guns join in the fun, too."

"God," I said, "what a slaughter!"

"Go on," said Doug. "This'll give the bloody Sixth Div. something to think about."

"Well," said Ralph, "all the time the 17th is fighting an infantryman's battle, and my God did those boys fight! The bloody Jerries couldn't understand why, their tanks having gone straight through, the battle wasn't finished. The 17th got stuck right into the 8th Machine-gun regiment. They wiped most of 'em out, took two hundred and fifty prisoners, and most of the regiment's equipment.

There are dead everywhere inside the perimeter and God knows how many outside. Did those boys of ours fight? They went out with sticky bombs stalking Jerry tanks, and one bastard even shoved an iron bar between the tracks of one."

"It's marvellous," I said. "I knew the boys would do it. But what does it mean?"

"It means," said Ralph, "that we've beaten the worst they can do to us. They'll try again, but they're not in the race. It means we'll hold Tobruk."

CHAPTER XXVIII

CLIVE sat up suddenly on his folded blanket on the dugout floor. I turned towards him with faint interest. He was looking intently at the bare earth in front of him. He did not move.

"There it is!" he cried.

Jim looked up from a letter he was scribbling and asked, "What?"

"A flea," said Clive, and his finger darted out and descended with grim inevitability. I heard a faint crunching sound.

"Got the bastard!" cried Clive triumphantly.

"You wouldn't have said that before you joined the army," said Gordon.

"A fat lot er good that'll do," said Jim. "There's only eight hundred and fifty-nine of 'em left."

A low booming came from outside, but nobody seemed to notice it. I got slowly to my feet. I had not shaved for three days.

"They're killing people down at the harbour again," I said. "Anybody coming up to the escarpment to have a look at the Stuka Parade?"

"*Mahlish*," said Jim.

"Too hot," said Gordon.

"Too busy," said Eddie.

Harry was down at the sea, fishing—with grenades. Clive merely shook his head. Eddie was sitting on his blankets, leaning against the wall and doing, as the boys expressed it, "a bit of perving". He was looking at his gallery of nudes and semi-nudes, and trying, as usual, to reach a decision about the one he would prefer to sleep with.

I went out into the harsh sunlight. I remembered how I had gone out into the light from the rehearsal of one of Margaret's shows back in Nerridale. It seemed so long ago. Why, it was back in the days when there were no bombs dropping on you out of the night, no accurate mortar fire to make you crouch in your holes. And although there were no bombs and no mortar fire and you could get fresh water to drink, I had thought it was futile to go on living. I kicked a stone out of my way and grinned wryly. I had come ten thousand miles across the world to Tobruk, but I had gone farther into my own mind.

It was hot. It was nearly always hot in the day-time. I looked around at the familiar scene of dirt and dust and desolation, the barren waste of Tobruk. This is my home, I told myself, ironically.

I passed a few Australians with their battered slouch hats, unshaven faces and sunburnt chests. They're fit, I thought, and full of fight. The officers tried to make us shave every day, sometimes even in the front line, and if we said we had no razor blades they gave us some; but we were still an army of scarecrows.

"G'day, Rat," they said, and I replied, "How are you, George? Liking this summer health resort by the blue Mediterranean? Going dancing tonight or just down to the pub?" And we grinned.

"Got a meet on with a good sort," said one; and another said, "Mary wants me to take her to dinner at Menzies's Silver Grill, but I'm sick of all this night life."

I climbed to the top of the escarpment and sat down in the dirt. It was hot all right, too hot, but the sun would go down soon and we would shiver all night. That was the trouble with this place, its crass malignity. It hit you with everything it had, and it had plenty.

I looked down towards the harbour littered with the gaunt shapes of sunken ships. There was what had once been the Italian liner *Liguria*; and there, down towards the point, the hulk of the cruiser *San Giorgio*, once a gleaming unit of Mussolini's fleet, stood out clearly. The Italians had used it as a sea fort protected by torpedo nets after the R.A.F. sank it, and they had set it on fire when the port fell.

"So are we humbled but not in the dust," I misquoted, and wondered who wrote it. Above the harbour I could see, gleaming in the sun, about a dozen planes. Too high for Jerries. Must be Eyeties. The Jerries came down through the barrage all right, but some of the boys reckoned the Eyeties dived upwards. I could hear the *whoomp* of the ack-ack fire bursting below the planes and an intermittent crunching as a stick of their bombs exploded.

The boys were right. It was not worth watching. They were only Eyeties. Suddenly I saw something that was not the white puff of a shellburst. A finger of black smoke became a smudge and then a stream, and the gleaming white toy in front of it seemed to lurch. Then it dived with black smoke gushing from it as it hurtled down.

I remembered a kite I used to fly in Nerridale Park. I would get it into the air by a short dash, and it would hover there, dipping, swaying and soaring, tugging at the string, and suddenly it would turn and dive straight to the ground. This plane was like that, but its tail was a black stream, not a ribbon of linen.

I had sprung to my feet, and I cheered as that plane went down. "You bloody beaut!" I yelled. "You bloody bobby-dazzler!"

It went down, down, down, and when it hit the sea there was a vivid flash, the dull boom of the explosion, and then nothing. They always disappeared when the bombs were still on.

"That's one less," I said to myself. "Raid Tobruk, would you, you bastards? Well, cop that for your corner!"

My elation was soon over. I remembered that there had been men in that plane, men who had tried frantically to regain control or get out. I felt sorry for humanity, and for myself for being part of it. I started to worry again.

It was all over down at the harbour. The bombers had gone back, perhaps for more loads of death, and the gunners were getting ready for the next raid. And somewhere in England or Australia, and in Italy, too, people would receive telegrams—"The Government regrets to inform you . . . ."

I sat there for a while, brooding. I looked down at the shattered town, the cream shells of buildings and the scarred earth. It's pretty unhealthy down there, I thought, and then I remembered how the fellows working at the port pitied the fellows in the perimeter posts and how the boys in the perimeter posts pitied the fellows at the port. I recalled, too, a talk I had had with a naval rating and an air force pilot.

The pilot said, "You fellers on the sea are pretty tough fellers. You cop it from the air, the land, the sea and under the sea."

"Forget it, choom," said the naval rating, and he looked at me. "You fellers in the infantry have to take it from the air, the land and sometimes the sea. No, Aussie, you've got the worst job."

"You air force fellows have the real guts," I said. "You cop it from the air, the land and the sea, and, boy, you've got a long way to fall!"

We all went "home" happy.

I looked down again at what was left of Tobruk. Of all the God-forsaken spots known to man, of all the desolate wastes, of all the places on the earth's surface where man had chosen to build a home, surely this was the worst.

Eddie was right when he said, "Just to live in this lousy place is bad enough without all the rest."

I heard somebody singing, faintly at first. The song became

louder and I recognized it as "The Wizard of Oz", the song the Sixth Division had sung when it went into action at Bardia for the first time. I could hear somebody tramping along the escarpment behind me. I did not bother to look round. I heard him stop a few yards away and then the words came clearly.

"Oh we're off to see the Wizard, the Wizard of Nerridale."

I was dropping a couple of stones from one hand to the other. I dropped them slowly to the ground. So somebody knew.

In the A.I.F. introductions lack the formality of those in civilian life. "Ay, Blue, this is Darkie" was the usual thing. You knew Diggers as "Slim" and "Bill" and "Snowy" and "Tich" rather than Private Jones, Corporal Smith, Sergeant Thompson and Sergeant-Major Williams. With me, it was more a case of "Mick, meet Harry" than "I don't think you have met Corporal Reynolds, have you, Sergeant Johnson?"

It was five years since I had played cricket and I had never played for the State. "The Wizard of Nerridale" had been forgotten. I told those who did remember my name that the Wizard was a cousin of mine.

But now evidently the secret was out. It did not matter. A champion cricketer was not much use in Tobruk. Some of the boys played occasionally and we had read some rot in one of the papers about umpires with loaded rifles; but the presence of a good ack-ack gunner or a soldier with two bottles of beer would have aroused more interest than Don Bradman.

There was something familiar in the tone of the singer's voice. I turned to look at him.

For a moment I stared dully at him. "It's George Shammar," I said slowly.

He was standing there, grinning all over his face. His head was as shaggy as ever, his eyebrows as bushy and his dress as unkempt, but there was more than mockery in his beady eyes now.

After I had pumped his hand, clapped him on the shoulder and spluttered in amazement, he sat down beside me.

"That was a pretty heavy raid," he said.

I looked at him sharply. "Sorry, George. It was chicken-feed. Apart from bringing down that Eyetie, it wasn't worth watching."

I saw the crinkles deepen around his eyes. "Oh," he said. For the first time I felt superior to George. His tone acknowledged that superiority. To him I was a veteran, one of the "heroes of Tobruk".

"You ought to see the Jerries turn it on," I said. "They come straight down through that harbour barrage. You wouldn't think they'd live through it. Some of 'em don't."

"Oh," said George.

"Christ, it's good to see you. So you finally got round to it, eh? What about that hollow log out Alice Springs way? I just can't believe that you're here. What are you in?"

"The 54th. I couldn't get with you. I tried, but an officious bastard at base posted me to the 54th. Said the 93rd needed no reinforcements."

"Of course we don't. None of our fellows ever gets killed. We're all Speed Gordons. We're all immortal. Like hell we are! Some of the officers at the reinforcement depot are a lot of twirps. They get into it because they can't take it or they're rejects who were no bloody good in action or they're good men who kicked against authority. I'll see if I can get you a transfer to my platoon."

"Good. I was a sergeant in the reos, but lost my stripes, of course, when I got here."

I drew a line in the dirt with the toe of my boot. Then I looked up into his eyes. "What price Pacificism now?" I asked.

"You were right, Mick," he said. "It was too big for me."

I had him down and I wanted to see him suffer as he had made me suffer. I saw those crinkles deepen around his eyes again, and I knew I had scored a direct hit.

"You're not going to say 'I told you so', are you?" he asked.

"Of course I am. You had no mercy on me and I'll have none on you. Do you still believe it's easier to enlist than face the silent condemnation of the mob? Do you still think you can pacify a mad dog like Hitler? Do you still believe I'm the kind of man who causes wars?"

George was drawing figures in the dust with a stone. "You sound bitter," he said.

"I am bitter. And, by Christ, when you've been here a few months you'll be bitter, too. The iron of Tobruk will enter into your soul. It's no Sunday School picnic here, George. It's not like doing route marches in the Palestine fields here."

George jabbed at the dust with the stone, and looked up at me. He was pale.

"I'm sorry, Mick," he said. "I was wrong. I apologize. Let's forget it."

"O.K.," I said.

"I couldn't stand it any longer," said George.

"The only difference between us was that your conscience had a delayed-action fuse," I said. "The infantry will win the war in the end despite all their tanks and their fancy planes; but it's a bastard. Why didn't you get a job in brigade or divisional headquarters or ordnance or postal or pay or some base unit."

"Because I'm a bloody fool like you," he said quietly.

"It's funny. Everybody I spoke to who'd been to the last war seemed to have been in the trenches. I had the idea that if you joined the A.I.F. you had to fight in the front line. I know now how many men it takes to keep one in those trenches. Do you know our divisions have even got a mobile laundry and decontamination unit and mobile bath unit? Wouldn't it rip you?"

"Yeah. But I suppose we'll all be the same. Every old Digger who tries to bite you for a drink or sixpence for a pie and peas or some lousy verse will have been in Tobruk or Greece or Crete."

I asked him eagerly about Palestine, particularly Beit Hareed, but my questions about Nerridale were half-hearted. Nerridale was a long way behind me now.

"Remember Shirley?" asked George. "The pouter pigeon girl with the beautiful eyes who worked in that sundae shop next to the Mayfair Theatre. Well she's the 'elegant Mrs 'Aliburton' now. Her husband's over here somewhere."

"Oh," I said.

"Remember the night war broke out and Captain Rissay came and told us it was great news for him?" asked George.

"Yes. I often wonder what happened to him."

"He got killed at Bardia. He was a major."

"Did he? We never see any casualty lists except those sent from home, and most people don't like to send things like that. You might be out on the Bardia Road sector and somebody you knew back home might get killed in the El Adem sector and you'd never hear about it. You wouldn't even know he was in the A.I.F."

George told me he had not seen Margaret. "Is that still on?" he asked.

"Yes."

"Good. You know you've given me such a faint picture of her."

"Yes. But I've got such a faint picture of her myself. It's a funny business. I've hardly ever seen the girl, you know. Haven't seen her more than about thirty times in my life. It's like—it's like being in love with a stranger, with a shadow."

"It's tough," said George. "Life hasn't been kind to you, Mick."

"*Mahlish*. I'm alive, aren't I? Some day I'll make up for it all. Some day."

"Yeah. Some day."

"Did you bring a chess set with you?" I asked eagerly.

"Yes."

"Hooray! It must be the only one in Tobruk. I've tried everywhere to get one."

He told me about the meals he had had in Tel Aviv and Alexandria. "Chicken," he said, "and asparagus and lettuce. Grilled steak, poached eggs, chips and tomatoes. And remember how you used to like grilled kidneys? Well, I had a plate full of 'em in Alex. the other day."

I licked my dry lips. "Stop!" I cried. "You're killing me. It's practically all bully beef and biscuits here, George. No matter how cleverly the cook disguises the old bully we always see through it. And we get about a cigarette tin full of chlorinated water to wash, shave and clean our teeth in. I advise you to clean your teeth first, then wash, then shave. And I hope you like flies. To eat, I mean. Because, boy, you're going to eat 'em."

"Sounds grim," said George.

"Remember in *The Journal of a Disappointed Man* Barbellion disagrees with what Keats—or was it Shelley?—said was the most beautiful thing in the world? Barbellion said, 'The most beautiful thing in the world is a xenophor standing in a glass jar in the sun.' "

"Yes, I remember."

"Well they're both wrong, George. The most beautiful thing in the world is a grilled flounder standing on a white plate in the electric light."

George laughed. "You're right, Mick. I didn't realize the importance of food until I joined the army."

"Nobody did. George, what is the most significant thing the army has taught you?"

"That's easy. It has taught me something fundamental—the sheer delight of living. It has made me realize that all my life I've been ungrateful, that I've taken things for granted. Things like food and comfort and security and peace. I've been ungrateful. If I ever get home I'll never complain again."

"I knew you'd say that. It's what everybody says. The whole world has learned that lesson, but I'm afraid the world will, as usual, soon forget. Some of the boys are inarticulate, of course, but if I put it into words for them they agree. 'Yeah,' they say, 'it was a bloody good life we led back in Aussie on'y we didden seem ter think so then.' India, Palestine and Egypt have taught us to appreciate our own country, and our standard of living. And there's something else you've learned, too, and now you're here you'll learn it so well you'll never forget it. And that is that the only decent thing you'll ever get out of war is fellowship."

"Yes," said George, "I can well believe it."

"It must have been funny when you arrived in Palestine. I suppose you were amazed when the first Wog you saw said 'Syeeda, George'?"

George laughed. "Yes. I couldn't believe it was fair dinkum. I thought one of the boys was having a joke. A colonel named George came over with us. You should have seen his face when the first Wog he saw when he got off the ship at Tewfik held out his hand and said 'Bucksheesh, George'!"

We laughed. "Tell me," said George, "how do you feel about the chocos? And the munition workers?"

"Some of the boys are bitter," I said. "The trouble with the world today is inequality of sacrifice, just as it's always been inequality of distribution of wealth. I know the munition workers are doing an essential job, but I wish to hell they wouldn't pay 'em a tenner a week when we get five bob a day for holding the perimeter of Tobruk. Did you know that every Sunday morning some of the boys go up to the cemetery the engineers built out near the Bardia Road? They observe a minute's silence for the fellows injured in Saturday's football games at home. Bitter, isn't it?"

"Tobruk must have gone deep," said George.

"It's gone deep all right. I don't think any man who's been here for long will ever be the same again. You can't get away from it, George. You just can't escape it. Sometimes when you come out of the line you get hell bombed out of you and you're bloody glad to get back into it. Have you ever lived for months without seeing a woman, without hearing a woman's voice, except on the radio? You begin to wonder whether there are such things, whether you'll be game to talk to one when you see one. Have you ever lived weeks without having a bath, without putting water on any part of you except your face? Your feet stink, George, and you get desert sores, and the dirt is caked on your body with your sweat, and you feel ashamed. You count the days until you'll be able to emerge from your hole and go down to the sea. And days and weeks and months go past and there is no end to it. It just goes on and on, and you see the hopelessness in men's faces and know there is hopelessness in your own. And then you see the spirit shine through, you see men laugh it off, and if you believe in God you thank Him for men like these, men who will make bets on where the next bomb will fall, men who go in through enemy shell-fire with that high-shouldered, swinging Australian infantryman's walk, and laughter on their lips, and cry to each other, 'If the tucker doesn't improve I'm going to get out of this unit.' And you hope that some day you'll deserve to share the same bully beef and flies and fleas with them."

We did not say anything for a while. Then I said, "I'm getting maudlin. Let me tell you something about our perimeter defences, tell you why Jerry will never get into Tobruk. He's a no-hoper, George. He's just not in the race."

"Good," said George.

I told him how we had a system of defences based on the old Italian perimeter posts and of our defences in depth. I told him about the Red and Blue Lines, about the minefields, the booby-traps, anti-tank ditches, the artillery support. I told him of the intense firepower of our machine-guns on fixed lines.

"George," I said, "you'll be going out on patrol soon if you haven't been already."

"Only got here last night."

"Mind if I give you some hints?"

"Christ no. Tell me—I ask for an academic as well as a personal reason—how did you feel under fire for the first time?"

He was looking straight at me, and I noticed the grim line of his lips and the way his eyes had narrowed. I said, "Well, you'll come to curse the day you ever heard of William Shakespeare. I wish to Christ I had left school when I was twelve and become a boiler-maker's labourer. Some of these fellows are amazing. They haven't the slightest idea of what can happen to them. I see myself lying maimed and twisted out there fifty times a day. They never think of it."

"The divine gift of the clod," said George. "An utter lack of sensibility. If you don't recognize danger you can't be afraid."

"That's right. You know, back in Nerridale I must have been an insufferable snob. Always prided myself on knowing taxi-drivers and boxers and racecourse urgers and fellows who worked on pie carts, too. But inside I despised them because they'd think Cavour was a racehorse, *Sartor Resartus* a fellow in C. Company, and William Makepeace Thackeray a delegate to an armistice conference. I thought I was a better man than they were because I knew the composition of a sonnet and could quote from a score of writers. I used to think that a man who couldn't speak the King's English didn't deserve to be a subject of the King. They've made me ashamed. Here in Tobruk you don't worry about such things. Here you find the real man revealed, and the man whose ignorance I've sneered at is twice the man I'll ever be. Who was it who, the first time we went on patrol, hid in a disused observation hole when they opened up on us with Spandaus, Bredas and mortars? Was it Eddie Wilson or Jim Mills or Harry Creege, who didn't even get their Q.C.? No. It was Mick Reynolds—but a Mick Reynolds who wasn't sneering. It was a Mick Reynolds trembling with fear, a Mick Reynolds who hid there for three hours, a Mick Reynolds who, when he got back, said he had got lost."

George did not look up. "Did they swallow that?" he asked.

"The sergeant didn't. He took me aside and said, 'Don't worry, Mick. I know how you felt. She'll be jake next time.'"

"It must get better after a while," said George.

"Not with me it doesn't. Your nerves start to go. Look at that." I held out my hand and it trembled slightly. "Everybody's bomb happy. Some more, some less. You're all right on patrol as long as you're hitting back at the bastards. It takes your mind off your danger. But when they get stuck into you with mortars and shell or bombs in the dark, that's the time you get a real touch of 'em. Mortar bombs, shelling and bombing at night are bad, but ground strafing is worst of all."

George was drawing figures in the dirt with the stone. He still did not look up.

"You can trace it back to the child's fear of the dark," I said. "If you can't see you imagine all sorts of horrors, and if you can't hit back it's bloody awful."

"It must be," said George.

"For Christ's sake and your own be careful of their mortars. This war has proved the value of mortars. Ask anybody. All the boys hate them."

"Sounds grim," said George.

"It *is* grim. Shelling's worse than bombing, but the mortars are worse than shelling. No matter what they try to hit you with, don't run. Just burrow down into the great good earth. You'll wish it was all over you, and it will be, six feet of it, if you don't get down on Mother Nature's bosom. It's better than any bosom I've ever rested my head on, and I've rested my head on a few."

George grinned. "I'll say you have," he said. "I'll remember. Anything else?"

"Yeah. Get hold of a 'murder suit'. That's a long pair of overalls with deep pockets for carrying grenades, wire-cutters and ammo. Nothing will shine if you wear that. You just merge into the ground. And don't wear a tin hat. Take the risk of getting smacked in the head. Our tin hats are pretty futile, anyhow. It's typical of the War Office that we stick to tin hats that expose nearly all the head. The Germans, the Russians and the Yanks have got the right idea, but you couldn't expect the British General Staff to copy another nation. 'Such an admission of weakness, old boy. Just wouldn't do.' Even if your tin hat's camouflaged, don't wear it. Wear your slouch hat. Tin hats make a noise if you go to ground in a hurry. Wear sandshoes or tie a bit of old tyre around your boots. Watch out for mines and booby-traps, always carry your field dressing, and a bootlace and nail for use as a tourniquet. Don't pick up anything off the ground. Too many fellows who've bent down to pick up shaving-sticks or fountain-pens have had their hands blown off."

"There's a lot to remember," said George, still without looking at me.

"You want to live, don't you?" I said.

"Never more than now. All over the world people have found a new faith in living."

"Well, remember it. And if a flare goes up and you don't hear the plop of the pistol just stand where you are. They won't see you unless the flare drops behind you. And if you're counting the paces for the officer or N.C.O. in charge for Christ's sake don't make a mistake. If you do it might be your last. It might be the last of the whole patrol. You'll pick up practically all of this from your section mates and some more as well. It's elementary stuff. I'll get you into my platoon as soon as possible, which means as soon as somebody goes out on patrol and doesn't come back, or comes back an Alex. job. I'll come and see you as often as I can."

"I'll look you up, too."

"Good. Well good-bye, George."

We stood up and shook hands awkwardly. I could see his eyes now. The mocking smile was back, but his eyes were hard.

"Good-bye, Mick," he said.

As I went down the escarpment in the fading light I realized that we had said good-bye and shaken hands as if one of us were going on a long journey.

I kicked a stone viciously out of the way. Well perhaps one of us was. Perhaps both of us were.

CHAPTER XXIX

Clouds of dust were stirred up by my feet as I came down the wadi. It did not matter; my brown boots were filthy and it was impossible to keep your clothes clean.

As I came down to where the boys were sitting on packs, tin hats and stones I remembered the hut inspections at Ingleburn and Bathurst, the tent inspections in Palestine, the guard inspections at all three places. I remembered how annoyed the inspecting officer had been if boots were not gleaming or if a shave had been cursory. The Australian soldier has never been noted for tidiness, but now he was a member of a scarecrow army. They still tried to make us shave every day, but they could not enforce the rule.

The boys were sitting round with their sunburnt chests bare and their identity disks dangling on their chests. It was hot—it was always hot while the sun was up—but our dugouts held only two and if some of the Rats wanted to have a yarn with the others they had to come out of their holes.

"G'day, ya old bastard," said Jim, and I was amused again at the thought that the Tommies could never get used to our main term of endearment.

I sat down on the ground.

"Ay, Mick," said Gordon, "what's wrong with Doug? He's been acting queer since yesterday."

"Somebody musta sold him some shares in Gordon C. Harday Gold Mines Incorp.," said Harry.

Gordon stood up, walked a few yards away, turned, lifted his right arm above his head, bent his elbow, put the back of his hand above his left ear, put his head back, assumed an injured expression and said in a choking voice, "All right, all right. If that's what you think. And to think I called you my friends."

I often wished I had a camera to record some of Gordon's mannerisms, particularly this one.

We laughed—everybody except Pat. Pat had not laughed for two days.

"What *is* wrong with Doug?" asked Happy.

"The mail came in on Tuesday," I said.

"What's that got to do with it?"

"Everything," I said. "Like a bloody fool, I went over to his doover and asked him. It was like trampling on violets with hob-nailed boots. He's got a cable saying his wife was killed under a car in Sydney. He didn't say anything. Just handed it to me, and sat with his head in his hands, staring straight ahead. I read it, clapped him on the shoulder in the stupid way one does in these cases, and walked out."

Nobody said anything. Then Jim said, "There's nothin' we can do, is there?"

"No," I said hopelessly. "Nothing."

Pat caught my eye, jerked his head to one side, and got up and strolled away. I followed after a while. He walked well away from the others, and sat on an old petrol drum. I sat on another. Neither of us spoke. He sat with his elbows on his knees and his chin in his hands.

Finally I said, "Well, Pat? Out with it. Get it off your chest. Confession mightn't be good for the soul, but it's good for the heart. What was in the cable?"

He sat up. "You knew?"

"Knew? You can't live with a man for a year without knowing all about him. I reckon if I got stomach ache all you alecks would know almost before I did. We all knew. Saw you get it. Knew it was bad news."

"It's bad all right," he said, and then, looking up at me, he said simply, "I'm diced, Mick."

I stared at him. "Diced? Oh no!"

"Yeah. Or scrubbed or wiped, if you prefer 'em."

He handed me the cable. I looked first at the red map of the world under "Cable and Wireless Limited" and then at the stamp "C and W Ltd, 1941, Haifa" and wondered why it was stamped "M.C." in purple. "M.C." meant only one thing in the army. Then, slowly, I read "FOH86N, Sydney," then a couple of numbers that appeared to be the date and the words, and then "G.L.T." and Pat's number, name and unit, and "A.I.F., Abroad".

There was nothing else left to read. I had to read the message. It was: "FEEL DIFFERENT WROTE FEBRUARY FORGET ME PAMELA."

I looked up at him.

"Diced," he said. "Diced in Tobruk." He stood up and began to walk up and down, stirring up the dust with his feet.

"It's tough," I said. I picked up a stone and scratched at it with my fingernail.

"I can't believe it," said Pat. "I don't believe it."

"It's true," I said. "You can't argue with a bomb and you can't argue with a cable either. A cable's a dreadful thing. It can say so little and mean so much. It's true."

Pat shook his head as he walked.

"Have a cigarette," I said, handing him a packet. He took the last cigarette out of it and threw the packet away. I knew then how deep the hurt had gone. No normal man in Tobruk would have taken your last cigarette.

He took off his hat and wiped the sweat off his forehead. "But Mick, after three years."

"Three or thirty. It's just the same. It happens every day. Divorce court judges have got to live. It's better before marriage than after."

I could hear explosions from the direction of the town. Evidently the Stuka Parade was earlier than usual today.

"But Mick, she couldn't do it—not Pamela."

Pat stopped in front of me, and I saw that there were new lines in his face overnight, and I could see something new in his eyes, too.

"Look, Pat," I said, "you built your life around Pamela, I know. But you've just got to take these things. It's like one of your mates going out on patrol and not coming back. It's a bastard, but you can't do anything about it."

"But Mick," he said earnestly. His eyes were like those of a bewildered child. "Pamela couldn't do a thing like this. She was sweet, Mick."

"Sweet?" I laughed grimly. "Sweet? She's sweet all right. Three hammer blows between the eyes. 'Feel different. Wrote February. Forget me'. Not 'Sorry' or 'Forgive me'. Just 'Feel different. Wrote February. Forget me'."

Pat was walking up and down in front of me again. He was a giant of a man. I could see the swelling muscles in his sunburnt back as he strode away from me. His shorts were dirty, and so were his brown boots. He did not wear any socks. A lot of the boys did not wear them. The bigger they are, I thought, the harder they fall. I could feel the heat beating up from the ground. There was no breeze in the wadi, and I could see a heat haze shimmering up from the earth in the distance.

The racket down at the harbour was still going on. We did not take any notice of it. It had lost all its novelty long ago.

Pat threw his cigarette away. It was only half-smoked. Somebody would pick it up later and smoke it.

"Snap out of it, Pat," I said. "A pity you can't get roaring drunk and sleep with a couple of women. No chance of finding any of that Eyetie cognac we used to get blind on when we came here first?"

"Two chances," said Pat. "Mine and Buckley's."

"Yeah. Why don't you go down to the cabaret near the Plaza Benito Mussolini and go home with Fatima or Fifi?"

Pat laughed bitterly. "What a joint! A man can't even find a bint to help him forget when he's been diced. What a joint!"

"They reckon there were a couple of bints here when we arrived. Reckon the boys used to pass 'em from unit to unit. It all sounds like bullo to me."

"Yeah. The Sixth Div. boys reckon they found the dead bodies of a couple of Eyetie harlots here when they took the place. What a break it would've been to have captured 'em alive. Or would it? I dunno."

"What you need right now is a harlot, Eyetie or any kind."

"I can't believe it. I simply can't believe it. She must be sick or she's found out she can't have a baby or something. I can't believe she's stopped loving me."

"Your vanity's hurt, and if you hurt a man's vanity you hurt a man deeply. She's not sick. She can have a baby. Pat, women are as unpredictable as the weather in a decent country. I don't know about the Greeks but the Arabs have a word for 'em. It's *magnoon*[1]. You just can't expect rational behaviour from a woman."

[1] Mad.

"I'll never expect anything from them again. I'm really disillusioned this time."

"Disillusionment is not the discovery that your girl no longer loves you but the realization that you do not mind very much," I said. "One of life's great mysteries is why all the finest women marry all the worst bastards, and stick to them through thick and thin. Their unpredictability is their greatest charm. They scratch your eyes out one minute and start taking off their scanties the next. Reminds me of an old joke. 'Mr Smithers, I give you exactly a quarter of an hour to get out of my room.'"

"I'll never have faith in anyone again. Never."

"I don't blame you, after this. People are no good, Pat. They're rotten. You know it now. But, like me, you'll come up for more. I'm continually amazed at the amount of punishment the human body and mind can take."

"But I still can't believe it. When we were in Palestine I wrote and told her that three fellers in B Company of the eight in one tent had been diced by their girls. She replied that she couldn't believe that anybody could be so despicable. And now——"

"She's a woman," I said. "That explains everything."

"But if you've got such a low opinion of women, what about Margaret? If she wrote and told you she had found someone else you wouldn't feel too bloody hot, would you?"

I made the initials "M.M." and "M.R." in the dirt at my feet. I did not say anything for a while. "I'm strong on theory," I said at last, "but weak on practice. If it did happen to me I know I'd wish I was dead; but then again I've wished I was dead over other girls, girls I wouldn't walk across the street to talk to now."

I thought of Doug sitting in his cave with his head in his hands, and Pat walking up and down, walking up and down with that look in his eyes.

The raid was over. It could not have been much of a raid.

"If a bomb drops on me tonight or I get killed next time I go out on patrol Pamela will get about £1000, which is what I'm worth as a corpse," said Pat, with a bitter laugh. "I wonder how she'd feel then?"

I remembered how I had made my will in Margaret's favour a few weeks after I entered camp, how I had made it out laboriously on the blue army form. The army had a form for everything. Even for dying.

Pat pulled a couple of letters out of his pocket. "Listen to this, Mick," he said. "Two days ago I wouldn't have read this to anybody. Now it doesn't matter. On January the sixth she wrote: 'I can't tell you how much I miss you. Sometimes I feel as though I can't bear this loneliness any longer. I have met no one whom I trust implicitly and love as I do you.' And on January the tenth: 'I didn't think it was possible to love you any more than I did when you left Australia, but that was mere infatuation to what I feel now, darling. I have planned my whole life, thinking of you. I can't bear this loneliness much longer, dear, so please God finish this war soon.' "

I jabbed the stone viciously into the dirt. "She couldn't bear the loneliness any longer," I said.

"And listen to this. On January the seventeenth she wrote: 'I know our marriage will be fine and loyal and blissfully happy. I love you, dear, more than anything else in the world. Darling, if you were married while you are away it would break my heart. It would break my very soul and life. We'll never hurt each other because we mean so much to be happy. I'll just have to look after our little home and wait for you to come home.' "

I jabbed the stone into the dirt again. A spasm of excruciating doubt seized me. Margaret was writing me letters like that. What would I do if Margaret—I had not had a letter lately, either. But no. I shook my head, and my doubts were gone. She could not do it. Not my Margaret.

"It's amazing," I said. "A month later she writes to tell you it's all over."

"I didn't get the letter. It must have gone west with that lot the sub. sank. Didn't hear from her so I sent a cable. I can't believe it. I just can't believe it. Diced in Tobruk."

"Tobruk or Greece or Palestine. It's the same the whole world over."

"But Mick. When I met her it was the most beautiful thing that ever happened. It was, really. But you wouldn't understand."

"No," I said, scraping the stone across the dirt. "I wouldn't understand."

"Do you know what I'm going to do?" said Pat suddenly. He leaned over and glared at me with shining eyes. "Next time I'm on patrol I'm going out and I'm going on and on till they get me."

I shook my head. "No," I said. "Don't be a bloody fool. It'd be funny if nobody got you and you had to surrender to their Corps Headquarters. You heard about the company commander—I forget which battalion—who took his company out the other night and made a sweep behind Jerry's front line? Came back with a couple of hundred prisoners. They reckon he'll get the D.S.O."

"I heard something about it. What of it?"

"Nothing. Just remembered it. Don't do it, Pat. What good would it do you? Things look pretty black now, but it'll be all right later. Time does heal, thank God."

Pat scraped a line in the dirt with his boot. "All right," he said. "I s'pose a man would be a fool to go and get himself killed over any girl."

"A bloody fool."

"All right. Do a favour, Mick?"

"Oh course. What is it?"

"Will you tell the boys for me? And they won't rock it into me, will they? I couldn't stand it."

"I'll tell them. And I'll see they don't say anything."

"Thanks. Some day I'll do the same for you."

I looked up with a grin. "Break that down," I said. "It's not going to happen to me." Then my grin faded. "Nothing's going to happen to me," I said defiantly.

Pat was walking up and down again, reading the letters. Suddenly he stopped in front of me and whipped something out of his pocket. I had seen it before. It was a school badge Pamela had given him.

He threw it down and ground it savagely into the dust with his heel.

"I swear to you, Mick," he said earnestly. "I swear to you by what little I've got left that I hold sacred that no girl's going to hurt me again."

I looked up at him as he towered over me in his dirty boots, his filthy shorts, with his brown chest bare and his face covered with stubble.

"If you really mean that," I said, "you really mean a great deal."

CHAPTER XXX

I AWOKE with a start and sat up quickly, my heart hammering for a moment. I had been lying in a sleeping bay. I was waiting for Clive and Jim to come back from patrol, and I was ashamed to find that I had gone to sleep. I could see a dim shape in the darkness.

"It's me—Lionel," said the platoon sergeant. "They've just sent a runner over. Harry's been out helping bring in the hot boxes and he's copped a bit of shrap. An air-burst. He's asking for you."

I put my hand wearily to my forehead and breathed out through my mouth, "Oh Christ," I said. "Is he bad?"

"Dunno," said Lionel, and I knew he was lying. You could always tell.

I got up, went down the passage, hit my head on the roof, climbed the iron rungs, went out through the manhole, through the reserve company lines and across the dirt and camel bush to B.H.Q. I was challenged twice but merely answered, "Mick Reynolds, C. Company. A cobber got knocked. Going to see him", and hurried on.

B.H.Q. was behind a ridge. It was a series of dugouts, and a few camouflaged tents dug in. It was a bad place because the enemy searched behind the ridge with shellfire nearly every day. Old Gutsache was going to change the position, but we were moving back to the Blue Line in a few days, so he did not bother.

The M.O., Captain Neil Hull, was waiting for me outside the R.A.P. "That you Mick?" he asked.

"Yeah. Bad?"

"Yes." He gave me some medical details.

"Which means?"

"Probably have to have both legs amputated. Can't tell yet."

I did not say anything. They brought Harry out on a stretcher and put him in an ambulance. I got in too.

"That you, Mick?" asked Harry in a faint voice.

"Yeah." I did not know what to say. Funny how a man could make apt quotations from dozens of authors, but when words really mattered he searched the cupboard of his mind and found it bare.

"Mick—this time—they got—me."

"Bullo," I said. "You'll be O.K."

"No. They got me. Doesn't mat—ter much. Didn't have much —to live for, I never—told—but—the wife left—me. I couldn't— keep off the—grog. I lied—to—you—too, Mick."

The ambulance was bumping over ruts, and I heard Harry groan.

"You never lied to anybody in your life, Harry."

"Yes I did. Lie—about why—I joined—up. Done me—bit last— time. Had a—gutful—too. Never wanted—it over—again—but me son—he joined up—an' I wanted—to be—near him—to see if—he was all—right. Ya see—we doan get—on too well together—me an' him. Will ya—tell him, Mick—for me? Wanter see—him before —wanter see him—2/87th—B Company. Name—of Jim."

"I'll tell him," I said.

"Thanks, Mick. Ya been—a good friend—right through. Dunno how—we'd all of—got along—without ya."

"Bullo," I said.

"If ya—ever have—a kid, Mick—doan rein him—in too hard."

"I'll remember," I said.

As soon as it was light I went out along the Derna Road, past the Eagle, a dead eagle tied to two posts near the food dump at the junction of the road to Fort Pilastrino, and found the 87th, which was in reserve. I asked a sentry for B Company and another for Jim Creege. "Fourth doover down on the left," he said. "He'll be spine bashing."

Jim was spine bashing. He had a furtive, shifty face. He looked at me suspiciously.

"Jim Creege?" I asked.

"Yeah. What's up?"

"Got a message for you, private."

"Christ, can't a bloke get some bloody sleep round here? Get it off ya chest."

I glanced at his mate, who was blinking sleepily at me. Then I looked back at Jim and wondered how this rat-faced youth could have been Harry's son."

"Get out of that doover," I said slowly, and something in my tone made him look at me sharply. He got to his feet and clambered out, muttering to himself. I led him away from the company lines, and then I turned and, looking him straight in the eye, I said, "Your father got hit last night. Pretty bad, too. Might lose both legs. Wants to see you."

A sneer twisted his lips and his eyes became hard. "Serve the old bastard right," he said. "Comin' spyin' on me."

I reached out with both hands and grasped him by the throat and into my arms there came a power I had never known before. I wanted to kill Jim Creege more than I had wanted to kill any German or Italian, even when I went in with the bayonet. I forced him down on to the ground, and when his face began to go purple I let him go. He lay there, clutching at his throat and choking.

"Next time," I said, "I won't let you go so soon," and I turned and went away.

That night Doug called me. "The three men from the reserve company are here," he said. "You can go now."

"I'll get Eddie and Pat," I said. We went out of the post and kept going until we came to the truck. Eddie drove. We did not say anything until we got to the town. Then I said, "Eddie, promise me something. Promise me you won't kill this bastard. I told Harry I'd look after him."

"Can't promise nothin'," said Eddie. "Try not to."

Pat and I waited in the darkness while Eddie went over to Jim's doover. We heard him say, "Private Creege? Ya wanted at B.H.Q."

"Who the bloody hell wants me?" asked Jim.

"The C.O. never tole me," said Eddie. "Musta forgot. Usually tells the runner everythin', too."

"Aw right," said Jim. "No need to be funny. I'm comin'."

When they came near us Eddie shoved a Luger in Jim's back and said, "One word outa ya, George, an' you're deader'n the Jerry I took this orf of."

"What the bloody hell's wrong with you?" asked Jim.

I stepped forward and grabbed him by the shoulder. "Shut up," I said, "and come on."

"So you're in this, too," snarled Jim. "I'm a wake-up now."

Eddie jabbed the Luger into his back. "Listen, mate," he said, "I'm just hopin' ya'll put on an act, that's all. Just put on an act. I never killed no Eyetie with greater bloody joy than I'll kill you."

Eddie and Jim climbed into the back of the truck. Pat drove. I sat next to him, but we did not speak. We got out at the hospital. "Listen," I said to Jim, "you're going in here and you're going to say you're sorry for all you've done. I think your father's still alive. He's staying alive to see you. You're going to say you're going back to live with him after the war. Got all that?"

"What if I doan say it?"

"If you don't say it," I said, "I'll give you my word you'll never say anything again."

Eddie jabbed the Luger into Jim's stomach. "Mate," he said, "in one way I hope you doan say it."

"I'll say it," said Jim quickly. "I'll say it all right."

He went into the hospital. We stood around in the darkness.

"Mick," said Eddie, "if Harry doan pull through can I give this bastard the works?"

"No," I said. "I promised Harry I'd look after him."

Jim came out, and we went over. "I done it," he said. "I tole him I was sorry I run away. Tole him I was sorry for everythin'. He tole me to find me mother when I got home and tell her he was sorry he got drunk so much. I said I would an' he said 'Good-o', an' to tell Mick 'Thanks for everythin'.'"

"I'll go in for a minute," I said.

"It's no use," wailed Jim, and started to sob. "He's dead."

I was glad it was dark. Eddie, Pat and I went back to the truck. Eddie got in the driver's seat, and Pat and I got in the front too. Eddie started the engine.

Jim came over. "Ya'll give me a lift back to me company, won't ya?" he blubbered.

"I'll give ya a lift under the ear," said Eddie, and he pushed him in the chest and sent him sprawling in the dust.

We drove off. Nobody said anything for a while. Then Eddie

said, "Doan know much about proverbs. More in yer line, Mick. But there's one, 'Like father like son'. Funny isn't it?"

"Yeah," I said. "Funny."

"God stiffen the bloody crows," said Eddie. "Medals doan do ya no good."

When we got out Pat said the first thing he had said all night. "Seems to me," he said, "that tonight we saw a real rat of Tobruk."

"Yeah," I said.

CHAPTER XXXI

I went into the cave. It was an immediate relief to get out of the stifling heat. I took off my slouch hat and used it as a fan. The sweat was pouring down my face.

"Ay, Mick," said Gordon, "Bluey brought a perv book back from Cairo with him."

I did not bother to ask which Bluey. Every fellow in the A.I.F. with ginger hair was called Bluey.

"One of those misguided, misinformed, misspelt mysterious paper things, I suppose," I said. "I remember one called *A Night in Paris*. An abortion of a thing. It had nothing to do with night and nothing to do with Paris. In blue type, evidently roneoed. Only about ten small pages."

"I don't know how you can read such things," said Clive. "They're absolutely disgusting."

"I dunno," I said. "They're amazing. As simple as a schoolboy's essay on the sunset. And, strangely enough, some of them are well written. Some of the fellows who write 'em really can write. They achieve what so many writers try so hard to do and fail— they give a vivid picture. Anyhow, a man's got to read something. Admittedly, they're not exactly the right thing for a place like this where, if a man feels carnal, there's ———— all he can do about it."

"It's not one of them," said Gordon, and I let the "them" pass. "This one's an example of American—American————"

"Pornography?"

"Yeah. That's it. Perving. It's *Saucy Stories* and it cost twenty-five cents, whatever that is. Would you like 'Purloined Passion', 'Conceited Virgin' or 'Wife Traders'?"

"President Roosevelt ought to stop them publishing such things," said Clive.

"Listen to this," said Gordon. "Wait till I find the perv parts. This is 'Lady Chaser'. Listen to this: 'He buried his head in the warm fragrance of her bosom.' So-and-so, so-and-so. It gets pervy again here. 'His hungry kisses were returned with passionate abandon, and while he could not see the lustrous curves which must have been revealed as he stripped off the silken underclothes'—he's turned off the light—'his hands could feel the rise and fall of the girl's charms; his fingers could feel the flawless quality of the skin; his very heart seemed to ache with longing as he felt the burning fire of his visitor's desires.'"

"Oh Jesus," said Eddie quietly. "Oh Jesus."

"Stop," said Jim.

"It's disgusting," said Clive, and went out.

"Wait a minute," said Gordon. "So-an-so, so-and-so. No, the rest's harmless. Let's try 'Conceited Virgin'. Christ! Look at this illustration of 'Broken Romance'. Underneath it says, 'Opening the door quietly, he found his wife and lover in a passionate embrace.' Wait a minute. Cripes, this is a story about a feller who finds his wife with another joker and puts them both in prison for ten years and tortures them. Finally he throws himself under a herd of wild elephants. Then 'his black-faced companion in sin' finds a 'mass of bloody pulp and matter'—that's what's left. Jesus, what a silly coot he was! If a girl ever diced me I wouldn't do anything like that. I'd just go on living the same way. I wouldn't give her the satisfaction of knowing I was hurt."

"That's sound enough in theory," I said. "I always remember someone saying, 'Dames are like buses. If you miss one you catch the next.' But it's always so hard when you miss one. It's so hard to get away from that fixation complex."

"Shut up and listen to this," said Gordon. "'His eyes slowly descended to her alluring bosom, where two plump jutting hillocks'—whacko!—'pushed proudly and stiffly forward beneath her grey dress. He shut his eyes for an instant, trying to blot out the sight of those tempting mounds. He opened them again—they were still there to taunt him, to tease his eager hands with their prominent erectness.'"

"Don't," said Jim. "You're killing me. I can't stand it. I was all right until ya started this. Never thought about sheilas."

"Christ, break it down, will ya?" said Eddie. "I'm just rememberin' I'm still a man."

"'Impulsively, uncontrollably, his left hand swiftly dropped inside her low neckline, slipped beneath a silk brassiere.'"

"Stop it! For Christ's sake——" wailed Eddie.

"She stops him, poor bastard," said Gordon. "Wait a minute till

I see. He grabs her, turns her over and—listen to this!—'raised her dress up to her slim waist, revealing her bare thighs, and a handkerchief size pair of filmy, pink silk panties.'"

"Panties," said Eddie. "Filmy, pink silk. Jesus, I'd forgotten there was such things."

"Christ," said Gordon. "He spanks her bare arse, calls her a 'damned prude' and a 'conceited virgin'."

"What happened then?" asked Jim.

"Thought you didn't want to listen," said Gordon. "She comes across. Turns it on like steam. She pulls her dress off. Listen to this. 'He saw her slender fingers unhook her scanty brassiere and toss it away from the prominent globes of her breasts. And, finally, he saw her glorious young body lying irresistibly nude across his lap.'"

"Can't stand it," said Eddie. "Just can't stand it." And, while the rest of us started to chant "Stars and Stripes Forever", he got up and went outside.

"'Her soft smooth arms slid about his neck,' and she says, 'I can see how much fun I missed by remaining a virgin. And I positively do not intend to be one any longer.'"

"Had a few virgins in me time," said Jim slowly, "but never one like that. It don't seem natural somehow. It was usually pretty tough goin' before they come across."

"Funny thing," I said, "but a virgin never forgets her first man. He has a place in her heart nobody else can fill."

"How dare you cold-bloodedly discuss this sacred question," said Gordon in mock annoyance. "Often thought how shocked sheilas'd be if they could only listen in for five minutes to the conversation of any group of men."

"I've often wondered how shocked men'd be if they could only listen in for five minutes to the conversation of any group of women," I said.

"Cripes," said Gordon. "Never thought of that. Listen to this though. So-and-so, so-and-so"—he skipped over the lines quickly— "'And, Renee concluded, quivering ecstatically to the touch of his daring hands, 'we're going to do something about it right now.' So-and-so, so-and-so. 'As there were no clothes to take from the lady'— lady, mind you—'his arms crept over her soft flesh, caressing the pink-tipped breasts, moulding her warm thighs and teaching her things that she had never before known of.'"

"Oh Jesus," said Jim, and Happy, who had not spoken before, said quietly, "I hope that's the end."

CHAPTER XXXII

"THE fellows who brought the rations up last night reckon Tobruk H.Q. was hit by a couple of thousand-pounders yesterday," I said. "It's in the town, near the harbour. In the Plaza Mussolini. There's only the shell of the building standing, they reckon. You can see the fins of a bomb sticking out of a road, too. An unexploded one, of course."

"Yeah?" said Eddie.

"Yeah," I said. "They reckon the Eyeties down at the hospital expected a blitz yesterday because it was Musso's birthday. We only had those three morning raids. None of 'em were much chop, apart from hitting H.Q. What's the date?"

"I dunno," said Eddie. "Hey," he called, "any of you mugs know the date?"

Nobody answered. We found out the date only when we had to put it on a letter.

"Wonder how old the old codger is?" said Eddie. "He certainly tried to come in on the grouter, didden he?"

"Yeah," I said. "He'll cop something for his corner before it's over. They sank a hospital ship a few days ago. And up at the hospital we're giving their M.Os anaesthetics for operations, too. We ought to let the bastards die. There's no theatre. Just take off arms and legs on a table."

"Ay, Mick," said Happy. "That was a pretty hot raid a few nights ago. Hit the workshops, too. D'ya reckon we'll get any worse than that?"

I looked at him. He was not laughing now. There was something new in his eyes, too. I realized suddenly that of us all he had changed the most. "I dunno," I said. "Christ only knows. It was pretty hot all right. Nobody got any sleep. I dunno. They might just be warming up. They've got the planes all right. Talking of raids reminds me. In case any of you get hit, I've got to check up on meat tickets."

"Mine are sweet," said Pat, looking down to where his red and green identity disks hung on his sunburnt chest.

"What blood group?" I asked.

Pat turned the round one over. "O4," he said.

I checked the others. All except Eddie. I turned to him. "And yours, Alphonse?" I asked.

There was something strange in his eyes, something furtive. "Mine're jake, too," he said. "Me blood group's A2. Doncher remember? Same as yours." Our eyes met for a moment and then I smiled and looked away. I was glad to know that if ever the time came for someone to give me his blood it would be Eddie Wilson. "I remember," I said.

"By the way," I said. "Why aren't you wearing 'em? I've been meaning to speak to you about it."

Eddie looked away. "They're in me haversack," he said. "They're O.K."

"Listen, Eddie," I said quietly. "These disks are important. You know that. Say you get knocked on patrol or by a bomb splinter and need a transfusion, and your disks are in your haversack. By the time we get the disks out to see your blood group you mightn't need a bloody transfusion. Your blood might have stopped running."

"He's right, Eddie," said Pat.

Eddie turned on him in swift anger. "Keep outa this!" he cried. "Mind ya own bloody business, will ya?"

Everybody stared at Eddie in amazement. Then Pat shrugged his bare shoulders. "*Mahlish*," he said, "if that's how it is. If you want to go and get yourself killed, well *mahlish*." And he turned and walked away. The others went away, too.

"Listen, Eddie," I said quietly. "Don't lets lose our tempers over a simple thing like this. I'm asking you to wear your disks. If you won't do it when I ask you I'll have to order you, that's all."

I looked into his eyes, and his gaze wavered and he looked away. "Do me a favour, Mick, will ya?" he said at last. "Doan make me wear 'em. Ya know me group's A2."

"Yes, I know," I said, "but I might forget. Or I might get knocked, too. We can't afford to take any risks."

"All right, Mick," he said reluctantly. "I'll wear 'em in future."

"You'll wear them now," I said.

He looked up at me, and I saw again that strange furtive look in his eyes.

"Now," I said.

He turned and went down the passage to the air-raid shelter. I waited till he came back, trying to puzzle it out. He was wearing the disks. He went up to near the end of the post, and then he turned and faced me. "Are you satisfied now?" he asked defiantly.

"No," I said. "Give me a look at those disks." I reached out for them, but he backed away, and I saw fear in his eyes.

"No, Mick," he said in a strained voice. "No. Don't touch 'em!"

"You're hiding something from me," I said. "By Christ, they're not your disks! Give me a look at them!"

"They're mine, Mick!" he cried. "I tell ya they're mine! For Christ's sake take my word for it! I tell ya they're mine!"

"There's something wrong here," I said. "Eddie," I said slowly, "I'm ordering you to show me those disks! And, by Christ, if you don't I'll report it to Doug. Show—me—those—disks!"

His mouth was working, and he licked his lips. "I won't!" he cried defiantly. "I won't!" And then suddenly his will collapsed and he held the disks out to me. His hand was trembling.

They were his disks all right. I turned the green octagon one over, and then I knew. In big letters across it was the word "Bleeder".

I looked up at him. He had his right thumb in his mouth and his whole arm was trembling. I waited till I got my voice back. "You know what this means?" I said at last.

"Yeah," he said, without taking his thumb away.

"It means," I said slowly, "that you're a haemophilic, that if you get knocked by a bullet or a piece of shrapnel you won't have a dog's chance. Your life will just run away into the dust."

He took his thumb away. "I know," he said.

"But how did you get into the infantry?" I asked incredulously. "How did you do it?"

"Wangled it. Went inter brigade headquarters at first as a driver, an' later, when they'd forgotten, I transferred. I wanted ter fight."

"Oh. You know what it means, too? It means that you've got to get out of this battalion, that you might have to get out of Tobruk."

He reached out and took me by both shoulders. I looked up from the disks and saw his eyes blazing into mine. "No! no!" he cried. "Ya can't do it, Mick. You know what we swore, back in Ingleburn Camp. That we woulden be like other sections, we woulden split up. Well, we've all kept our word, even Clive, an' by Christ, I'm goin' ter keep mine!"

I looked away. "I'm sorry, Eddie," I said at last. "I can't do it. If anything happened to you I'd never forgive myself." I looked up at him, and then looked down into the dust at our feet again.

"But, Mick, ya must help me. I can't leave the section. I can't leave ya. I won't leave ya. Ya can't ask me ter do that. We swore, back in Ingleburn Camp, we'd stick together, no matter what happened. Ya swore it too."

I looked at him again, and in my sigh there was all my hatred of Tobruk, all my despair, all my anxiety about my responsibilities. It was too much to bear, too much to ask any man to hold another man's life in his hand, but it was happening every day. Lieutenants controlled the lives of tens, captains the lives of scores, lieutenant-colonels the lives of hundreds, generals the lives of thousands. Human life, nurtured so gently in peace, was thrown away as if it were grains of sand.

"I can't do it," I said at last. "It's too much to ask me. I'm sorry
I ever became a corporal. I'm worried stiff now with my great
little responsibility. Christ, Eddie, if anything happened to you
I'd never sleep easy again."

Eddie tightened his grip on my shoulders. "Mick," he said, "ya
me mate. I've lived with ya an' I've fought with ya, I've been drunk
with ya and I've laid in the dust with ya when we didden know if
we'd be alive a second later. I've gone in with the bayonet with ya.
An' I tell ya, now, as God is me witness, that if ya report this I'll
never speak to ya again as long as I live, that as long as I live I'll
hate the name of Mick Reynolds. An' if ya do this ter me I swear
I won't live long ter hate ya. First chance I get I'll take a rifle
an' I'll go out into them Jerry lines an' I'll go on till they get me.
But, by Christ, I'll get a few er them bastards first!"

I looked into his eyes and I knew he was speaking the truth. I
did not say anything.

"Ya'll do it, Mick?" he asked desperately. "Ya won't say
nothin'?"

I knew suddenly that if Eddie Wilson died I would never leave
Tobruk because I would know in my heart that I had killed him.
This was the world our forefathers had given us, a world in which
men pleaded for a chance to die.

I nodded my head wearily. "All right," I said. "I won't say
anything."

I saw the relief come flooding into his face.

"There's one thing I must tell you," I said. "You're the bravest
man I've ever known."

"Bullo," he said awkwardly. And then a strange thing happened.
Blood seeped up into his sunburnt, hard-bitten face. Eddie Wilson
was blushing.

CHAPTER XXXIII

"Eddie," I said, "like to come for a stroll over to the 54th to see
George?"

"No thanks, Mick. Do you reckon Jean has the best brace and
bits?"

"Doing a bit of perving again?" I asked, looking at the gallery
of nudes he had gathered from all sorts of magazines. There were
thirty-five of them. Eddie had them pinned on a sheet of cardboard

leaning against the side of our dugout, and there was a sign over the top—WILSON'S PERV GALLERY. Soldiers came from all over Tobruk to see them.

There were slim women, normal women, buxom women. Eddie had given them all names and still spent most of his spare time trying to decide the eternal question about the best one to sleep with. I did not look at them much. I could not stand it.

"I don't know," I said. "What about this one?" I pointed to a strapping wench with her shoulders thrown back and her breasts thrust forward. "She flaunts her breasts in front of her like a banner," I said. "The morals and morale of this section haven't been the same since you started this perv gallery. We never feel that way until we see these gorgeous creatures. What's her name?"

"That's Eunice. She's got pretty good tit for tats, hasn't she?"

"Most of 'em have a pretty decent sort of an upper deck," I said. "It's woman's most valuable visible asset. It's the tangible manifestation of feminity."

"What?"

"*Mahlish.* See you later."

A khamsin was blowing. I could not see more than a few yards. A pair of anti-gas shields protected my eyes, but the dust got into my nostrils, mouth and hair, and down my shirt and into my boots. It was impossible to escape it. The fine particles were driven against me by a wind that was like a blast from a furnace.

I found my way to George's doover after trudging about in the dust for half an hour. His company had come out of the line last night and I knew he would be in his old home in the sand. It was bigger than the usual two-man one, and four lived in it.

I went in. It was darker inside, but not so hot, and for a while I could not see anything. I took off my eye shields and looked around. There were three fellows there. One of them said "G'day, Mick", and I said, "Good day, Rat."

I sat down against the wall, and took my hat off. My hair was full of dust, and I could feel it in my ears, my eyes and against my chest.

"Where's George?" I asked.

Nobody spoke. Skinny Johnson shifted his feet. Hughie Fitzgerald got up and went out into the khamsin. I watched him go. That's funny, I thought. He went out without a hat.

"Where's George?" I asked again, and this time my voice was louder than I intended it to be.

"He's—he's not here," said Skinny.

"You silly bastard!" I cried. "Anybody can see that. Where is he?"

Skinny did not answer, and I was about to ask him what the bloody hell was wrong with him when Jack Halliday got up and went out. I stared after him stupidly. Had all the section gone mad, or was walking about in a khamsin without hats and eye shields part of some new joke? Had I done anything to offend them? Nothing could have happened to George because I had seen him three days ago, gone up to his post through the reserve company's lines in the darkness and had a good yarn, and he had told me he was not on patrol the next night either.

Skinny cleared his throat nervously. I got up, went over, grabbed him by the front of his shirt, pulled him to his feet and said slowly "Skinny, tell me when George will be back or, by Christ, I'll knock your bloody head off!"

Words came gushing from him so fast it seemed that they were pressing insistently against his lips.

"He won't be back, Mick. He'll never be back. They got him on patrol the night before last. He took Merv's place when Merv got crook. The padre dug his grave for him yesterday morning. Up in the cemetery it was. Dug it himself, he did. In the khamsin, too. Nobody was game to take a message to ya." His tone was close to hysteria. I let him go, and he slumped down on his blankets.

I went back and sat against the wall. We had to be ready to defend as well as attack and only a couple of men could be spared from each section each night. The others waited for their mates to come back, and sometimes they did not come.

War has been described as ninety-five per cent waiting and about five per cent fighting. This waiting was the worst of all, this waiting through the night for your friends to come back. Sometimes the patrol was late getting back or the firing out in front was more intense than usual, and then nerves became frayed, talk almost ceased, and the closest mates found themselves being abrupt with each other.

And when the shots were fired by the protective patrol, the shots indicating that the main patrol was coming in, you held your breath and you hoped, and if you believed in God you prayed.

Then you heard them coming across the anti-tank ditch and through the gap in the wire and you might hear a man's voice or his laugh and your heart leapt and you wiped your forehead with a clammy hand and were happy again. But if you heard the others speak and did not hear him you waited there in the darkness until they came into the post, and you peered at them, looking quickly from one to another, and then you saw the blurred outline of a face you knew so well and you were glad because it was dark and he could not see the look in your eyes.

And sometimes he would say, "Yeah, Eustace. It's me. Ya doan think them Jerry bastards are smart enough to get me, do ya?" and laugh, and you would laugh, too, a short awkward laugh.

I shook these thoughts off. I could hear the fine dust rattling against the doorway and seeping down into the dugout. I could hear our twenty-five pounders booming in the distance. Fancy firing in weather like this! I thought. Oh well, it was just as good a day as any other for killing people. The driving sand would probably bury the bodies before you could dig a grave. I felt for something to get my hands on to. I picked up a spoon from a mess tin and began to twist it in my hands. Skinny was talking again. I had better listen.

". . . found it that night after a helluva lotta trouble, but it was too late to do anythin' so we went back the next night to clean it up. We were nearly there when we heard a desert bird cry to the right. Ya know them birds, Mick?"

I did not say anything. I could see George pulling in a fish at Lake Carraday with the confident prediction, "It's a squire this time," and I could see his crestfallen stare when it was a trumpeter again. I could see despair breaking through when I hooked my drive again on the third tee at the Grosvenor Club. I could see his embarrassment when I gave him *The Fortunes of Richard Mahony*, the greatest Australian novel, for Christmas. "You shouldn't have done that, lad," he said.

It was funny how you remembered the little things about a man —how he looked when he smiled, the way he drank a mug of beer, his taste in ties.

"Well," said Skinny, "we went on and then we heard another bird, to the left this time. Then we heard another bird in front. Even then we weren't awake-up. It was a signal all right, for the bastards opened up on us with everythin' they had. They blew hell out of us with artillery, mortars, machine-guns and every bloody thing. Only me an' another joker got out alive. George—well George didn't."

I was turning the spoon over and over in my hands. I could see George waking me from a drunken sleep in his room in Nerridale and telling me that he had rung my mother the night before and told her I was staying with him. I could see him telling me that he would never go to a war, that it was men like me who made wars. I could see the look on his face in his room when I was on final leave, and I could hear him saying, "That's all you understand. Force." There was another thing he had said, too. "There's nothing romantic about a shell splinter in the guts, Mick. There's nothing romantic about that."

"Oh Christ!" cried Skinny. "Why didden they get me, too? They got Ossie an' Mark an' Eric an' Cliff. Why didden they get me, too?"

I did not speak. I had bent the spoon out of shape between my hands. I could see Harry Courtenay leaning over the counter of his hamburger shop. I could see his pale blue eyes gleaming through his glasses and I could hear him saying, "If you join the infantry, Mick, for Christ's sake don't make any friends. It's easier if you don't make any friends."

What could a man do? You couldn't live and growl and curse and sweat and march and laugh and fight with a group of soldiers, live under the same canvas, fight in the same trench with them, shelter from death in the same hole, without making them your friends. For that was the only decent thing any man ever got out of war—fellowship. You wished to hell you could regard them as strangers, but you couldn't.

"I know," said Skinny. "I know what ya thinkin'. I was a silly bastard not to be awake-up to their game. We all were. We heard them birds whistle and we didden do nothin' about it."

I did not say anything.

"Ya doan blame me, Mick?" he asked suddenly, urgently.

I looked up at him slowly. He was leaning forward, and his hands were pressed against the dirt floor.

"Tell me ya doan blame me, Mick," he said. "For Christ's sake say somethin', will ya?"

"I don't blame anybody, Skinny," I said. "It was just bad luck, that's all."

I dropped the twisted spoon and it clattered faintly on the ground. I got up and went out into the khamsin. The dust was thicker than ever, and a scorching wind drove it into my face. The bare waste of Tobruk was blotted out by it.

I fought my way towards my section. Eddie and Gordon and Clive and Pat and Jim were still alive, thank God—so far.

But were they? I could hear the sound of shelling coming from our sector. I bent lower and hurried on, stumbling through the dust.

CHAPTER XXXIV

As I tramped through the driving dust I realized that I did not believe I could go on much longer. A few weeks ago they had got Harry, a few days ago Happy had killed himself, the night before last they had got George, and soon they would get us. I blamed myself for Happy's death. I had noticed that he had been transformed into a brooding introvert, but I had done nothing about it. One day we heard six shots in quick succession. We ran over to his doover and he was lying there, dead, with a Luger in his hand. Evidently he had pulled his head away the first five times, for there were five bullet holes in the wall. That night Eddie said to me, "Ya know, Mick, his old woman'll think he died a hero." "Mothers always do," I said.

I was down as low as I had ever been. There had been no letters for me in the last two mails and I was worrying about Margaret. A friend had written to tell me she had pneumonia. A cheerful sort of a correspondent he was, the sort of fellow who believed in keeping up the morale of the troops. The day before we came out of the Red Line into a reserve position the enemy bombers switched from the harbour to the perimeter. It was the worst bombing we had ever known, and God knows we had had some bad ones. For two hours they gave us everything they had—high-level bombing, dive-bombing and strafing—and all we could do was huddle in our holes and take it. The men on the Bren guns did what they could, but it was hopeless. There is nothing so bad as that feeling of impotence you know when you cannot hit back, for then you have time to think. We just huddled in our holes, and perhaps some of us prayed.

If you could take the noise out of war you could take away much of its horror, too—the whistle and scream of bombs, the sinister swish of mortars, the staccato repetition of machine-guns, the smashing crash of explosions. For two hours they attacked the perimeter posts. The result was two men wounded and a ninety per cent slump in morale.

My old frustration of the Nerridale days was nothing to the feeling I had now as I fought my way through the khamsin. This time I felt I was doomed physically. My mental stagnation was allied with fear. It was too much for flesh and blood to stand. We were trapped like the rats Lord Haw-Haw called us. We were in the Germans' trap, and they sat out there in the desert gloating over our inevitable doom. Help had been so long coming that it would never come. Any day now they would make a third attempt on Tobruk, with an overwhelming mass of tanks this time, and we would go down fighting—if we were stupid enough to fight.

The horror of Greece had been superseded by the horror of Crete, where death came from the sky, where armed men fell like rain. My friends had died in Crete as they had died in Greece and were dying in Tobruk and Syria.

We could not win the war. I was certain of that now. Germany was too powerful, too well prepared, and Britain was alone again. Greece and Yugoslavia had tried to help and had been slain. It was no use going on. Why didn't Churchill give in? Why didn't he stop this murder? If the Nazis owned the world there would be no wars; they could not fight themselves. Perhaps they would make a better job of it than we had, with our poverty and slums. And now George was dead, George who was with me the day I met Margaret.

Eddie was waiting for me in the driving dust outside the dugout. "Doan say nothin' to Clive," he said, wiping the sweat wearily from his forehead. "He's just got the drum his brother was killed in Crete."

"Oh Christ," I said. I could not fight against this overwhelming series of misfortunes. It was too much to bear. I went into the dugout. It was remarkably big. Practically everywhere in Tobruk there is rock just under the surface, but here we had found a softer spot and we had made a big dugout because we wanted to be together. The only light came from a hurricane lamp. Clive was sitting in a corner with his head in his hands. He was staring through the wall, staring back to the Australia he had known so long ago—before the war. I did not say anything. I knew what so many millions of people will never learn—that sympathy cannot be proferred in words, that if you are a man's friend you do not have to tell him you are sorry.

Gordon was lying on his side on his blankets, tracing figures moodily in the dust. Jim was leaning against the wall with his slouch hat pulled down over his eyes. Pat was lying on his back with his hands under his head. I could see his lips moving, but he was not speaking aloud. I could read the words. He was cursing the Germans, cursing them over and over again.

Nobody looked up when Eddie and I came in. I could not tell them about George now. They were down. They were just as far down as I was. I sat down on my blankets, and Eddie slumped down on his. We were through, the whole bloody lot of us. Eddie did not even glance at Wilson's Perv Gallery.

"They killed my brother," said Clive suddenly. And then over and over again he said, "They killed my brother." I had expected anger or grief or defiance or fear, but not this utter hopelessness. In it was mirrored the general conviction of the inevitability of our own doom.

I got up, went over and shook his shoulder gently. He looked up. I shook my head and he stopped.

Pat sat up. "They'll get us all, too," he said, "every bloody one

of us. They're too good for us. Only a silly bastard won't admit
when he's beaten."

The others were looking up, too, now, and I saw that awful hopelessness in their eyes. I looked away.

Gordon stopped tracing figures in the dust. "They'll get us, too,"
he said, "One by one. What's the use of my ability if I'm dead? A
dead man can't make smash. We'll never leave Tobruk alive."

"That's right," said Jim quietly. "Why did we ever bloody well
enlist at all? We can't beat these bastards. They're too good for us.
It's no use going on like this."

"I hate to say it, but all of yous are right," said Eddie. It was the
first time I had ever heard him agree with Jim. "We're buggered.
It's just heat an' flies an' bombs an' ya mates gettin' knocked, day
after day, month in month out. I doan mind a fair fight, but this
ain't no fair fight. Hitler's got the game sewn up.

"It's always the same," he continued. "No bloody planes. God
stiffen the bleedin' crows, the bloody war's been goin' on two years
now. No planes in Greece, no planes in Crete, no planes in Tobruk.
What the hell do they do with their bloody planes? I'll tell ya
what they do. They save 'em up in England for the invasion that'll
never come, while we sit here in our holes in Tobruk like the
rats we are an' take it just as the Diggers and Kiwis took it in
Greece and Crete. Those bog-bred bastards in England think only
of themselves. Let the poor bloody Dominions do all the fightin'.
It's the old army sayin', 'Bugger you, George, I'm all right.'" He
glared around. "What d'ya think, Mick?"

I wiped the sweat and dust off my face with the same weary
movement Eddie had used. Their heads swung round to me. I knew
they were right. I was about to tell them so when I remembered
something. In a flash of clear perception I realized that in this
dugout there was starting something that might sweep Tobruk. It
was the first crack in the wall of Tobruk's morale. It was what
the Germans wanted.

I realized, too, that it was only unusually sustained bad luck, a
series of quick calamities, that had got us down so low; that packed
into a few days had come more bad news than we would probably
experience in the whole of our time here. I realized, too, that I was
their corporal, that I was responsible for morale, and that if I did
not get them out of this depression anything might happen. They
would be murdered on patrol with their nerves gone and that
utter hopelessness in their eyes. There was only one thing to do:
I had to taunt them into fighting back.

"What d'ya think, Mick?" asked Eddie again.

I felt my head come up and my shoulders come square, and I

let them have it. "I think you're a lot of yellow rats," I said. "Lord Haw-Haw said you were rats, and by Christ he was right! And not only because you live in holes. And I called you all my friends! Why, there's not threepenn'orth of guts in the whole bloody lot of you."

They were gaping at me. I saw their jaws drop and their mouths come open as if they were a lot of marionettes.

"You give me a touch of 'em," I said, jumping to my feet and striding up and down. "So you can't take it, eh? Just because things aren't so hot you drop your bundles and talk a lot of rot about losing the war. Well, let me tell you this. It'll take more than a few Aussies dropping their bloody bundles to beat Britain. Let me tell you this, my fine feathered friends—there'll always be an England whether you bastards drop your bundles or not!"

"But, Mick——" said Eddie, "the Eyeties aren't much chop, but these bloody Jerries are good. It's all bullo that they're starvin' or feelin' the heat. Ya know as well as I do that the prisoners we've taken are as fit as Christ. Ya know they've got fresh brown bread wrapped in cellophane, an' Nestles chocolate. Ya know they can take the heat as well as we can. The bastards 've been trained in hot houses, an' they're *magnoon* blokes who think it's an honour to die for their Fuehrer. We can't beat men like that."

"You poor misguided bastards!" I cried. "We don't have to beat them here. We've got to hold on, that's all. Just hold on, and the victory is ours. We only know one thing—that they can't beat us despite all their planes and all their bombs and all their tanks. They'll never take Tobruk. This is the test that has shown the world can be saved. If they were supermen they'd overwhelm us; but they're not supermen and we're the first people in the world who've proved it."

I looked at them eagerly, but that hopelessness was still in their eyes.

"What've we got to hope for?" said Jim slowly. "A man's just a crumpet. That's what he is, a crumpet. We're fighting for democracy, I suppose. Oh yeah? That's why you can't buy a whisky in Tel Aviv if you're not a sergeant. Democracy, eh?"

"That's why so many cabarets in Cairo are for officers only, and you can't get into Shepheard's Hotel, the swankiest in the Middle East, if you haven't got pips," said Gordon. "A machine-gunner in the Northumberland Fusiliers told me there's eleven hundred officers at G.H.Q. in Cairo, that there's a major and a sergeant whose only job is to look after the bloody clocks. The rotten bludgers. And we're here in Tobruk fighting for them."

"Listen," I said, "I know what you say is true; but remember this

—we're fighting, not only for ourselves, not only for bludgers at
G.H.Q., but for humanity. We're fighting a tyrant who wants to
dominate the world. By holding Tobruk, by killing Jerries out on
patrol, we're hitting back at Hitler, we're striking a blow for
civilization, for all that decent men hold dear."

"You're right, Mick," said Clive, and I glanced at him quickly.
I could see his eyes gleaming through the gloom. I remembered
that this was the only line to use to win him over, yet I was amazed
that it could get him when he had just heard of his brother's
death. Good old Clive! Why, the little fellow had more guts than
all the rest of them after all.

He jumped to his feet, and then it was Clive and I against the
rest.

"Mick's right," he said. "We ought to be grateful we're in Tobruk.
What has Hitler brought to the nations he's conquered by his shame-
less aggression? Nothing but misery and devastation and bondage.
A dreadful weight of wretchedness has settled on the conquered
peoples, but it has not broken their spirit; and some day the huge
mass of hatred Hitler has built up for himself will overflow and
overwhelm him. They can well say with Macduff:

> O nation miserable,
> With an untitled tyrant bloody-scepter'd,
> When shalt thou see thy wholesome days again?"

"Yes," I said, "and

> Blood and destruction shall be so in use
> And dreadful objects so familiar
> That mothers shall but smile when they behold
> Their infants quarter'd with the hands of war;
> All pity choked with custom of fell deeds."

"You're clever, aren't you?" sneered Gordon, but I knew that
he was hurt. They all were.

"And listen to what Rupert Brooke wrote in nineteen fourteen,"
I said. "He died in the Aegean while he was with the British
Mediterranean Expeditionary Force. See if this will inspire you to
find the guts he had." And I began:

> "If I should die, think only this of me:
> That there's some corner of a foreign field
> That is for ever England."

and went on to the end.

Nobody spoke. Outside I could hear the distant rumble of artillery
fire. I wondered again why they were wasting ammunition on a
day like this. The faint swishing of the dust could be heard, too,
as it came through the dugout door. Nobody spoke.

We had them! I could see the anger in their eyes and the spirit coming back into them as the light came when the sun slid up over the bare rim of Tobruk. Sweat was pouring down my face, and there was a throbbing exultation in my heart. You cannot live with men for months without knowing them, and I knew we had them going. It hurt to do it, but we were making them ashamed.

"We're men," said Eddie, leaning forward defiantly and glaring at me, "an' we gotta right to live like men, not like rats stayin' in our holes."

"Men?" I cried. "They were men who fought in Poland, men who went singing down the streets of Dunkirk, men who, from sheer exhaustion, had to be lifted back into their planes in the Battle for Britain when they saved the world. They were men who went from the burning desert of Libya to the snowy mountains of Greece, and they were men who stood in Crete, defying death that dropped on them from the sky. Guts! Have you ever heard of guts! It's what the women and children of London had when hundreds of Jerry planes came over and smashed their homes. They were men then, and, by Christ, that's more than you are!"

"Listen, Mick," said Eddie, leaning forward so that his face was thrust into mine, "if ya weren't me mate I'd push ya bloody face in." He tapped me on the shoulder. "I'm givin' ya the drum now. Break it down, Mick. For Christ's sake break it down. There's no other bastard in the world can talk to me like that. For Christ's sake break it down or I'll lose me grip on meself. I'm tellin' ya now. Break it down, see."

"Earn my respect, then," I said. "Don't plead for it. Why, you're Morshead's men. You're the Rats of Tobruk."

I pointed to Wilson's Perv Gallery and I saw Eddie's head turn sideways and the old longing come back into his eyes. "They're worth fighting for, aren't they? There are girls like that waiting for you when you get out of here. Girls like that in Alex. and Cairo, and girls in Australia just waiting to turn it on for the 'heroes of Tobruk'."

"By Christ, you're right!" cried Eddie, and his eyes were glistening.

"Listen, Eddie," I said, and I could feel my heart pounding. I had him. I had him. "They've got you down. The bloody Jerries are just too good for you. They've got more guts than you have. You said so yourself."

"I never said it!" he cried. "It took guts to dong them two big M.Ps the night A Company stacked on a blue in Tel Aviv, didden it? You seen me do 'em over. That took guts, didden it?"

"Yes," I said, "that took guts." I remembered what a Tommy

commando had told me when he came back from a patrol with
Eddie. I had dysentery, and it was the only patrol I had missed
with Eddie.

"Blimey," said the commando. "You mookin' Aussies are mookin'
daft luds. We go out, me and the big bloke, and we destroy the
objective, like we was told to, and then the big Aussie, 'e says,
'There's a machine-gun nest over there,' 'e says. 'Let's do bastard
oop.' And ——— me if he doesn't get stook into it with grenades
and then 'e goes in with the bayonet and cleans oop the survivors,
and I 'as to go in with 'im, too. 'E woulda got V.C. if officer 'ad
seen 'im. No more for mine, choom. I stick to me commandos. You
mookin' Aussies are mookin' daft, lud." And, shaking his head,
he went away.

But Eddie did not mention this now. He mentioned instead the
night he did over the M.Ps in the blue in Tel Aviv.

"Eddie," I said, "you like laying off with girls better than
anything in the world, don't you?"

"Well, what if I do?"

"It's O.K. It's your life and if that's your way to live it nobody's
got the right to tell you what you should do. To do it, though,
you've got to get out of here, you've got to stop those Jerries getting
in. And what about your daughter? You want to see her, don't
you?"

Eddie ran a hand through his untidy hair. "Yeah," he said. "I
been thinkin' a lot about the kid lately. I doan like kids when they're
only a few months old. Ugly little codgers. Like a lotta red beetroot,
and always squawkin'. But young Alice—she tells me she was goin'
to call her Alice if it's a girl and Eddie if it's a boy—will be pretty
well grown outa this when I get home. You know, Mick, there's
somethin' to havin' a kid, even if it's not yer own. Not all yer own,
I mean. See, I gotta kid, but not much responsibility. I just gotta
see its old man—the bloke what thinks he's its old man, I mean
—don't neglect it. I'm not crooked on ya no more, Mick. I'm just
crooked on that bastard Hitler for keepin' me in this bloody place
without lettin' me get home to see me own kid."

That was the second off the list. I turned to Jim. "Jim," I said,
"you used to tell me how beautiful it was at Wattle Creek in
the early morning when you were bringing the cows in; how the
green fields were wet with dew and that old kookaburra used to
laugh at you every morning."

Jim looked up from rolling a cigarette. "Yeah," he said gruffly.
He paused, then went on slowly, "I'm not much of a hand at
apologizin', Mick—reckon I go better with a plough—but I'm

tellin' ya I'm sorry. Mr Hitler had us on the run for a while and we thought we was beat. We doan think so now."

"Thanks, Jim," I said.

I turned to Gordon. "Well?" I asked. "Think you can make smash in hell?"

He grinned. "As long as Harday retains his health and strength Harday can make smash anywhere," he said. "A fit Harday is a formidable Harday."

"You've got the world in front of you," I said. "You reckon you're good. Well if you are and you leave Tobruk a 'fit Harday' nothing should stop you. And 'hero of Tobruk' should amass smash, particularly a fellow like you who will exploit it so ruthlessly."

"A Harday does not need Tobruk to help him amass smash," he said. "A Harday just amasses smash naturally."

"I gather that you've ceased belly-aching?"

"I am seriously displeased. A Harday never belly-aches. A Harday never had anything so crude as a belly."

"All right, all right. Come back to the field. You're not still crooked on Tobruk?"

"Tobruk to me is just an unfortunate incident, a pause in the Harday career. If I voiced my displeasure on this occasion, I withdraw it and express regret."

"Oh Christ!" I said, and somebody cried, "Shut the poor misguided bastard up."

There was only Pat left. I thought that wild Irish spirit might still be holding out, glorying in a lone cause. I looked at him in the dim lamp-light. "Well," I said, "Are you through or are you still back in the dark and afraid of it?"

Pat scratched his head. "My grandfather died because he fought the Black and Tans," he said, "so I s'pose if it was good enough for him to fight against injustice I won't be a grape on the business. Anyway, I'm beginning to believe that the Jerries out there are an even lower lot of bog-bred bastards than the bloody Black and Tans."

"That's an admission, coming from you," I said.

"You know what got me, Mick," said Pat. "It was that feller Rupert Brooke. I reckon he must have been a pretty decent sort of bloke."

"He was," I said, "but women gave him hell."

There was a chorus of questions, and I knew my section had come back from the abyss. "Some other time," I said.

"Hey," said Eddie suddenly. "I want to go on patrol as soon as we get back to the Red Line. I want to get this war over."

"Me, too," said Gordon.

"Corporal," said Jim, "I'm making an official application."

Clive made a sign to me, and I put my eye shields on and went outside with him, leaving them arguing about who was going on patrol. The dust was being driven harder now and the scorching intensity of the heat had increased. Clive took me by the elbow and we stopped. He had forgotten his hat, and I saw the dust gathering in his hair and moustache.

"Mick," he said, looking up at me earnestly through his eye shields, "I want to tell you how sorry I am for what happened today. I'm ashamed of myself. I'm sorry I was weak. You were right. I'm not really tough enough for the infantry."

I could not speak for a while. "Forget it, Clive," I said at last. "Forget it. You're tough, all right. Much tougher than I ever thought you would be. You're a man, Clive, and I'm glad to have had you as my friend."

He shook his head, and the fine dust shot out of his hair and joined the driving particles.

"No, Mick," he said. "The war has taught me how many better men than me there are. I wish I were as tough as you. You're never afraid. You're like a great oak-tree. Nothing ever disturbs or frightens you. You're strong."

I stared at him. I remembered all the nights I had lain in my hole and shivered with fear as planes droned overhead and the bombs came whistling down, how many times my heart had pounded in my chest, how, that first night, I had come back from patrol with my shirt wet with the sweat of fear.

I could not say anything.

"You were marvellous, the way you spoke, Mick. You made me feel so ashamed."

Christ, he had believed all that rot. He had believed it, with months of dirt and dust and horror in Tobruk behind him and his brother lying dead in Crete.

"You made me feel ashamed of my poor selfish fears," he said earnestly. "I'll never forget what you did for me today. Now I'm going over to the A.S.C. to see if I can get the boys a drink. They've rigged up a distillery out of the radiator of an old truck."

I watched him as, without a hat, he disappeared into the driving dust, his slim body bent against the wind. And *he* thought *I* was brave. Why the little fellow had more guts than the whole lot of us.

I had brought them back from the abyss, bolstered up their flagging morale. I wondered desperately what I could do to bolster up my own.

I kicked a stone savagely out of my way and went back into the dugout.

CHAPTER XXXV

Most of our posts in the Salient were just holes in the ground. All the enemy had achieved in his two big attacks in April and the beginning of May was the capture of the old Italian concrete perimeter posts, which meant that we had to man what were originally supporting posts scraped hurriedly out of the rocky earth of Tobruk. Some of them were only big enough to hold a section. They were the liveliest places in Tobruk, for although the enemy lines were over four thousand yards apart in other sectors, in the Salient they were less than two hundred.

Neither side would have been able to man the Salient forward posts if there had been no unofficial truce each night so that the rations could be brought up. It was curious. At ten o'clock each night both sides ceased firing, and for the next two hours an eerie silence settled over the area. Each side could hear the other's ration trucks driving up, but they held their fire, for a man must eat, even in war. Then, at midnight, after the hotboxes had been brought up full and taken away empty, one of the boys would say, "It's on again. Might as well show them Jerry bastards we're still fair dinkum", and let go a burst of Bren-gun fire.

Nobody liked the Salient. We cursed when we were told we had to go there, we cursed while we were there, and we were elated when we came out. One day my section had had a nerve-racking time in a Salient post.

"Them Jerries oughta hunk a few lumps of ——— off their livers," said Eddie, and I think he was right. They did not let up on us all day, sweeping the area with Spandau fire and lobbing mortar bombs all round us. I was afraid. I was so afraid I did not talk; I knew my voice would give me away. We did not merely sit and take it, of course, and I found myself wondering whether I would rather be where I was or over in one of the German posts. It was impossible to leave the post, so we used a corner of it as a latrine.

About nine o'clock that night, in a lull in the firing, we heard somebody call out in English. At first we thought the voice came from one of our supporting posts, but then we realized that a German was calling, "Can you hear us, Aussies?"

"What the hell's wrong with ya, yer square-headed bastard?" yelled Eddie.

The German asked us, coarsely, did we want to go to the latrine. We told him, coarsely, that we did.

"Well what about calling it off for five minutes so we can all go?" called the German.

"Don't agree, Mick," said Gordon. "It's a trick. They want to get us out in the open and then we'll cop the lot."

"I don't think it's a trick," I said. "Even a poor misguided bastard like a Jerry must find these conditions disgusting."

"Are yous square-headed Jerry bastards fair dinkum?" called Eddie.

"Yes," came the reply. "We mean it."

"It's nine o'clock," said Clive. "We've only an hour to wait. I wouldn't trust them, Mick."

"But perhaps they can't wait that hour," I said. "I trust them. To show you I trust them I'll go first."

"No, you won't," said Eddie quickly. "I bags first." And he called, "All right yous rotten Jerry bastards, we agree, but if you try any funny business yous'll wish you'd never been foaled."

"There is no funny business," replied the German. "We give you our word."

"Yer word?" cried Eddie. "Why you——" but I put my hand over his mouth because I knew the sort of thing he would say.

"All right," I called. "It's off for five minutes from now," and I clambered out the back of the post.

"Be careful, Mick," said Eddie, climbing out after me. "For Christ's sake be careful."

His words made me afraid, afraid that I would fall with a burst of Spandau fire through me, but then I heard a German call clearly, "You see, Aussies, we are men of our word," and I knew that at least one of them was out of their post too.

All my section except Gordon and Jim, who had Bren guns at their shoulders, got out of the post then, and when the five minutes were up we were back in it and I called, "Are you O.K. Jerries? Is it on again?" and they replied, "Yes, Aussies. You can resume the war now." A burst of machine-gun fire made us duck our heads. We fired a few shots, but there was not much spirit in us now. It seemed unnatural to fire on men who, for a moment, had cast aside the discipline of war and had made a bargain and kept it.

"Ay, Aussies," called one of the Germans. "Give us a song, Aussies."

"They gotta hide," said Gordon. "What do they think Harday is? Do they think Harday would fraternize with the lower German orders?" and Eddie called "Give ya a song? We woulden give ya the smell off the —— we just had."

"Come on, Aussie," called the German. "Be what you call a sport. Sing us a song."

"Listen Jerry," yelled Eddie, "we'll give yous nothin' except the bloody cane every time we meet yous. Yous give us a song."

"All right," called the German, and as we crouched there, straining our ears, across the bare ground in front of us came the sound of the Germans singing. They were singing:

"We're gonna hang out our washing on the Siegfried Line."

"It's half past two," I said. "Let's buzz off down to sigs and hear Germany."

Eddie and I made ourselves a home in a wadi. We were out of the Red Line for a while and we had scooped a hole out of the ground, put a sheet of old iron over the roof and covered it with dirt. It was hot and stuffy, but it was underground and that was all that counted. All over Tobruk men were living like that, living in holes in the ground.

"You go, Mick," said Eddie. "Ya doan mind if I dice it, do ya? Gonna have a snooze. Them bloody fleas give me hell last night and they doan seem ter be so bad now. Fair dinkum, if they doan bite ya ter death they keep ya awake crunchin' the bloody flea powder."

I laughed. It was nearly as bad as that. We rubbed brown flea powder into the blankets, but it did not make much difference.

"Can't understand why ya so interested in the bloody news all the time," said Eddie. "S'pose ya can't help it, ya poor misguided bastard. Ya been like it right from the start. Why, in Palestine a man always had ter miss the early show at the flicks 'cause ya wanted ter listen ter the news. Few more planes down over England, patrol activity continued at Tobruk. It's always the bloody same. A watched pot never boils, Mick. Listenin' ter the news won't help none."

I laughed. "If you were playing in a football match," I said, "you'd want to know the score, wouldn't you? Anyhow, this is Germany. They never lose any planes. They put over a lot of bullo, but I like to hear it because then I know the real news can't be worse than that. I'll get Clive to go. Might take his mind off the night before last."

Eddie scratched himself, and I smiled at the thought that probably he would not be able to sleep anyhow.

"Funny bloke," he said. "I just doan give a continental. Ya know, Mick, why didden you an' Clive get together straight away, back in Ingleburn Camp, instead of ya pickin' on a poor ignorant coot like me?"

I pushed my slouch hat back with one finger. "I dunno," I said. "He's certainly my type in many ways, but a little of him goes a bloody long way. I dunno. You and I get on pretty well together; I amaze you at times and you amaze me. We keep each other amused by the things we do and say. No, I don't think I did the wrong thing the day I sat you on your arse back in Ingleburn Camp."

Eddie looked at me in mock concern. "Hey, just a minute, Mick," he said. "The day ya did whatta? Cop this, mug. If Old Gutsache hadn't come along they'd have taken ya to the C.R.S. in an ambulance. Why——"

"Go and jump in the lake," I said, grinning, and went through the sandbags at the entrance into the sunlight.

I went over to Clive's doover. Jim was asleep. Clive said he would like to go. I tried not to stare morbidly at his face. I could see that look in his eyes again. The shock had gone deeper this time.

"We're early," I said. "Want to go for a stroll? They tell me there are some pretty snappy lines in low-necked costumes down at the beach."

Clive smiled. I was glad he was smiling. "You know me, Mick," he said. "I wouldn't be able to resist them. I'd be asking them to sleep with me in my summer villa in the Ritz-Carlton Wadi."

"You wouldn't have said that before you joined the army," I said.

"Go to hell," said Clive amiably.

"You wouldn't have said——" I began but he was picking up stones.

On the way over to the sigs dugout we met a driver I knew.

"Ay, Mick," he said, "have a *shufti* at this. Jerry dropped it over the front line yesterday. He handed me a sheet of paper, it read:

AUSSIES

After the Crete disaster, Anzac troops are now being ruthlessly sacrificed by England in Tobruk and Syria.

Turkey has concluded a pact of friendship with Germany. England will shortly be driven out of the Mediterranean.

The offensive from Egypt to relieve you has been totally smashed. YOU CANNOT ESCAPE. Our dive bombers are waiting to sink your transports. Think of your people at home.

Come forward and show white flags and you will be out of danger.

SURRENDER

"Wouldn't it?" I said. "The poor misguided bastards."

"Now you know what to do, Mick," said the driver, grinning. "Just go out and wave your singlet—if you can find one that's clean enough—and you'll live happily ever after."

"They have the simplicity of children," I said. "A strange combination is Jerry, O King. General Wavell tells the story of the Germans publishing one of Bruce Bairnsfather's pictures—'Old Bill' sitting in a room with a big shell-hole in the wall. Somebody asks him what made the hole and he says, 'Mice.' But the Germans added a footnote, 'It wasn't mice. It was a shell.'"

"The poor bastards," said the driver.

"Ay, Tom," I said, "got any more of those pamphlets?"

"Take that one," said Tom. "I was going to use it for a certain purpose, but *mahlish*."

"Naughty, naughty," I said. "Thanks."

"There was a ship in a couple of nights ago," I said to Clive as we walked on. "Wonder did it bring any beer?"

"Cripes, you got half a bottle a few weeks ago. That makes a bottle and a half since the siege started. You'll want port-holes in your coffin next. When I was a kid, I used to wish that I owned the lolly shop on the corner. Hoping for beer in Tobruk is much the same thing."

"Yeah," I said, "but hope springs infernal in the human beast."

We went down into the dugout, pushing aside the hessian hanging at the bottom of the steps. Brian Hill was on duty. "You're too early to-day," he said.

"Yes," I said. "Anything worth listening to now?"

"No, unless you like the children's session from Berlin?"

I glanced quickly at Clive. I could not see him properly in the faint light, but I saw his expression change. His face seemed to tighten. "The children's session from Berlin," he said.

"We don't want to listen to it," I said quickly.

"I do," said Clive.

"Clive ——" I said.

"I do," he said.

Brian was looking at us queerly. "There's two pairs of headphones," he said. "Go ahead. It's only a woman and a lot of girls talking and laughing."

"They're laughing," said Clive bitterly. He put on the headphones. I stood there for a moment; then I put another pair on.

I had never heard German spoken until I went to a picture show in Tel Aviv. It was a Richard Tauber film. The words were shown in English on the bottom of the screen and in Hebrew and Arabic on a small screen next to the big one. I enjoyed listening to the strange language I had always imagined was guttural. When the child spoke, it had a beauty, a new lightness.

It was the same again. A woman spoke, and every time she stopped one of the girls said something. The woman's voice was cultured, but the children's! Their voices were clear, gay, lilting, delicious. And when they laughed, then I was back in Nerridale, with my friends' children around my knee, all listening wide-eyed to preposterous stories about Bogeywomps and Mumbledoops, Wild Garages and Ziggle Zoggles, all reminding me that I had no children of my own, that I had to borrow my friends'.

I could not understand a word of it, but it did not matter. The language of laughter transcended all barriers of race and language; and the children were laughing, high musical laughter.

And they were Germans. Any night now our big bombers would be over Berlin, and down would come death from the sky. Perhaps one of these girls, perhaps all of them——

I looked at Clive. I could see him better now in the light from a ventilator above. He was listening intently, and his hands were clutching the edge of the table. His lips were pressed together, and I could see the hardness in his eyes.

One of the girls spoke again, and then they laughed, captivating, bubbling laughter. There is nothing in the world like children's laughter.

Clive pulled the earphones off and threw them on the table.

"Hey, break it down," cried Brian. "You'll break the phones." But Clive did not hear. He was out of the dugout already.

I took my earphones off and followed him. He was walking straight ahead, walking fast. I ran after him and caught him by the shoulder. "Clive," I said, "don't take it like that, Clive."

He shook my hand off roughly, and turned to face me, "Go away!" he said intensely. "For God's sake go away!"

I did not know what to say, but I had to say something. "We can't help it, Clive," I said. "It's not our fault. We've got a job to do and no sentiment should stop us doing it."

The words sounded so flat, so banal, after the gaiety of that laughter. I was goaded into anger by my own impotence.

"He had two children," said Clive dully. "You saw the pictures didn't you? You saw them?"

"Yes, I saw them. But we can't help it. They started it. They killed thousands of men with children in Warsaw, Belgrade, Rotterdam. Killed the children too."

Clive's face was white, his lips were trembling. I could not look into his eyes. "I didn't kill anybody there," he said. "No, not there."

I scraped my boot in the dust, and looked down at the mark it made. "It's hard," I said. "I know it's hard. But we can't help it. It's our heritage; and Clive, don't let them beat you. It's their diabolical cunning that makes them put the children's session on just before the news. So that if you tune in a bit early you hear the children. Don't let them beat you, Clive. Don't let them get under your guard."

"You saw the pictures," he said again. "You saw them, didn't you?" he demanded. "I took them out of his pocket. And his eyes were staring. I always thought men's eyes closed when they died. But they don't. Sometimes they don't. They stare at you, and when you try to sleep at night you see them, staring, always staring."

"Don't, Clive, don't."

"And last night—last night when I went to sleep I dreamt I was in bed with a woman, making love to her. And suddenly she turned into that German, that German with the staring eyes."

"Clive! Please don't!"

"Do you know what was on the back of those pictures? No? Well I'll tell you. It was hard to read the words through the blood, his blood, but the I.O. read them all right. They were: 'Daddy, this is Gretchen and Mummy and me. Please, Daddy, hurry up and finish the war so that you can come home to all of us. Lots of love from Johann.' "

I was looking down at my boot as I made a line with it in the dust. I did not say anything.

"You'd laugh at that," said Clive. "You'd say it was senti-mentality. You wouldn't understand. You've got no children of your own. You're just a cynic with a heart of stone. You're hard all through. You just wouldn't understand. You wouldn't care two hoots if you'd killed their father."

He turned, and as he walked away I could hear him sobbing. I took a step after him, and then I stopped and stood there, looking down. I drew another line in the dust with my boot. What was the use anyway? I just wouldn't understand.

CHAPTER XXXVI

"THEY'RE killing people down at the harbour again," I said.

"They're killing people out in front, too," said Clive, and I glanced up.

"Jerry's a bugger for Very lights," said Eddie.

He certainly was. If you dropped your tin hat half a mile from the nearest German position up would go the Very lights, filling the sky with brilliant, cascading stars. They were all colours; they would have been beautiful if they had not been the eyes of a crouching, waiting enemy.

"I hope the boys are all right," said Clive. As he spoke we heard a few bursts of machine-gun fire and ducked instinctively. When we put our heads up cautiously we saw a flash from the enemy lines, and down we went again. We heard a shell scream by over our heads, but when it landed well behind us there was no explosion.

"God starve the lizards," said Eddie, "another dud. Reckon half their bloody shells are duds."

"Unseen hands are working for us," said Clive. "We need them. It's good to know it, isn't it? They dug a dud one out in the Salient the other day and opened it up. Found a note reading 'This is all I can do. Czech' in it. It was full of dirt."

Another shell screamed overhead. This one was not a dud.

"They're after our batteries again," I said unnecessarily. It was always a relief to talk. You stopped, for a moment, seeing yourself crushed and broken out there.

We heard explosions out in front, and an occasional burst of machine-gun or Tommy-gun fire. Our artillery had opened up now, with counter-battery fire, and shells were shrieking over our heads, intermittently and both ways.

From the harbour all the time there came the *whoomph* of ack-ack fire and the crunch of bombs. It was Tobruk. It was our home. We were used to this now, as used as a man can become to such insanity.

"Mick?" asked Clive.

"Yes?"

"What do you think of Francis Thompson?"

"Who d'ya mean?" asked Eddie. "That bloke in B Company?"

Clive and I laughed. We could not help it. It was too dark to see Eddie properly, but I felt him stiffen.

"All right, all right," he said. "I'm just a poor ignorant bastard." And he moved out of the weapon pit, down the concrete steps and disappeared in the darkness.

"Will I go and apologize?" asked Clive.

"Forget it," I said. "It's hopeless. It's not a tragedy to be uneducated, but it's a tragedy to be conscious of it."

"Mick, tell me this," said Clive. "How do you manage to get on so well with people at the top and bottom of the social scale?"

We crouched down again as a shell wailed over us, and as we came up I thought that if anybody blew a whistle or burst a paper bag behind me after the war I would flop in the gutter as a reflex action.

"Sometimes I don't think I get away with it," I said. "It's purely a matter of adjustment. I've known so many taxi-drivers and cricketers and bookmakers and footballers and second-rate boxers and barmen and boilermakers that I fall naturally into their idiom. I talk like them and even almost think like them when I'm with them."

"I see. I wish I could do it. I'm never at ease with them, except Jim, and they're never at ease with me. I worry about it, but I just can't help it."

We listened for a while to machine-gun fire out in front and the deeper noise of mortar bombs.

"I wanted to go with Jim tonight, but they only wanted one," said Clive.

"Bad luck," I said, and grinned to myself in the darkness. "You know, Clive. About this getting on well with people. The trouble with you is that you've the face of a cultured man as well as the mind. You wouldn't deceive a child. Now me, for instance. With my rugged dial I'd pass for a bricklayer's labourer any day."

The raid on the harbour seemed more intense than usual tonight. They were after the destroyer that came in with food and ammunition, but they would not get it. It was never there long enough. It slid in, unloaded, loaded, and slid out again—all in less than an hour. No matter what happened, it never berthed for longer than half an hour.

Two soldiers came up the concrete steps behind us.

"Time for you bastards to do some spine bashing," said one. "Are you going to sit there ear bashing all night?"

We laughed. "*Mahlish* the condys, Mac," I said. "Go back to bed. And take your cobber with you. I'll do the next shift, too. Clive and I've got a lot to talk about. Wouldn't sleep for the fleas, anyway."

"O.K." He put his rifle down and rubbed his hands together. "Cold as Christ, isn't it?" he said. "What a place to live in. Hot as hell all day and cold as a polar bear's backside all night. Looks as though somebody's copping it out in front tonight. Down at the harbour too. But they always cop it down there. 'Night boys."

"Mick," said Clive suddenly, "what do you think of the brothels?"

I glanced sharply at him. He was staring towards where Jim and the other Rats were nibbling at the enemy lines, and in the darkness I could see the sensitive outline of his face. We bobbed down as another shell went over. It landed much closer this time, and we felt the ground shake and heard loose earth slide down into the post.

"You're the only person I can talk frankly to," said Clive, "and

I never seem able to get you alone. There's always Jim or Eddie hanging around."

There was something doing out in front tonight all right. We could hear the rattle of automatic weapons and the dull boom of explosions. Down at the harbour, too, the eternal battle went on. I glanced over my shoulder. The ack-ack fire was like exploding stars.

"Think of them?" I asked. "I don't think of them. They're inevitable."

"But because men fight like animals they don't have to live like animals, too."

"War merely gives man an excuse. It gives woman an excuse too, as history has shown us. Beats me why there's so much hypocrisy about such a natural function."

Clive did not say anything for a while. Then he said, "The fact that you're at a war doesn't give you a licence to act like a dog. God, people make me sick. There's no restraint about them. Anything will do as an excuse."

"Ah, that's the word. An excuse. I believe that woman is an extremely emotional creature and that at times of acute danger and stress she's simply not responsible for her behaviour. It's only her conscience and innate modesty she's got to satisfy, and when the danger and stress are there the conscience and modesty aren't."

"Good heavens, Mick. Anyone would think you approve of all this."

I took off my tin hat and scratched my head. "I dunno," I said. "I approve of it in theory, particularly in wartime, when life's given people such a raw deal they're entitled to get what they can back out of it. But the trouble is that it attacks the sanctity of the married state—there's a sententious phrase for you—and I still can't envisage any state of society better than one based on the home. Christ, what am I talking about? Ah well, *mahlish*."

The bombing of the harbour had ceased now; the men down there, or what was left of them, could sleep. It was cold, bitterly cold. I remembered again how cold it had been that first night at Ingleburn Camp, and I smiled wryly to myself in the darkness. I knew now that it was nothing to be cold or hot or hungry. All that really mattered was not to be afraid; not to have your heart pounding in your chest and your hands clammy and the sweat on your forehead and that caving-in feeling at the pit of your stomach; not to start and tremble at every strange sound; not to feel certain that, when they came back from patrol, somebody would be missing, somebody you knew.

It was Jim who was out tonight—Jim the self-effacing, who loved the land so deeply. I remembered how one day I had asked him what kind of girl he wanted to marry. "I dunno," he had said. "There's really only one sheila I ever seen who got under me skin. I dunno. I reckon with sheilas I always draw the crow. But there was a sheila once. I come to Sydney on holidays—down to see the cows at the Royal Show. Well, I goes up to the Carlton Hotel— I wasn't stayin' there, of course, but I wanted to see what a posh pub was like, so I goes up there for a drink. I'm goin' up in the lift. There's a sheila an' an old joker in the lift with me, an' I takes a look at the sheila. A blonde, she was, with a white thing on her head. A waitress or a maid. She's leanin' back against the wall. She looks like as if she's been scrubbin' floors for six weeks without stoppin'. 'Somebody's tired,' I says, and then I thinks she'll go crook on me for speakin', seein' that we ain't been introduced."

"Yes? What happened?" I had asked.

"Nothin'. She just smiles—she smiles a bonzer smile—and says 'Somebody is', an' she gets out at the next floor an' I never seen her again. But here, in Tobruk, I gets to thinkin' about that sheila, an' maybe some day I'll go back to the Carlton Hotel—maybe stay there a few days if I have a good season with the cows—an' maybe I'll see that sheila again. An' maybe I won't. . . ."

"I don't know, Mick," Clive was saying. "I'm too tired to argue with you, but you're wrong, hopelessly wrong. You're wrong about the church and about men being hypocrites, and your cynicism about man is all wrong, too. Things aren't the best, I know, but after all this is over there'll be a new order. They'll put the world right again."

I pulled up the collar of my greatcoat and rubbed my hands together to try to drive out the cold. The shelling had stopped now, too, and for a while it was possible to forget that there was potential death all round you and that it was Tobruk.

I laughed the bitter laugh my friends had come to know so well. "New order?" I asked. "There'll be no new order. We're the little people, Clive. The gullible little people. The world takes things away from us; it doesn't give anything in return. They fought for a better world last time and what did they get? Another war for their sons. Some day, when we get home, I'll stop selling furniture for a while and get down on paper all this bitterness that's in my heart."

Suddenly Clive said, "Mick, I'm glad I've known you. I'm glad you're my friend."

"I'm glad you're mine too, Clive," I said, and we talked of other things.

He told me that the things he missed most were music, the ballet, and clean clothes.

"What about your wife?" I asked.

He did not answer for a while. Then he said, "I wouldn't say this to any man but you Mick, but your wife grows out of your heart, your child grows into it."

So it went on, this talking through the night, this passing of the time away. At last I told Clive to go out and get some sleep.

"I'd rather stay up, Mick. I want to see that Jim gets in all right."

"She's sweet," I said. "Go and do some spine bashing."

"I won't go to sleep," he said, "but I'll lie down." He went grudgingly.

Half an hour later I was standing there by myself, peering through the darkness for any sign of life, when I heard somebody stumbling along the trench behind me. I grabbed my rifle instinctively.

"Who is it?" I challenged.

"It's me, Dick Martin. Who's that?" Dick was one of our stretcher-bearers.

"It's Mick," I said, "Mick Reynolds. Anything wrong?"

"Christ, Mick, I'm glad I've found you so quickly. I need help bad."

I felt my fingers tighten around my rifle. I wanted to ask a question, but I could not ask it.

"Quick, man!" I cried. "What's happened? Where's Ron?" I had come out of the pit now and was standing next to him. I could see his face faintly in the darkness. He turned his head away.

"Ron's—Ron's dead," he said. "Went out like a light."

"That's the way to go out," I said. "Go on. Make it snappy."

"Well we were out there with our stretcher. We shouldn't have been out there, I know, but we got sick of doing nothing and we thought we'd trail the patrol. Thought we might be of some use. We heard somebody groan. Just then up went a whole bloody lot of flares. Before we could do anything they had opened up on us. They—they got Ron straight away. A mortar bomb got him. I went to earth and heard the stuff whistling past me. As soon as they stopped I went over to Ron but—but he was dead."

He stopped. "For Christ's sake go on, Dick," I said. "Get to the bloody point, for Christ's sake."

"Well I heard the groaning again, and after a bit of a search I found him."

I took a deep breath. "You found—who?" I asked.

"Millsy," he said.

I closed my eyes and tightened my grip on my rifle. I did not speak for a moment. "Is he bad?" I asked.

"A no-hoper, Mick. Copped two in the guts. I had to leave him there. Couldn't carry him with wounds like these. Fixed him up as best I could and came for help. You'll send someone back with me? I'll be waiting at the gap in the wire."

He turned, and I heard him moving down the trench. Somebody pushed past me in the darkness and followed him.

"No you don't!" I cried. "I'm corporal here. You get into that weapon pit. I'll go." I took five quick strides, grabbed him by the shoulder and swung him roughly round so that his face was within a few inches of my own.

"Listen you——" I began, and stopped.

It was Eddie.

For a moment I was too surprised to say anything. "But Eddie," I said at last, "it's Jim."

"Let me go!" he cried, pushing my arm away from his shoulder. "He done me guard for me, didden he?" and, turning, he vanished in the darkness.

I stood there for a while, scratching my head under my balaclava and thinking about Eddie Wilson, and then I remembered Jim, and I drew a deep breath and went down the trench to tell Clive.

CHAPTER XXXVII

I HAD heard about it, so I went looking for one of them. I tracked him down to his doover. He was sitting on a rock near it, pulling his rifle through. His bare chest was brown as coffee from months in the Tobruk sun, and standing there watching him I suddenly thought I was back on Nerridale beach, and that at any moment he would get lazily to his feet and saunter down for a surf.

He glanced up and saw me, and grinned. "Take a good bo-peep, Dig," he said. "Ya'll know me next time."

"I know you now," I said, and I told him his name. "I'm Mick Reynolds, of the 93rd. How's things?"

"She's jake," he said.

I sat down on the ground and found myself looking around for a piece of grass to chew. Then I remembered I was in Tobruk. "They tell me you were in a bit of a blue the other night," I said.

He looked up, but did not grin this time. "Yeah," he said.

"What happened?"

He pulled his rifle through with a vicious jerk, held it up to the sun, and peered down the barrel. "If they say there's a bird's nest in that," he said, "they've got another think comin'.""

"What happened the other night?" I asked again. He did not reply for a long time and I thought he was not going to reply at all. I cursed myself for being too hasty. Then he told me.

"Well," he said, "there's not much to tell. We was ordered to attack this post, see, and they knew it was goin' to be pretty tough so they put jest about the whole company on the job. There was about a hundred and thirty of us—a hundred and twenty-seven, I think, was the right number—an' for two nights we go out and recce the ground. Not a shot's fired. Well, we put the tapes out, an' the next night she's on. It's fair dinkum this time. Well, we get well out then they open up with everythin' they got. They hit us with everythin' but the kitchen sink—arty, mortars, M.Gs, everythin'. We copped the lot. There was about a hundred and twenty-seven of us went out, and there's seven of us come back, an' three of them's walkin' wounded. I was one of them the bastards missed, touch wood." He reached down and touched the butt of his rifle. "Well that's all, mate. It ain't much of a story."

"It's a story," I said. "Don't worry about that. You haven't finished yet."

"Finished? Course I've finished. There ain't no more."

"There's more. What about next day? Didn't the padre go out with a white flag to bury the dead?"

"Oh, that? Yeah. He went out all right."

"Well, what happened? You weren't with him, I suppose?"

"With him? Yeah, I was with him."

I tried to keep my elation down, but it must have been shining in my eyes. I was elated, but I was disappointed too. It always seemed my fate to miss these things. I had missed the tank battles that decided whether we would hold Tobruk, and now I had missed this.

"What happened?" I asked.

I saw the look I knew so well come into his eyes, and he did not speak for a while. He found a sudden interest in the breech of his rifle and began to wipe it with an oily piece of service flannelette, bending over it so that I could not see his face.

"Well," he said, "nothing much happened. We goes out there with the padre. There's dead and wounded all over the joint. They sends their sappers out to clear the minefield, an' then we goes into the post."

"Jerries?"

"Yeah."

"Good."

"Well, they take the padre away to see the trump an' we stand there talkin' to the Jerries."

"What did they say?"

"First thing they said was to ask us to have a cup of tea. We didn't think they was fair dinkum at first but they was. Bonzer tea, too. Nearly all of 'em could speak English, an' they starts to rock it in about the war."

"What did they rock it in about?"

"Well, there's one big bastard there. There's a word for him. Just can't think of it, but it suits him down to the ground. Somethin' like 'conceited'."

" 'Arrogant'?"

"Yeah. That's it. An arrogant bastard."

I remembered a story a private in the 17th Battalion had told me. He told me how a giant German stood up in the turret of a tank in the first battle for Tobruk, crying, "Surrender, Australians. Surrender!" how a corporal shouted "Surrender be buggered!" and how the German died with a burst of Tommy-gun fire in his chest.

"Well, he tells us we might be Aussies but we can't take a trick. He says we got a canin' in Greece an' had to get out, an' then they beat us by just droppin' from the sky on us in Crete an' we had to get out again. An' then we was driven back from Benghazi to Tobruk, takin' a hidin' at Mechili on the way, an' that Lord Haw-Haw was right when he calls us self-supportin' P.O.Ws, that we'd starve to death in here. He said maybe we weren't such pansies as the English. There was another word he used, too. As—as——"

" 'Decadent'?"

"Yeah, that's it. Maybe we weren't as decadent as the English, but we wasn't as good as we thought we was an' we weren't in the race with the great German—he used another big word here. Buggered if I can remember it though."

" 'Wehrmacht'?"

"Yeah. How do ya know all them words?"

"I've talked to 'em—up at the P.O.W. cage. They're all the same. Arrogant bastards."

"Yeah. Funny ain't it? Well then he tells us nothin' can stop 'em, that Hitler is the greatest bloke ever foaled, an' that what they done to Poland an' France an' Holland an' Belgium an' all the rest they was going to do to England too. There was a lot more bullo like this, but I doan remember it. An' all the time he's turnin' to the few Jerries what doan speak English an' tellin' 'em how he's rockin' it into us and they're grinning an' jabberin' away to 'emselves. 'Look out there,' he says, an' points out in front where all our cobbers are lyin' an' says, 'That's what happens to anyone who tries to stop our Fuehrer from conquerin' the world.' "

I felt sick then, sick deep down in me, for this arrogant German was a symbol of the madness that was in the German soul, the madness that, someday, if we could only hold out long enough, would destroy them. If only I had been there to reply to their sneers. If only I had been there.

"You had a go back?" I asked. "You didn't let him get away with it?"

"Not on your life," he said. "We rocked it back all right. We asked him had he finished and when he says 'Yes' we gets stuck into him proper. We tells him about what the Sixth Div. done to the Eyeties, how we haven't got much ground back in Egypt where there ain't prison camps. 'But,' he says, 'they was only Italians. They have no place in our new order.'

"Then we tells him that if they're so hot why doan they come in an' take Tobruk, why doan they come in an' get us. We say we're waitin', that we won't go away, that they got hundreds of planes an' we got none, that they got us surrounded, that we're not P.O.Ws at all and that even if we are we're self-supportin' all right 'cause they can't stop the British Navy gettin' supplies in an' out. We tell 'em they've been sittin' on their arses out in the desert for five months now an' that if they're so bloody hot they're gonna conquer the world they better soon get on with the job of conquerin' this little bit of it. An' then we say they're sittin' out here not 'cause it's part of their plan to rule the world, but for the simple reason we won't let 'em come in, an' that the only twice they tried it they got such a helluva canin' they haven come back for no more."

"You beaut!" I cried. "You bloody beaut!"

"We give it back to 'em all right. We wasn't gonna take that from no Jerries. Funny thing, too—the big bloke didden translate what we said to the Jerries who didden understand our lingo. They was at him to do it, but he just barked somethin' at 'em an' then he sulked an' woulden say nothin'."

"What happened then?"

"Well bugger me if them mad Poles don't open up on us with their arty. The Jerries go stone mad. Did they scream? We didden have nothin' with us, of course, but I got a commando's knuckle-duster in me pocket, an' slips me fingers into it an' feels the good hard feel of it around me fingers an' I think that if they're gonna get me I'll get a couple of them bastards first."

It was typical of the Poles. They wanted only one thing in life —to kill Germans. I remembered how they had acted when they came into the front line for the first time, how they had been

impatient when we told them the Italians were there, there and
there, pointing to spots on the map. "Never mind ze Italians,"
they had said. "Show us ze Germans." I remembered the night, too,
when hell broke loose on the perimeter and we started up out
of our holes like frightened rabbits. We thought it was a big attack,
but it was only the Poles, who had moved all their artillery right
up behind the forward posts and used their fortnight's supply of
ammunition in one night. Afterwards they were given only one day's
supply at a time or they would fire it all off at once.

He was speaking again now. ". . . so they tells us to get out, so
we goes. An' we comes back, an' that's about all there is to it. It's
not much of a story."

"It's a story," I said. "Don't worry about that. There's only one
thing that matters. You rocked it back into them, all right, didn't
you? You didn't let them get away with it?"

"Yeah. We done that all right. We told 'em where they got off."

"Then everything's all right," I said. "As long as you rocked
it back into them everything's all right."

CHAPTER XXXVIII

I was standing in a strongpoint in the Derna Road sector, looking
out over the bare desert. I had my greatcoat on, but I was shivering.
I touched the bolt of my rifle. It was like a piece of ice. What a
place! I thought. Burning heat all day; bitter cold all night. Why
didn't we let the Germans have it?

Our patrols were out in front somewhere, nibbling at the enemy
lines, harassing them, goading them. So the Germans were the
greatest soldiers in the world? Well if that was so why had they
failed to stop our patrols? Why, the other night we penetrated
eight thousand yards behind his lines in the El Adem sector and
he could not do anything to stop us. Evidently the Germans were
trained for blitzkrieg war and did not know how to cope with static
operations. They were always busy at night laying mines, wiring
and digging in.

Australians were funny blokes. If we were told to go out two
thousand yards we always stepped out another fifty as a point of
honour. I could not imagine the Germans doing that. Strange we
never called the stretch between our lines and his no-man's-land. It
was not no-man's-land! It was ours. We regarded it as our property.
We knew every inch of it; we had his minefields taped and knew

where the gaps in them were. Why, the other night we wanted a thousand mines, so the C.O. of one of the field companies sent his boys out to dig them up from a German minefield. Who said the Germans were the best soldiers in the world?

You could not be a good soldier unless you could laugh. That was what I liked about our fellows, their ability to laugh even when things looked black. I'll bet if the Germans had a paper of their own they wouldn't have a page of sketches, verse and stories contributed by the troops, like the Ack-I-Foofs page the *A.I.F. News* had just started. I had never seen a German soldier laugh yet or heard of one laughing, the arrogant bastards. Why——

I shook my head and came back to earth. That was what this place did to you; you found that you were arguing with yourself. Ah well, *mahlish*. You had to have someone to argue with or you'd go crazy.

It was getting late. They should be back soon. There had been one violent flare-up a long way out in front. We had heard explosions and seen the fiery streams of tracers. Very lights had gone up, too, and had burst in coloured cascades.

Although a fighting patrol was out, there was only one in it from my section. That was Clive. I did not like to see him go out alone, but orders were orders and there were plenty of other fellows from our platoon with him.

I noticed that he was pale when he left us. Evidently he preferred to be with one of us. I thought his nerves were beginning to go. Several times in the last week I had found him irritable and preoccupied. I had done what I could to get him out of it, but it was no use. He had just sat by himself, staring moodily into space and dropping a stone from one hand to the other and back again.

He did not eat much. Even when hot tinned meat and vegetables made a delicious break from bully beef he just ate a few mouthfuls and threw the rest away. He spent hours writing something. I thought it must be a short story—it seemed too long for a letter —but this morning he had come to me and said, "Mick, you've been a good friend to me and I appreciate it."

I murmured something depreciatory.

"No. I mean that," said Clive. "You've done a lot for us all."

"Bullo!" I said. "I've tried to keep our spirits up, but I'm afraid I've failed because I've been unable to keep up my own."

"You've done wonders," said Clive. The lines around his eyes had deepened and he was pale beneath his tan. I noticed that he had not had a shave. Something must be wrong. I could not remember the last time he had not shaved. Clive insisted on doing things like that, even in Tobruk. The lack of water—we went for weeks without a bath, without even taking our clothes off—hurt him deeply. "It's been pretty hard for us all," he said, "but I wouldn't have missed it for the world. To be here in Tobruk, to have helped to hold this barren bit of desert has been a rare privilege."

I laughed hollowly. "A rare privilege? Oh yeah?"

"You don't mean that, Mick. You'll always be glad you were here."

"To my dying day," I said slowly, "I'll curse the name of Tobruk."

"You don't mean it, Mick. I know you don't mean it." He stood there awkwardly for a while, and I could see that he wanted to say something and could not make up his mind.

"What is it, Clive?" I asked.

He hesitated. "Mick," he said, "I hate to ask this, but would you do me a favour?"

"A favour? Certainly. What is it?"

"Well, it's—it's a letter. It's a letter to my wife. If anything happens to me——"

I laughed, but my laugh did not seem convincing even to me. "Nothing's going to happen to you," I said. "Don't be ridiculous."

My words mocked me. He was here in Tobruk, out in the Red Line, and nothing was going to happen to him. He was going out on a fighting patrol that night.

"In case it does," said Clive, "will you see that my wife gets the letter? It's in my pack."

"Of course I will. But it's a promise I'll never have to keep."

"Thanks," said Clive, and I noticed that he looked relieved. "Mick," he said suddenly, looking me in the eyes, "I just want to tell you that it's been good knowing you. We haven't agreed on some things and perhaps we've hurt each other over them, but I'm glad I met you and I'm proud to have had you as a friend."

Before I could say anything he had pressed my hand, turned away and disappeared around a corner of the post. I stood there, staring stupidly after him.

Now he was somewhere out in front, and the sun would soon be coming up over the escarpment.

"Ay, Eddie?" I said.

Eddie yawned. "I was nearly havin' a snooze, Mick," he said. "Jesus, it's cold. What's eatin' ya?"

"What's wrong with Clive lately? Worried about something, isn't he?"

"Yeah. Must be. Somethin' on his mind. This bloody place gets everybody down sooner or later. He's had a gutful of Tobruk, that's all."

"Perhaps you're right, but I dunno. Why don't you buzz off to bed? Or to that hole scraped out of the side of the trench that masquerades as a bed in these parts. What the hell are you hanging around for? Go and do some spine bashing. It's warmer there."

"Can't seem to settle down. Wish those bastards'd get back."

I looked at him as he stood near the Bren gun set on a fixed line along the northern wire. "I'm like that, too," I said. "What's wrong with us tonight? Clive's been out without any of us before."

"Yeah, I know. But it's somethin' else, somethin' different."

I knew he was right, but I did not know what it was. "What's different?" I asked.

"Dunno. Somethin' different in the way he's been actin'. He's sorta scared. Suddenly gone bomb happy or somethin'. You shoulda seen him this mornin'. Every time someone goes near him he looks up like a dog that's gonna be hit. Brave but scared. Like as if he knew he was a moral to cop a crack, but had a hope he wouldn't."

"I was asleep," I said; "but I know what you mean."

"Yeah. An' when Doug tells him he's on patrol tonight he goes pale. White as a sheet he was, an' I think he sways a bit, but he pulls himself together an' says 'Yes, sir.' 'It's a fighting patrol,' says Doug. 'Yes, sir,' Clive says just the same as he always does. I go over and I ask him does he feel crook an' can I go on patrol for him, but he says he's O.K. an' he's gotta go through with it.

"'Go through with what?' I asks, puzzled-like, an' he says, 'Nothin'. I'm all right now.'"

I took my slouch hat off and scratched my head. "I can't work it out," I said. "I just can't work it out. Why the hell didn't you tell me this before? Clive's a case for a psychiatrist not a fighting patrol. I'd have gone in his place if I'd known."

"Didn't want ter bother yer. But wait'll I tell ya." Eddie was looking out through the wire and across the waste in front. It was getting lighter now. They should be back soon. "Then a funny thing happened," said Eddie. "Clive stands lookin' at me with a funny look and then he starts to say somethin'. He stops, an' then he had another go. I could see his mouth movin' but he wasn't sayin' nothin', and then he shakes his head an' bites his lip."

"Yes?" I said. "Go on." I was trying to work it out. There was fear in my heart now, an awful, unreasonable, nagging fear. There was something wrong somewhere, something queer. If only I could bring it out into the open, only get my hands on it.

I remembered the first day I had met Clive; how horrified he had been at the prospect of sharing the latrine with half a dozen other soldiers without barriers between them. How, ever since then, we had said, "You wouldn't have said that before you joined the army." How, coming back to the tent alone one night in Palestine, I had found him sobbing.

"Go on," I said.

"Well, it was kinda queer," said Eddie. "He was sorta strugglin' with himself, tryin' ter tell me somethin'. 'Eddie,' he says at last, 'I just wanter say—I just wanter tell ya—well, you musta thought I was a queer sorta feller with me French plays an' me Bach fugues' —ya know them things he's often ear bashin' about—'an' the way I laughs at ya when ya doan understand me. But I wasn't laughin' at ya, Eddie. It was a—a friendly sorta laughter.' "

I saw Clive with me on leave in Tel Aviv, smiling with indulgent amusement at my absorption in the lilting cadence of Bing Crosby. I remembered how I had said, "It's almost incredible that a man with a face like a fish can have a voice like an angel", and how he had called me a moron, attacked the crooners of the world, and talked of Gigli and Fleta, Caruso and Chaliapin, Tauber and Herbert Ernst Groh.

"It was kinda queer," said Eddie. "An' then he says, 'An' all the time I was laughin' at meself, like Mick does. Ya see, he an' me see things different, an' when we laugh at things an' people we laugh at ourselves, too. We laugh at mankind. That's what ya gotta do Eddie. Laugh at yaself. Ya get pretty close ter reality here in Tobruk,' he says, 'an' ya see things from a new, from a new— er——' "

" 'Perspective'?"

"Yeah. That's the word he used. How'd ya know? Reckon ya know him so well ya even know what he is thinkin' 'cause ya his kind. 'Ya gotta laugh at yaself,' he says, 'but mind ya doan die laughin'.' He said that bit in a queer sorta way like as if his throat was hurtin' him.

"An' then he says, 'Can't speak ter Mick meself. Just can't seem ter do it again, but I want ya ter tell him I've always prayed for him an' I know some day he'll believe. S'pose he'll laugh when ya tell him, but tell him all the same. I want him ter know. An' I want ya ter know, Eddie, that I been ya friend an' I appreciate all ya done for me although I didden deserve it.' Queer it was. All *I* done for *him*. I never done nothin' for him, Mick, 'cept get full an' abuse him an' come home blind an' wake him up with a lotta bullo—when he was sick. I done nothin' for him."

I could see Clive in Ingleburn Camp the day they handed him his rifle, see him plodding doggedly over the Blue Mountains on the march to Bathurst. I could see him in Palestine tramping along the wet white roads, and digging slit trenches with muscles, real muscles, showing on his brown back, digging till his frail frame must have throbbed with pain.

I saw him lending the others money when they had spent their pay on beer at the canteen or lost it at two-up, saw him struggling across country on gruelling route marches, saw him that day in Deir Al Balah Cemetery copying out the names of dead Diggers from the last war so that he could write to their people and tell them their men were lying in tidy graves.

Funny how he had sobbed that day, sobbed in hysteria, and how Eddie had had to knock him out when I could not do it. What was it all about? It seemed so long ago. Something about reading of his own death on a tombstone. Queer the way these hypersensitive people behaved at times. Unnecessary suffering was their destiny. A pity. Perhaps it was better to be like Eddie or Jim. It was better in wartime, anyhow.

Fancy reading the date of your own death on a tombstone! Your own death. The date was there, too. Now what date was it? Damned if I could remember. Somewhere near Eddie's birthday. Two days after, I think Eddie had said.

Suddenly my latent fear swept over me in one mad throb. A prickly shudder ran up my spine. My hands were trembling and I could feel my heart thudding in my chest. Eddie was talking, but I could not understand a word of it.

I tried to speak, but could not. I had to wait a moment and lick my dry lips.

"Eddie," I said at last, "when's your—when's your birthday?"

"Birthday?" he said, puzzled. "When was it, ya mean. I didden mention it, didden seem no point in mentionin' it, but it was two days ago."

I did not speak.

"Why?" he asked.

"Clive," I said. "Clive and the cemetery."

A puzzled look spread over his face, and then his mouth dropped open as comprehension dawned.

"Oh Christ," he said quietly. "What bloody fools we've been."

CHAPTER XXXIX

IT could not have been the food because it was bully beef as usual, and the biscuits were the same biscuits, and just as hard. The fleas had been as irritating the previous night and the flies as persistent all day.

I looked back across the day that had passed, but it was no different from most of the others, a day of heat shimmering over the dun expanse in front of the strongpost, a day of watching, waiting, a day of sporadic shelling and machine-gun and mortar fire.

I could not find the reason, but the fact was there. A strange gaiety had seized us and was wringing laughter from the hearts of men who had known fear and death, dirt and bombs, cold and hunger, heat and misery, loneliness and despair.

I did not have much at which to laugh. Only Eddie, Pat, Gordon and I were left now, and I had not had a letter from Margaret for a fortnight, but I was laughing too. You could not help laughing at Gordon when he was at his best, and he was at his best tonight. We were getting our murder suits ready and pulling our rifles through and cleaning our Tommy guns, getting ready for the night's patrol, when suddenly Gordon jumped up and yelled the old yell "Who'll carry the mail through?" in an urgent tone.

We responded, as usual, with "*I will!*"

"And who are you?" he bellowed with the same gravity in his voice.

"Dick Tracey of the United States Marines!" we roared, and then we broke into the usual rapid singing of the tune of "Stars and Stripes Forever".

It was our stock joke, and it had made us laugh since the days when we sang it on parade back in Ingleburn Camp while Old Gutsache fumed and roared.

Gordon took out a pack of cards and broke into his patter. "Prepare the Opera House," he said. "Ah, well I remember the Wintergarden, Berlin, the Folies in Paris. Twenty-two curtains each night. Wilson! The drums!"

"Right," said Eddie, and imitated a roll of drums.

Gordon came tripping down the trench on his toes, smiled that fatuous entertainer's smile, bowed obsequiously to all points of the compass, riffled the cards, and said, "Take a card, gentlemen. Any card will do. Don't let me see it. Place it back in the pack. At least ten cards from the top. So. Thank you."

He was swaggering and bowing, and we crowded around, unshaven, unkempt, grinning, our slouch hats pushed back on our heads.

Somebody was shelling on the Derna Road sector, but we did not take any notice.

"Now select a number from one to ten. Four. Thank you, sir." He riffled the cards once. "Now sir, you will find the card you selected is the fourth from the top. One, two, three, four. Is that the card? Thank you, sir."

He bowed and smiled smugly. He did more tricks. His pudgy hands moved smoothly over the cards and the gold ring gleamed as he manipulated his fat little finger. I knew he did a lot with it, but he moved it too fast for me to see exactly what.

Somebody put the two of spades in the middle of the pack and somebody else told Gordon when to stop shuffling. The two of spades was always on top. "Thank you, sir. And you, my lad, you put the two of spades somewhere. The quickness of the hand deceives the eye. On the top again. The two of spades. Thank you, sir."

We stood round grinning. The news had spread that Gordon was doing card tricks, and the boys came crowding out of their holes in the sides of the trenches.

Then Gordon, ungainly as a water buffalo, began to sing "All Round the Town", his signature tune. He cleared a space and began to sing in his raucous voice "All round the town they run her down. They call her Dixie Dinah."

That was all he knew, but he went over it again and again, stamping up and down in the one place, swinging his arms awkwardly and bending farther back all the time. His legs went higher and higher. His fat face was pink with pleasure and exertion, and he was grinning.

"All round the town they run her down. They call her Dixie Dinah!" he bellowed.

I was screaming with laughter before it was over. He had his tin hat on at a rakish angle, and his plump face was so pink, his marking time so awkward, his voice so harsh. Then we got the call to get ready, for it was nearly dark and, still grinning, we put grenades and wire clippers in the pockets of our murder suits and finished pulling our rifles through and cleaning our Tommy guns.

Later we got the call to go, and we made our way out of the strong-post, and through the wire and across the anti-tank ditch.

There were about fifteen of us. We went out in arrowhead formation, with Doug leading and a couple of scouts well in front of

him, and a man at the back to keep our rear covered. Each man
kept the man in front of him just within sight. That meant that when
the enemy caught sight of the man in front he could not see you.
Doug had a compass and had detailed a man to count the paces.
Most of us had rifles, with fixed bayonets of course, but some had
Tommy guns. We were going out looking for trouble.

We had gone about a thousand yards when suddenly a flare went
up. We went down automatically, down to the good earth.

A burst of machine-gun fire swept over the bare ground. I heard
a few rounds zipp by and heard others kick up a few spurts of dust.
Then silence came down on the desert again, dead, uncanny.

We lay there for a while, and then got to our feet. I turned to
Gordon.

"That was close, George," I said softly; but he was still lying
there. "Come on," I said. "It's all over now. We've got to find that
trouble."

He did not move. Suddenly I heard him groan. I stood there,
looking down at him, and involuntarily I closed my eyes and put
my hand up and pressed it hard against my forehead. When I
opened my eyes I saw his hands clawing at the ground.

Then I went back the few yards to where he lay, put my rifle
down, knelt down next to him and turned him over gently. Doug
had come back to see what was wrong.

"It's Gordon," I said. "They got him."

"Oh Christ!" said Doug. "Did he get it badly?"

I looked down at Gordon's pale face in my lap. He was trying
to smile. His face twisted in pain and he was biting his lip. His top
lip was drawn up and I could see his white teeth. He moved his
left hand limply to the right.

I slid my hand down from under his armpit, down his right
side. I felt the warm dampness of his blood, felt it trickling through
my fingers.

"It's bad," I whispered to Doug. "It's bad all right." I whipped
out my field dressing, tore it open, pulled his overalls and shirt
away from the wound, and put the dressing on.

"Oh Christ," said Doug again. "We've got to get on. We'll have to
pick him up on the way back."

I looked up, and in the darkness I could see his worried face
and the bitter set of his lips. The others had come back, too, and
were standing about, dim shapes in the darkness. They did not
speak.

Doug turned and noticed them. "Jesus Christ, men!" he said

quietly but emphatically. "Get down on the ground! Do you all want to get killed?"

I looked down again at Gordon. His eyes were closed and his mouth had fallen open grotesquely. For a moment I thought he was dead. Then I felt his heart beating faintly under my right hand.

"One M.O. to a battalion," I said. "No stretcher-bearers with patrols."

"Come on," said Doug. "You'll have to leave him. You can't do anything."

I looked up into his lined face. His eyes were hard. The boy had become a man.

"I won't go," I said. "I won't go, Doug."

He knelt there for a moment, and I saw him drag his hand wearily across his forehead. "I could order you to come," he said quietly. "We didn't have enough men when we started out. Now we've lost Harday. We can't spare you, too. This is a fighting patrol, Mick."

I had my knees under Gordon's shoulders. I had torn his shirt off, and was trying to tie the bandage round his chest.

"You—go—Mick," he said faintly. "They can't—do this—to Harday. They've got a—bloody hide."

I could feel the warm, sticky blood, Gordon's blood, running down my arms.

"Order me?" I said to Doug. "Well go on. Order me. They got Gordon and you talk about orders!"

Doug knelt there, looking at me. "Go on," I said. "Go on and kill people. That's what we're here for, isn't it? Go on and kill!"

Doug got to his feet. "All right, Mick," he said. "You can stay."

"Thanks," I said bitterly, and glanced up as he went over to the others. They went forward into the darkness.

"You—you broke—the rules," said Gordon faintly. "You used—your—field dressing."

"Bugger the rules," I said. The blood, Gordon's blood, had seeped through the dressing already. I felt in his pocket, and took his dressing out. I put it on over the first one.

"You were—right—Mick," he said. "Smash—doesn't matter. You can't—amass smash—if you're—dead."

I shook my head, but I could not shake the fear out of my heart. "Don't be silly," I said. "You're going to be all right."

Gordon shook his head slightly. It seemed to take a great effort. "It's no good—bluffing," he said. "I don't—hold any—aces. This is —the last—card in the—deck. They got—a bloody hide." He bit his lip and I saw his teeth gleam. "They can't—do this—to Harday."

He coughed, and I saw blood trickling from the corner of his mouth and running down his chin. I tried to tell myself that it was coming from his lip.

"You'll be all right," I said. "A few weeks in hospital and you'll be O.K. again."

"No," he said. "This is—it. I know." His hands were clenching and unclenching in the dirt at his sides.

"It's not," I said fiercely. "I tell you it's not. Think of all the things you've got to do in the world yet. You can't die. You can't. You'll be all right. Lots of fellows get wounded. You don't die if you get wounded."

Gordon smiled faintly. "Sometimes—you do. Funny—but I—wanted to die—gloriously. The—Harday way. Leading—a bayonet—charge. This way—isn't good enough—for Harday."

"Don't say that," I said. "You're not going to die. I tell you you're not going to die!"

"I didn't—get the M.M.—Mick. It would—have helped—in my —organization—after—the war. Would have—helped me—to amass —smash. Mick?"

"Yes?"

"You were right—Mick. Hate to—admit it. Wanted to be hard—right through. There was—someone. There's—a letter—in my—pack. You'll see—she—she gets it?"

"I'll see she gets it," I said.

"I didn't—think she was—good enough for me. You see—she had no smash. But now—I know you—were right. All the—smash in—the world can't—help me—now."

I had his head in my lap. I could feel the blood seeping through the second dressing and running down my fingers, running down my arms. I pressed the sodden dressings against his side and felt the warm blood well out.

I saw his face twist into a grimace, and I knew he was trying to smile.

"Harday—speaking," he said. "Stick to me—buddy—and you—won't—wear diamonds. You'll tell—people at—home—about me? You won't—let them—forget?"

"I'll tell them," I said.

A shudder went through him. I had cramp in my legs from the weight of his head and shoulders. I had to get him back somehow, had to stop his life running away through my fingers. But I could not leave him, leave him alone to die.

"Mick?"

"Yes, Gordon?"

"Tell me—one thing. I had—had—ability—didn't I?"

I bit my lip hard. "Yes," I said. "You had ability."

I saw the pain in his face disappear, and for a moment he smiled, the old Harday smile.

"I had—ability," he said, and his head rolled over against my knee and I knew he was dead.

CHAPTER XL

WE were sitting on stones in the wadi eating our tea. It was bully beef again, bully beef stew and those hard tasteless biscuits we had come to know so well.

"They reckon they're goin' to start a cookin' school here to teach the cooks twenty different ways of cookin' bully beef," said Eddie. "They reckon the W.O. in charge used to be a cook at the Hotel Australia."

"What're you moaning about?" asked Pat. "You've got pickles with your bully tonight, haven't you?"

"I'm not moanin'," said Eddie with a grin. "You know an Aussie never moans."

"Of course not," I said. "No soldier does."

"Termorrer," said Eddie, "we oughter have some goldfish." Goldfish were herrings.

"I didn't think," said Pat, "that I'd ever see the day when I'd bless the name of goldfish."

Eddie spluttered, and spat out a fly. There were flies everywhere. We had to brush them off the food before we put it in our mouths. The food was dusty enough without having flies in it. They were as bad in the day-time as the fleas were at night.

I handed Pat and Eddie two white anti-scorbutic pills each.

"Don't want 'em," said Eddie.

"Naughty, naughty," I said. "Take nice lollies."

"Nice lollies?" said Eddie. "Oh yeah?"

"They put lead in your pencil," I said.

"Fat lot of good that is," said Pat. "Save 'em up till we get back to Alex."

"Where's our reos?" asked Eddie. He could not hide his contempt when he talked of them. I was sorry for them. It was not their fault that they came late into a platoon, that they took the place of soldiers who had been killed or wounded. They could not take their place—that was a tragedy. No matter what we went through with them, they would never take the place of Clive and Harry and

Jim and Gordon and Happy and Bert. Most of them were young, inexperienced, frightened, pathetically anxious to learn. We were uncomfortable when we spoke to them, for they reminded us of things we were trying to forget.

"They've gone up to watch the Stuka parade," said Pat. It was a rebuke when he said it.

"Don't be too hard on them," I said. "The poor coots can't help it."

I looked at Pat and Eddie, sitting there with their mess tins on their laps. Their clothes were dirty, their boots caked with dust, their faces unshaven. It was impossible to keep clean with the meagre water ration. They were so different from the youths who had come laughing into the desert and stumbling, with fear in their eyes, back to Tobruk.

It was hard to realize that they were killers, skilful, deadly killers, these young men from desk and taxi. I looked at Pat. He was smiling that irresistible Irish smile as he took the anti-scorbutic pills. I shook my head. I could not realize that this was the same man who had bayoneted eight Italians in an anti-tank ditch as they clawed frantically at the sides, squealing in terror as they tried to escape.

Since he received the cable from Pamela, Pat had changed. He was a killer now, a cold-blooded, merciless killer. He went out on patrol to kill. Even on a reconnaissance patrol he insisted on probing at the enemy lines until he found a spot where he could kill.

"I've got nothing to lose now," he told me one morning when he came back from patrol. "I'm going to get as many of the bastards as I can before they get me."

I did not say anything. I pointed to his bayonet as it glistened in the morning sun. He glanced at it, said "Sorry", wiped it with a handkerchief, and threw the handkerchief away.

"The girl who packed that in a Comforts Fund parcel thought somebody'd blow his nose on it," he said. He laughed, and went down the passage to have a sleep.

He won the M.M. shortly afterwards. Our new company commander had taken out twenty men to get prisoners, for identification purposes. As soon as they attacked their objective, they found it had about fifty men in it instead of the fifteen Intelligence had estimated. The patrol went into them with everything it had. Pat mowed them down with grenades. He bayoneted three Germans, and his bayonet broke off in a fourth. Then he fired at them from the hip. The patrol got its prisoners. Pat went into a dugout and dragged two Germans out, one in each hand. I will never forget how he looked when he came in. When the Intelligence Officer questioned him all he could say was, "The bayonet. I used the bayonet. The bayonet. It broke. The bayonet." His eyes were dulled, his mouth set, his mind stunned. "The bayonet. I used the bayonet. It broke. It broke off, in him. The bayonet." Eventually I led him away.

I looked at Eddie. He was brushing the flies off his face and cursing. He was like Pat. I managed to keep him off some patrols, but he had to do the others. Pat killed because he was hurt. Eddie killed because it was his job. "I reckon it's like this, Mick," he said one day. "Some day the Springboks are gonna come up from Bardia way and we're gonna push out El Duda way to meet 'em. After we meet 'em we're gonna get outa this place. Every Jerry or Eyetie I kill now will make it easier for us all then. Every one I kill brings me closer to goin' home and seein' me kid. That's how I work it out."

I was drawing pictures in the dust with a stone. I told myself I would have to get out of this habit of drifting into introspection. I was always studying the reactions of other people and my own reactions. I remembered what Gordon had said, "Don't psychologize me." I would have to stop psychologizing people. Suddenly I realized that I must be a killer, too.

I heard footsteps and looked up. It was Doug. I do not know how he managed to look so immaculate. His fair hair was blowing about, and he was grinning a huge grin.

"I've got some good news for you, Mick," he said. "Like to hear a secret?"

"Don't say we're getting out of this seaside resort," I said in a flat voice. I had given up hope long ago. We would never get out. I could not conceive that there was any other kind of life but this life of dust, heat, flies, fleas, bully beef, bombs and death.

"No, it's not that," said Doug. "It's better, in a way. You're going to get the M.M."

I stared at him as he stood there grinning. Eddie and Pat jumped up, strode over to me and pumped my limp hands.

"Christ, Doug," I said. "What have you done?"

"I've done you a good turn," he said. "You did me one the other night. I've shown my gratitude."

I got slowly to my feet and shook off Eddie and Pat. "Gratitude?" I asked. "A bloody nice way to show gratitude."

Doug's grin faded. "But Mick, I—what's wrong? Aren't you pleased?"

Eddie and Pat were staring at me in amazement.

"Pleased? Christ, Doug, you ought to know. You've been censoring my letters for bloody months. You ought to know I've kept up the illusion of being in Palestine. For months I've written to

Margaret about Palestine until I'm heartily sick of the bloody word. I've questioned every reo for the latest news about the weather and the pictures and the crops and camp sports and donkey races. And now at one stroke you mess everything up. If I get the M.M. it'll be in all the papers at home and she'll realize I've been in danger, I'm still in danger. I won't have it, I tell you, I won't have it."

I was trembling. For six months I had tended the plant of subterfuge. I had planted it in Margaret's mind, nurtured it gently, watered it, protected it from the scorching impact of truth. What was an M.M. compared with peace of mind for Margaret?

"I'm sorry, Mick," said Doug. "I forgot. I don't know how I came to forget. I was so pleased to be able to help you get an M.M. you deserved I forgot all about your girl."

"You forgot," I said bitterly. "Everybody forgets about me. I seem to do everything for everybody around here. When a man's got two stripes he's everybody's fool. The platoon commanders pass the buck to the sergeants and the sergeants pass it to the poor bloody corporals. Who looks after my section? I do. Who sees they're tucked in at night and on duty on time and who helps the poor bloody reos when they come here straight from base? I do. Who writes letters of half the bloody battalion? I do. Who writes to their wives and girl-friends and mothers when the boys get knocked? I do. 'Don't worry. Get Reynolds. He's willing.' That's right. Work the poor bloody willing horse to death."

Doug was staring at me with troubled eyes. "You've been a good friend to me, Mick, and I'm grateful," he said slowly. "I wouldn't be alive now only for you."

"Well, why in Christ don't you think of me?" I asked. I kicked a stone away viciously. "If you'd had the—the tenderness to hide the fact of being in Tobruk from your wife you wouldn't want some fool to come blundering in and telling her, would you?"

I saw his face working as soon as I said "wife" and I hated myself for my brutality, but I plunged on.

"I told her the truth," he said. "She was proud to know I was here."

"Well Margaret wouldn't be. She'd be worried stiff. I won't have her worried, I tell you. It's bad enough now when she thinks I'm in Palestine. I won't have her worried. You'll have to cancel your recommendation."

"I can't do that. It's gone through. Old Gutsache's got it by now."

"Well, you'll have to do something. I won't have it, I tell you. Say you want to withdraw your recommendation. Say you exaggerated."

He bit his lip. "But I can't do that, Mick. I made the statement on oath. I'd lose my commission if I said I was wrong. I can't do it."

"All right," I said. "If you won't do anything I'll go and see Old Gutsache myself. I'll tell him I won't accept it."

"You'll tell him what? You've got to accept it, Mick. He'll go mad if you say that."

Eddie grabbed my arm. "Mick," he said, "ya can't stop it now. Old Gutsache'll have a stroke if you say that. He'll want to know why and you'll have to tell him. Then the whole works'll go up. Let it ride, Mick."

I shook his hand off. "Go to hell, the whole bloody lot of you," I said, and walked away.

I strode into B.H.Q. "Is the C.O. in?" I asked.

"Well, yes," said Jack Mason. "Just about to go to mess. You can't——"

"Who can't?" I said, and brushed past him to the doorway.

"Ay, Mick," he said, grabbing at me. I shook him off, and went in.

Old Gutsache was poring over a big map of the perimeter. "Who the bloody hell is it?" he growled without looking up.

I stepped up to the table, saluted, and said, "Corporal Reynolds, sir. I want to talk to you."

He looked up, his mouth was even tighter than usual. "How the bloody hell did you get in here, Reynolds?" he barked. "There are bloody ways to do these things, you know. Going to mess in a minute. See the bloody adjutant."

"I won't see the adjutant, sir," I said. "I want to talk to you and I'm going to talk to you now."

Old Gutsache laughed, but there was no mirth in his laugh. "Congratulations, Reynolds," he said. "I didn't know you had taken over command of this battalion. You'll give me your two stripes, I suppose? Now get to hell out of here before I put you on a bloody charge."

He bent over the map again. I felt like a man stranded on a desert island. I put my hands on the table and leaned over it.

"You can put me on a charge, sir," I said; "but, by Christ, I'll have my say first."

He looked up and said wearily, "Will you please go away?"

"No," I said doggedly. "Not till I've had my say."

He shook his head and sighed. "Reynolds," he said, "why can't you behave like an ordinary soldier? You give me more trouble than any other five men in this battalion. All right. I'll give you two minutes. If I hadn't known your father—— Go on, man. Get it off your chest."

"I understand I've been recommended for the M.M."

His eyes brightened. "Yes. Congratulations. Got the papers here now. All ready to go on to brigade. You saved Mr Jackson's life. Good show. We can't spare officers. Losing too many. Well, what are you belly-aching about? Isn't the M.M. good enough for you? Want the bloody V.C. I suppose?"

I shook my head. "I don't want anything. I only want you to tear the papers up."

He pushed his lips out and ground his teeth. He always did that when he was surprised. "You're joking," he said, "and I've got no bloody time to spare for jokes."

"I'm not joking. I don't want the M.M. I don't want anything. I just want to be left alone."

"You're mad," he said. "You're raving mad. Practically every man in Tobruk'd give his right arm to have the M.M. Don't talk rot."

"It's not rot. It's the truth. I don't want the M.M."

"Reynolds," he said, "if you're pulling my leg you'll pay for this."

"I'm not pulling your leg, sir. I'm serious. I tell you, I'm deadly serious."

"But why, man? Why?"

"My girl thinks I'm in Palestine. If I get the M.M. she'll know I'm not there. I won't have her know."

Old Gutsache did not say anything for a while, and I could hear him grinding his teeth. When he spoke he had all the arrogant anger of the man who cannot understand.

"Your girl thinks you're in Palestine, so you refuse to accept an M.M. Good God man, you can't get away with a paltry excuse like that! Why don't you tell her you're in Tobruk? She'd be proud to know it if she's half a woman. When I was in France I used to write to my wife and tell her all about the battle I'd been in. She was proud of me."

"Margaret would be horrified. She'd worry terribly. I won't have her know. I won't have it."

"*You* won't have it?" he said.

Suddenly something dawned on Old Gutsache. "By the way," he said quietly, "what gave her the idea you were in Palestine?"

I drew a deep breath. "I did, sir. I wrote and told her."

His hands came up on to the table. "You told her, eh? And who censored the letter?"

It was coming now. I could see a grim light in his eyes.

"Nobody, sir."

"Nobody? What do you mean by 'nobody'."

"Nobody did. I wrote it in a green envelope. I told her the 93rd was doing garrison work in Palestine. I wasn't going to have her worried."

He was out of his chair in a flash, levering himself swiftly to his feet by the pressure of his hands on the table.

"Gr—green envelope? Garr—garrison work?" he spluttered. I saw the colour flaming in his cheeks. He had thrust his head out towards me and I could see his jaw working. "You told her—told her the 93rd—my battalion—was doing garrison work? Garrison work, in Palestine?"

"That's it."

He tried to speak and failed. I could hear my heart thumping and hear the grinding of his teeth.

"Jesus Christ, man, it's incredible! Absolutely incredible! By Christ, Reynolds, you'll pay for this! I'll have you in bloody Jerusalem jail next week! You won't get away with this. Disclosing military information in a green envelope. You know you signed a declaration on the outside that the letter contained only private and personal matter?"

"I know."

"Garrison work in Palestine! What the bloody hell am I supposed to be commanding—a troop of Girl Guides, a battalion of bloody pansies? The 93rd doing garrison work in Palestine! It's incredible!"

"I won't have her worried," I said.

"You can be court-martialled for this."

"That wouldn't be published at home. I wouldn't mind that. But I won't have her worried."

"Don't stand there saying it like a parrot. 'I won't have her worried. I won't have her worried.'" He slumped down in his chair. "Reynolds," he said, "your father was just the same. Wild, head-strong, always doing the unexpected thing. I ought to have known. I ought to have sent you to another battalion. Good God man, I've got enough worries without having madmen like you coming barging into B.H.Q. refusing to accept M.Ms and telling me they've used green envelopes to tell their girls the battalion's doing—doing garrison work in Palestine." He spat the last few words out as though they tasted foul.

"Now get out before I put you on a charge. If it was anyone else I'd drum him out of the unit. But seeing you're Mick Reynolds's son I'll overlook it. Now get out. We're going back into the Salient tomorrow. I've got work to do and I'm late for mess."

"I take it, sir, that I don't get the M.M.?"

"You deserve the cat-o'-nine-tails, but you'll get the M.M. Now get out." He was mopping his face with a handkerchief.

"All right, sir," I said, "if you insist. But you'll regret it. I won't be here to receive it."

"You mean you'll act the silly arse and go out and get yourself killed?"

"I don't mean killed, sir."

He got to his feet slowly. "Do I take it that you will desert, Reynolds?" he asked.

"I didn't say so, sir," I said.

"No, but, by Christ, you mean it!" he cried. "I'll have you on a charge for this, you won't get away with it. No, by God, you won't."

"You've got no proof. I didn't say it. And do you think a court-martial would believe that a man could earn the M.M. one day and say he was going to desert the next?"

Old Gutsache sat down. "You're clever," he said, "damn clever." He picked up a pen and tapped the desk with it. Suddenly he glanced up. "Reynolds," he said, "what do you think of my daughter?"

"Your daughter? She's a nice girl, sir."

"Oh. That's all, eh? A nice girl."

"Yes, that's all."

"Oh. When I sent you out to my home that time I hoped—well, you know, I knew your father pretty well, and I—— Oh well, let's forget it. Heard from her lately?"

"Had a letter the other day. She's keen on some fellow in the Armoured Division."

"Armoured Division, eh?" He was still tapping the table with the pen. "Well, that's A.I.F., isn't it?"

He sat there, twiddling the pen with his fingers. I waited a while. Then I said, "Well, sir, what about it?"

He looked up. "Eh? Oh you're still here. What about what?"

"The M.M.," I said. "Is it jake?"

He gave one of his rare quick smiles. "It's jake," he said. "Now get to bloody hell out of here or I'll put you on a bloody charge."

I turned at the doorway. "Thanks," I said.

He was sitting with his head in his hands. He was saying to himself, over and over again, "Garrison duty in Palestine. Garrison duty in Palestine."

I smiled, and let the tent flap fall behind me as I went out.

CHAPTER XLI

It happened when we were on the way back. It would not have happened at all only for our vanity. We always made it a point of honour to go fifty yards more than ordered, and so this night, on a reconnaissance patrol on the El Adem sector, we went the extra fifty yards. When Pat, who was counting the paces, moved up to Doug and whispered, "That's the three thousand, George", Doug just nodded, and we went the other fifty.

Suddenly we heard the *plop* of a Very light pistol and knew again the reflex action of going down to earth. There was a burst of machine-gun fire—we heard it zipping over our heads—and then I felt my left hand jar, and a sudden pain in it as if somebody had jabbed it with a red hot needle. Then it was gone, and I was lying there, with my heart beating wildly against the dust. For a moment I thought it was imagination—I had believed I was hit before—but then I knew my hand was wet and sticky, and that dust came away with it when I lifted it slightly. Panic gripped me then, a flaring panic, and over and over again, as we lay there waiting for the Very light to drift down and go out, the words "I've been hit, I've been hit" drummed in my mind. I pressed hard against the rifle I was holding in my right hand. It was something to hold on to.

The light went out, and we waited. The words were still drumming in my mind, beating themselves against my skull like a bird caught there, and my heart was pounding so hard I thought the Germans would hear it. Blood was beating in my ears, too, and I could feel it forced out of my hand with each wild pulse of my heart. I could hear the stealthy movements of the others as they got up, but I just lay there. I tried to move, but could not. I heard somebody come close to me, and I let my rifle go and sat up suddenly, and said, "I'm all right. I'm all right."

"Sssh," whispered Pat. " 'Course you are. Just nervous, that's all. Do you want every bloody Jerry around Tobruk to open up on us? Come on. Don't muck round the fountain."

I thought he had seen my hand—I could feel the blood dripping off my fingers—but it seemed darker than ever after the Very light, and the blood made no sound in the dust. I tried to speak. My lips moved, but no sound came. I swallowed, gritted my teeth so hard the tendons sprang to life in my throat, licked my lips quickly, and got my voice back.

"You go on," I whispered. "I'll follow. Going to snoop around for a while."

"I'll come," he said.

"No, you go. I want to be left alone."

A hand came out of the darkness and took me by the left forearm. I felt the firm pressure of his hand, the only gesture we allowed to escape from the rigid censorship of our fellowship, and I knew he was smiling. "All right, Mick," he said. "I know that tone. But don't do anything rash. I'll tell Doug." And then he was gone. I was glad he was gone because I could not stop whimpering any longer. He had set my hand throbbing, and the blood flowing faster, too. I sank down on my knees and took my left wrist in my hand, pressing hard on it, and there were tears in my eyes from the pain. It was a funny thing about wounds. We all knew now why men showed "great fortitude" when badly wounded, why they smoked casually while trams were lifted off their mutilated legs. We knew they did not feel anything after the first impact. It was later, when the paralysed nervous system recovered from the shock, that the pain came back. But this was different; my wound had been shaken. The blood was running fast now, and the salty smell of it was in my nostrils. I was holding my hand up. The blood ran down my wrist on both sides and wet my thumb and forefinger.

I'm going to die, I thought. I'm bleeding to death. I'm going to die here in the dust like a dog. I took my right hand away and wiped it on the side of my murder suit. As I did it I felt the Luger in my pocket, and I knew then I was going to die all right, for I was going to kill myself. From the first time I went out on patrol I had always taken the Luger with me. Whenever anyone noticed it I tried to grin and said, "Might come in handy if I run out of ammo some time." Once I did run out of ammunition, and I killed two Germans with it. I remember saying when I got back, "Killed the bloody Jerries with their own gun," and trying to laugh over it. But that was not why I always took it with me. I took it so that a broken thing would not go back to Margaret. I would go back to her whole or not at all. And now I had the way out. They would not have to amputate what was left of my hand now, the hand with a throbbing hole through it, and if the boys came back and found me they would not tell, for they were my friends and you did not tell things like that about your friends. They would just scrape a hole in the hard ground and put me in it, and perhaps one of them would mumble a prayer, and that would be all that would ever be known of how I died.

I whipped my hand into my pocket and took out the Luger. I put it up against the side of my head and I was just about to say good-bye to Margaret when something fell off the top of it into my face. It was the bootlace I always took with me to use as a tourniquet. The bootlace saved me. Habit was stronger than my wavering will, for every time I took that bootlace I practised making a tourniquet with it, and now, before I knew I was doing it, I had put the Luger away and was putting a tourniquet on my arm and twisting it tight with a nail. The bleeding had stopped before I remembered my abandoned resolve. I hooked the nail into the sleeve of my shirt, took the Luger out, and threw it away.

I knocked my hand getting into the anti-tank ditch and up the other side on the way back, but it did not hurt because I was numb from the elbow down. Somebody challenged me. It was one of the standing patrols. I had to use my right hand to put my left into my pocket. I answered.

"How's things, Mick?" asked the sentry when I came up. "Pat said you were taking a butcher's hook around. See anything?"

"Sweet ——— all," I said.

"A bloody good definition of the desert," he said, and chuckled. "Will I fire the shot to let 'em know you're comin' in or will you?"

I could not fire a shot. "You do it," I said.

When I went through our wire Eddie was waiting for me. "You O.K., Mick?" he asked.

"Yeah," I said.

"I was just comin' out to look for ya. Them commando stunts are all right for some blokes, but we got a date in Cairo with a coupler bints."

We went down into the post. I looked for somewhere to hide, for I had remembered that if anyone found out about my hand I would be sent to the hospital and my name would appear in the list of wounded in the Australian papers. I saw Margaret's face as she read it. I looked around desperately. I would hide somewhere and treat myself. It would soon be better. I would treat it myself. I noticed one of the sleeping bays indented into the concrete. That would do. I would roll into one of those where nobody would find me.

I looked up and found Eddie watching me. "Have a cigarette, Mick," he said, and held out a packet. I had reached out to take one before I noticed it was the last. "I wouldn't take a man's last smoke," I said. "Not in Tobruk."

"Take it," he said, and his voice was hard.

I put my right hand out again but he pulled the packet away. "Take it with your left hand," he said slowly. I could not see his eyes clearly—he had his back to the moon—but I knew what they looked like.

"You know?"

"Yeah. There's blood on your murder suit. You got hit and you didn't say nothin'. Come on. You gotta see Neil."

"I won't go," I said. "They'll see me. Everyone'll know then. Bring him here. I'll talk to him. I'll make him keep it dark."

"For Christ's sake," said Eddie. "What's up? What's on your mind? Come an' see Neil. She'll be jake."

"I won't go," I said, and my voice was high and strained. "Bring Neil here."

"But, Mick. Doan give me the screamin' ———. He can't come. He's got wounded to see to. He can't leave 'em."

"I can wait. Tell him I said to come when he can. I can wait." And I lay down and edged my way into the sleeping bay.

"Jesus Christ," said Eddie in disgust, and I heard him walk away.

It was a long time before Neil Hull came. I edged my way out of the sleeping bay and got to my feet. "Now what's all this?" he said in that weary, exasperated tone he used when he was harassed.

"It's simple. I got hit in the hand. I want you to have a look at it, but I don't want you to report it."

"You're mad," he said. "I must report it. You're mad."

"If you're my friend you won't report it. I won't have Margaret worried, I tell you. It'll soon be all right. Just slap some sulphanilamide or something on it and it'll soon be jake."

"You're mad," he said. "You're delirious. Give me a look at it."

I took my hand out of my pocket, with my right hand. "You should have put your field dressing on this," he said.

"I forgot about it," I said.

He shone a torch on the wound. The bullet had gone in the back at an angle and come out the palm. The parts of my hand not clotted or stained with blood were white from lack of it. He turned it over and peered at it.

"It'll soon be O.K., won't it?" I said.

"O.K. be damned!" said Neil. "The bone's shattered. There's dirt in it, too. There's a nice little bed for you down at the Fourth A.G.H."

"Neil," I said, "let's get this straight. Are you my friend?"

"Yeah. I'm also your M.O., and I say you're going into the Fourth A.G.H."

"And I say I'm not. I won't have Margaret worried," I tell you.

"But Mick——" said Eddie, and I turned on him and snarled, "Keep outa this. Mind your own bloody business!" and he sighed and walked away.

"Mick," said Neil, "you're a headstrong, conceited, mad bastard.

I can't do this for you. I'd be court-martialled. I'd finish up in Jerusalem jail."

"I won't have Margaret worried," I said. "That's all there is to it. I won't have her worried. You'll do this for me or, by God, I'll never speak to you again."

Neil shifted his feet uneasily on the concrete floor. "I tell you I can't," he said. "It'll be all right eventually, but you've got to have it treated straight away."

"I won't come," I said, "and I'll rub dirt into it so it gets infected and I'll say your treatment did it. You rotten bastard. I thought you were my friend."

"Oh Christ," said Neil, rubbing his hand wearily over his face. "I'd do it for you if I could, but I can't. I can't do it, that's all. You ought to be in bed. You'll know what pain is when that tourniquet comes off, and you'll feel as sick as a dog. I can't do it."

"You selfish bastard. I thought you were my friend. You can do it all right, only you won't."

"I could hide it for a while, but it'll take months. You've got a nasty wound there, Mick. Everyone'd soon know."

"Say it's desert sores."

"Desert sores. A hand like that? You're delirious. I'm sure you're delirious." He put his hand up to my forehead, but I struck it down with my right hand.

I reached down and scooped up all the dust I could off the concrete floor. "You'll do it," I said. "You'll do it or I'll rub this dirt into it, and I'll go on rubbing dirt into it until they'll carry me to you, and you'll be able to treat me all right. You'll be able to amputate my arm at the shoulder, and I hope you enjoy it."

Our wills met then, and I knew that it was the crisis. In the pale light I could see his face working. He brought his right hand up with the fist clenched, and moved it up and down in front of his chest, and I thought he was going to knock me down. I could not do anything to stop him because I had only one hand. Then his hand fell back to his side. He shook his head as though he could shake the torment out of it, and said, "I'll do it. I'll go to jail for it, but I'll do it. We'll see who's your friend."

"Good," I said, and then I fainted.

CHAPTER XLII

"Excuse me, corporal," said a shy voice. "Sorry to trouble you, but could you spare a minute?"

I was trying to sleep, but the heat, the fleas and the flies would not let me. There were other reasons, too. I was lying on a blanket in the air-raid shelter at the back of the post, lying there with dysentery clawing at my inside, lying there wondering how long it would be before I would have to get up and go wearily out to our improvised latrine again.

I looked up testily. "What's the trouble?" I snapped. Through the gloom I noticed that it was Dick Eyres, our latest reinforcement. He had taken Gordon's place. That was what the records showed, but Eddie, Pat and I knew differently. He had fair curly hair, fresh young face and an eager air. He looked as though he should have been at home with his mother. We had been dive-bombed the previous day and I had looked covertly at him. He was green with fear and I could see his hands trembling. Eddie and Pat were laughing at the dive-bombers—they knew how little damage fifty Stukas could do if you were underground—and cracking jokes.

But Eyres did not laugh. It was probably the first time he had been under fire. He did not curse or whimper as I had the first time. And he did not run to the air-raid shelter at the back. He just stood there, biting his lip and fighting against the terrible thing that was trying to beat him. And when the air was full of the mighty explosions of the bombs and great spouts of dirt went up and the post shook as though a giant hand had jerked it about, he stood there, and I could see him trying to smile.

"I'm sorry to worry you, corporal, but I want to ask a favour of you if you don't mind," he said.

I had bumped my hand when I sat up. It was throbbing. "Christ, what's wrong, now? All right," I growled. "Out with it, man."

"Thanks. I—er—you see——"

"Come on, come on. I haven't got all bloody day to waste. Speak up." My tone was harsh, peremptory.

"Well I——" and then it came out in a rush—"I'm going out on patrol tonight for the first time and I thought you might be able to help me. You know, give me some hints that'd help."

He stood there, ashamed at his confession. He was swinging his tin hat nervously by the chin strap, and his eyes were troubled.

"Oh," I growled, "is that all? Christ, man, you're a soldier, aren't you? You're fully trained, aren't you, or you wouldn't be here? We can't start training men in the front line. What the bloody hell are all those base-wallopers for?"

He took the tin hat in both hands and twisted the chin strap around his finger. "I'm sorry, corporal," he said.

"And don't keep calling me corporal," I growled.

He shifted his feet uncomfortably. "I'm sorry," he said. "You see, I'm so new to—to all this. It's not for me I'm asking. I don't want to let the other fellows down."

I was ashamed then. When I had gone out for the first time I had not thought of the others. I had been thinking too much, too frantically, of Mick Reynolds.

Something was clawing at my inside again. I looked up at the fresh face of the eager youth standing in front of me. He shifted his feet again.

"I came to you," he said, "because I think you can give me the dinkum oil better than the others. You see, I think—I think you've got guts to carry on after you got that knock on the hand. Gee, I wish I was like you. I wish I didn't know what it was to be afraid."

I laughed—a short, bitter laugh that was more like a snarl. "Listen, mate," I said, "I've been more afraid than I'd ever dare admit. I've practically wet myself with fear."

He shook his head slowly. "I don't believe it," he said.

I lay back on the blanket as a twinge of pain racked me. When I sat up again he was walking away.

"Hey, Eyres," I called. "Don't you want that advice?"

He flushed because the others had heard and were looking at him, but his eyes were gleaming with eagerness and he came back quickly.

"My oath," he said.

I told him the conventional stuff—muffled boots, slouch hats instead of tin ones, keeping right distances, alertness for minefields and booby-traps, going down as soon as you heard the *plop* of a Very pistol, staying close to the earth if under fire.

He listened carefully and asked a few questions. His gratitude embarrassed me.

"How old are you?" I asked. His face had the fresh tints of boyhood.

"Twenty last week," he said.

"You lied to get in, then," I said.

He flushed. "Yes, I couldn't stand it any longer."

"I know," I said.

He licked his lips and made two attempts to say something. Then he blurted out, "Got married before I left." He pulled out a wallet, took out a photograph and thrust it into my hand. I was sitting up and he was kneeling in front of me.

"That's the missus," he said shyly.

I took it. In the light from the doorway I saw that it was his wedding photograph. His wife had the fatuous, self-complacent smile of a young bride. He was looking stern and determined, like a man who faced an ordeal but would see it through at any cost.

"Feel like writing to Ripley," he said, lowering his voice. "Believe it or not, met her on the Manly ferry. Yeah. Fell for each other straight away. And they reckon there's no such thing as love at first sight."

"Yeah," I said. "That's what they reckon."

"You wouldn't understand it. Took one look at her and was head over heels."

"No. I wouldn't understand it."

Another inward struggle was mirrored in his pink face, and then he stammered, "She's—she's going to have a baby."

"Oh," I said. I wished the throbbing in my hand would stop. Why did these fools rush off and get married just before they sailed? Tobruk must be full of the morons. What did they think they were going to? A Sunday School picnic or something? I knew I was expected to say something, so I said it. "Congratulations," I said.

"Wish you could come with me tonight," he said. "I'd feel O.K. if I knew you were there."

"Bullo. There's nothing to it. I've been laid up with this hand. Most of the boys have had more experience than me. She'll be jake."

Eyres stammered his thanks, and went away. I did not sleep well that night. I lay awake for hours, with that clawing inside me, that throbbing in my hand, and thought of Eyres and his smiling young wife. I was sorry I had been so gruff with the kid. I told myself I would apologize in the morning.

I got up three times and dragged myself out to the latrine. I had to get up again at dawn. A member of the patrol was sitting in one of the sleeping bays. He had taken his boots off and was prizing bully beef out of a tin with a fork.

"How'd it go, Jack?" I asked. "Any fun and games?"

"Not bad," he said. I noticed a scratch down his forearm. There was dark dried blood around the edges.

"Wire?" I asked.

"No. A close one, that's all. They made it bloody hot when we were getting through the wire."

"A fighting patrol, eh? I thought it was only a recce."

"They're bastards for Very lights, aren't they?"

"Yeah. Lose any men?"

"Yeah. One killed."

I did not have to ask who it was. I knew.

CHAPTER XLIII

It was strange how, sometimes, you knew something had happened. I was waiting for the patrol to come in, and long before I heard the warning shot from the standing patrol I knew less men would come back through the wire than had gone out through it.

One man was missing when the boys came in. I knew from counting them. I went up to the corporal, Sam Russell, and asked him who it was. Sam put his Tommy gun down and wiped a weary hand over his sweaty face. I liked Sam. He had worked in an architect's office in Melbourne, and one night he said to me as, kept awake by fleas, we lay in one of the rooms off a perimeter post in the El Adem sector, and yarned, "Funny thing, Mick, back in Aussie I used to draw plans to build things up; here I tear things down."

"Yeah," I replied, "but you've got to cut the rottenness of things before you can build anew. You were going to be an architect, so you must know you can't build anything decent on a rotten foundation. Some day we'll all be able to build anew." He scratched his back where a flea was biting him and said, "Yeah, Mick. I s'pose that's right."

There was a bond between us, as there is between all section leaders, and sometimes he drew me aside and asked my advice about how to handle reinforcements who, fresh from a training battalion back in Palestine, thought they knew how to run the war.

I asked Sam who it was. "Blue Carter," he said. "His body's hanging on their wire."

"Blue," I said. "Oh." I knew Blue well. I remembered how worried he was the time his wife was sick, how he pestered the postal corporal for mail, and how he had come to me once, talked awkwardly for a few minutes, and then said, "Hope you don't mind me asking, Mick, but I heard about the letters you used to write to Clive's nipper. You know, about Bogeywomps and Ziggle Zoggles and Wild Garages and all those other queer things. Well, I was wondering if you'd mind writing one—a short one will do—to young Peter. He's got the mumps and you know how kids like getting letters, 'specially ones with drawings in 'em like yours. Hope it's not too much trouble."

"Trouble?" I said. "Why, Blue, if it'd cheer the kid up it's no trouble. And I'll sign it 'Uncle Mick'."

That was how it started. Often, after that, I wrote a letter to young Peter, and sometimes a letter came back. "When the war is all finished," he wrote, "you and Daddy and me will go fishing and have plenty of ice creams and catch a lot of fish."

Sam told me all about it. "We tried to get his body," he said, "but they pinned us down with M.Gs and mortars. We weren't in the race. But we'll get to him all right. We'll go back tomorrow night.".

"Let me come, Sam," I said.

"Sorry, Mick," he said, "but this is a section show." He glanced down at my wounded hand. "Anyhow you wouldn't be much use."

"Thanks," I said bitterly. He reached out, and I felt the firm grip of his fingers on my shoulder.

"Sorry, Mick," he said, "but you know how it is. It's a section show."

I knew all right. I would have done exactly the same if I had been in his place. You could not ask an outsider, even a man in your platoon, to risk his life for a man in your section. I knew that Sam knew, too. I knew that the Germans would leave the body there, hoping that we would try to get to it, and that they would have fixed lines trained on it and would be sitting there, waiting.

Sam led his section mates out the next night, and when they came back one of them was being carried. He had a bullet through the thigh.

"Fixed lines," said Sam. "We'll try again tomorrow."

They went out again the next night, and this time another was carried in. A bullet had gone right through him, probably through his lung, but it was not as bad as it sounded. We knew now that those "sucking wounds"—the air was sucked in and out as the wounded man breathed—were not nearly as serious as a hole in the stomach. They lived with sucking wounds, they even came back to Tobruk.

"Fixed lines," said Sam. "Those Jerry bastards."

I heard the voice of Captain Herbertson, the company commander, and Old Gutsache's peevish voice in reply. Somebody said, "Christ, the trump", and then we were all being called together.

"The C.O.," said Captain Herbertson, "would like to have a word with you all."

Old Gutsache cleared his throat, put his finger along the side of his nose in his characteristic way, and said, "Er—it has come to my notice that patrols have been going out from this post the last two nights to bring in the body of a dead comrade, Private Carter. I understand, too, that two men have been wounded in this futile but heroic—er—gesture. Well—er—all I want to say is this; I deplore this as a soldier—it's reprehensible to have men wounded in a fruitless venture like this—I deplore it as a soldier, I say, but, by God, I admire it as a man. For truly it has been said 'Greater love hath no man than this—that he give up his life for his friend.' Er—that's all, men. Carry on."

"Can I say something, sir?" asked Sam.

"Yes, corporal. Speak up, man."

"Well sir, it's not much. It's just this: You've got most of the story right, but there's one part that's skew-whiff. We didn't go out to get Blue Carter's body. What's the use of bodies anyhow once they're dead? We didn't go out for his body. We went out to get thirty-five pounds he won at two-up. We wanted to send it home to his wife."

CHAPTER XLIV

I WENT into the dug-in tent. Neil had asked me to come earlier than usual. He had said he wanted to play chess. I could play chess again now so I brought the set with me. He was sitting on a chair, with his elbows on his knees and his chin in his hands.

"Hullo, Neil," I said as I went in. He did not seem to hear me so I said it again, louder this time. He glanced up at me with a start, sat up and said "Hullo, Mick" in that slow voice of his I would have known anywhere. He was small and muscular, but his hands were a surgeon's hands. Sometimes I noticed them trembling slightly, and knew that, however hard he might try to hide it, he was bomb happy, too. What did it matter? Everyone in Tobruk was bomb happy. It was only a question of degree, and when he was working his hands were steady enough. They had to be. He could not patch up broken men if his hands trembled, for he was there because of what his hands could do; his hands took the pain out of men's wounds and kept them alive until other hands could start to build the flesh anew. His mind directed them, but his hands did the work.

Suddenly I wondered what would happen one night if an M.O. had one of his hands blown off. I thought of the line of wounded from a fighting patrol, the line coming into the tent and finding the M.O. on one of the stretchers instead of bending over it. I saw the faces of those men as they saw him there and realized he could not help them. I looked down at my own hand then, my left one, and wondered whether I would have killed myself the night I got hit if it had been blown off. Suddenly I knew I would have killed myself because I could not have gone on any longer, maimed like that. Other men did it, and smiled, too, a sardonic smile; but not me. I was too afraid. Perhaps I was a coward after all.

I looked at Neil. His head was back in his hands again, and his thoughts were far away. Suddenly I saw how old he had grown. There was grey in his hair, and the lines were etched deeper into his face. M.O. of a battalion at twenty-five. What a job! About eight hundred men to keep well, to keep alive. It would be a big task in civil life; it was much more in Tobruk.

He sat up and smiled that bright smile I saw so rarely these days. "Not much of a welcome on the mat, eh, Mick? You see, a man gets to thinking here. The desert's a hell of a place for thinking. When they issue you with your uniform they should give you a non-thinking apparatus. You should be able to press your navel and stop that goading mechanism we call the mind.

"We won't play tonight. You know, Mick, I've had enough. I want to get back to a base hospital. I'm sick of the dust and fleas and flies and dysentery and death. It's ugly to die as these men die. At least there should be some dignity about it. You know, white sheets, and flowers beside the bed." He laughed. I did not like that laugh.

"We all want to go back," I said, "but you wouldn't go if you could. None of us would."

"Yeah," he said. "I suppose you're right. I wouldn't go if I could. I'd like to talk. You're always pestering me for information about gangrene, syphilis, typhus and God knows what. Ask me something. Let me amaze you by my vast medical knowledge."

I put the set down and pulled the chair round so that I could rest my arms on the back of it. "All right," I said. "There's one thing I want to know. Tell me about sulphanilamide."

His eyes lit up. "Ah," he said, "You speak of strange alchemy, sir. The magic drug, the Aladdin's lamp, the open sesame to healing."

We sat there for a long time, talking and thinking, and then the medical orderlies arrived, nodding curtly to me—they resented my attempt to help and my intimacy with Neil—and saying "Good night, sir" to Neil. I sat there and watched them getting ready. Neil was preparing, too.

"It's a fighting patrol tonight," he said.

"Yeah," I said. "Just about the whole company out. More an attack than a patrol. The O.C. went, too."

"I know," he said, and turned away. I found myself straining my ears as the minutes passed. They would soon be coming in, and, judging by the noise we had heard earlier, some of them would not be walking. Then we heard the first stretcher-bearers, and turned to face the tent flap. For a moment I was plagued by the fear that Eddie or Pat would be carried in—both were out—but I shook it off angrily. I saw Neil's face grow set and his thumbs and forefingers rub against each other quickly, twice, and then he was ready. The Arabs did that when they wanted money; Neil did it when he wanted strength.

They brought them in, these things that had been men. I knew some of them well, others by sight, some not at all. I saw no fear, only unquestioning acceptance. I did what I could, which was not much—I had had no medical training and could not use my left hand.

The first stretcher-bearer nodded and said "They're O.K., Mick" as he went past and I did not care what happened then, for I knew Eddie and Pat were safe. A private was sitting near the door, awaiting his turn for attention. We called him "Snow". I did not know his other name. He had his left arm in a sling and he was trying to balance a writing pad on his knees and write a letter. Blood kept getting on the paper, and he had to throw sheets away.

"How's things, Snow?" I asked. "Where'd you cop it?"

He looked up and grinned. "Got three of 'em, Mick," he said. "Only flesh wounds. Just writin' to the missus so's she won't be too worried. She'll get a telegram."

"Good idea. I'll write it for you after if you like."

"Thanks Mick, but she'd be worried if she read someone else's writin'. Thanks though. Ya know, they worry, women, don't they?"

"Yeah. They worry."

"A man's jake. Just a couple of fleshies. Be back again in a few weeks, dealing it out to old Jerry again. But I dunno. Strike me pink, women worry."

Then they brought him in. Somehow I knew it was Captain Herbertson before I saw him. At first I thought he was dead. You could see death in his face. There was a field dressing on each of his shoulders and one on his neck. The front of his shirt was stained with bloody water, and the hairs on his chest clotted with purple blood. I could not understand where the water had come from. Perhaps he had vomited as they were giving him a drink. One of the stretcher-bearers saw the puzzled look on my face and said,

"We gave him a drink, Mick, but it just ran out the hole in his neck."

"Oh," I said.

"He can't talk unless you press the edges together."

"Oh," I said.

The other stretcher-bearer went up behind Neil and said, " 'Scuse me, sir."

"Don't bother me," Neil snapped.

"But, sir," said the stretcher-bearer, "he's hurt bad."

I saw Neil's back stiffen. "Christ, man," he said, "isn't this poor bastard hurt bad, too? He's only got an M.G. burst in his chest, that's all. Shut up, for Christ's sake!"

The stretcher-bearer licked his dry lips, for he knew what I knew. "But, sir," he said, "it's Captain Herbertson."

Neil's hands stopped moving. He did not say anything. I was glad I could not see his face. "It's Captain Herbertson, and he's hurt bad," said the stretcher-bearer.

Neil's voice was hard when he spoke at last. "He'll have to take his turn," he said. "There's no rank here. He'll have to take his turn."

The stretcher-bearer turned away. I looked at Captain Herbertson again, and suddenly, I saw him as he stood before us that first day, a giant of a man, confident and grinning. His round face was like that of a child, and it had a child's big ginger freckles.

"I'm your new company commander," he had said. "My name's Herbertson and my first name's Archie, so see what you can make of that. You'll call me something rude, I know, so you might as well get the facts to work on. Well, I inspected your huts this morning, and they looked like a brothel on New Year's morning. Of course, I've never seen a brothel on New Year's morning or at any other time, but I understand it would look like what your huts looked like this morning."

There were cries of "You beaut!" and somebody started to sing "Bull ——— bull ———, it all sounds like bull ——— to me, to me", and the whole company took it up, with Herbertson standing there grinning, and eventually joining in the song, too. We all knew then that if we had to die it would be easier to do it following a man like that.

His turn came at last. Before Neil turned to look at him I saw him draw a deep breath, and saw again the rapid nervous rubbing of the fingers. His face was set in the old grim lines when he turned. I saw recognition flicker in Herbertson's eyes and his lips moved, but no sound came. Neil took the field dressing off each shoulder and peered at the wounds. As they undid the bandage from around his throat I noticed a red furrow across the back of his neck. It looked as if he had been lashed by a whip. That one had been close. When they took the bandage away the bottom part of his throat fell away and thick blood oozed out. A round had torn a big gap across his throat.

Neil looked at it for a moment, felt Captain Herbertson's pulse, and stood up. I held my breath. The groan of a wounded man was the only sound in the tent. We were all waiting to hear what Neil would say.

"Put him over in the corner," he said. "Put him over in the corner to die."

And then I saw a miracle happen. I saw a man's hands slide up along a stretcher, I saw his elbows take the strain, and then his hands, and I saw him come upright. I saw him panting as he sat there, with staring men all around him, and I saw the blood begin to flow anew from the ragged hole in his throat. I saw his teeth clench, his lips come down over them, and then I saw his hands come up and take the bloody, tattered edges of the wound and press them together, and I heard him say, "Die? Like bloody hell I'll die!" and I knew he was going to live, because you could not kill a man like that unless you shot him through the heart.

Later, when it was all over for another night and Neil and I were the only ones left, I stopped in the doorway. "Good night, Neil," I said.

He did not speak at first, and just when I was about to speak again he said, "Good night, Mick."

I opened the flap of the tent and let it fall again. "Neil," I said, "I'm sorry about Johnson's leg. I didn't mean to hurt him."

He turned around then, and I saw how old he looked. I used to think men could not age overnight. I used to think a lot of things. "It's all right, Mick," he said dully. "You couldn't help it. You've only got one hand anyhow. I shouldn't have talked to you like that. I didn't know what I was saying. I don't know whether you know this, but Archie Herbertson and I joined up together."

"Yes," I said, "I know that."

"He married my sister."

"Yes. He was my friend, too."

"You see, Mick, when you know them it's hard. Back home, when they used to bring accident cases in they were just cases, names on a card; but here it's different. To see Archie here tonight and know that I couldn't do anything for him—well, that made it hard. I could only tell them to put him in the corner to die. It hurts to be impotent, Mick. I sit here at night and wonder who's going to come through that flap. You only know the fellows in your company, but I know them all. There's not one of them who hasn't come to me at some time or other for a recipe for a hangover, or a weak story so's he could be put on light duties. And sometimes they ask me how to cure their kids' whooping cough or what advice they should give their wives so they can have a baby easier. And when they're brought in and they look at me the way they do and I can't help them, well it just seems that it's my fault, that I've let them down. And when they come to me with a temperature and I know they've been chewing cordite to get them out of the front line I can't give them away because I want to chew cordite myself. And so you see that if I lose my temper well it's not really me, it's the man they've made me. I'm sorry."

"It's all right, Neil," I said. "I never thought of it like that. I'm sorry I worried you that night I got hit."

"Forget it. You made me do it. I couldn't let you down. You'll come again tomorrow night? It stops me thinking if I've got you to talk to."

I wanted to say I would not come, but I could not say it.

"All right," I said, "I'll come," and, opening the flap, I went out into the dawn. The bare waste of Tobruk stretched around me, and a chill wind stirred the dust at my feet.

As I trudged through the dust towards the perimeter post the strong tide of my weariness came back and the wound in my hand began to throb again. I was so tired I could think of only one thing. It went round and round in my brain—when I go to sleep I must not dream about Herbertson's throat. I must not dream about Herbertson's throat. It was no good; I did dream about it, only it was Margaret whose throat had that ragged hole in it and it was I who could not help her.

CHAPTER XLV

WE did not believe it when they told us. There are some things you simply cannot believe, and this was one of them.

We thought it was merely another latrine rumour. We had heard so many of them and so few of them had been true.

Eddie shook his head doggedly and tried to keep the gleam of hope out of his eyes. "Mick," he said earnestly, "it's a furphy. It's the same ole furphy, all over again, an', stone the bleedin' crows, it's not funny no more."

It had never been funny to me. Leaving Tobruk? Why, it would be like coming to the end of a prison sentence. It would be like coming out of a dungeon into a flood of sunlight and seeing children playing on a beach with the white surf behind them. Children? We had not seen a child for seven months, had not seen a girl, either. It would be strange to hear a girl's voice, even a Wog's. I wondered whether I would be gauche when I spoke to a girl again.

And then we found it was true. We *were* leaving Tobruk. There was no exultation in me, only wonder. I was stunned. I could scarcely comprehend what it meant. Going back to Palestine, to Beit Hareed—why, it would be like going home. To see green fields, and patient donkeys plodding down the chocolate hillsides, and to have a sky above you with no German bombers in it. No, such things were not for men like Pat McDonald, and Eddie Wilson and me. As long as there was a Tobruk and Germans sitting in a semicircle around it we would stay here, prodding them occasionally, holding grimly to it always.

But the day came. We were issued with our emergency rations, the Poles took over our flea-bitten doovers and one afternoon we put our haversacks and packs on, and those who had kit-bags lifted them on to the shoulders, and we climbed into trucks and were driven down to a beach near the old village on the Derna Road side of the town. We had to wait there for twenty-four hours. It was the longest twenty-four hours I have ever known. The night passed, and the next day. We were supposed to go on board a destroyer at midnight. At seven-thirty we heard the bombers coming over and as we huddled there Eddie said, "God stone the bleedin' crows. It'd be just our luck to cop one now", and I moved near him so that I could try to shield his body with mine if they dropped any close. The flares came down over the harbour, lighting it up like day, and the ack-ack fire went up. Then we heard the eerie whistle of the bombs, and the crunching sound as they burst. The bombers went away, and the black night came down around us again.

At nine we were given the order to move, and I got my section together. As we drove through the battered shell of the town I tried to convince myself that I would never see it again, that all that had happened here would soon be only a memory. I could not believe it, and I knew I would never forget it, either, or the men I had seen die here.

We got out of the trucks and lay down above Number Four Wharf. It was just a wharf, but to the men who had worked there it was much more than that. They would never forget it, either, and some time, later, they would be able to talk about it, and the men they had known there.

We were not allowed to smoke and were told to talk as quietly as possible. "Anyone would think bloody Jerry had a battalion of ghosts to fly over us an' give him the drum," said Eddie. Pat did not say anything, and I knew that his Irish heart was stirred. I realized, too, that Eddie and I were going out of Tobruk together, just as we had come in, but Pat was alone. Gordon was not going out with him, for Gordon would never go anywhere again.

The three hours we waited above Number Four Wharf were the longest I have ever known, longer than the half hours I had waited for my friends to come back from patrol. We expected that at any moment the big bombers would be over to pound the harbour or that Bardia Bill would hurl shells at us from twelve miles away. But nothing happened; there were no bombers, and no shells; there was only peace.

Suddenly someone said, "Here she comes," and a ripple of excitement, of relief, went along the line of waiting men. A black shadow loomed up behind it, and soon we heard the tramp of marching men, and the sound of English troops singing "She'll be Comin' Round the Mountain When She Comes".

"Yi yi yippy yaselves," cried Eddie. "You'll be sorry!" And the others took up the cry. "You'll be sorry!" they yelled, "You'll be ———— sorry!" and suddenly I was back in Ingleburn Camp, walking down to the 2/93rd Battalion lines in my new suit and new overcoat, going forth to the war.

"Don't worry, luds. We can take it," the English troops called back, and somebody said, "By God, if they're like the Royal Horse Artillery and the Northumberland Fusiliers they can, too."

I got my section together, and we went on to the wharf.

"There's no doubt about the bloody navy," said Eddie. "Look at the bastards." There was no doubt about the navy all right. For seven months it had been our life-line, through it had flowed the strength that sustained us, the food we ate, the rounds we fired, the mail that kept us going. While we were going up the gangplank on one side Australian troops, stripped to the waist, were unloading supplies and ammunition on to lighters on the other. The navy had a time limit, and when that limit was up the ship would steam out of Tobruk. Nothing could stop the navy from keeping to that schedule. They left a major behind one night, and they would have left General Wavell behind, too, if he had wanted to go out by sea and had been a minute late.

When we reached the top of the gangplank I noticed a dark figure standing on the deck. "Well, Aussies," he said in a broad

English dialect, "you held her." And suddenly it was all worth while, all the flies and the fleas and the bombs and the death and the scars, all made worth while by the words of a man whose face I never saw. I knew that in that darkness I had found a friend. And suddenly I was proud, too, fiercely proud, that after seven months the Germans had captured only three square miles of the one hundred and thirty-four square miles inside the perimeter.

"Yes, mate," I said, "we held her." And I followed Eddie and Pat down on to the deck to look for a place to sleep.

BOOK FOUR

AFTER TOBRUK

★

CHAPTER XLVI

WE went out of the Victoria Hotel to have a look at Cairo, to which we had come on leave from Syria, where we had been stationed after Tobruk. In the blue sky the inevitable black kites sailed on still wings. They dipped and soared all day, banked and turned, hardly ever moving their wings. You could go out on to any balcony in Cairo, and if you could not see a kite gliding about within two minutes there was something wrong with your eyes.

Pat looked up and grinned. "Bettr'n M.Es and Stukas, eh?" he said.

"Yeah," I said. "I hope the sirens don't go while we're here. I'll probably leap out of bed and rush downstairs."

"Me, too," said Pat. "Just a trio of bomb happies, eh?"

We went down the street, pestered every few yards by hawkers, touts for barber and curio shops, beggars and boot-black boys. We learned later that there were three thousand street hawkers in Cairo, five thousand five hundred barbers, and eight thousand donkey boys and cart drivers. Gharries went clip-clopping by, the drivers calling out for custom. All car drivers, as in Bombay, blew their horns incessantly.

"This place," said Eddie, "makes Tobruk seem peaceful."

We stopped outside Shepheard's Hotel, and looked at the old, low, long building. "So this is it," said Pat. "The famous Shepheard's, one of the abodes of the white masters."

"Don't be a cad," I said, with an exaggerated accent. "After all, old boy, there's a code."

We laughed and looked up at the men who would use those phrases. Officers were sitting about on the wide veranda that stretched from the building to the footpath. They were drinking tea, coffee or lemonade, lolling languidly with women who varied from colourless Englishwomen to exotic Egyptians, Greeks and Syrians.

A simpering hawker, with a great show of caution, gave us a

glimpse of a set of obscene photographs. Eddie was immediately interested. He told us that his interest was impersonal, that it was merely professional, because he wanted to compare these with the choicest of Wilson's Perv Gallery.

After a lot of haggling, Eddie beat the hawker down from fifty piastres to five. "Keep them down," said the hawker furtively. "If policeman see me, me go calaboose."

We turned the corner. "Take a bo-peep at these perv snaps," said Eddie, taking them out of the envelope. They were photographs of fully clothed English soldiers. Eddie stood staring stupidly at them, then made a dash towards the corner. He disappeared round it, and a few minutes later he came back.

"Not a bloody sign of him," he said. "And if yous laugh I'll push your bloody faces in."

There were hundreds of beggars. A man was sitting on the footpath. His arm had been chopped off near the shoulder and he had the stump outside his clothes. He pointed at it with a grimace and cried "*Bucksheesh!*" If he had not had the stump exposed I would have given him something, but instead I went on, sickened.

A woman kept following us with a filthy baby with flies all around its lips. Every time the baby moved its head a cloud of flies rose and settled down again. "*Ana muskeen*[1]," wailed the woman. "Gibbit *bucksheesh*. Gibbit *mungareer*[2]."

We gave her a piastre. "It's not our responsibility," said Pat defiantly. "Why don't some of these pashas give them something? We've got our own poor at home and after the war we'll have plenty of widows to look after. Why don't the rich people here do something about it?"

"When the world does something about poverty," I said, "I'll believe we've made one step towards not having a war every twenty-five years."

"We only get six bob a day," said Eddie. I knew they felt ashamed, as I did, because we could not do more for these people.

"Let's get on a tram," said Pat, "and take a look at the Pyramids."

When we got to Gizeh we changed trams, and watched the green fields and houses slipping by. We could see the Pyramids pointing to the sky in the distance. They did not seem to get any closer. Eventually we reached the terminus, shook off the guides who insisted that they show us the Pyramids and the "Sphinkus", abused natives who wanted us to ride camels and donkeys, and trudged up the hill to the Pyramid of Cheops.

"I dunno," said Eddie, staring up at the rugged triangle of stones. "It's just a heap of rocks."

[1] I am poor.
[2] Food.

That was what it was, just a heap of rocks, old weather-worn rocks piled on each other and stretching hundreds of feet into the air.

We climbed up. It took us a long time. The rocks were so big we had to climb from each one to the next. They were a dirty brown and were worn by countless feet. We were hot and puffing when we reached the top, a few square yards of flat rock.

There was, of course, a magnificent view from the top. Here the ancient met the modern, antiquity rubbed its weary shoulders with the future. Stretching away towards the horizon was the undulating desert. At first there were the inevitable tents of a military camp, and, beyond, the drabness of the desert. On the other side the ribbon of the tram lines ran straight as an arrow back to Gizeh. It amused me to think of going to see the Pyramids in an electric tram.

"It's the new world that matters, not the old," I said. "These relics of the ancient past leave me cold."

"We're just three poor ignorant blokes," said Eddie. "Let's go back to Cairo and have a drink."

That night we looked in at a cabaret. It was a big room full of tables and chairs and it had a bar down one side. On the stage a girl was dancing to music that was a weird sequence of mournful sounds, a wailing protest against a malign fate. It always seemed to be working to a climax, but never reached it. Yet behind it there was something, something elemental, a plaintive longing for something unattainable, the gnawing hunger of a starving world.

The dancer was wearing a scanty brassiere of spangles the colour of brass, and her only other garment was a narrow sheath of the same spangles covering her hips. We could see the dark channel between her full breasts. Her copper body gleamed in the electric light as she twisted it to and fro, and her navel showed black against the corpulent mound of the stomach. She held her hands level with her head, and the staccato crack of castanets filled the air about her.

She moved slowly around the stage, waggling her hips up and down to the rhythm of the castanets in her hand and the howling Arabic music. The faint pelvic movement induced in most women by walking was accentuated in this dance. Up and down went her hips, flicking their weight from one side to the other.

Then she stopped. She remained still, apart from the movement of her fingers with the castanets and the changed motion of her hips. She was moving her pelvis backwards and forwards now amidst the raucous cheers and coarse remarks of the troops.

"Christ," said Eddie.

A fat girl in a pink evening dress sidled up to us and said, "Nice Aussies. You buy me drink, Aussies?" She had full lips, black eyes she was trying to make alluring, and a sloppy amplitude of flesh. I shuddered.

"Cripes," said Eddie, "I could go for this."

The Scot in Pat spoke. "*Kam fuloose?*" he asked.

"Ten piastres," she replied. She lost attraction for Eddie. We ignored her and went to the bar.

"Well," said Eddie, "what about it?"

"What about what?" I asked.

"Berka Street," said Eddie. "Now doan say ya doan wanter see it."

"Eddie," I said, "I'm willing to see anything. If people live that way, any way, I'm willing to see them."

"O.K.," said Pat. "Let's go."

We got up and went out into the street. "It's a great black-out," said Eddie, looking round at the lighted doorways and windows. "Imagine showin' them lights in Tobruk!"

The blue street lights were like those in Bombay. The stench of decaying manure was the same, too. We walked down a filthy street to where a sign told the world that here was Sharia El Berka. The buildings were old and dingy, and wide brick pillars made the footpath like a tunnel. We had scarcely entered the street before a dirty native urchin who was lurking in the shadows said, " 'Ullo, Aussie. 'Ullo, George. You want to see exhibisheeon?" and he told us what sort of exhibition it was. He also rattled off a long series of remarkable demonstrations we would see for fifty piastres for each of us. Most of the words were English, but some were Arabic. We understood the Arabic ones.

I stared at him in amazement. He could not have been more than ten. I asked him to repeat the programme. "Exhibisheeon," he said. "Very good, very nice, very clean, very syphilitic. Exhibisheeon can can. Exhibisheeon——" and the list followed.

"No," said Pat. "*Imshi.*"

"Me make special price," said the boy. "Special price for Aussies. Thirty piastres each. Very good, very nice, very clean."

"What do you do?" I asked.

He grinned. "Me band," he said. "Me play, like this," and he went over to the wall and beat a tune on it with his hands and chanted.

We shook him off and went on. The street was full of troops. Many were drunk, most had been drinking.

Berka Street has an assertive patriotism. Crudely painted flags
were on the wall of almost every building, outside and inside.

We went through a dingy doorway. There was an open latrine
at the bottom of the stone stairs. We went up the stairs, passing
many soldiers on the way down. At the first floor landing there
was a sign "Mimi House". About twenty soldiers, mainly Tommies,
were sitting on settees. Some had their arms round girls. Three girls
were sitting down and two were standing. One was trying to drag
a Tommy into a room. When she saw us she cried, "Aussie! Aussie!"
and came mincing over. She had black kinky hair and a painted
face, and her only garment was a white slip. She was singularly
unattractive.

"She leaves nothing to the imagination," I said.

"My oath," said Eddie.

"———?" she asked, with devastating candour. It was the old
word again, the word C.Os had tried to stamp out in Australia,
Palestine and Tobruk. It was the ugliest word in the world. I
recoiled, for I had never heard a woman say it before.

"———?" she asked again. "No? Well ——— off!" and she
laughed a wild, high-pitched laugh.

Most of the soldiers laughed. We soon learned that it was one
of their stock jokes, like their use of an Arabic expression which
ordered you to do something physically impossible.

"Let's go upstairs," I said.

Every floor in every building was a brothel. We saw them all.
We went to London House, Fatma House, Amina House, King
George House, Churchill House, Fifi House, Love House, and
Tiger Lil's. We saw girls in dresses, slips, kimonos, and bathing
costumes. We saw Egyptian girls, Greek girls, Maltese girls, Syrian
girls, French girls, Jewish girls. Some were repugnant, and some
were strangely attractive.

One girl, a Syrian, had dewy eyes and a skin like ivory. I was
amazed to find such beauty flowering in such a cesspit. I was
talking to her in my halting Arabic when a Tommy interrupted.
He was drunk, and his persistence irritated me. I lost my temper.
"What the bloody hell's wrong with you?" I snarled.

"Orright, Aussie. Everything's O.K., Digger," he said, and
staggered away.

Suddenly I realized that I was squabbling over a harlot in a
Cairo brothel. The girl walked away. A little later she went into
a room with a South African. An unshaven servant knocked on
the door, and she opened it. She was wearing only a slip now. She
took a jug from him, and smiled winsomely at me.

"Condys," she said.

I turned and walked down the stairs. Eddie and Pat followed. We went out into the filthy street.

"What do you think of it?" asked Pat.

"Well," I said, "it's unfortunate, but it's a necessity. All they've got to sell is their bodies. At least they're frank about it—not like a lot of amateur harlots I know back home. We've seen enough. Let's go back to the Empire and have a drink."

Eddie and Pat looked at me, and then at each other. Eddie pushed his slouch hat back with his forefinger.

"Mick," he said. "I got twenty ackers that's burnin' a hole in me pocket."

"Oh?" I said. I turned to Pat. "You, too, I suppose?"

"Yeah," said Pat quietly. "There's a girl named Fatma up in London House. I've got to go back."

"Mine's Fifi," said Eddie. "She's in Tiger Lil's. I've gotta go back, too."

I stood there, looking at them. We ignored touts for shooting galleries, bars and curio shops who were clamouring for our custom.

"Ya won't come with us?" asked Eddie.

I shook my head. I was frightened to go with them. "No, I won't go back," I said.

Eddie scratched his head. "Yer a funny joker, Mick," he said. "There's hardly a married man who hasn't been here, and ya not even engaged. Why, more soldiers've been with bints in Berka Street than've seen the bloody Sphinx. Why doan ya give yaself a break? Ya gotta long way to go. Yer a funny bloke."

"I'll see you later," I said, turning away.

"Hey, Mick," called Pat after me. "Go back to the pub and write to Pamela. And tell her where you left me. Tell her I think it's funny." I heard him laughing bitterly as I walked away.

I walked on, and my steps got faster and faster. Exaltation was pulsing deep in me. It would be useless trying to explain it to anybody but Clive.

CHAPTER XLVII

I was tiring of the cabarets already. The girls were exotic, but as predatory as the kites that floated, black against the cloudless sky, above the Cairo roof-tops.

I watched the writhing body of a girl dressed in a few shimmering scales and found it dull. Pat had buttonholed a drunken English lieutenant and was telling him how the Black and Tans hanged his great grandfather or his grandfather—he did not seem to know which—and the lieutenant beamed back at him and said "Oh quaite, quaite" whenever Pat paused.

Eddie came back, and the sultry brunette sitting opposite me shrugged her bare shoulders, spat out something derogatory in Arabic, stood up, and wandered away.

"Where've you been, Eddie?" I asked listlessly.

"Just takin' a bo-peep outside," said Eddie. "Met a bloke from the *A.I.F. News.* Did ya know their office was just up the street?"

"No. Any news about the Japs?"

"The Japs? Yeah, he did say somethin'. The Japs bombed some joint or other. Ay, Mick, how d'ya reckon I'd go with that dark sheila over there? The one with the Springbok loot."

"Mademoiselle Fifi," blared the amplifiers, "in an Oriental dance."

"Eddie," I said slowly, "where did the Japs bomb?" I tried to tell myself that it was Chungking or somewhere else in China, but the short hairs on the back of my neck were bristling and I felt my hands go clammy.

"Now's me chance," said Eddie. "The loot's gone through."

I reached over and took his arm as he was about to rise, and he said, "Lemme go, Mick, or I won't be in the race with this bint."

"Eddie," I said, "this is important. Where—did—the—Japs— bomb?" The cold hand of fear had closed around my heart now, and in my mind were the words, "Malaya. Our Aussies in Malaya."

"I dunno," said Eddie testily. "Some place beginnin' with a sheila's name. Priscilla or Merle or somethin'. Yeah, I remember now—Pearl—Pearl Harbour. I'm gonna buy this bint a drink." And he stood up and went over to her.

Pearl Harbour. The Japs had bombed Pearl Harbour. I closed my eyes as hard as I could and shook my head, but it was still true, it was still clamouring in my head.

"Sare," said an ingratiating voice at my elbow. "You want a drink, sare?"

I glanced up into the smiling face of a native waiter. "Drink, George? You want a nice drink?"

"George," I said, "I've never wanted a drink more than I want a drink now."

I stopped near the corner of Sharia Galal and Haret Galal Pascha and listened to the clanking of the linotype machines in the squat white office of the Société Orientale de Publicité, publishers of the *Egyptian Mail* and *Egyptian Gazette.* I wanted to go in and hear the details, but I could not face them,

Eddie and Pat, their arms around each other's shoulders, were singing raucously a coarse parody of the Egyptian National Anthem, that merry-go-round tune, including:

> Oh we're all black bastards and we dearly love the King,
> *Enter kwyess, kwyess kateer, mungareer badin.*[1]
> Queen Farida, gibbit *bucksheesh,*
> Queen Farida, plenty *bucksheesh,*
> Oh she's queen of the Wogs and the jackals and the dogs,
> *Enter kwyess, kwyess kateer, mungareer badin.*

Filling the gutter and spreading over the footpath of Haret Galal Pascha, about twenty-five yards from the newspaper office and near Emad El Dine, one of the main streets, there was a heap of dirt and rubbish. I could see cabbage leaves, dried orange peel, broken glass. It looked as if it had been there for a long time. The wall was stained with the urine of dogs and humans, and the little street stank with it. There were droppings on the footpath too, and they had not all come from dogs. Suddenly the heap of dirt and the stains and the smell were symbolical of the degradation of Egypt, the debasement of a once-great land. I knew that if I came back in three months the heap of dirt would still be there.

"Eddie, Pat," I said, "let's go back. Let's go back to Syria. It will be beautiful going up through the cedars of the Lebanon, and the air will be fresh and sweet and the snow white and clean. Let's go back."

"Aw right, Eustace," said Eddie, swaying on his feet, "Le's go back. Tell 'em ——— 'em."

"Shertenly, Alphonse," said Pat. "Go anywhere. Go anywhere except England. I think you're Christ. They hanged my great grandfather. Le's dice rest of our leave. Le's go back."

I knew I could not run away from the news I had heard that night, but I could try. I could always try.

It is strange how, all through life, the big things happen unexpectedly and the eagerly-anticipated things always have the staleness of anti-climax. I was lying in my hut in Syria watching the snow drifting down when I heard the news. I had just been listening to the B.B.C. I had learned that Singapore had fallen, bringing down with it half my world. A whole division of Australians, one of our only four overseas—Peter, Joan's husband, among them—killed, wounded or prisoner. I was stunned. I saw the men I knew—and there were many in the Eighth Division—stumbling back through the dark jungle, and as I sat there, watching the snow drifting down, I smiled bitterly.

[1] You are good, very good, food later.

But this was not the news I mean. The news was that some of us, "specially selected N.C.Os and men who have proved themselves in action", as the official direction expressed it, were going home to strengthen infantry battalions. Pat, Eddie and I were included.

Going home? I knew it was true, but I found it hard to believe. To see again the lighthouse on Rottnest Island, the last part of Australia that had disappeared; to see the gaunt, grey shape of the Sydney Harbour Bridge with its reassuring permanence, its ends clamped solidly on each side of the harbour; to see the yellow sand of Nerridale beach and the still beauty of Lake Carraday glistening in the morning sun—why these were things to long for but never to expect to see until the last arrogant German had been killed, the last pitiful Italian taken prisoner.

"I'm not going," said Pat suddenly.

I rolled over to face him. "Not going?" I said incredulously. "Don't be *magnoon*. What's wrong?"

"I'm not going. There's nothing for me to go home to, Mick. I know we swore we'd stick together and I've stuck till now, but I don't want to go home. It's a big place, Australia, but it's empty, Mick. It'd be like going home to an empty house. There's nothing there for me any more. I'm not going."

"Oh," I said. "I know why. There's a girl. I've often seen you sneaking off through the trees with a sugar-bag of rations. There's a girl."

Pat went red. "Well, what if there is?" he said defiantly. "That's my business, isn't it?"

"Of course," I said. "*Mahlish*. I'm not your master. I'm only your friend." It would never be the same without Pat.

I watched the struggle in Pat's mind mirrored in his face. "I'm sorry, Mick," he said, "but you know how it is."

"Yeah," I said, "I know how it is." I turned suddenly to look at Eddie, and then I felt ashamed of my fears. He knew what I was thinking, for he grinned, reached over and gripped my arm, and said, "As long as we're alive an' kickin', Mick, we stick together. We'll give them yellow bastards somethin'."

I smiled and said, "My oath. We'll give 'em Singapore."

"With knobs on," said Eddie Wilson.

CHAPTER XLVIII

WE left the ship at Adelaide, and most of the boys sent telegrams. All we were allowed to say was that we had arrived. I did not send anything. I wanted to surprise Margaret.

It was late when I arrived in Sydney, too late to go to see Margaret. After all, there was plenty of time. A man who had waited eighteen months could wait a few more hours.

I got a taxi to the King George Hotel in Elizabeth Street, where I always stayed, and was surprised to find that I did not know the sleepy night porter. It was the first symbol of change.

"Sorry, Dig," he said, "but we haven't got a single room. There's hardly any room anywhere since the Yanks got here. They've taken a lot of the grouse pubs, you know. I can put you in with another soldier if you like."

"O.K." I said. I wanted a room to myself, but I had shared too many holes in the ground to worry about sharing a room with a soldier.

When I reached the room I glanced at the soldier's uniform. "A soldier?" I said to myself. "Why it's only a choco."

He sat up in bed and rubbed his eyes.

"Sorry to disturb you," I said, "but I couldn't get a single room."

He grinned. He had an engaging grin and frank blue eyes. He was only a boy. "Forget it, pal," he said. He noticed my colour patch. "Cripes," he said, sitting up in bed, "not the 2/93rd? Ay, were you in Tobruk with them?" The youthful zest in his tone was delightful after the cynicism of scores of jaded soldiers.

"Er-yes," I said reluctantly. But the clarity of his blue eyes, the engaging candour of his manner, the sheer youth of him, swept all my hesitancy away.

"I've often wanted to meet someone from Tobruk," he said. "Gee, would you tell me about it? You fellows certainly copped it all right, but you dished it out, too."

"Well," I said, "it was a bit tough at times but——" and I found myself talking, slowly at first, and then with a youthful relish that matched the zest in his tone, a relish that I had not known for a long time. I even told him about the scar on my hand, and spoke about Harry and the inordinate ambition of Gordon, the faith of Clive. He did not ask me what happened to them, and I was grateful for his rare understanding.

I found myself drawing rough maps on pieces of paper and

telling him I could not understand why the Germans did not bomb
Kantara out of existence, how they could have changed the whole
course of the war if they had sent the Afrika Korps to Egypt six
months earlier, how strange it was that such fine soldiers were incapable of stopping our patrols at Tobruk.

He listened with eager interest, asked intelligent questions, made
intelligent comments.

I told myself that I had misjudged the chocos. After all, they
had stayed at home to defend Australia and we would have been
in a sorry mess without them if Japan had attacked. Any day now
Japan might attack, and then we would thank God for them, and
the Yanks.

"You make us feel ashamed of being chocos," he said suddenly,
looking at me with shining eyes. He was sitting up in bed with
his arms around his knees. "You don't know how much I admire
you fellows."

"Forget it," I said, looking away. It was the first expression of
gratitude I had heard since returning to Australia. "You fellows'll
get your chance soon, perhaps. Somebody had to stay behind in
case the Japs got rough. Forget it."

"I want you to know," he said, "that we'll never forget what
you've done for us."

"Forget it," I said awkwardly. I was getting into bed when I
remembered something. I stood there, thinking.

"What's the trouble, pal?" he asked.

I turned and looked at him. "I drew eighty-five quid out of my
paybook yesterday," I said. "It's the money I saved in Tobruk.
I—I've got a girl, you see, and I want to hand it to her and tell
her that it represents Tobruk. Might sound funny to you, but I
want to do it that way. Be more real if I've got the notes instead of
entries in my paybook. I forgot all about it. Think I ought to go
down and shove it in the safe?"

The youth said, "That's an idea—handing your girl the money.
She'll get a great kick out of that. Well, I dunno about taking it
downstairs. It's your dough, mate, but don't you think if you lock
the door and stick it under your pillow it'll be sweet? But don't
let me influence you. After all, it's your dough."

"Yeah," I said. "Maybe you're right. S'pose nobody's going to
batter the door down while I'm asleep, eh?" and I laughed, and
the youth laughed too. I had not seen such an engaging smile since
I was with the girl in the light blue sari in Bombay. Like her smile,
it reached out and took you by the hand.

I took the money out of my uniform and put it under the pillow.

"Good night," I said.

"Good night, mate," he said. "It's been bonzer meeting you."

"Thanks," I said.

He had gone when I woke in the morning. I was disappointed. There were a few things I wanted to tell him about mistakes the Germans had made. I lay back and abandoned myself to the sensuous delight of the soft bed. It was so different from the ground, bed boards, and palliasses on the deck of a troopship. We had often joked about preferring the floor when we got home, but they could have the floor.

A pity the kid had gone. Wanted to tell him about what the Germans could have done to stop our patrols, and what merry hell the Luftwaffe would have played with our convoys in the Red Sea if it had been operating from Eyetie bases instead of the Eyeties. Nice kid, that. Probably had to get back to camp in a hurry. Bad luck. I had a week, a full week of freedom—and Margaret.

I sat up quickly. Margaret. I had forgotten Margaret. I looked at my watch. Ten past eight. Good heavens, this was what happened when there was no Eddie to wake me. I was wasting time I could be spending with Margaret.

I jumped out of bed, grabbed my towel, and was about to go to the bathroom when I remembered something. I smiled as I thought of the eighty-five pounds and how surprised Margaret would be when I counted it into her lap.

I went over to the bed and turned back the pillow. I stared dully at the bare sheet. The money was gone.

It was a new Sydney I had come to, a Sydney at war. It had seemed natural in Palestine, Egypt, Libya, and Syria to see slit trenches and gun emplacements, sandbags and dimmed lights, but Sydney —well Sydney was different, Sydney was home.

We had expected to come home with the war ended, with Hitler overthrown, but we had come home to a country full of Yanks and Dutchmen, a country called suddenly to arms.

I had never seen so many pregnant women. I asked a soldier for the explanation.

"Well mate," he said, "I reckon it's like this: Blokes with no kids want to have one so they'll be a bit more exempt, blokes with one want to have a second so they'll be even more exempt, and so on. I reckon that's how it is."

"Oh," I said.

I went out to Croydon, smiled as I passed the spot where I had helped Margaret out of the bus the week before I joined the A.I.F., and tried to appear casual as I drew a deep breath and rang her door-bell.

She was not there. She was at Epping, visiting my Aunt Maude. I went back to the station and caught another train. Nearly all the men were in some kind of uniform. I listened to the slow pleasant drawl of a group of Yanks. And they said overseas that we had an Australian accent!

Three women were sitting opposite me and two beside me. I noticed one staring at my left hand and put it in my pocket.

A middle-aged woman with an incipient moustache clucked to her friend, "Johnny's joined up, you know. He's in the A.I.F. He was to be called up next week, so he got in first."

"Now, isn't that nice," said her friend. "I do admire the boys who see their duty and do it."

I looked out the window. We were out of Sydney now, out where the trees grew straight and tall, and the grass was green.

That was what we resented—this sneaking into the A.I.F. just before being called up. Her Johnny was a soldier, too, just like Eddie and Pat, like Gordon and Clive and Jim and Bert and Harry, like the Diggers who had been in Greece and Crete and Syria, in Malaya, and Singapore.

"There's a long casualty list in the paper this morning," said a woman sitting next to me. "Oh, look at this in the next column. 'Pastel silk frocks. Styles to flatter the matron. Pastel silk frocks with embroidery trims. Basque at the waist. Pleats. Variety of shades.' And only seven guineas too! Well what do you think of that?"

"I think it's so noble of your husband to put five hundred pounds in the War Loan," said a woman sitting opposite. "Such a great sacrifice to make. But we must all help, mustn't we? Must all help to make it a real war effort."

I looked out of the window at the green grass slipping by, and thought how we would have gathered round and stared at one blade of it in Tobruk. A sacrifice? Yes, a sacrifice at three per cent.

When I got out at Epping a man came up to me and said, "Excuse me, corporal, but I notice by your colour patch that you're in the 2/93rd. My son was—was killed in Tobruk. He was in your battalion. I wonder could you tell us anything about it. The wife, you know. She wants to know. Just can't seem to sleep much until she knows."

I looked down into his anxious face. He was a little man, and he kept turning his hat over in his hands. His suit was shabby. His air was eager but apologetic.

I shifted my feet uncomfortably. "What was his name and what company was he in?" I asked gruffly.

He told me. Suddenly the memories I had pushed away came flooding back to me, memories of men I had seen die.

I was in a slit trench and I saw a soldier cut in half by a piece of shell, cut in two at the waist. His legs and hips stood there incongruously for a moment before they fell.

I saw the body of a young pilot, one half five yards away from the other.

I saw a stretcher-bearer go on working mechanically with his entrails trailing on the ground.

I saw a rifle bullet cut both eyes out of a youth's face as cleanly as if a surgeon had done it with a magic knife.

I saw Eddie, goaded to action by the persistent tune played by a German on his Spandau after each burst, send a message back to the artillery, and I saw a shell land on the machine-gun position and blow the German and his Spandau to pieces.

I saw Gordon lying in the dust of Tobruk, and felt his blood trickling down my arms.

I saw a ward of the hospital, or what was left of it, after a direct hit by a bomb. I saw the bits we found of some of the patients and M.Os.

The man was talking to me. "I'm sorry," I said, coming back to Epping. "What was his name and company?"

He told me again. I knew his son. He was only a boy. I had seen him die in Tobruk hospital one day I went to visit Harry. He was in agony from a bullet wound in the stomach. We were glad he died.

"I knew your son," I said. "You can tell your wife that he was hit in the head by two machine-gun bullets and died instantly."

The little man did not say anything for a while. He just stood there, turning his hat over and over in his hands. "Thanks," he said at last. "I'm grateful to you. I'll tell my wife. She'll rest easy now."

I shook the hand he held out. "You won't ask anybody else how he died?" I said. "You see, we—we don't like talking about these things. They make us remember."

"I won't ask anybody else," he said. "I'm satisfied now I know. You've been very kind. I'll give you my address. If it wouldn't be too much trouble the wife and I'd appreciate it if you'd look us up."

"Thanks," I said. "I'll do that some time." I could not go to see them. I could not go to see Clive's wife or Gordon's girl.

"I'll tell my wife," said the little man. "She'll rest easy now."

I walked over the railway bridge and up the street to where my aunt lived. It was eighteen months since I had seen Margaret. It was a new world I had come back to; it might be a new Margaret. I had not had a letter from her for months. Perhaps she did not care any more.

Then back to torment me came an even more goading possibility;

perhaps *I* did not care any more. Perhaps I could never care for anybody else. Perhaps, in living like a brute, I had come down to a brutish level. Perhaps I was hard right through, instead of just on the surface.

I shook my head, but the thought persisted, driving me to quicken my pace to find a truth I scarcely dared to face. This was what I had feared most of all, this exchange of other men's lives for my own soul.

I had found when I joined the army that I could not read any more. I simply had no desire to read. Most other soldiers told me the same thing. We were using our rifles, our bayonets, our arms, our feet; our minds were stagnating. Perhaps we would never be able to use our minds again. Perhaps none of us would.

I stopped at the gate, fear in my heart, then quickly opened the gate and went down the path.

The front door was open. I hesitated, drew a deep breath, and went in. I found myself, involuntarily, moving like a cat, moving silently as I had moved with old tyre tubes around my feet on patrol in Tobruk. I could hear voices. I could hear Margaret's voice.

I had taken off my slouch hat and was holding it by the chin strap to hide the scar on my hand. I stood in the doorway, leaning against the woodwork and looking at her. She was sitting on the lounge. She was talking. I did not know what she was saying: I was content to listen to the lilting cadence of her voice. She was speaking in that precise way I knew so well.

She was wearing a blue dress. She was talking. I could see her golden hair beneath the daintiest hat I had ever seen. I could see the delicate texture of her skin, its pink richness. That had not changed, anyhow.

I did not feel anything at first. Then, suddenly sweeping over me, came the realization that there was only one woman in the world for me, had been only one woman since that day, nearly six years ago, when she had walked out on to a Nerridale stage and into my heart.

Margaret turned her head slowly and looked at me. For a moment fear gripped me, for I knew that I cared, but did she?

She looked at me for a moment without recognition, and then a light flared in her eyes, and, with a cry, she was on her feet and running towards me. I took three strides into the room, and she was in my arms and I knew that I had come home.

My hat dropped to the floor. Aunt Maude came over. I felt her lips touch my scarred hand, and then she was gone.

"Oh, Mick darling! Mick," Margaret was saying. Her voice was so low I could scarcely hear it. "You've come home to me. Oh Mick. You've come home to me."

She was crying now, with her head on my shoulder. I smoothed back her golden hair from her forehead.

"I told you I'd come back," I said. "I told you I'd come back."

CHAPTER LXIII

"This, Mrs Reynolds," I said, "is where we are going to spend our honeymoon."

"Oh, Mick!" cried Margaret. "I don't care where I spend my honeymoon as long as it's with you!"

"That," I said, "is the stuff to give the troops. Or this one, anyhow."

I opened the high back gate and led the way down the gravel path and down the rough steps leading to the house. It was just a "week-ender", just like any of the other thousands scattered sparsely around the edge of Lake Carraday; but to us it was more than that.

I had chosen it well. It was just around the corner of Eldslie Point, which separated the wide sweep of Hugo Bay from the western end of the lake. There were no houses for half a mile, and to get food and mail we had to climb the hill behind the house, follow the winding track through the towering gums and go down the hill the other side to the yellow gravel road.

We laughed like children as I carried her over the threshold, and as soon as I had put her down and kissed her I told her about the money.

"So you see," I said, "apart from the money from my allotment that has been paid into the bank all the time I was away we've hardly got anything. Old J.B. couldn't afford to make up my pay and before you—er—before I joined the A.I.F. I just didn't have any reason to save. Oh darling, we've got such a bad start and it's all my fault for being such a fool."

She was looking at me, and her eyes were shining. "Oh, Mick," she whispered, "it doesn't matter. Money doesn't matter any more. It's having you and being free—free from fear and worry—that's what matters. Being certain of the future. It wasn't your fault, dear. It's not your fault if you trust people."

"I was going to send twenty-five pounds to Clive's wife," I said. "That's what hurts. Just put it in an envelope and send it."

"We'll still send it. We'll save it somehow."

"Good," I said. "We'll forget all about it. I don't want to spoil our—our honeymoon."

I sat on the veranda with my feet on a chair, a cushion behind my head and a cigarette in my hand, and I watched a few mullet breaking the surface near the edge of the lake. It had been raining and the air was heavy with the lush smell of the grass. The wireless was switched on, and an orchestra was playing softly. The lake was like a sheet of black glass.

I could hear Margaret—I could hear my wife—busy in the kitchen, cooking, and the smell of food, fresh, delicious food, came drifting out to me. First I thought of the bully beef and biscuits in Tobruk, and then I remembered how, years before, I had stood in the lounge of a girl's home and been struck by the analogy between the rich smell of food and her opulent self. Her Royal Australian Air Force friend about whom I had been plagued by the bitter pangs of jealousy had gone out to bomb Bremen one night and had not come back.

How long ago was it since that night? Seven years. It seemed so much more than that. I had lived through twenty years of experience in those seven years. I thought again of Beryl and how little she meant to me now. That was how things always were; even the fairest flowers faded, even the richest beauty died.

Strange how little Beryl meant to me now. She was probably as big as a house.

"What are you smiling about, dear?" asked Margaret. She had come in quietly and was watching me.

I beckoned her over with one finger and put my feet down and my cigarette out. She came over and sat on my knee. I kissed her forehead.

"What were you smiling at, Mick?"

"Just something I remembered. Something—something funny that happened in Palestine."

"What was it, darling?"

Lots of funny things must have happened in Palestine. I tried to think of one. "Well, it happened while we were in camp at Beit Hareed," I said.

"Yes, dear. Go on."

" 'Beit' is the Arabic word for 'house' so 'Beit Hareed' means the House of Hareed, whoever he was."

"Yes?"

I could not think of anything funny. "There was another A.I.F. camp not far away named Beit Jirja, evidently the house of Mr Jirja years before, and Bethlehem means the 'House of Bread'."

"Yes, dear. But what about the funny incident?"

"What funny incident?" I had to keep stalling. I could not think of anything funny.

"The one you were going to tell me about."

"Oh that. Well——" She had her arms around my neck and her head on my shoulder. Her blonde hair was streaming down my khaki shirt. I looked around wildly and saw the wireless. "Only that one night we switched the wireless on in the recreation hut on the hillside and the first thing we heard was a lot of Arabic. Bert Trevine listened intently until the announcer finished, and then he turned to us. 'Cripes, boys,' he said, 'it run second.' "

Margaret laughed, and I could feel her breath against my cheek. "Tell me more, dear," she said. "You talk so little about those days overseas."

"There's another one I can tell you about Bert. He was a jockey once. When our platoon commander was checking up on his ammunition on parade in Palestine one day—it was before we got the basic pouches and were still using 1908 equipment—he found that Bert had put his twenty rounds in all the pouches, five in some, two in others, one in a few. When he complained Bert said, 'It's all right, sir. I'm carrying the weight all the same.' "

She laughed. "What happened to Bert?" she asked.

"He got lost in the Benghazi Derby," I said. "He didn't come back."

"Oh. You came back," she said.

"Yes," I said, "I came back."

"And at Beit Hareed one day," I said, "one of our jittery machine-gunners opened up on an R.A.F. plane. The R.A.F. sent back a cryptic message—'We are not amused.' "

I could feel her breath tickling my neck as she laughed. "More, Mick," she said.

"In Tobruk one night the C.S.M. got hold of a jar of rum. I don't know where he got it. Nobody did. He wouldn't have had it long if we'd known about it. He could've sold it for a fortune. Well, he finished the jar off and staggered about, cursing the Germans and ranting about what he'd do to them if he could get his hands on them. We were back on the Blue Line at the time so it did not matter what noise he made.

"Well, finally he fell into a funk hole and went to sleep. Later when one of the sentries found him and prodded him with the butt of his rifle he jumped up and cried 'Kamerad! Kamerad! I surrender!' so loudly he woke us all up. We certainly pulled his leg over that. He was soon surrounded by a jeering crowd of Diggers. You know, we had some fun in Tobruk."

"Yes," she said quietly. "I'll bet you did."

The look was back in her eyes again. I kissed her and tickled her. "Mick," she said, laughing again. "Let me go. The water will boil over."

"Let it boil over," I said. It did.

For once in my life realization fulfilled the expectation; that week at Lake Carraday was worth all the burning days and long nights at Tobruk, all the chlorinated water and bully beef, the Stukas and mortar fire.

People might prate about spring, that pretty painted thing, but autumn had the mellowness of maturity, its rich ripeness, and it was tinged with the melancholy awareness of its own transience. It had the kind dignity, the sweet serenity, of a painless death.

I was happy at Lake Carraday because, for the first time for years, there was peace in my soul. I had come through to a simple appreciation of the elemental things in life—things like food and shelter and warmth, the fresh breeze in my face, the strength in my muscles as I pulled at the oars, the light in a woman's eyes. All the things I had always taken for granted, the things everybody takes for granted.

All these things were so precious because I had seen Death look me in the face and pass me by. Nearly a thousand Diggers who were in Tobruk with me would never leave it, but I had come through, and every time I looked at Margaret and saw the clarity of her eyes and felt the touch of her hand on my forehead I knew that I had come home.

We did something I had wanted to do all my life—we got up before the sun and, strolling along the shore of the lake with an arm around each other's waist, we watched the sun slide up over the purple hills and saw it gleaming deep in the black stillness of the water.

And, at sunset, we drifted down the bay. I lay with my head in her lap and listened to the cheeky chuckling of the water against the sides of the boat, and was content. Margaret always held my left hand in hers and ran her fingers gently over the scar as though she would wipe it away, wipe away all it stood for.

Only once in that week did reality smash roughly through the defences of our little world. Laughing at something—we were always laughing—we climbed the track to the top of the hill hand in hand, threading our way through the giant white gums. I told her how, just outside Tel Aviv, we had come suddenly on an avenue of gums, and how that breath of home prodded our nagging nostalgia.

I stopped at the top to kiss her, and for a while we looked out

across the lake with its wooded hills all round and its blue sky
above. To the east, behind a gleaming stretch of sand, there was
the channel that led to the Pacific, and there, past that green point,
was the mining village of Denniston, dreaming in the sun. We
could hear that friendly sound, a motor-boat chug-chugging in the
distance, and far to the south there was the smoke of the Murranda
ferry.

We turned, and I helped her through a barbed-wire fence. As I
was getting through, my shorts caught just as they had caught one
night in Tobruk ten months before. Suddenly I saw the Very lights
go up as they had gone up that night, and the outline of stones and
sangars standing out sharply against the sky, and I heard the
enemy upon us.

"Christ, Eddie!" I cried. "Quick! Help me for God's sake! Get
me free!"

I cried out as I had cried out that night so long ago.

I saw Eddie whipping his bayonet off and hacking me free with
it amid the enemy fire.

"Oh no!" cried Margaret, and there must have been fear in my
face for I saw her shudder when she looked into my eyes. "No, Mick,
no!" she cried, and she grabbed me and pulled me free.

Then her arms were around me, and she was trying to stop my
trembling. I must have fainted then because I woke up underneath
the rustling branches of a great white gum, and I could see the
clear blue sky through gaps in the leaves and hear a lizard scuttling
through the dry grass.

Margaret was smoothing my forehead with her cool fingers and
her cheek was against mine. She was crying softly.

"It's all right, dear," I said. "I'm sorry. I'm all right now."

"Oh Mick, oh Mick," she said. "I should never have let you go.
I should never have let you go."

We might have been in another world. We *were* in another
world. The second day I changed from khaki to a white shirt and
old blue shorts. All I had to remind me that I was a soldier was
my slouch hat, and I usually wore that on the back of my head
with the strap dangling down my neck.

We drifted through those golden days without any news of the
world of men and guns. Occasionally an R.A.A.F. plane droned
overhead, but I did not bother to look up. I had seen enough planes
to do me for the rest of my life.

We had no newspapers. The first time the radio music stopped
and the announcer said, "You are now about to hear a news
bulletin," Margaret switched to another station. She turned and

her eyes met mine, and we smiled. After that the one nearer the wireless stopped the news every time.

I had left the telephone number of the shop over the hill with my new company commander and I had told the old man in the shop that if anybody rang me to come and get me immediately. One day we saw him hobbling down the track and waving, and I heard Margaret catch her breath and felt her hand grasp mine, but the old man had only come to tell us that he had heard that flathead were biting among the weeds in Hugo Bay and he had brought us some mullet for bait. He did not come back again.

We went fishing in the early mornings and late afternoons, the only times of the day that are really worth while. Sometimes we caught fish—mainly squire with a sprinkling of whiting and flat-head—and sometimes we did not catch any. We did not care much whether we did or not.

Often I caught Margaret watching me when she thought I was not looking, and often she caught me watching her. When I saw how she looked at me I felt humble. It became a game after that, with both of us trying to catch the other.

Sometimes, when she turned, the sun gleamed on her golden hair, and I remembered a fugitive phrase, "her hair, always blowing a little wild", and wondered if I were right in believing that Shelley wrote it.

After nearly two years of living with men in huts and tents and holes in the ground I had forgotten what tenderness was, but now I knew again. I was elated to find that I had shed my uncouth words, my uncouth habits, as a snake sheds its skin. Margaret surpassed my wildest hopes, even those ardent forecasts I had made desperately to myself as I lay in the dirt and darkness of Tobruk and let my imagination play with the future.

It was autumn, but we went swimming every day, splashing through the shallow water at the point, and then we lay in the sun and I felt the salt caking on my body, still brown from the sun of Tobruk.

We were always gay, and often we laughed uproariously at nothing at all. I had never known the world to be so delightful before. Since the afternoon I became caught in the barbed wire we had not talked of Tobruk any more. We did not even mention the war. We did not talk much about anything, for we had learned a new language, a language of the eyes.

I had put my rifle in the tool shed. One afternoon I was pulling it through when Margaret came looking for me. I looked up and saw her standing in the doorway. She was staring at the rifle, and the old fear was back in her eyes. She stood there for a moment, and then she turned and went back to the house.

The end came suddenly. First it was the day after tomorrow, then tomorrow, and then—today. We got up even earlier than usual, and walked along the edge of the lake. I had my left arm around her waist and she was holding my left hand with hers. I felt her hand tremble as she ran her fingers over the scar.

I changed to her left side and put my right arm around her. At times we stopped, and I took her face between my hands and kissed her lips. I remembered how, so long ago, she had turned her cheek. She did not turn her cheek now. She would never turn her cheek again unless it was to hide the tears in her eyes.

We watched the sun come sliding up over the purple hills, and the shadows vanished, all except the shadows in our hearts. I did not look at her. I could not. We went back to the house, and as she cooked breakfast I sat in a chair on the veranda and smoked, and watched her as she moved about.

She was wearing a floral dress—a woman never looks more attractive than when she is wearing a floral dress—and she had a blue ribbon in her golden hair. I could not watch her for long. I had to look away.

The taxi came. I helped the driver carry my bags up the steps and along the gravel path. Margaret stood in the doorway and watched me. The driver was a little man with glasses and thinning sandy hair. He bent his head and peered over his glasses when he spoke.

"Thanks, corp.," he said, and nothing that had happened did more to make me realize that it was all over, that I was Cpl H. W. Reynolds, formerly of C Company, 2/93rd Battalion, A.I.F.

"You know what to do?" I asked.

"Yeah. I've got everything O.K., corp. I dump the stuff at the garage and come back for you in half an hour. I wait round the first corner till you come. She's jake. Ay, corp. Was you ever in Tobruk?"

I ran a hand through my hair and nodded. "Yes," I said.

"You was, eh? Must have been pretty berluddy. Where you got that, I s'pose?" He pointed with the stem of his pipe at my left hand. "I seen it straight away. Observant bloke, ain't I?"

"Yes," I said, and put the hand in my pocket. Somehow I felt ashamed.

"You didden happen to know Bluey Humbert in Tobruk, did you?" he asked.

"No. Can't say I did."

"A nephew of me partner's, he is. Or was, I should say. He's

still there, an' not likely to be leavin' in a hurry. He got buried
be a bomb."

"Did he? Well I'll see you later."

He opened his mouth to say something, and shut it with the
something unsaid. He peered suspiciously at me over his glasses
with his head on one side. I could see him telling a few of his
mates in the public bar at Denniston: "This joker reckons he was
in Tobruk, but I'm a wake-up to him. Probably come in on the
grouter and bludged in a base job somewhere or other. One of
them base wallopers. Got a scar on his hand, but probably he's
had it since he was a little snork. He's on the nose. A.I.F. all right
—I seen his colour patch—but he don't know nothin' about Tobruk.
They all say they was there, the whole bloody lot of 'em. Oh well,
Tom, all the best, mate."

I went back to the house, and sat down in a chair on the veranda.
Margaret came and sat on my knee. She put her arms around my
neck and her head on my shoulder. I could see the sun sparkling
on a patch of water the breeze had ruffled. The patch widened and
came towards us, and soon there was a sparkling path of sunshine
across the bay.

"Oh, Mick," cried Margaret, "why do you have to go? Haven't
you done enough? Seven months in Tobruk should be enough
sacrifice for any man to make. It's so unfair. They're taking the
best years of our lives away from us. Why do you have to go?"

" 'Man was born free'," I said, " 'but is everywhere in chains'."

"Who said that, Mick?"

"I think it was Rousseau. It doesn't matter."

"But, Mick, why do you have to go? We *were* born free, but
nobody's free any more. We don't ask for much—just for freedom,
just for the right to live in peace, just for the certainty that our
children won't have to leave their homes and kill other people's
children, kill people they've never seen before. Oh, Mick, why
is it so?"

I recognized it for what it was—the tormented cry of a suffering
world. Throughout the British Empire, throughout America,
throughout Russia, throughout China, throughout enslaved Europe,
yes even in Germany, Italy and Japan, the cry went up, and thinking
men turned their heads in shame.

"It's our heritage," I said. "That's all. It's our heritage from a
long line of fools who've 'poured out the red sweet wine of youth'.
Don't worry, dear. Some day, perhaps, there will be sanity on
earth, and then there will be peace. Good-bye, dear."

"Oh no, darling! Don't go yet, Mick. I waited so long for you to
come home. I can't let you go yet."

"I'm sorry, dear, but I'm a soldier. I promised the C.O. I'd be back in camp this afternoon, and I've just got to be there, that's all."

Her arms went round my neck and her lips met mine. We clung to each other desperately, as a swimmer clings to a rock in a treacherous sea, and then we stood up and I got my rifle, loosened the sling, put the rifle on my shoulder, and put on my slouch hat, and we went out to the back gate. We did not speak. I could hear her sobbing quietly.

I turned to face her, and her arms went round my neck and my arms around her shoulders. "You'll be careful, won't you, dearest?" she asked. "Wherever you are, be careful, dear. I'll be waiting for you to come back."

"I'll be careful," I said, "and I'll come back."

I took her arms from around my neck, and kissed her gently on the forehead. For a moment I looked deeply into her eyes.

"Good-bye, Mrs Reynolds," I said, and turned away.

"Good-bye, Corporal Reynolds," she said.

I hitched the rifle on my shoulder, looked straight ahead and started to walk down the road. Suddenly I heard the patter of her feet on the gravel and heard her crying "Mick! Oh Mick!" I turned, and she was running towards me.

"Oh Mick! Oh Mick!" she cried. She came up and took my left hand between hers and kissed the back of it. "I nearly forgot," she said, and her eyes held mine for a moment before I turned away.

When I reached the corner I stopped, turned and looked back. She was standing where I had left her, in the middle of the yellow road, and her floral dress was flapping in the breeze. She waved, and I waved, too.

Suddenly I realized that I was resigned to all this. I did not like it—I never would—but I accepted it. It was as I had said, our heritage. This was our world. We could not help what it was like, but by God, we would take it as it was, as it had been left to us, and some day, perhaps, we would "shatter it to bits and then remould it nearer to our heart's desire".

Eddie, good old Eddie, would be standing in the doorway, waving and grinning, as the express glided into Nerridale. His rifle would be close to his hand and he was still the best shot I had ever seen. Then, a little later, the old firm would be doing business again, but not at the same old stand.

Things were not so bad after all. I was still alive. I was in one piece, and I had had a week with my wife. A man could not expect any more than that. I had had that week. Let them do what they liked with me but, by God, they could not take that away from me. They could not take that away.

When I came back from Broome or Wyndham or Darwin or New Guinea or Java or Manila or Tokio, or wherever it was I was going to kill Japanese, perhaps there would be two people waiting for me instead of just the one standing in the yellow road. Fear gripped me again for a moment, for I feared we would have a son and that twenty-five years later we would know the agony of waving him good-bye. But then I squared my shoulders, lifted my head, and threw the fear off. We would see, somehow, I thought, that this would never happen again.

I moved the rifle to a more comfortable position on my shoulder, waved again to my wife, and turned to face the future.